Royal Mysteries of the Tudor Period

Royal Mysteries of the Tudor Period

Timothy Venning

PEN & SWORD
HISTORY

First published in Great Britain in 2023 by
Pen & Sword History
An imprint of Pen & Sword Books Limited
Yorkshire – Philadelphia

ISBN 978 1 39905 429 4

A CIP catalogue record for this book is available from the British Library

Typeset by Mac Style
Printed in the UK by CPI Group (UK) Ltd, Croydon, CR0 4YY.

MIX
Paper | Supporting responsible forestry
FSC® C013604

Pen & Sword Books Limited incorporates the imprints of After the Battle, Atlas, Archaeology, Aviation, Discovery, Family History, Fiction, History, Maritime, Military, Military Classics, Politics, Select, Transport, True Crime, Air World, Frontline Publishing, Leo Cooper, Remember When, Seaforth Publishing, The Praetorian Press, Wharncliffe Local History, Wharncliffe Transport, Wharncliffe True Crime and White Owl.

For a complete list of Pen & Sword titles please contact

PEN & SWORD BOOKS LIMITED
47 Church Street, Barnsley, South Yorkshire, S70 2AS, England
E-mail: enquiries@pen-and-sword.co.uk
Website: www.pen-and-sword.co.uk
or
PEN AND SWORD BOOKS
1950 Lawrence Rd, Havertown, PA 19083, USA
E-mail: Uspen-and-sword@casematepublishers.com
Website: www.penandswordbooks.com

Contents

Introduction

Compared to earlier periods of English history (and even more so to any period of non-English British history pre-1707), Tudor history is an era with which at least part of modern reading and viewing public has some degree of familiarity. The same applies to the 'basics' of some of its more intriguing problems – and its mysteries. This is due to the greater number of books, TV series, and films made about the period, which has always been attractive to creators in the media world due to a mixture of drama, Royal Family and political scandal and violence, and visual sumptuousness in an age of excess in dress and lifestyles – with the brooding and literally gigantic figure of Henry VIII, one of Britain's most recognizable monarchs, at the centre of it all. (Even at the collection of royal militaria at the Royal Armouries at the Tower of London, the huge suits of armour made for the corpulent ageing Henry dominate the scene – as I discovered when I first went round it aged about ten.)

The sheer swaggering panache and the outsize personality – and brutality – of the man who has been called 'the British Stalin' have long been on object of popular myth and recognition. Few other countries able to match a man who not only arranged his country's first 'Exit From Europe' in defiance of a continent-wide international bureaucracy (an inspiration for 'Brexit'?) but had no fewer than six wives and rid himself of two of them by judicial murder after 'show trials'. He ran though his ministers, waged war, remade his country's physical and intellectual landscape, and slaughtered his nearest aides and real or supposed rebels with enthusiasm. The long-running 'soap opera' of his court, with its swift rises and falls in favour, was replayed in that of his equally famous and equally flamboyant younger daughter, the 'Virgin Queen' Elizabeth I.

In her case, the highlight of her equally crisis-hit reign (with its prototype 'cold war' against a hostile Europe-wide ideology, i.e. Counter-Reformationary Catholicism, and plethora of spy stories and real, exaggerated, or imaginary plots) was another confrontation with the dominant force in Europe – the 'evil empire' of Spain, led by her brother-in-law King Philip II, at the time of the Spanish Armada in 1588. In the case of Elizabeth, parallels could be drawn for modern times between the failed subversion of the 'Catholic menace' and the 1945–89 'Cold War threat of Communism led by the USSR, the submerged iceberg or exaggerated 'hype' of a network of 'Islamist'-style 'home-grown terrorists' (in this case fanatical young Catholics motivated to murder their sovereign and stage a coup backed by Spain and the Papacy), and the successful defiance of a bloodthirstily aggressive European superpower in 1588 as in 1940. Some of the political and court dramas of the era have long been seen as similar to those of modern times, with Elizabeth I portrayed in the media as a prototype for Nazi-defying Winston Churchill or Argentina-defeating Margaret Thatcher, and Tudor dramas were a staple of historical plays and films long before TV was invented.

Back in the 1930s, there was *The Private Life of Henry VIII* with Charles Laughton (best known as the equally violent and despotic Captain Bligh from Mutiny on the Bounty) as the obese, gormandizing, callously wife-murdering king; a more nuanced psychological drama about Henry's relationship with Sir/St Thomas More appeared in Robert Bolt's 1954/1957 play *A Man For All Seasons*, filmed in 1966 with Robert Schofield as More, Robert Shaw as the king, and the film-director Orson Welles as Cardinal Wolsey. The perennially interesting and dramatic story of the rise and fall of Henry's second queen, Anne Boleyn – variously seen as an 'empowering' and modern-style 'achieving' heroine and victim of male chauvinism by feminists, as well as a political and intellectual player or adventurer, or as a greedy and seductive schemer out for what she could get – has also long been well-known on the film and TV screen. In 1969 there was the film *Anne Of A Thousand Days* starring Genevieve Bujold and Richard Burton, based on Maxwell Anderson's 1948 play; in 2003 there was the TV version of Philippa Gregory's 2001 novel *The Other Boleyn Girl*, told from the point of view of Anne's little-known sister Mary, starring Natascha McElhone as Mary Boleyn, Jodhi May as the scheming Anne, and Jared Harris as the King (remade as a film in 2008). (Philippa Gregory's imaginative retelling of the Boleyn/Howard/Tudor saga ran to a whole series of books, including *The Boleyn Inheritance* in 2003, *The Queen's Fool* in 2004, and *The Virgin's Lover* about Elizabeth

I and her admirer Robert Dudley in 2006.) The whole saga of Henry and all of his wives was presented by the BBC as *Henry VIII And His Six Wives* in 1970, one of its earliest lavish historical costume-dramas, with Keith Michell as the King (ageing and fattening as appropriate over 35 or so years), Annett Crosbie as Catherine of Aragon, Dorothy Tutin as Anne Boleyn, Anne Stallybrass as Jane Seymour, and Angela Pleasence as Catherine Howard, with Bernard Hepton as Archbishop Cranmer – a stellar cast of leading TV actors of the era. This was then followed by the hugely influential *Elizabeth R* in 1971, which launched the top-level career of its star Glenda Jackson and also featured perennial favourites Robert Hardy as Robert Dudley, and Robin Ellis, aka the first 'Ross Poldark', as the Earl of Essex. The third part of the BBC Tudor trilogy of the 1970s – and my own introduction to the televisations – was *The Shadow of the Tower* in 1972 about the less-well-known tribulations of intrigue –afflicted Henry VII, starring James Maxwell and Norma West.

More recently the focus of best-selling Tudor era historical novels about the 'snake-pit' of Henry VIII's court, has been the controversial career of Henry's master-fixer' and chief minister Thomas Cromwell, as written up from his viewpoint by Hilary Mantel in her Booker-Prize-winning masterpieces *Wolf Hall* (2009) and *Bring Up The Bodies (*2012), followed by *The Mirror And The Light* (2020). The first of these was televised in 2015, starring Mark Rylance as Cromwell, Damian Lewis as Henry, and Claire Foy as Anne. There is also the notably 'soapy' and 'over the top' Anglo-US-Canadian dramatic adaptation of Henrican court politics and royal marital relationships in *The Tudors* (2007–10), starring Jonathan Rhys Myers (Henry), Natalie Dormer (Anne), Annabelle Wallis (Jane Seymour), and Joss Stone (Anne of Cleves), which had Elizabethan rather than strictly 1530s-1540s-style costumes and took more liberties with the real events than did the 1970s BBC versions. (Notably the equally dramatic and bloody career of Mary Queen of Scots has attracted less high-profile adaptations, though it was the subject of two nineteenth-century operas and a 1971 film with Vanessa Redgrave and Glenda Jackson).

The changing manner and focus of re-telling the royal Tudor story, indeed, is a reflection on what is seen to matter more to and be most 'appealing' for varying audiences over centuries, and commenced with Shakespeare's (and Fletcher's?) carefully laudatory play 'Henry VIII' in 1613 – an early production of which was the occasion of a misfiring cannon burning down the Globe playhouse in Southwark. All this shows that the royal drama of Tudor politics has always been of public and 'cultural world' interest, and not only in the UK – but this is not to say that we 'know' what happened much more than we do about earlier royal/court politics and their mysteries, personal or political (and the two were usually intertwined in this era). The exact motivations of major and minor 'players' to act as they did can be assessed with a reasonable amount of evidence, but can still only be guessed at – and debate rages among historians on such matters as to what extent Henry VIII was carefully 'guided' and influenced by ministers such as Cromwell or his predecessor Wolsey. The extent of Anne Boleyn's personal, political, and religious goals are also a matter of dispute – was she a clever and idealistic figure, as has been argued by her admirers ever since the reign of her daughter Elizabeth I when she was portrayed as a 'reformist' proto-Protestant, or was she a misunderstood and ruthlessly maligned character, as ruthless and scheming as some of Henry's male ministers, only with the added advantage of being able to sexually manipulate the king, or even a callous murderess who removed several of her rivals? Her sudden and dramatic fall and the bizarre – and unique – circumstances of a 'self-made' queen, being accused of committing incest with her brother and ending up on the execution-block, have been pored over in great detail for centuries and seen from diverse viewpoints. Though we can probably dismiss much of the worst stories about her – often made up by her Catholic detractors or her daughter's enemies, who had their own agendas – some of them still linger and reappear in modern novels and TV dramas. Why exactly were these charges laid against her, and was it just due to the fevered politico-religious atmosphere of the era and a desire to ruin her reputation – and 'shut down debate' – by presenting the most damaging allegations possible? 'Spin' and 'fake news' were as important political weapons in damaging reputations and distorting the public perception of people and events in the sixteenth century as in the twenty-first century, and the sources have to be examined for bias as rigorously as for the medieval era.

There may be more of them – but that is not to say that they all (or most) get anywhere near the truth or can be safely used as 'objective'. This also applies to the many scandals and mysteries of the interwined careers and reigns of the cousins Elizabeth I and Mary Queen of Scots. The first seen as being mixed-up in the suspicious death of her admirer and potential husband Robert Dudley's ailing first wife, the second accused of luring her weak and drunken second husband Lord Darnley to a place where her allies (her admirer Bothwell?) could blow him up and later accused of trying to have Elizabeth murdered so she could take her throne. Again, the most outrageous allegations have been plausibly identified as 'smears' based on lies or distorted rumours but there are still fundamental questions to be asked, plus any number of potential suspects. Even back in the lesser-known reign of the dynastic founder Henry VII – a man who came to the throne after the disappearance, still unresolved, of his wife's brothers, the 'Princes in the Tower', who were variously seen as either the rightful legal heirs to the throne or bastards – we are no nearer to solving the question of who exactly were the two challengers to his throne who could have deposed him 'Lambert Simnel' and 'Perkin Warbeck'. The clouds of mystery and the murk of dubious 'smears' and spin' still hang around our assessments of the 'reality' of goings-on at the Tudor – and Stuart – courts in the late fifteenth and sixteenth centuries.

Chapter One

Were Either Of Henry VII's Challengers Genuine?

'Lambert Simnel'. Was he Edward V?

Contrary to later simplification, the battle of Bosworth was not the 'end of the Wars of the Roses'. This was the image presented by Shakespeare, with the battle of Bosworth at the end of 'Richard III' as the climax of his cycle of history plays and an epilogue celebrating the restoration of peace by Henry VII's marriage to Elizabeth of York, and in doing so, he followed the similar story-line of Edward Hall's 1548 chronicle. It was a neat and logical ending to the story of the York-Lancaster feud; but the reality is rather different. Bosworth solved very little, and would have looked very different to contemporaries who had no means of knowing that it was more than just another of the frequent political upheavals in fifteenth-century England. In a sense it was less decisive than Edward IV's victory at Tewkesbury in May 1471, which resulted in the deaths of his rival (Henry VI) and the latter's heir and a 'cull' of surviving Lancastrian commanders. It left Richard III's heir – his adult nephew John, Earl of Lincoln – and other senior Yorkist partisans such as Lord Lovell either at large or only superficially reconciled to the Tudor dynasty, and Henry Tudor had a far weaker claim to the throne than Edward IV had done. Henry's wife, transmitter of the stronger Yorkist claim, had been declared illegitimate by the previous regime and the swift reversal of this could not erase doubts over her parents' marriage. Bosworth was followed by several serious attempts to overthrow the government during the next decades.

As far as contemporaries were concerned, the surprise victory of Henry Tudor (though he did not use that surname, calling himself 'Richmond' due to his title as its earl) was merely another reversal of fortunes in the unstable world of English politics, and more plots and invasions could follow. Would Henry's government be as short-lived as that of his uncle

Henry VI, temporarily restored in October 1470 but removed within six months by exiled Yorkists? This background of instability helps to explain why so many people were prepared to gamble on overthrowing Henry in the Yorkist cause after August 1485, irrespective of the actual merit or 'legitimacy' of his challengers – it was an era of many swift reversals of fortune when political gambles were rife and some unexpectedly paid off. Desertions of a seemingly strong ruler by his closest followers were also becoming a habit – Edward IV, who had overthrown the regime of his father Duke Richard of York's killers at the age of eighteen in 1461, had been attacked and arrested by his cousin and chief aide Warwick 'the Kingmaker' in 1469, had driven him out of the country in 1470, and had then been driven out by him in turn. Warwick had then returned in an unlikely alliance with the Lancastrians who had killed his father, brother, and uncle, aided by Edward's own brother Duke George of Clarence – who in turn had abandoned Warwick to help Edward get his throne back in 1471. Another swift reversal of fortune was quite possible as seen from the perspective of the English elite in autumn 1485 – and Henry Tudor's declared claim to the throne, that of the junior Lancastrian Beaufort line (the founder of which had been the eldest son of Lancastrian founder Henry IV's father's third marriage) had been barred from the throne by Act of Parliament in 1396. Henry quickly married the eldest daughter and heiress of Edward IV, Elizabeth of York, as he had promised to do when his partisans joined up with hers in 1483 – but were her two brothers, Edward V and Richard of York (the 'Princes in the Tower'), really dead at the hands of her usurping uncle Richard III? Their bodies had never been found, although rumours about who had killed them (usually blamed on Richard) had been going around since they were last seen at the inner windows of the Tower of London shortly after Edward V's deposition. Nor did Henry ever find their bodies and openly declare them dead, though he made unspecified charges of infanticide against Richard.

The 'White Rose' Yorkist plotters put up their first alternative candidate in 1486–7 in the person of the boy known as 'Lambert Simnel', initially claiming to be Edward, Earl of Warwick (born 1475), the son of Edward IV's next brother the Duke of Clarence. The treacherous Duke George had been Edward IV's nearest adult heir if his children were regarded as illegitimate due to Edward being a bigamist, as Richard III had alleged when he deposed Edward V in June 1483, but by this time he was dead, condemned for supposed treason by Edward IV in 1478 and probably killed in the Tower by being drowned in a butt of wine. Technically, the charge of attainder forfeiting his rights and property barred his young son Edward of Warwick from the throne and so Clarence's next brother Richard (III) had claimed the throne not handed it to Edward when Edward V was deposed – but this could be reversed. Edward and his elder sister Margaret (born 1473), who Henry VIII was later to execute, were still alive and fell into Henry VII's hands at his accession, and he put Edward in the Tower but the boy's escape was rumoured. Could a boy – who would need a regency and so be a source of political instability – be preferred to an adult, but genealogically junior male relative, as the rightful king? This point was uncertain in fifteenth-century politics, not least as in 1399 the deposed King Richard II's nearest genealogical heir had been a boy, Edmund Mortimer (aged seven), but he had been pushed aside to make way for the adult Henry, Duke of Hereford and Lancaster (King Henry IV), who had led the invasion that deposed the king. This was claimed by the Yorkists – the backers of the descendants of the childless Edmund's sister Anne and her husband – to have been illegal and unjust and to have sparked off the Yorkist challenge to the mentally unstable King Henry VI in the 1450s. So was it illegal or inviting Divine wrath for another new King Henry to push the 'rightful' boy claimant to the throne aside?

Richard III's other nephew (his sister Anne's eldest son) and heir John de la Pole, Earl of Lincoln (born 1464), in a stronger position than Edward of Warwick as an adult, had been pardoned by Henry after Bosworth but subsequently fled to the Continent, while Richard's close friend Francis, Lord Lovell was at large along with other Yorkist stalwarts. Two of the latter, the Stafford brothers Humphrey and Thomas, started a revolt in Warwickshire in 1486 but were pursued and dragged out of sanctuary at Abingdon Abbey, whose Abbot Sante was a Yorkist partisan and was later to offer money to Yorkist plotters who planned to 'spring' Warwick from the Tower of London. Thomas Stafford was pardoned at the last minute on the scaffold in a shameless piece of public theatre but Humphrey was executed. Meanwhile Henry had had a troubled first visit to York, which was the centre of Richard's power whose council dared to write their regrets at his killing into their official records, and was nearly killed by assassins while in the city. One story had it that Lord Lovell, at large at the time after escaping from sanctuary in Colchester unnoticed, was linked to this plot and contacted Richard III's nephew and heir. Lincoln, who was at court, asking for help but was turned down.[1] Had they acted together, could they have murdered Henry and seized his throne for Lincoln? Henry lacked loyal northern magnates and had to rely for control of the north on the Earl of Northumberland (head of the Percy clan) who came from an old Lancastrian dynasty and had hung back from taking his wing of the royal force to assist Richard at the crucial moment at Bosworth. Northumberland duly carried out exemplary executions and cowed the region, but Lovell escaped over the Pennines to the Furness Yorkist stalwart Sir Thomas Broughton's home near Cartmel and later made his way south to East Anglia, clearly protected by a network of allies. Later that year 'Simnel' appeared in Burgundy under the protection of a shady Yorkist priest called Richard Simon (or Simmonds). He was subsequently identified as the son of an Oxford organ-maker/joiner, and given his youth (he was aged somewhere between ten and sixteen) and low birth[2] was seemingly the puppet of powerful figures with an interest in overthrowing Richard – possibly Lincoln. But if so, why did Lincoln not claim the throne in his own name? Did he think that more people would rally to the 'unjustly deprived of his rights' and supposedly 'real' claimant to be Warwick, i.e. Simnel? In the summer to autumn time of 1483, more of the former supporters of the late Edward IV had rallied to the cause of the (already missing) deposed Edward V and his brother, than to that of their then ally, Henry Tudor, or to Richard III's defecting chief lieutenant, Duke Henry of Buckingham. So was Lincoln hoping for a more successful 'replay' of the 1483 rebellion in the name of an 'appealing' and 'innocent' boy-king denied his rights by a 'usurper'?

Oxford was not far from Abingdon Abbey whose Yorkist abbot had given refuge to the Stafford brothers and from Minster Lovell, principal residence and possible post-Bosworth refuge of Lord Lovell. Presumably selected as a pretender by one of these enemies of Henry, as he resembled Warwick who was eleven in 1486, 'Simnel' (an unusual surname, possibly a pseudonym which has given rise to all sorts of speculation about his real identity) was smuggled out of England to Burgundy, supplied with troops and men by Richard III's younger sister Duchess Margaret of Burgundy, and sent to Ireland.[3] The chief magnate of the 'Pale', the only region (near Dublin) in secure English hands but still dominated by various powerful

Anglo-Irish noblemen with private armies of tenants who overshadowed the government, was a Yorkist partisan – Gerald Fitzgerald, the Earl of Kildare, a former 'strongman' for Edward IV and Richard III who Henry VII had not dared to sack as chief minister (Lord Deputy) or arrest. He duly backed the invaders and lent them troops. These basic details of the story come from the 'official' story as known – i.e. as circulated by the government? – in early Tudor England and picked up by contemporary historian Polydore Vergil, so it may hide important information that Henry VII suppressed. None of the principal actors survived the debacle at the battle of Stoke in 1487 except 'Simnel' himself (who was kept under control in the king's household as a servant thereafter), and a few of the minor Northern gentry – involved in the revolt after 'Simnel' and his entourage landed – who survived and were pardoned, would not have known much about the earlier stages of the plot. There has even been doubt if the boy who was captured at Stoke and put in the royal household was the same one as the 'original' pretender, given that the latter was about ten and the captured boy who Henry paraded was possibly around fifteen. By that reckoning, the rebel leadership might not have entrusted the valuable person of the actual pretender to the battlefield but kept him safely away from it ready to be spirited away if the battle was lost. In that case, had the 'real' Simnel – i.e. a genuine Yorkist prince? – been smuggled away safely, and a younger 'stand-in' been captured by Henry VII and taken by the relieved king for a semi-harmless working-class pawn of Lincoln's who could be kept in semi-custody with patronising scorn in his household? For that matter, with Lincoln and most of his senior 'staff' dead and Lovell disappeared, was anyone who could definitely identify the 'real Simnel' in custody after the battle, so Henry could be bamboozled into accepting the 'stand-in' as genuine? Or did Henry fail to find the real Simnel, so he quickly arranged for a 'fake' to be produced in order to reassure his allies and frustrate his foes by showing that he had the pretender in custody? In that vein, John Ashdown-Hill has suggested that it is significant that when the famous incident took place of Henry making 'Simnel', now a Household kitchen servant, serve up wine to a party of visiting ex-rebel Irish lords around four years later – 'My lords, you will crown apes next' – the Irish did not recognise 'Simnel' until Henry identified him. Was this because the 'servant', i.e. the ten-year-old boy captured in 1487, was not the 'Simnel' who they had fought for?[4]

This is, however, modern not fifteenth-century speculation, and may make too much of genuine muddle and erroneous gossip about ages at the time. The scenario of an escaped Yorkist claimant receiving mercenary assistance from the English 'Lancastrian' regime's Burgundy foes resembled that of the invasion of England by Edward IV and a small army in 1471, with Lincoln (aged c.23) as the equivalent of the then 28-year-old Edward IV – and that invasion had succeeded. Edward's target Henry VI had been a mentally feeble 'puppet' of his advisers, which Henry VII was not; but Edward IV had had no more troops when he invaded than Lincoln did. The advantages of an incumbent sovereign's position in dissuading hesitant potential rebels might have saved Henry VI in 1471, had Edward's brother Clarence not defected back to him and the Percies refrained from attacking the invaders when they had a chance. Lincoln's chances of success seem less with hindsight than they would have done at the time; ironically the crucial piece of luck that had won Edward IV victory over the Neville brothers in March 1471 at Barnet had centred on a muddle in battle involving the man who was now Henry VII's chief commander, the Earl of Oxford.

The government in Dublin and its local Anglo-Irish aristocratic backers could be expected to back Henry's foes. The Yorkists had been careful to win their support, and Edward IV's father Duke Richard of York was remembered with affection as a capable – and, unusually, resident – Lord Deputy from the late 1440s. Richard had also been the heir of his mother's Mortimer dynasty (based in Shropshire and Herefordshire) to the lordship of Trim in Meath, Ireland. The Anglo-Irish warlords who traditionally backed the English regime in Dublin had sent troops to support the Yorkists in England in 1460–1, and the only major pro-Lancastrian Anglo-Irish dynasty were the Fitzgeralds of Desmond (Munster, south-west Ireland), heirs of the Earl of Desmond executed by Edward IV's regime in 1468 and currently not in power. The Lord Deputy who controlled the Irish regime in Dublin as of 1485 was currently Gerald Fitzgerald, Earl of Kildare, head of one of the Anglo-Irish territorial lordships whose power overshadowed that of the government and foe of their cousins the Earls of Desmond. He was a Yorkist loyalist and had not been replaced yet by the wary Henry, in case he launched a revolt and seized control of the regime in the name of York – presumably recognising Lincoln as king. The central government in

Dublin was so militarily weak that Henry had not dared risk immediate revolt by replacing Richard's Irish office-holders, headed by Kildare, in 1485. Simnel was accepted as king by Kildare, and was duly crowned as 'Edward VI' in Dublin (with a coronet borrowed from a statue of the Virgin Mary) on 24 May 1487.[5] He had some support in northern England during his subsequent invasion, in which Lincoln and Lovell's exiles and Kildare's Irishmen were assisted by a body of German mercenaries headed by Martin Schwartz (sent by Margaret of Burgundy). Landing at Barrow-in-Furness and received by local ally Sir Thomas Broughton, they penetrated across the Pennines into Yorkshire with no major support but no attempts to stop them either; as in 1485, a pretender with a force of English exiles, Anglo-Celtic lords' tenants, and foreign mercenaries were able to reach the Midlands where the incumbent King waited for them. Henry's army was not noticeably larger than the rebels', and was headed by the same veteran Lancastrian commander who had captained his force at Bosworth – the Earl of Oxford, formerly a lieutenant of the 'Kingmaker' at Barnet in 1471 and long held captive by Edward IV after seizing St Michael's Mount in the mid-1470s.

Unlike Richard, Henry could rely on his principal supporters in the crucial battle, although the small number of magnates fighting for him would suggest that many were wary of committing themselves to the royal cause in case the king lost and there was another change of dynasty. The rebels advanced south to the Trent, and Henry emerged from Nottingham with his army to march east and meet them on the river's southern banks near Newark. Notably, he had a relatively small and compact army led by the Tudor 'main wing' commander at Bosworth, the Earl of Oxford (also a veteran of Warwick 'the Kingmaker's Neville/Lancastrian army at Barnet in 1471 and probably the best general in England) rather than having called up a larger host of potentially unreliable lords. This gave his army more 'impact' in battle than a large and potentially muddle-prone force of unseasoned local gentry and nobles, but it has been suggested that he was wary of calling up lords who he did not trust lest they defect as part of the late king's army had done before Bosworth. His or Oxford's tactic was to present a solid and impenetrable infantry 'square' bristling with pikes, against which a rebel charge would break itself, and Henry kept back from the scene of action – ready to flee if he had to? After a fierce and initially evenly-balanced battle at Stoke near Newark on 16 June, the rebels failed to break the king's defensive 'square' and were picked off by a demoralising shower of arrows. They broke, and were driven into the nearby River Trent and slaughtered; Lincoln was killed, Simnel and Simon captured, and Lovell last seen trying to ride his horse across the river and presumed drowned. (According to one famous legend, he died later in hiding at Minster Lovell).[6]

The fact that some rebels claimed to be fighting to 'restore' the king and the confusion over the age of Simnel, apparently believed by some observers in Ireland to be around fifteen but aged around eleven when captured at Stoke, has led to a theory that it was the exiled Edward V that was crowned in Dublin but not risked to invade England in case the invasion failed.[7] The (not always accurate) early Tudor historian Bernard Andre referred to Simnel's supporters as backing 'Edward V', but was this just a slip? The very unusual names of the pretender, with no known late fifteenth-century 'Simnel' relatives ever traced, might also suggest that the mysterious boy was only using a pseudonym. In support, it is argued that Lincoln would hardly have foregone his own claim to the throne in favour of a clearly fake 11-year-old from a low social class but would have done so for Edward V. But why then was Simnel not crowned as 'Edward V' and the rebellion carried out in the latter's name? According to this theory, it was too risky in case the deposed king was captured by Henry when he ventured to England.[8] But it would have been rather difficult to proclaim a victorious Simnel, already crowned as 'Edward VI' (i.e. Warwick), as 'Edward V' instead once Henry had been overthrown – as was perfectly possible given the even nature of the sides at Stoke. If the divergence in ages between the 'sightings' of Simnel by observers – aged around fifteen or sixteen in Dublin but much younger when captured at Stoke – implies that there were two boys not one, with the more valuable and older pretender (Edward V?) crowned in Dublin and the ten-year-old brought to England as expendable, why did Lincoln's plotters not at least find a second boy the same age as the first? At the time or in subsequent decades, it was rumoured that if 'Simnel' had won at Stoke, Lincoln intended to supersede him as king, which Henry VII's 1620s biographer Sir Francis Bacon reported.[9] This is a logical explanation, and possibly Lincoln felt that more Yorkists would rise in the name of Warwick (as heir of Richard III's older brother Clarence, the heir to England until the birth of Edward V in 1470, so closer to Edward IV in blood than he was as son of Edward's sister). Also, it is possible that some Yorkists believed in Edward IV's marriage to Elizabeth Woodville being invalid as the 1484 Ricardian Act of Parliament '*Titulus Regius*' stated, so they might feel that Clarence and his son Warwick had been cheated of the throne but regard Lincoln as having an inferior claim. They might thus prefer not to fight for any real or fake 'Edward V', as under this Act he was illegitimate – and the cleric who had supposedly witnessed or carried out the 'secret first marriage' of Edward IV to Eleanor Butler c. 1462, Bishop Robert Stillington of Bath and Wells, was still alive in 1486–7 to bring the issue up again. '*Titulus Regius*' was suppressed and 'airbrushed out of history' by Henry VII in 1485–6 and he called in all copies of it and banned it from being cited in legal documents and Stillington was presumably 'persuaded' to keep quiet about why he had 'lied' earlier to assist Richard III in bastardising Edward V, but that does not mean that no ex-Yorkists believed that its story of Edward IV's children being bastards was true.

After the defeat of the revolt it was said that Henry had wanted to capture Lincoln alive in order to find out 'the bottom of his danger', and it is clear that the king believed that there was more to the plot than a simple plan by Lincoln to set up a 'lookalike' organ-maker's son as his pretender to be Lincoln's cousin the 'rightful King'. But this may refer to a search for other traitors at court – Edward V's mother Elizabeth Woodville, who was pushed into a nunnery and had her property transferred to her eldest daughter during the plot, and her allies? – rather than to Lincoln knowing the real whereabouts of Edward V. The number of senior lords who were involved with the next pretender, 'Perkin Warbeck', in the early 1490s – or at least sought to find out if he was genuinely Prince Richard – shows that Henry was not paranoid to suspect that many people who had accepted his regime in 1485 hankered after a Yorkist restoration. The doubts over the fate of the Princes meant that some could accept a plausible claimant to be one of them, not least as Henry's restoration of the legitimacy of Edward IV's children made one or other of his wife's brothers rightful sovereign again if alive. The seizure of Elizabeth Woodville's estates at the time of the Simnel rebellion is another source of excited speculation. In February 1487 she was required to retire to the royal apartments at Bermondsey Abbey, and her estates were transferred to her daughter the queen. The excuse was that Henry was angry with her because she had endangered his chances of seizing the throne in early 1484 by coming out of sanctuary at Westminster Abbey and handing her daughters over to their mutual foe, Richard III.[9] Having agreed at Christmas 1483 to let Henry marry her eldest daughter Elizabeth, she was now risking Richard preventing this by marrying Elizabeth off to another candidate – and when Richard's wife Anne died in March 1485 he was widely suspected of intending to marry her himself to deny her to rivals. He was even suspected of poisoning Anne to hasten her demise and make Elizabeth or another wife available for him quicker – and Elizabeth was rumoured to favour the match herself. A letter was unearthed in which she urged Richard's close ally John Howard, Duke of Norfolk, to help her obtain her desired marriage quickly. (Possibly this was a mistake for a plan to marry off Elizabeth abroad – probably in Portugal given the contemporary presence of a Portuguese embassy in London in spring 1485) As seen above, Richard had to swear an oath that he was not intending this, under pressure from his most loyal lieutenants who had warned him of the threat of revolt if he did marry his niece. Henry would have been informed of all this by his spies at court, led by his mother Margaret Beaufort – then married to Richard's supposed supporter Thomas Stanley, earl of Derby, who notoriously abandoned Richard and attacked his army at the battle of Bosworth despite Richard threatening to execute his hostage son if he did so.

But if Henry suspected Elizabeth Woodville of double-dealing, why wait to punish her until February 1487? This may have been due to prudence, in that he needed her to rally Woodville and Edward IV loyalists to his cause on his accession, and when his son Arthur was born in late summer 1486 a clearly non-disgraced Elizabeth Woodville was named as godmother. But the same surely applied to February 1487 when there was a threat of defections to 'Simnel' in Flanders; Henry was equally insecure then – though he needed money more to raise troops. The excuse was a rather harsh judgement on the ex-queen's actions, as Richard could have dragged her out of sanctuary whenever he chose – the Yorkist leadership had violated sanctuary to round up Lancastrian commanders at Tewkesbury Abbey after the battle in May 1471 and Richard had already forced her to hand over her younger son from Westminster Abbey in June 1483. She had to come to terms with him, and had evidently made the best bargain that she could as Richard had had to swear to treat her and her daughters honourably and find the latter suitable dowries and husbands. The reason Henry gave for her deprivation may have been partly true, and the issue quoted may have symbolised his resentment at her past double-dealing, but hinted that he feared she was doing so again. Given that he could not prove this latest alleged plan, he quoted an earlier one by her – also aimed at betraying him – instead. But her behaviour towards him in 1486–7 was clearly more vital to such a shrewd politician than her past activities in 1484–5, and the fact that her daughter the queen had still not been crowned has been cited as evidence that Henry mistrusted and sought to marginalise her family in general in 1486–7 – his wife included. Notably her son by her first marriage, Thomas Grey, marquis of Dorset – who had tried to defect from Henry's court in exile to return home in 1484–5 and so was proven unreliable already – was kept in custody during the Simnel invasion, as if Henry knew he could not trust him. It is possible, however, that Henry was merely aiming to add a 'safety-net' to his position in 1486–7 by not crowning his wife so if she was kidnapped by or defected to invading Yorkists she could not be re-married to someone else (Lincoln or Warwick?) as the already crowned i.e. legitimate co-sovereign. He had claimed his throne in 1485 via his own descent from the Beauforts, not via his then fiancée (and soon wife) Elizabeth of York, as if making her role less vital to him.

It was unusual for a politically active 'queen-mother' figure still only aged around fifty to 'retire' from administering her property with no hint of ill-health. Elizabeth also left court to reside at Bermondsey Abbey down the Thames from London, which had extensive royal apartments used by a previous 'retired' queen-mother, Henry VII's grandmother Catherine of Valois (only in her thirties but apparently ill) in the mid-1430s. Catherine had been in a degree of disgrace for her secret marriage (if such it was) to her ex-squire Owen Tudor, a minor Anglesey landowner far inferior to her in social 'station', and may have fallen ill after giving birth to the last of their children. Among previous dowager queens who had lived in retirement away from court, Edward III's mother Isabella (mostly resident at Castle Rising, a secular estate, from 1330 to her death in 1357) had been 'banished' in her late thirties but had been in disgrace for her affair with Roger Mortimer. Edward had overthrown their joint government to seize power, denied him by his mother, in October 1330; her affair with Mortimer, the man rumoured to have disposed of her husband Edward II, had been notorious and her presence at court would have been an embarrassment. Even so, the extent of her disgrace has been exaggerated by later legend. In Edward I's reign, his mother Eleanor of Provence had increasingly resided at her favourite convent, Amesbury, in the later 1270s and 1280s (and died in 1291) but she had been aged over sixty. In Henry III's reign, his mother Isabella of Angouleme (rumoured to be as promiscuous as her husband John, and still young) had voluntarily left England to marry again – to her ex-fiancee's son, Hugh of Lusignan – and had never come back. Henry VII was supposed to have considered removing Elizabeth Woodville in a similar manner, as a new wife for his ally James III of Scotland, in the two countries' negotiations in December 1487 – which was after her 'disgrace' and so indicated that he still regarded her as a diplomatic asset.[10]

As Elizabeth Woodville had been a major political actor throughout her career since 1464 it could be assumed that her sudden 'retirement' in her early fifties was involuntary and linked to the Simnel plot. Her subsequent – very occasional – appearances at court, as at Christmas 1489, and some polite official documentary references to her could be written off as necessary for the sake of appearances to reassure domestic and foreign observers. The only foreign visitor she definitely received was her distant relative, the Count of Luxembourg, who would have been suspicious if he had not been allowed to see her.[11] Had she contacted Lincoln and Duchess Margaret of Burgundy out of revenge against her long-term rival Margaret Beaufort, now more powerful than her at court as Henry's mother, and edging her out of any remaining influence? Or was the long delay by Henry VII in crowning his wife, her eldest daughter Elizabeth, doing more than irritating her? (A queen was usually crowned at or close to her marriage; Elizabeth Woodville herself had not had this advantage but that had been due to the secret nature of her wedding, only announced months after the event.) It is surprising that Elizabeth Woodville, with her eldest daughter Henry VII's wife and a grandson already born, would have jeopardised her position as the grandmother of the next king. This would install the supposed son of her mortal enemy Clarence on the throne. Clarence had abandoned her husband and sought to supersede both him and her son by allying with Henry VI in 1470, and in 1477 George had been claiming that he should be Edward IV's rightful heir. This can be interpreted as a hint that he had acquired details of the claim that Edward had been 'pre-contracted' to or had married Eleanor Butler before he married Elizabeth, and hence that she forced Edward to execute him to remove the threat to her and her children. In addition, Clarence's wife –like Richard III's – was the daughter of the 'Kingmaker' Earl of Warwick, who had opposed Elizabeth's marriage to Edward in 1464 and in 1469 tried to rid the court of Woodville influence by executing her father Earl Rivers and brother Sir John Woodville. Elizabeth was not a natural ally for any cause designed to put Clarence's son on the throne.

Hence it has been argued that she would have assisted the Simnel rebellion only if she had known that her own son Edward V would be the eventual beneficiary. (This is Bertram Fields' argument for Edward V being still alive and involved in the Simnel plot).[12] But Lincoln's and Elizabeth's motives may have been more complicated than at first apparent. The latter was denied any effective power at court by her rival Lady Margaret Beaufort, Henry's mother, and the Yorkist dynasty had suffered the 'snub' of Queen Elizabeth not yet having been crowned a year after her marriage. Elizabeth Woodville could have sought to rid herself of the Tudors and then remarry her daughter the queen to the 'restored' Warwick (Simnel) or Lincoln as her protégé. She could be the power behind Warwick's throne as she was not for Henry VII's. It is still not clear that Elizabeth Woodville's 'retirement' to Bermondsey Abbey and the transfer of her lands to her eldest daughter soon after the Simnel rebellion *were* connected to intrigues in favour of Simnel. But a voluntary retirement is perhaps unlikely for this most ambitious and 'meddling' of queens and the involvement of her rival Margaret Beaufort is probable if her withdrawal was forced by Henry VII. The fact that the belated crowning of her daughter followed Simnel's defeat and Elizabeth Woodville's 'retirement' may indicate that Henry only then felt secure enough to grant his wife this honour. Had he delayed it in case the Woodvilles sought to play up the role of a crowned queen as his political equal, the heiress to whom he owed his throne, or even to depose him in her favour? And did the fact that he made it a priority to secure a Papal ruling that his right to the Crown rested solely on his – not his wife's –genealogy indicate a desire not to rely on the untrustworthy Woodvilles? The key to this Papal case may be uncertainty over the status of Edward IV's and Elizabeth Woodville's marriage, which Henry had re-legalised by cancelling the

Act '*Titulus Regius*'. Having it announced by the highest source of church law that he was the rightful sovereign without relying on his wife's claims may have been a shrewd 'insurance policy' in case more evidence came to light invalidating the Edward-Elizabeth Woodville marriage, but would have infuriated his wife and her mother.

Was it possible for Elizabeth of York to reign as the sovereign in her own right, the logical result of any 'plot' to remove Henry VII by Elizabeth Woodville? The only case of a 'Queen Regnant' in English history had been the brief regime of the usurping – or legitimate – Empress Matilda in London in 1141, an arrogant and controversial woman who had quickly been deposed. It is unclear if Edward IV had intended Elizabeth as his heiress before his son Edward V was born in autumn 1470 – though the fact that his brother Clarence was plotting against him before Elizabeth Woodville had had a son may indicate this. But two queens had reigned – and changed husbands – in southern Italy in the past century or so, most notably the adulterous virago Joanna I of Naples (r. 1343–82). The younger line of Aragon in Sicily had ended with an heiress, Mary (r. 1377–1402); in north-eastern Europe Louis 'the Great' of Hungary and Poland had been succeeded in 1370 by one daughter (Mary) in Hungary and the other (Hedwig) in Poland. The minor state of Navarre had been transmitted by female descent (into the French royal family) by Queen Joanna in the early fourteenth century, by a second queen (Blanche) in the early fifteenth century; and by a third (Eleanor) in the mid-late fifteenth century. The phenomenon was thus not unknown. Henry could have feared eclipse and/or deposition by a faction led by his mother-in-law, and her son Dorset's 'preventive' arrest at the time of the Simnel revolt indicates that Henry suspected his loyalty too. The 'disgrace' of Elizabeth Woodville may not necessarily be linked to Simnel, but was probably political.

'Perkin Warbeck': was he Prince Richard? Or at least an illegitimate Yorkist?

The plots and the invasions

The next pretender to invade – 'Perkin Warbeck', claiming to be Edward V's brother Richard, Duke of York – had a limited degree of support in south-west England, though arguably this was as much regional autonomism from a staunchly 'separatist' society in Cornwall as Yorkist sentiment and it was in the immediate aftermath of a damaging anti-tax rebellion in 1497. This mysterious young man, of apparently regal bearing and tall fair good looks resembling Edward IV, first appeared in 1490 at Cork, a servant fresh off a Breton trading-ship displaying the rich robes on sale from his master Pregent Meno. He had come from a poor household in Tournai in Flanders originally, but according to the latter's 1496 story, he had been taken on by a neighbour of Portuguese-born Yorkist merchant Edward Brampton (Duarte Brandao) and his wife in Middleburg, after running away from his first job with an organist to find work in the larger city of Bruges. This was with a man who sold pins and needles. He was fourteen or fifteen at the time, i.e. 1487 at the latest, according to an ex-neighbour who had talked to his 'father' – a man who Brampton called 'Bernal Uberque'. 'Piers' was then taken on by Brampton as a servant at Middleburg after becoming friendly with Brampton's children, and at his own request accompanied him and his wife back by sea to the Iberian peninsula in search of a more adventurous life. He was then in service in a noble household in Portugal owned by one Pedro Vaz da Cunha, and a noble who had seen him with his master at court and been struck by his good looks, which he told to the 1496 investigators and confirmed that he had come to Portugal with the Bramptons. He remained with Vaz da Cunha for a year and then changed masters several times by his own 1497 'official' account, apparently voyaging overseas during a period of four or five years based in Portugal.

But the account of Brampton in 1496 differed from this, and had it that other pages' tales of adventure inspired Warbeck to ask for a job with Brampton for voyages (the adventurer sailed to Africa in these years of intense Portuguese exploration) but he was turned down. According to Brampton, Warbeck then decided to return home to Flanders, missed his intended ship, and ended up on the same ship as merchant Pregent Meno who paid him to display his fine clothes in ports. His arrival in Cork in autumn 1490, and decision to stop off there, was thus not his original intention – i.e. it was a whim, not a careful Yorkist plan to 'launch' him in a region known for its Yorkist sympathies (which cleared Brampton of any Tudor suspicions that he had advised his ex-protégé where to go and why he then claimed to be a Plantagenet prince). Brampton himself was a former unofficial 'agent' for and on the payroll of both Edward IV and Richard III, so his motives were likely to be questioned by the ever-vigilant Henry VII – and indeed as a close 'contact' of the late King Edward IV in 1483 with trading interests in London he had been in a position to smuggle Edward V and/or his brother Richard of York out of London on one of his ships if they had escaped from the Tower of London when they 'disappeared'. Was it just a coincidence that a boy who 'happened' to look like a Yorkist prince had taken service in Flanders with a former agent of two Yorkist kings? Warbeck was allegedly 'recognised' as a Yorkist prince by the locals in Cork, though according to his own 1497 confessions after he was captured by Henry VII, they originally thought he must be the Duke of Clarence's son Warwick – whose first impersonator had been 'Lambert Simnel', crowned in Dublin in 1487. He would thus have been aged around fifteen at the time,Warwick having been born in 1475. He took an oath on holy relics that he was not Warwick, but they persisted that he must be a Yorkist prince and he then had to deny that he was a bastard son of Richard III. He finally agreed that their third identification of him, as the Duke of York, was correct.[13]

Brampton's 1496 story was told to Spanish investigators sent to Setubal in Portugal to meet him and try to find out if 'Warbeck' was genuine, and so was not under Henry VII's control – though it was possibly 'doctored'by the Spanish sovereigns, King Ferdinand of Aragon and his wife Queen Isabella of Castile, who were uncertain enough if the pretender was genuine in the mid-1490s to refer to him in their secret diplomatic code in the manner reserved for legitimate kings, but who eventually backed their ally Henry VII and accepted him as a fake. The 'Setubal Testimonies' also included interviews with Spanish citizens who had met Warbeck in Portugal in the late 1480s – and one who had earlier seen the real Duke of York in England obligingly said that Warbeck looked different. The 1497 confessions by Warbeck after his capture by Henry (definitely approved and probably 'doctored' by the government), and the other sources, contemporary London chronicles not controlled by the government but using officially sanctioned statements plus current gossip, agree that 'Warbeck' sailed to Ireland from Portugal with Brampton. He was then approached in Cork by Yorkist sympathisers with a proposition to assist their attempt to overthrow the king by acting as a pretender. The confessions named the guilty parties – John Atwater, a local merchant who had been Lord Mayor of Cork; John Taylor, an

Englishman and a former servant of Clarence; and possibly also another Englishman, Stephen Poytron. They allegedly persuaded Warbeck to play the role of a Yorkist pretender – the confessions say an illegitimate son of Richard III, though Henry himself wrote in 1493 that Clarence's son Warwick was the first identity and Richard's bastard the second. He was to be the centrepiece in a new plot to depose Henry.[14] Somehow this identity soon changed to Richard of York, a couple of years older than Warwick – possibly the fact that the real Warwick was known to be in the Tower of London persuaded the plotters that Henry would just produce him to show up their candidate as he had done to Simnel.

Henry told the Milanese ambassador in 1499 that he would rather have Taylor in his hands than 100,000 crowns – he was thus a principal leader of the initial plot.[15] As with wanting to get his hands on the Earl of Lincoln in 1487, he clearly felt that there were 'undercurrents' in the plot beyond what was immediately obvious. Significantly, back in 1477/8 Taylor had been involved in an alleged plan by the soon-to-be arrested Clarence to smuggle his son Warwick out of England to preserve him from Edward IV for future plots. The young duke was then to be replaced with a 'strange child'.[16] Taylor was indicted for this plot by Parliament at the time of Clarence's trial and execution but was pardoned and he and his son continued to receive lucrative local posts from Edward IV's regime, but he was sacked by the new king in 1485 and soon after being granted a pardon for unspecified crimes in 1489 appeared in exile in Rouen (Edward IV's birthplace) plotting against Henry. When Atwater and Taylor were captured by Henry in 1499 the latter was only imprisoned and was duly released however, and instead Henry referred to Atwater as 'first mover and half-inventor' of the plot in a letter to Louis XII.[17] The other inventor was no doubt Richard III's sister, Dowager Duchess Margaret of Burgundy, as Henry's historians Bernard Andre and Polydore Vergil agreed. Vergil, writing at the Tudor court in the years after 1502, wrote that Margaret had been sending spies around to look for plausible boys to pass off as a Yorkist pretender for years before 'Warbeck's appearance c. 1490. They came across 'Warbeck'- a youth of unknown background, identified as clever and quick to learn and already speaking English– in Tournai.

Andre identified 'Peter of Tournai's' local patron as a converted Jew called 'Edward' who had been in Edward IV's service – a correct identification of the person and role of the adventurer Edward Brampton (Duarte Brandao), as will be seen.[18] The records show that Margaret was in contact with the government of the young King James IV of Scotland, which was hostile to Henry, and with exiled Yorkists there – Lovell, co-organiser of the Simnel revolt, was granted a safe-conduct to Scotland by the regime in 1487 but never arrived – and was with pro-Yorkists in Ireland from 1488 onwards. Did she send Taylor to Ireland to look for a suitable candidate to be the duke, or did she already have one in mind? Andre also named Stephen Frion, the former 'French language secretary' to Edward IV and Richard III (of Burgundian birth) who had deserted Henry for Margaret's service in 1489, as training Warbeck on her behalf and coaching him in the details which a Yorkist court resident should know. Records show that Frion had been complaining to Henry VII about overdue pay for years and he defected to France during a mission to the Continent before his next due payment (at Michaelmas) was handed over, soon going on to Margaret's court.[19] But it is uncertain if money was the defining factor in his desertion; he may have been assisting Margaret with information for years, dating back to the time of her alliance with her brothers' regime in England pre-1485. Frion and his unnamed friends then sent 'Warbeck' to Ireland in 1490 to appeal to local Yorkists. He returned to Ireland on Charles VIII's behalf to collect Warbeck for use as a pawn by the French government in 1492, but it is unclear if he had already informed Charles of the imposture back in 1489–90.

Frion would have known all the details of court life in the late 1470s and early 1480s that Warbeck was to recite to 'prove' his genuineness, whereas Taylor had not been so well-connected. The extent of the pretender's knowledge of court life was to be an important factor in persuading people to back him, adding to the argument presented by his personal appearance. But, as with physically plausible royal claimants as late as Anna Anderson ('Grand Duchess Anastasia' of Russia in the 1920s), it could be explained away by doubters as down to careful coaching by an 'insider'. Frion was the likeliest candidate for this role with Warbeck; Duchess Margaret had not lived in England since 1467 and had only paid one brief visit home in 1480. Despite all the allegations by Andre that she was the person who coached Warbeck, she was not in possession of enough information about English court life to assist him with intimate details and she had left England over twenty years before to marry the late Duke Charles, returning for one visit. Her support would have been mainly psychological, giving him the confidence to carry out his role and believe in himself as 'Prince Richard'. Again, it was to be alleged in the case of Anna Anderson that she certainly believed that she was 'Anastasia', even when facts suggested the contrary, and could absorb new details she had been given and add them to her story. Was Warbeck similarly suggestible?

In 1491 the rising antagonism between Henry and his one-time patrons in France led to King Charles VIII joining with Richard's sister, Margaret of Burgundy, and James IV in Scotland in alliance against England. James had been a former (sporadic) Yorkist ally too, promised Edward IV's daughter Cecily by that king while he was heir to the Scots throne and later offered a De La Pole niece of Richard III. Margaret had already been in diplomatic contact with James on his accession in 1488, sending him refugee Yorkists and receiving envoys in return, and it has been speculated that these plans centred on a (real or fake) 'Yorkist prince' now resident at her court in Flanders. According to Sir Francis Bacon's life of Henry VII, Margaret had been spreading rumours that Richard of York was alive in Ireland for at least a year before Warbeck arrived – suggesting that she had a pretender in mind to impersonate him. A grant of wine had been made to a 'son of Clarence' at Margaret's court back in 1486, when neither the real Warwick nor the fake 'Simnel' was there. Had this boy been a pretender she was nurturing?[20] It was possibly Warbeck, and Charles was now to tell James IV that Margaret had been nurturing him for years.[21] But this nurturing need not have been at her court, merely somewhere under her governance (Tournai?), and as there is no record of Warbeck at her court in 1486, it may have been another pretender. Was there any link to Taylor's activities in planning to smuggle Clarence's son abroad in 1477?

Given Taylor's part in the 'Warbeck' plot, his past activities might suggest that he thought up the idea of identifying the pretender as a son of his old employer – he knew all the details of Clarence's household which a plausible 'son of Clarence' would have to recite to questioners to seem genuine. There is even a possibility that Taylor had actually smuggled Clarence's son abroad in 1477 and the 'real' Earl of Warwick was brought up by Margaret (and /or sent to Ireland later) so the one put in the Tower by Henry in 1485 was a fake, as has been suggested in recent years[22] – but this must be reckoned unlikely. If Taylor had taken the 'real' Warwick abroad, then he and his allies in Cork in 1491 would have known precisely who 'Warbeck' was and would presumably have advertised him under his real identity – assuming that they had kept traces on the 'real' Warwick throughout his exile so they would have known that the boy who Brampton had taken up was him. There have also been suggestions in a claim by the leading Irish 1486–7 rebel, the Earl of Kildare, that 'Simnel' had been brought up by him in Ireland (rather than arrived there from Flanders in 1487) which implies that this boy – who might have evaded capture at the battle of Stoke, as suggested earlier – could be 'Warbeck'. But this is even less probable, given that the main witness to the early career of 'the' Warbeck was Sir Edward Brampton, according to whom in 1496 'Warbeck' had never set foot in Ireland until 1490.

In 1491–2 Charles sent a small force to southern Ireland to start a rising, on the scale of that which had seen 'Simnel' and his lordly sponsors in control of Dublin five years earlier, but this time the main nobles – crucially the ex-Yorkist Earl of Kildare and his faction – did not join in. Taylor was on a French ship which arrived in Ireland in autumn 1491, and significantly wrote to a fellow-ex-servant of Clarence's in England (John Hayes) saying that Charles was backing the cause of Clarence's son Warwick, now a Tudor prisoner in the Tower of London. Hayes, as 'receiver' (rent-collector) for the earl's estates in the south-west under the new regime in 1485, was asked to ready himself and collect other Clarence-Warwick partisans to aid the scheme.[23] Nothing came of this – but the focus of Charles' and Taylor's attention was thus on Warwick, not on Warbeck. It was apparently changed to backing Warbeck when the pretender arrived in Cork, but the reason for and timing of the change in candidate is unclear. The fact that the Taylor-Hayes group initially backed Warwick might imply that Taylor was not yet ready to use Warbeck, assuming that he knew his location in Flanders – or else that Warbeck was Brampton's protégé, not Taylor's, in 1491. Nor did Henry VII 's first mention of Warbeck, in a letter to Gilbert Talbot in 1493, provide much information on this issue. He claimed correctly that Margaret was at the bottom of it and had set Warbeck, the 'feigned lad', up in his role, but said that the pretender had initially played the role of Richard III's bastard son, then of Clarence's son (Warwick), and finally of Richard of York.[24] Richard III's son John of Gloucester had been imprisoned in the Tower in obscure circumstances connected to a plot in 1490 and executed[25] – but had Warbeck been claiming to be him before or after the execution? There is also the question of whether Richard III had had other illegitimate sons unknown to history and that Warbeck was intended at first to impersonate one of them who Taylor knew about, but could not get his hands on in 1490–1. The likeliest of these was the enigmatic 'Richard Plantagenet of Eastwell, Kent' – a mysterious figure, a skilled stonemason (able to write and read Latin, so well-educated) who was recorded in a much later history of Eastwell manor (the then home of the Moyle family) in the eighteenth century as having told Sir Thomas Moyle well into the sixteenth century that he was an illegitimate son of Richard III's. Apparently he had been brought up in obscurity by a schoolmaster/priest in the Midlands under the guardianship of an anonymous Yorkist lord who had taken him to see his father the king on the eve of the battle of Bosworth, but after the disaster he had hidden away in the countryside and trained as a builder. He had ended up working at Eastwell, and his tomb (dated 1550) was extant there in the eighteenth century – so was his patron someone such as Lord Lovell, and did Taylor think of putting him (or a boy claiming to be him) on the throne?

The identification of Warbeck's first impersonation with John or another son of Richard III's was to be changed in the 'confessions' that he made in 1497 – instead it was claimed that various people in Cork had identified him with Clarence's 'son', the 'fake' Warwick who had been in Dublin in 1487 (Simnel). Taylor's associates John Atwater (ex-Mayor of Cork) and Stephen Poytron (and Englishman), then intervened to tell him that they knew he was Richard III's bastard son John and persuaded him to change his 'identity' to this person. They trained him up in the sort of behaviour and knowledge that would be expected of a young man familiar with the Yorkist Court, before deciding to change his identity to Richard of York as John was known to be in prison in England.[26] Presumably they feared that Henry would produce John to confound them if they launched a revolt, as he had produced Warwick in 1487.

The timing of this was therefore before news of John's execution in 1490 reached Cork. But in Warbeck's own account of his visit to Cork to Queen Isabella of Castile – written of his free will, while he was at liberty and not 'doctored' – he had gone purposely to Cork claiming to be Richard of

York, rather than being spontaneously 'recognised' to his surprise on the quayside. He had sent letters ahead announcing his arrival, and had been greeted by expectant Yorkist partisans – presumably led by Atwater, as a leading citizen – as 'Richard'. If his purpose in sailing to Cork was this, Charles VIII, who authorised his sailing on a French ship and sent the Clarence partisan Taylor with him, had sent him. In any case, Atwater and his supporters probably took him to the leading local pro-Yorkist magnate, the Earl of Desmond. A rebellion failed to materialise, and they had to think again about where to launch his campaign against Henry.

Whatever happened in Ireland, in summer 1492 Warbeck was brought to France and placed in the charge of James IV's ambassador to France, Alexander Moneypenny, in Paris.[27] His escourt included Taylor and his son, Frion, and a bastard member of the Neville family (related to Clarence's wife Isabel). Ironically, France had been Henry VII's own chief backer against Richard III in 1485; their relationship had soured since then, over Henry's support for Breton independence as France endeavoured to take it over when Duke Francis II, Henry's old patron, died in 1488 (Henry's failed expedition to save Brittany had been led by Sir Edward Woodville, the ex-Queen Mother's brother and a mainstay of the resistance to Richard III in 1483.) Henry invaded France in retaliation that autumn of 1492 and besieged Boulogne, and in a private 'annex' to the resulting peace-treaty it was agreed that Warbeck should be expelled. He left Paris secretly for Flanders, possibly to avoid kidnap by Tudor agents *en route* as he claimed that Charles made sure that each of the places he stayed in overnight had an extra exit in case of emergency.

Having joined – or re-joined? – Margaret of Burgundy at Malines in winter 1492/3, Warbeck received his own household as the real 'Duke of York' and was recognised as legitimate king by her stepson-in-law Maximilian, son and heir to the Holy Roman Emperor Frederick III (who he was soon to succeed). The devious and calculating Maximilian was regent of Burgundy for his son Philip, his late wife Duchess Mary having died in a riding-accident in 1482. Writing to Queen Isabella of Castile on the pretender's arrival, Margaret said that the earls of Desmond and Kildare – Warbeck's partisans and hosts in Ireland – had informed her of his identity and sworn to its veracity. (As far as is known, neither had ever seen Prince Richard before 1483.) Before receiving him, she had sent anonymous people who knew the real Prince Richard to check him out in France and they had recognised him.[28] This letter left out the fact that Warbeck came from Flanders, although this would have swiftly become known to her (from his Flemish 'minder' Frion) even if he was not her direct 'plant' as a pretender in Ireland. There was no mention of Warbeck having been at her court as a boy, as would have been the case had he been smuggled out of England in 1483/4 at the time of the Princes' disappearance – which would have been the case if the money Richard III paid to Sir James Tyrrell at this point was really to pay for his taking the Duke of York to Margaret's court. If he had been in Flanders since 1483/4, why did Margaret not tell Isabella how she knew York/Warbeck's real identity from that fact, not from the sworn oaths of men in England and France? Her lack of honesty was probably due to a desire to hide her involvement – which would make Isabella aware that Warbeck was serving her political interests – and to imply that he had 'spontaneously' appeared in Ireland without outside help and was a miraculous sign of God helping the Yorkist cause.

Warbeck's current story, as given in a letter to Queen Isabella in 1493 and thus not 'doctored' as with the 1496 and 1497 accounts, spoke of him being 'about nine' – a peculiar reference, as the real Prince's precise age was well-known and he was ten at the time in 1483 – when an unidentified lord was ordered to kill the Princes and let him escape to Flanders but made him swear to keep his identity secret for some years.[29] Richard should have known his own age, although people unconnected to court – e.g. the chronicler Robert Fabyan, who made him aged seven in 1483 – were often vague about royal ages.[30] Probably this version of events and/or the stories current at Margaret's court in the 1490s lay behind the version of the 'Divisie Chronicle' of Holland, Zealand, and Friesland of c.1500 which had Buckingham as the lordly killer who spared one boy and smuggled him abroad, with 'Richard' being in the care firstly of Louis XI of France (i.e. before that King died on 30 August 1483) and then of Duchess Margaret.[31] The involvement of Louis would fit in with a statement by his chronicler Commignes that he heard about the killings, which altered his view of Richard III – but in this case Louis had heard of Edward V being killed and knew that Richard of York was alive. One version, recorded by Jean Molinet, gave details of Richard of York begging for his life with the killers and being smuggled out to safety – presumably retailed by Warbeck himself.[32] Assuming Warbeck left France on Louis' death as he did not mention help from Charles' regency after that date, he would have been too young in 1485–7 to be useful to Margaret as a pretender and in any case 'Simnel' was fulfilling that role. Accordingly, it would be logical for her to lodge Warbeck with a friendly family in the town of Tournai until he was needed. Warbeck spoke vaguely of two men who had come with him from England looking after him, until one died and the other left Flanders – but he did not name them.

Assorted English exiles lived at Margaret's court, and malcontents visited there from England in secret to obtain aid for new Yorkist plots. Warbeck now served as a focus for their efforts, but in practical terms Margaret – only a dowager duchess, not the ruler of the area – was short of money to aid him. Hence presumably the appeals to sovereigns such as Isabella, which were carefully 'spun' to minimalise Warbeck's Burgundian patronage from the start of his exile. He was put up at a mansion in Malines, and later at the house of the English Merchant Adventurers in Antwerp where he displayed his arms as 'Prince of Wales and Duke of York' – and had pro-Tudor English visitors throwing mud at the latter. Hugh de Melun, governor of Dendermonde, took charge of his affairs on Maximilian's behalf and organized a bodyguard of thirty men wearing the Yorkist 'White Rose' livery. According to Maximilian, Warbeck alleged that bodily marks proved that he was the prince and he showed them to anyone who doubted him – which fits in with the 1496 Portuguese testimony about the marks being how a visiting Portuguese herald checked out the 'Prince's identity with Jean Osbeck, the father of 'Warbeck' according to Henry Tudor, in Tournai.[33] Maximilian, Margaret's stepson-in-law, was convinced – or was eager to overthrow Henry due to the latter's reconciliation with France, the Habsburgs' enemy. He received Warbeck with royal honours in Vienna as the funeral of Maximilian's father, Emperor Frederick, took place at the end of 1493 and he married Bianca Sforza the following spring.

Now that Maximilian had control of the Habsburg empire and resources, he admitted Warbeck to his court as a favoured friend and rightful king, gave him the resources which the politically weaker Margaret (who had only the funding of a duke's widow in Burgundy/Flanders) could not, and attached him to his son Philip's new ducal court in Flanders. Maximilian accompanied Philip to Flanders in September 1494 for his inauguration-ceremonies, as did Warbeck who took part in the ceremonial. All Henry could do was to send an ambassador to Margaret in autumn 1493 to warn that royal honours were being given to a 'cooking-pot' boy of base birth;[34] Margaret was said to have tried to assault him. In spring 1495 the captain of Henry's bodyguard and his (illegitimate) Beaufort cousin, Sir Charles Somerset, disparaged Warbeck during an official visit to Maximilian's Flemish court, and refused to bow to him. When Maximilian protested, he said that Richard of York was dead and buried and claimed he could show anyone who doubted it the site of his burial – which was inaccurate unless he meant one of the Tower of London chapels.[35] Does this tie in with the story by Thomas More in his unpublished biography of Richard III (written c. 1510) that the Princes had been secretly buried in consecrated ground? If so, the story that More heard c. 1510 of murder in the Tower by hired assassins, a temporary burial under some stairs nearby, plus a secret reburial by a priest was known to Henry and his court by 1494. Logically, if Somerset knew the location so did his king – but Henry had not made it publicly known, possibly as the priest had soon died (as More said) so finding the site would have entailed an embarrassing and public quest to dig up the chapel floor. Nor was the chief assassin named by More, John Dighton, ever put on trial for regicide by Henry who would have found him a useful scapegoat – so had Henry dismissed the Dighton story (preserved by More so presumably told him by one of Henry's ministers/courtiers, such as More's ex-employer Archbishop John Morton) as a fake, after not finding any bodies at the right spot? Maximilian always insisted that Warbeck was genuine, and it would have been by his instructions that Warbeck was allowed to mint coins (containing the words of the 'writing on the wall' that Daniel interpreted for the doomed tyrant Belshazzar, here meant as Henry) and to use a royal seal as 'Richard IV' in 1494. This was going beyond the normal encouragement for a resident pretender to the English throne given by European sovereigns, e.g. Louis XI's to Margaret of Anjou and her son in the 1460s and by Charles VIII to Henry in 1485; the cautious Duke Charles of Burgundy, Margaret's husband, had conspicuously refrained from recognising her deposed brother Edward IV as rightful King in 1470–1.

Maximilian was a wily politician, not an idealistic romantic, so his open snub to Henry VII was a political rather than a chivalrous act – a gambit in a game of high stakes. He made ruthless use of Warbeck for his own aims, by forcing him to sign a document bequeathing his rights to the English throne to the 'King of the Romans' (Maximilian was not yet crowned Emperor) and his son Philip before he set sail to claim it. If Warbeck was captured and killed Maximilian had a legal claim on England, and if he succeeded he was 'Richard IV's heir until the new King had a child.[36] Genealogically speaking, the only legal Habsburg claimant to the English throne could be Maximilian's son Philip when he married Princess Juana of Spain – Juana was the descendant of John 'of Gaunt's second marriage, whose offspring had been legitimate unlike the children of his third marriage, ancestors of Henry VII's mother. Philip's claim by matrimonial right was no worse than that of Henry himself, given that Henry's direct Plantagenet ancestry was from John of Gaunt's third marriage, to Catherine Swynford – and that John and Catherine's children had been barred from the succession by Act of Parliament in 1396. These children, unlike Philip's ancestress, had been conceived out of wedlock.

But in practical terms Henry could counter conspiracy within England if not persuade Maximilian and Philip to abandon their protégé. In spring 1493 the plotters included former royal household men and Ricardian loyalists such as Robert Clifford and the current Steward of the Household, Lord Fitzwater, who consulted with Sir William Stanley (Lord Chamberlain and brother to King Henry's stepfather, who had notoriously turned on Richard III in the nick of time as the armies clashed at Bosworth). The latter might be assumed to be content with his eminence at the Tudor court but evidently was not, and Henry may indeed have distrusted him already and complained about the slowness he had shown in coming over to him at the battle. Stanley promised the 'White Rose' cause his secret support, and with his agreement Clifford went to Malines to enter Warbeck's service. The Prior of the Order of Knights of St John (the Hospitallers) in England, John Kendal, the order's head in Ireland Sir James Keating, Thomas Langton (Bishop of Winchester), Archdeacon Hussey of London, and other senior clerics were involved along with a sprinkling of Londoners and Yorkist gentry, and Kendal set about turning his money-raising expertise for the order for Warbeck's cause. Concurrently still a trusted royal diplomat, he allegedly used a visit to Rome to consult astrologers about their success and was offered, but declined to use, a 'magical' potion to poison the king and his family (according to a 1496 confession by his agent De Vignolles). Apparently this was so toxic that he feared to touch it, and instead of smearing it on a doorpost at Henry's palace to drive anyone who smelt it into a regicidal frenzy he threw it away.[37]

Also involved were men close to Richard III's and Duchess Margaret's mother (i.e. Richard of York's grandmother) Cecily Neville, now in her late seventies and living in retirement at Berkhamsted Castle, including the dean of her chapel (Richard Lessy) and the prior of the nearby Dominican priory of King's Langley; some local gentry arrived at Malines in 1493.[38] Her attitude to their activities is unclear. There were traitors in the garrison at Calais, as well as men with more obvious Yorkist connections such as Sir James Tyrell's cousin Thomas, Suffolk landowner Sir Gilbert Debenham (pardoned in 1486), and the Cumbrian ex-Ricardian Skeltons. Henry VII's historian Bernard Andre categorised them as a mixture of desperate penniless adventurers, outlaws, ex-Yorkists, men brooding that Henry had not rewarded them sufficiently for past service, and bored gamblers seeking excitement. The involvement of a network of clerics was particularly troubling, showing that such men disregarded Henry's acquisition of a Papal Bull backing his rights and excommunicating all rebels (1486). At a previous time of uncertainty over an ex-king's alleged survival, a clerical network had backed pretenders to the name of the murdered Richard II against his replacement Henry IV. More men than were openly involved were said to be passing on money to Warbeck secretly.

The court of exiles that Warbeck was gathering around him in Malines seems to have been penetrated by royal agents who gained access to lists of supporters in England, and in 1493 their clerical allies were already being hunted down, and a circle of inflammatory London pamphleteers rounded up too.[39] Clifford seems to have taken the lead in England in approaching the most valuable recruit, Sir William Stanley, in spring 1493; according to the 'official' story he discussed Warbeck's appearance in Flanders with Stanley who said he would not oppose a genuine 'Prince Richard'. He asked Clifford – who was trusted by the regime, having fought for Henry at Stoke and received confiscated lands of Lord Lovell's, and was used to going abroad on minor diplomatic missions for the king – to enter Warbeck's service. Clifford was to tell Warbeck that Stanley was sympathetic but would not declare for him yet, an echo of Sir William's caution in standing aside from both armies at Bosworth (and allegedly dressing his men up in Simnel's livery at Stoke ready to defect if advantageous).[40] Clifford was also offered troops by Henry's steward of the household, Lord Atwater. Clifford duly appeared at Malines, and during 1494 became trusted by Warbeck so that he was able to act as witness to his secret treaties with Margaret and Maximilian that December; but he also visited Calais without attracting suspicion. Presumably the authorities there had orders not to arrest him, as Henry was being kept informed of who was at Warbeck's court; but was Clifford passing on details of events at Malines to Henry's men there? Or was he pretending to serve the king while really working for Warbeck?

The question also arises of whether he had let the English government know of his arrangement to work for Stanley at Malines and await their prearranged signal for Sir William to revolt. Henry VII may not have been taken by surprise by the extent of treachery close to him in 1494–5, but have been drawing up a list of suspects based on what Clifford was telling his agents in Calais. He was also collecting information about Warbeck – or drawing up his false identity for him, as the latter's backers would have claimed. His 1494 instructions to his embassy in France show that Henry was now aware that Warbeck was the son of a boatman. The instructions referred to research among those who had known Warbeck in earlier years as well as among defectors from the court in Malines.[41] One source may have been the merchant Pregent Meno, on whose ship Warbeck had first arrived in Cork; he was captured by an English ship in late 1491, never punished, and ended up with a regular Royal grant and valuable employment in Ireland.[42] In July 1494 Henry's envoy to Duke Philip's court, the Garter Herald, boldly proclaimed that Henry had proof that Warbeck was a low-born impostor and when Philip and Margaret ignored him, and announced it in the public square.

Already in April 1493 two pro-Warbeck plotters in London, Stanley's young relative Humphrey Savage and the Suffolk knight Sir Gilbert Debenham, had been detected and forced to flee to sanctuary in Westminster Abbey. Possibly the Welshman who had brought them a letter from Warbeck was a 'double agent'. They were allowed to stay there and watched not removed, but early in 1494 a more humbly-born group of London plotters (who had been putting out seditious papers) were dragged out of sanctuary at St.Martin-le-Grand's. Hangings followed. Later in

1494 a major round-up of plotters in England, including Lord Fitzwater and the churchmen, broke the back of the first serious attempt to start a rebellion.[43] Either this success or the following defection of Clifford was linked to the story circulated by the Flemish chronicler Molinet, that three members of a group of Tudor court defectors to Warbeck were government 'plants' who re-defected to Henry after collecting useful information. (These three men can be traced as arriving from Warbeck's court at Calais in October).[44] Late that year Clifford 'defected' back to Henry and exposed other plotters, leading to the arrest of Stanley and others early in 1495. According to the London citizen Robert Fabyn's account, he had spent two years at Warbeck's court, initially believing in his Royal identity, before becoming disillusioned.

Clifford's swift pardon on 22 December, almost as soon as he had arrived in London,[45] had aroused suspicion; why would Henry pardon him so quickly if he was a genuine rebel whose complete conversion and total confession could not be guaranteed? Surely he would normally have been 'lent on' and threatened with execution for some time, to induce him to co-operate fully? He was in fact still being referred to as a prisoner in January; Polydore Vergil's version has him so terrified that he threw himself at Henry's feet when the king arrived at the Tower for his Christmas stay and named his principal 'contacts' (including Stanley).[46] The early pardon is not conclusive, and may suggest that he had to be reassured as to his fate before he would talk. The Lord Chamberlain's execution (14 February) showed the immediacy of the threat close to Henry; Fitzwater was kept in prison near Calais for a year before being executed, possibly for a further plot. The churchmen, having benefit of clergy, escaped with their lives but had to pay heavy fines; Kendall was not even removed from office but had to pay a large bond (£60) for his future good behaviour. It was subsequently alleged that Clifford (soon made Master of the Ordnance) had been a 'double agent' all along, and that his supposed disillusionment with Warbeck and discovery that he was a fake was by arrangement with his masters in London. It is more likely that he genuinely had second thoughts, and that in 1494 the king still regarded him as an enemy. Bernard Andre, Henry's court panegyricist, wrote that Clifford had been persuaded to abandon the plotters by his friends to save himself from ruin; he was not showered with rewards in 1495 as might be expected for a master-agent apart from an initial £500.[47]

It is not impossible that he had been working for both sides during 1494, intending to decide on who to back by their chances of winning. Nor had Stanley done much to help Warbeck in practical terms, though his verbal approval of him in the event that he was Edward IVs' son and his encouragement to Clifford to go to the pretender's court technically amounted to treason; he was duly charged, pleaded not guilty to no avail, and was executed.[48] A further round of mass-trials and executions of the London plotters and gentry followed, with French chronicler Molinet hearing that Henry showed them the hijacked letters they had written to Warbeck adorned with their seals to silence any attempts by them to argue their innocence.[49] The church plotters were given gaol-sentences in line with the usual 'benefit of clergy' leniency normal since Henry II's clash with St Thomas Becket – but the avaricious Henry made Dean Worsley of St Paul's Cathedral pay a large sum to have his death-sentence commuted.

Warbeck belatedly sailed across the Channel with Flemish ships lent by Archduke Philip in July 1495 to try his luck in Kent – a centre of the summer 1483 revolt on the Princes' behalf. Maximilian was short of money but had managed to borrow a reasonably sized sum for him, as had Margaret and some sympathetic Flemish bankers and lent Warbeck some mercenaries, but they lacked a skilled captain like the 1487 commander Schwartz and Warbeck had few experienced men with local knowledge of south-east England beyond a handful of exiled Yorkist captains and gentry. His attempted landing at Deal was a fiasco and lacked Simnel's and Lincoln's capacity in 1487 to rally local support and march on the capital, though Kent was closer to London so the royalists found defence easier and the rebels had no respite to set up a base (or a major local figure to host them as Sir Thomas Broughton had done in 1487 Furness). His small 'army' of mostly European mercenaries had only a few English renegades and no nobles, with no major conspirator except Kendal still at large to organise within England. His men were initially unopposed and appeared to be welcomed, but even the inexperienced Warbeck was too cautious to go ashore, which was wise as the invaders were soon ambushed. They were ignominiously defeated with around 150 killed, and the survivors were rounded up and executed. At the best, the local gentry had been slow to attack his men when they landed – but that might have been due to anxiety in case any more rebels landed to intercept them, rather than a hesitation about fighting for Henry.[50] Maximilian hoped in vain that Warbeck had landed successfully and would soon be in a position to send him English help to fight his foes in France. He continued to hedge about joining Henry in a new international alliance in diplomatic talks that summer and autumn in case Warbeck won after all, but sent no more money or troops; having succeeded his father as Emperor in December 1493, he had other more pressing priorities. His son Philip in Flanders could or would not help either, and even Margaret had to give up any meaningful support after Henry's negotiators exercised the 'power of the purse' in the new Anglo-Flemish trade-negotiations that now led to the 'Intercursus Magnus' treaty in 1496. The treaty explicitly banned the maintenance of any rebels against Henry's authority in Philip's domains and required the expulsion of any who the king named, and Margaret had to sign up to this to save the treaty and preserve the region's economy which depended heavily on exports from England.

In fact Warbeck returned to Ireland in the hope of receiving as good a reception as Simnel had had in 1487, but the formerly pro-Yorkist Earl of Kildare had evidently learnt his lesson and in return for his pardon in 1489 kept away from all subsequent Yorkist plots. The new Lord Deputy, the centralising English military commander Sir Edward Poynings – author of 'Poynings' Law which required the Irish Parliament to act subject to an English veto on its legislation – had brought an end to the slack governance of the 1480s, and the turbulent nobility were now under his watchful eye and knew that any plotting would face a ruthless response. Had Charles VIII or Maximilian sent an expedition before Poynings' arrival, the Yorkists would have had a better chance. The poorly-financed and manned expedition received no major support except for the Earl of Desmond (a supporter in 1491), the city of Cork (thanks to local stalwart Atwater, Warbeck's backer in 1491) and the out-of-reach Gaelic magnates O'Neill of Clandeboye and Tyrconnell in the north. Warbeck struck lucky at first as his small squadron of seven ships arrived at Youghal to capture a passing English merchant-ship, impound it, and sell its cargo to buy arms and hire local mercenaries, but he could not take any major town. He was beaten off as he and Desmond tried to storm loyalist Waterford, four of his ships were captured by local loyalists with better cannon on their ships, and after drifting across western Ireland northwards for two or three months and achieving nothing (one story had it that he had been shipwrecked *en route*) he gave up on the campaign. As the king's troops closed in, he set sail for Scotland.[51] He was accepted by Margaret's ally James IV as rightful king of England and was granted James' kinswoman Lady Katherine Gordon as his wife.[52] He joined in James' brief incursion into Northumberland to attack Norham Castle in 1496, but this was repulsed within days and the pretender's complaints at the Scots ill-treating his invaded countrymen were not welcome.[53] Left to his own resources, as James received envoys from Henry proposing an alliance in return for handing him over, he evaded attempts by Ferdinand and Isabella to lure him to Spain as their pawn. Apparently they and their ambassador in England, De Puebla, were hoping that once they had 'Richard IV' safe in Spain that would induce Henry to accept their terms for the long-discussed marriage of their daughter, Catherine of Aragon, to Henry's elder son and heir Prince Arthur –a piece of genteel blackmail for Spain's and not Warbeck's benefit. In line with that, their ambassador in Scotland, De Ayala, pretended to James IV that his sending Warbeck to Spain would assist the latter's cause, and tried to hoodwink him into acting as the Spanish sovereigns' ally in this. Instead, James appears to have left it up to Warbeck what he did – though he offered him no further aid.

Meanwhile Ayala warned Warbeck that once James' impending negotiations with Henry got underway the Scots king would accept an offer of Henry's elder daughter Margaret for his wife and hand over Warbeck, so he should head to Spain. The pretender did set sail on a Spanish ship, but not to Spain. Instead he now landed at Land's End on 7 September 1497, with minimal support offered beforehand or when he landed from local gentry and none from any nobles. Already he had had to hide from English government searchers on board his (Spanish) ship as they boarded it looking for him *en route* from Ireland, and had boldly – and wisely? – turned down all suggestions that he head for safety in Castile to join Queen Isabella's court.[54] Ireland was now no use to him, as his main local supporter, Sir James Butler of Ormond (a cadet of the large Butler dynasty of the Tipperary region), was killed by his cousin and rival, the loyalist Sir Piers Butler, just before Warbeck arrived; O'Donnell and O'Neill followed Kildare's lead in keeping out of trouble.

By bad luck, he had arrived in Cornwall just after the suppression of a massive peasant rebellion against the high taxes raised by the king to pay for his Scots war against James IV and Warbeck. The rebels, led by the lawyer Thomas Flamank and the blacksmith Michael Joseph from the village of St Keverne, had started their rebellion like the 'Peasants' Revolt' in 1381 by killing a tax-collector, then fearing royal punishment, they went further. They had marched all the way from Bodmin to Kent in June before being surrounded and wiped out by Royal troops at Blackheath. Luckily for the Cornish, the king's army was currently *en route* to the Scottish border to tackle James as they marched east, and so they reached Kent unhindered; later questions were asked about why the royal commander, Lord Daubeny, had taken so long to arrive to rescue the government.[55] Had he been hedging his bets? If Warbeck had landed in time to put himself at their head with promises of tax-remission he would have had a formidable, if no more experienced or better-armed, force. His numbers might have persuaded a few pro-Yorkist gentry to join him, though the main network of his supporters across the country had been exposed by the king's agents in 1495. He landed at Whitesand Bay near Land's End – as far to the west as possible to keep his distance from any loyalist attack – with around eighty Irish mercenaries and a few dozen English and Scots supporters at most, and was only able to raise a few hundred men, none of them socially impressive gentry – at least the recent rebels had had one peer on their side.[56] Leaving his wife at St Michael's Mount, he marched as far as Exeter, which held out against his attack on 17–18 September thanks to the local Royal troops under the Earl of Devon. Warbeck's force managed to storm a gate but was driven out again in fierce fighting, and as Lord Daubeny's main royal army approached he marched on to confront him.[57] He got as far as Taunton on the 21st, but his ill-equipped army was clearly outnumbered and was becoming demoralised and Warbeck lost heart. Unwilling to face a hopeless battle, he abandoned his dwindling army and made for the Hampshire coast to find a boat.[58] He ended up in sanctuary at Beaulieu Abbey, where he was surrounded by Royal troops and persuaded to emerge of his own accord rather than being dragged out.[59] In one of the many ironies of late fifteenth-century history, the last important anti-government refugee to turn up there after a battle had been Richard III and Clarence's mother-in-law the Countess of Warwick, grandmother of the boy whose identity Warbeck had first assumed, in 1471.

The confessions: a pack of lies, or a mixture of truth and Tudor 'spin'?

Warbeck's confession to Henry VII after capture that he was not Prince Richard but a Flemish boatman's son from Ostend was full of mistakes and inconsistencies that cannot be explained away, due to imperfect Anglicizations of Flemish names and places or a hasty, muddled compilation of details by Henry's agents. Henry, a methodical and careful ruler who left nothing to chance, had had his men checking out details of 'Warbeck' for years, and had said he knew he was really called Warbeck and was from Tournai in 1494.[60] From 1495 his French allies had been assisting him in compiling information from local interviews within French-ruled Picardy, though their initial version had Warbeck as the son of a barber not a boatman. However, the King preferred to call the pretender '*le garcon*' without using his surname until 1497, which may indicate uncertainty as much as publicly reassuring contempt. Initial use of 'Warbeck' in English references to him – including Henry's own comments of 1493–4 – were then altered, as Henry referred to him as 'Osbeck' in a letter to Canterbury after the abortive landing in July 1495 and in a letter to Waterford in October 1497 he called him 'Piers Osbeck'.[61] Presumably some informant, either his own researchers or his French or Portuguese allies, had come up with the new name. Possibly Brampton, who was by 1499 acting as an ambassador from the King of Portugal to Henry and was given exemption from customs-dues for his goods at Southampton, had started to 'spill the beans' (or helped Henry to make up a plausible story in return for his past activities being overlooked?).

The captured rebel supposedly talked freely to Henry when he was taken to him at Exeter from Beaulieu, although Henry also made people who had known the real Richard of York (e.g. his half-brother the Marquis of Dorset and a royal household servant) testify that he was a fake. The accounts of the historian Bernard Andre and the Milanese ambassador Soncino make it clear that the confession was drawn up quickly in early October and sent around Europe (the version Soncino saw was in French).[62] This shows that Henry's men had done the basic work in compiling it already and the King did not have to wait to check out details that Warbeck had given them in Flanders; Henry's researches in 1494–6 were deemed adequate for the task. One French copy of the confession was sent overseas quickly via Calais, as a propaganda riposte to Warbeck's backers in Flanders, and is probably the one that survives at Courtrai. Its touches of the local Picard dialect, correct Flemish names, and lack of explanation of local geography has been taken as possible proof that it was a verbatim account by a native Fleming – i.e. the 'original' confession by Warbeck himself (or a compilation from details given by Henry's Flemish informants.) The alternative explanation is that it was the story compiled on Henry's behalf by the French investigators in Picardy since 1496, to which Henry hastily added a few extra details which Warbeck gave him in person. In that case, its linguistic accuracy does not show that Warbeck was a genuine Flemish boy.[63]

The English version of the 'confession' had more inaccuracies and was also full of legal language, as if translated by and for Henry's lawyers who were less familiar with Flanders and Flemish. Given the differences between it and the French version, it may be a separate document – from different sources – rather than a direct (but incompetent and hurried?) translation. This version of the confession may have been based on a document already prepared in London before 1499, as a result of Henry's own researches – and inventions? The divergence between the two is unusual, given Henry's usual carefulness to draw up a 'water-tight' case, but may indicate his need for haste to reassure Warbeck's Continental backers that the pretender had admitted that he was a fake. Accordingly, the English version may have been drawn up with less care for accuracy than the more important version that had to be sent abroad, and there was no time to collate the two before despatching them.

Even in the French version of the confession, the pretender's father was said to be 'John Osbek', the 'comptroller' of the Flemish river-port of Tournai – a post which did not exist. The man in question was in fact 'Jehan Warbecque'. The pretender's 'maternal step-grandfather', Pierart Flan – in fact he was only his godfather – was called the 'receiver' of Tournai and dean of the boatmen's guild; in fact the two offices could not be combined and he was only the latter. His maternal grandfather, Pierre Farou, was described as keeper of the keys at the gate of St Jean, whereas in fact there was only a 'wicket' entrance in a fence not a proper gate. Warbeck's supposed mother, who Jehan de Warbecque married in 1473, was Nicaise Farou, not 'Kathryn de Faro'.[63] The French version also included a long list of Warbeck's schoolfriends, teachers, and neighbours who could testify to his identity – evidently people contacted already by

Henry's agents and/or the French, and now cited so that Continental doubters reading the confession could go to Tournai and check with them. The addition made to the French version also contradicted the main text of both versions in saying that Warbeck had been educated at the cathedral school in Tournai, rather than hardly being educated at all (more normal for a boatman's son). In this version, instead of being shuttled around relatives in Tournai as the English version had it, at the age of ten he was suddenly sent away in some form of apprenticeship with a merchant called Berlo at Antwerp and passed on by him to a haberdasher (John Strewe) in Middleburg. Possibly this detail was added at the last minute as Henry received the information, and there was no time to re-write the earlier part of the statement to accommodate it. Nor was there time to add this detail to the English version.[64] But all this detail added to the mystery in one sense – how could an ordinary working-class Flemish boy with no courtly background or high social connections have passed himself off as the son of a king successfully to the sovereignsof Europe for so long, as chronicler Molinet for one asked (and Sir Francis Bacon did later).[65] There may be comparisons here with the surprise expressed in the late twentieth century when the Romanov pretender 'Anna Anderson', aka 'the Grand Duchesss Anastasia', was identified by others (she denied it) as the runaway Polish factory-worker Francisca Szanchowska. Could a plausible and adaptable ordinary person, with a flair for acting and a receptive memory, really pass themselves off as a royal provided they were given the right coaching – and did either believe their supposedly assumed identity? Or were their enemies trying to allege that they were working-class frauds and/or deluded fantasists to put their more snobbish backers off?

Another testimony to Warbeck's background with a different story came from Sir Edward Brampton (Duarte Brandao), the mysterious Anglo-Portuguese merchant adventurer, as retailed in 1496 to Don Alonso de Silva during an official investigation into the pretender's background. This version had not been tampered with by Henry's officials for propaganda reasons and preceded Warbeck's capture, and thus is more likely to be accurate. Brampton called 'Piers' Warbeck the son of 'Bernal Uberque', a boatman of the district of St Jean in Tournai, who had been educated at the Tournai cathedral choir-school and apprenticed to an organist. He had run away after a few years and ended up working for a needlemaker in Antwerp. ('Uberque' was presumably a phonetic rendering of the Flemish name by its Portuguese translator. A distant relative, Gaspar de Weerbecque of Oudenarde, was a distinguished musician – which might explain why a boatman had allowed his son to have such an education unusual for his background.) He had been running wild in the streets when the Bramptons first came into contact with him, but had clearly been eager to better himself. The boy had told some French friends his own age in the service of Brampton's wife, who was living near his employer's house in Tournai while a refugee from the plague, that he wanted to travel. Warbeck had secured a place in her service when she set out for Portugal to join her husband, presumably from the other dates that were given around 1488. There Warbeck had been placed with a nobleman called Pedro de Cunha, and had first appeared in public wearing fine clothes at a ceremony in honour of the Prince of Portugal – two facts testified to by other witnesses. Brampton testified that at the time Warbeck had only been able to speak French, which meant that he had learnt his courtly English (apparent by 1496) from his sponsors in Ireland in 1490–1, with probable refinements at the Burgundian court. This was at variance with earlier stories of Warbeck's linguistic accomplishments, that had said he could speak English before he was taken up by his political 'sponsors'.

At the time, Brampton had no clear reason to hide any fact that Warbeck spoke English when the boy entered his wife's service – Warbeck could still have successfully overthrown Henry at this point so Brampton did not need to please the latter in order to retain his business-status in England. After some time in Portugal the ambitious Warbeck, disgruntled by Brampton's failure to take him into his household as an adopted son, had proposed to return to Flanders with one of the latter's sons but had missed his ship and had to take one that was travelling via Ireland. There he had earned money by parading in port advertising the clothes of a merchant who was on the voyage (i.e. Pregent Meno), and had first been hailed by the locals as Duke Richard of York. (There is no mention here of Taylor and Atwater as suggesting the idea to Warbeck.) In another one of these 'Setubal Testimonies' passed on to Henry in 1496, a Portuguese court herald confirmed that he had heard that Warbeck was from Tournai and had come to Portugal with Brampton's wife, and that later when he had visited Tournai the boy's father 'Jean Osbeque' had confirmed that. 'Osbeque' had identified the boy, seen in Portugal and now acting as the pretender, as his son Piers from distinguishing marks on his body.[66] But even if 'Osbecque' knew that the boy was his 'son' from these marks, and thus had been his guardian before the boy left for Portugal, he might in reality only have been looking after 'Piers' for someone else rather than been his real father.

Alternative explanations: genuine muddle, cover-ups, false leads, or a 'Tudor plot'?

The 1497 confessions are full of mistakes, so some partisans claim that 'Warbeck' was really who he at first claimed. He had been smuggled out of England in 1483 and threatened or hoodwinked into remaining silent until 1490, whether it was the Duke of Buckingham (as of August 1483, shortly to rebel against his cousin and patron Richard III) or Sir James Tyrrell (the latter the man who Richard III gave large sums of money for unknown secret service in Flanders in 1484) who had done the smuggling. 'Warbeck' himself claimed to have been saved from Richard's malice by an unnamed lord who smuggled him abroad but told him to remain quiet about his true identity, or he would be hunted down and murdered. This could suggest a link with the story that the Princes had secretly lived at Tyrrell's Essex home at Gipping in 1483 before going abroad, which was picked up in local lore by historian Audrey Williamson in the late twentieth century, or identify the 'lord' as Tyrrell (or the shadowy adventurer Sir Edward Brampton, who had connections with Warbeck's home in Tournai and the merchant Pregent Meno). And what had happened to Edward V, or did 'Warbeck' genuinely not know as the boys had been separated by their kidnappers/rescuers? In the early sixteenth century Sir Thomas More's son-in-law John Rastell, producing a revised version of More's book on Richard III, had heard that Edward V had died, possibly being thrown into the sea by unknown persons – but was this just a rumour or a guess as to why he had totally disappeared? The alternative for the rescuer was Buckingham, who as a rival for the throne in 1483 might have devious reasons for terrifying the boy into keeping away from his relatives. Buckingham was married to Elizabeth Woodville's sister and so might have had a reason for preserving at least one of his nephews from Richard, and rose in rebellion against Richard III within weeks of the time of the presumed 'rescue' in late summer 1483. Could his apparent desire to have a private interview with Richard before he was executed in October have been due to information that he had about the Prince's whereabouts?

Buckingham is, however, less likely than Brampton to have had 'contacts' in Flanders who could hide the boy and pass him on to Jean de Osbeck in Tournai. It is also surprising that the pretender should allegedly be noticed parading in Meno's rich robes on a sales-visit to Ireland and 'happen' to be mistaken for Richard and taken up by unnamed Yorkist agitators – and recognised by senior rulers all over Europe as the Prince. The account of this seemingly haphazard process in Warbeck's 'confession' leaves many questions unanswered, and hints that his appearance in Ireland was probably 'stage-managed' in order to gauge possible support for a revolt. Sir Edward Brampton is the likeliest 'mastermind' as he had had close contacts at the Yorkist court in 1471–85, unless he was only acting for Duchess Margaret of Burgundy, Richard III's sister. By his own account in the 'Setubal Testimonies' in 1496, he had been responsible for bringing Warbeck to Portugal, and possibly to Ireland too. Had he done so in collusion with Taylor but kept quiet about the latter to protect him? Taylor is a vital link, particularly as he had been involved in a mysterious plot to smuggle a son of Clarence abroad in 1477/8. He had 'form' in the notion of hiding refugee royal Yorkist boys abroad. As a former member of Clarence's household, may have been involved in the appearance in Cork in 1490 as Brampton's agent.

By this date Sir James Tyrrell, the other possible 'rescuer' of Prince Richard and the recipient of a suspiciously large sum of money from Richard III early in 1484, was stationed at Guisnes Castle near Calais as Henry VII's governor, thus having easy access to Flanders too. But Henry, who had required him to sell up his Welsh estates and reside out of England so he clearly did not trust him, was to have him arrested for contacts with Lincoln's refugee brother Edmund de la Pole in 1502 and was probably having him watched already. Guisnes was a valuable fortress close to his enemy Duchess Margaret's Flanders and so at risk of subversion, and it is unlikely that Tyrrell could have risked taken part in the 1490 'appearance' of Warbeck in Ireland without fear of his activity leaking out. Pardoned in 1486, Tyrrell had every reason to keep out of trouble – and when he was finally arrested in 1502 there was no hint of his being linked to Warbeck as opposed to Edmund de la Pole, so his Yorkist sympathies seem to have been centred on Lincoln's family. Nor did Henry choose to charge him with knowing Taylor or any other plotters from the 1490s, despite the fact that many of them had passed through Calais *en route* to and from Warbeck's court at Malines in 1493–5. Henry VII's rivals such as Emperor Maximilian and the Yorkist princess Margaret, Duchess of Burgundy, could be presumed to have recognised 'Warbeck' as a useful tool to use against the King in case of conflict. Their personal reception of and gifts to him in the early 1490s is no indication that he had brought proof that he was the Duke of York. Henry's unexpected rapprochement with France after his 1492 invasion meant a diplomatic breach with Maximilian, and Margaret had already backed 'Simnel' in 1486–7. But it appears that even Ferdinand and Isabella of Spain, Henry's allies, referred to the boy in their diplomatic messages in the code normally restricted to genuine sovereigns. It has been suggested that if he was not Prince Richard he was an illegitimate son of Edward IV, possibly born abroad during the latter's Low Countries exile of 1470–1 or else smuggled out of England to serve as a focus for Yorkist plots by his one-time patron the ubiquitous Brampton. A more scandalous origin is also suggested, following Tudor 'smears' that he was the illegitimate son of his patron Margaret, Duchess of Burgundy, and the Bishop of Cambrai. This story seems to have originated with Maximilian, who told the Milanese ambassador Erasmo Brascha in 1495 that Clifford (the 'defector' who fled to Henry that winter) had informed him of the boy's identity.[67] But was this just an invention of Clifford's, designed to ruin Duchess Margaret's reputation and so ingratiate himself with Henry VII ahead of his defection back to Henry in December 1494?

The Warbecks' district of Tournai was within the Cambrai diocese so an illegitimate son of the Bishop's could logically have been hidden with them, though the current bishop had not held this office in the 1470s when Warbeck was born. The childless Margaret had certainly had a mysterious small boy called 'Jean le Sage' in her entourage from c.1478 to 1485, as shown by her household accounts, and made much of him with luxuries and a good education. He seems to have been regarded as some sort of unofficial adopted son. The boy's appearance had followed the death of her husband Duke Charles at the battle of Nancy in 1477, and hence it could be speculated that he was the product of a secret affair.[68]

As Charles had had a daughter (Mary) by his previous marriage, he must have been anxious to have a son when he married Margaret to secure the succession and preserve Burgundy's independence from its overlord Louis XI, his arch-enemy; as it turned out, they had no children and when he was killed Burgundy was forced to rely on Mary's marriage to secure outside help from a male military commander capable of defending it – Maximilian of Habsburg. There would have been every effort on Charles' part to secure a son by Margaret in c.1467–72, and the failure to do this would imply that unless he had become infertile recently she was unable to conceive. This would argue against her having a son by the Bishop of Cambrai or any other lover – but it is not decisive, as Charles could have contracted some fertility problem.

If this boy who appeared after 1477 was Warbeck, the apparent age of the latter in 1497 – around twenty-three or twenty-four – would indicate that he would have had to be born when Charles was still alive. Charles and Margaret had not been close, and the duke had notoriously refrained from supporting her exiled brothers Edward IV and Richard in their local exile in 1471. But it would surely have been very risky for her to have a relationship with, and a child, by someone else in the early 1470s, a scandal which her enemies could use against her to have her sent home in disgrace. It is not impossible that the boy was in her charge as the illegitimate son of a close friend or relative, who could not be acknowledged by his real parents. This raises the possibility that Edward IV – or, more likely as the King acknowledged his own bastards, the disgraced Clarence who was in no position to help his son and was executed in1478 – was the father. The latter might be inferred from the appearance of Clarence's ex-retainer Taylor, who had already been involved in a plan to smuggle Clarence's legitimate son out of England, at Margaret's court by 1490. That would account for why Warbeck looked like a Yorkist prince and took so many people in. If he as born around 1477, it would also explain his apparent lack of knowledge of English – he had left England as a baby and had not spoken it since then. The involvement of Taylor with his cause from the start, in 1490, was due to his having been the man who took the boy abroad and so knew his real identity. Having been pardoned for his part in the baby-smuggling plot in 1478, he was sacked from his offices as bailiff of the Clarence lands in Worcestershire and chief forester of a royal park in Gloucestershire after Bosworth and fled abroad. (His son, another Thomas, was chief surveyor of customs and subsidies in several Dorset and Devon ports to 1485 – useful for helping his father with smuggling small boys abroad?) He initially took refuge in Rouen, France, so he might have been able to offer his young protégé's services to Charles VIII. A son of Clarence might already have been abroad by then, as Warbeck apparently forgot any English he had known as an English resident – a major drawback for his story. This is more likely from a boy who had left England as an infant than as one still in his native land until Bosworth (when he would have been about eight). The emphasis that Warbeck placed on his long illness around 1484 in his 'confession' might indicate a 'cover-up' of the fact that he had been substituted for the real Piers Osbeck/Warbeck then; the 'original' had died and the replacement had been kept out of sight at the Warbeck family home until coached in his new role and his new language. But this can only be informed guesswork. Margaret may have taken Taylor into her employ as a loyal gesture towards her executed brother's supporters and a means of annoying or threatening Henry VII, and given him the task of taking her protégé to Ireland as a shrewd and determined Yorkist.

The victim of the Anglo-Spanish marriage agreement of 1489/1501?

After Warbeck had made his confessions – including to his wife Katherine Gordon – he was removed to London as a trophy, and was paraded in public in a number of processions before being kept under guard at court. He was treated neither with the deference customary for a guarded prisoner or hostage of noble birth – a status which Henry himself had held at the Breton court in the late 1470s and early 1480s – or the mixture of clemency and disdain which Henry had shown to the innocent, low-born pawn Lambert Simnel in 1487. Simnel had been younger and less dangerous, and the king had evidently feared Warbeck personally far more than he did the earlier pretender even if he publicly scorned him as a gullible low-born foreign boy used by Yorkist plotters. The anomaly of his position under guard at court in 1497–8 implies that Henry did not quite know what to make of him, and could not just send him back to his family as harmless or throw him in an ordinary prison in the capital as a base-born foreign plotter.[69]

Warbeck's confession appears in the *London Chronicle* for November 1497 and was also sent abroad, where the bizarre spelling of the names of Irish participants in the account of the revolt recorded in Burgundy shows that this came from the French text of the document. But Henry did not accept offers from France and Spain to arrange to send Warbeck's parents to London to publicly confirm his identity, which would have been standard procedure. (Warbeck's father died that autumn, but other relatives as well as Nicaise were available.) The letter – presumably dictated by Henry's officials – which Warbeck had to send to his mother on 13 October 1497 from Exeter compounded the mystery, by referring to her as 'Catherine' (which was what English sources pre-'Perkin's confession' had called her) not Nicaise, and giving their surname as 'Wezbeque', two elementary errors. The name of their 'home' parish of St Jean in Tournai was also muddled up. The language was stilted and awkward and contained references – some of questionable accuracy – which sound as if dictated by Henry's men from a list of their details of his background, and its terminology has been argued as being in 'court' French not the local Picardy dialect.[70] If a genuinely Flemish Warbeck was writing to his mother, why not use their own local dialect? The court French of the letter was thus more likely to result from it being drawn up word by word by English government officials who spoke French. But it is odd that Warbeck did not correct the name given to his 'mother' when it was presented to him to sign, as if he had pointed out the mistake the English would have probably corrected the wording so that it sounded more authentic to Flemish locals.

Did Henry refuse to accept a correction, thinking that it was a trick so that the letter's readers would see that it was inaccurate – and thus that Warbeck was not Katherine de Faro's son? Or did Warbeck let the mistake stand, in order to trick Henry by enabling the readers to observe the mistakes and realise that the King not him had drawn the letter up? Henry was a methodical man who had had several years to build up the 'official' story of Warbeck's origins; the 'slip' about Nicaise or Katherine de Faro was unlikely to have been mere carelessness. It is a vital clue that someone – Henry or Warbeck – was deliberately not telling the truth.

Whatever the truth about Warbeck's background or Henry's real opinion of him, he broke his 'parole' by attempting to flee from court at Westminster in June 1498. Two guards placed in his chamber were evaded at night as Warbeck slipped out and headed upriver, suggesting that Henry did not think his escape likely and relaxed his close watch over the prisoner. It would have made more sense for Warbeck to try to get on a ship for Flanders, but presumably he escaped on the spur of the moment – or at short notice – without contact with Yorkist agents in the City and thus could not arrange a ship. Polydore Vergil suggested that Margaret had put him up to it, out of a desire to use him further against Henry, but he had 'bolted' before when he apparently felt cornered – first as a boy from Middleburg, then to and later back from Portugal, and finally when his army was about to be confronted by Henry's at Taunton. Warbeck was clearly disorientated and had no help ready to find him a ship or a hideout, and seems to have wandered aimlessly up the Thames. A few days later he was cornered at the Charterhouse at Sheen and taken back to Westminster, where he was exhibited in fetters in the stocks as a common criminal before being removed to the Tower.[71] The lack of the usual punishment for incompetence for his 'gaolers', who had been publicly blamed for letting their vigilance slip, and the punishment inflicted on his wife (who lost her attendants and had her allowance reduced) suggests that his wife may have assisted him. Henry may even have arranged the escape in order to have an excuse for committing him to close custody in disgrace, as he was currently negotiating with Ferdinand and Isabella for the hand of their daughter Katherine for Prince Arthur and the Spanish sovereigns seem to have wanted the English throne secured by eliminating the pretender. Warbeck had to be induced to try to escape in order to put him in close custody, as if he was suddenly taken to the Tower without reason it might imply that Henry was taking his claim to be Prince Richard more seriously than he had done in 1497.

When Margaret of Burgundy sent over an ambassador to check up on Warbeck's welfare in the Tower in 1499, the choice was the Bishop of Cambrai – the man who Maximilian or Clifford had said was the boy's real father. Was this coincidence? Even if the bishop was not the boy's father, he may have known his real identity. At the interview in July, Warbeck had to confess to the bishop and to the Spanish ambassador and swear an oath that he was Margaret's pawn and that both of them knew that he was a fake. Henry then praised the Spanish sovereigns for not being taken in by him.[72] Logically, the scene was stage-managed by Henry as a warning to Margaret that he had found out her plots and she had better leave England alone or Warbeck, be he her 'son' or just her protégé, would be executed.

Later in 1499 a final obscure and rather risky plot enfolded the imprisoned pretender, who for whatever reason had been put in the cell underneath the Earl of Warwick – the other main challenge to Henry as Clarence's son. The Spanish ambassador De Puebla seems to have been relaying messages from his sovereigns of their concern at potential English stability as a stumbling-block to the Arthur/Katherine marriage, with the removal of both Warwick and Warbeck as necessary to reassure them. Accordingly, it is possible that the entire 'plot' that evolved in autumn 1499 for Warwick and Warbeck to escape with the aid of their gaolers – or even seize the Tower – was organised by Henry as an excuse to convict them of treason. Alternatively, it may have been more than coincidence that Maximilian was currently planning to send a fleet to rescue his protégé – which had to be preceded by his getting out of London. It is unlikely that Henry was so short of secure rooms in the Tower that he had to put the two most dangerous state prisoners in adjacent rooms, and it was logical to think that they might attempt to communicate. Warbeck, an adventurer who had attempted to escape once already, was more likely than Warwick – who the details of the 'plot' show to be a passive character open to his gaolers' suggestions – to initiate contact. Thus the location of their cells suggests strongly that Henry expected it to provide him with an opportunity to incriminate Warbeck further and to draw Warwick into punishable activity.

Earlier that year an obscure Cambridge student called Ralph Wilford had been executed for pretending to be Warwick. There were also a number of pro-Yorkist pamphleteers at large in London, though none with known connections to significant nobles who could have posed a political threat. Now for no apparent reason the two prisoners' gaolers – Robert Claymound, in charge of Warwick, and Thomas Astwood, in charge of Warbeck – coincidentally followed up an earlier meeting with a London Yorkist plotter in 1498 by proclaiming their loyalty to their charges. It is possible that Astwood was a genuine Yorkist and offered to look after Warbeck in order to free him, but the Tower authorities are more likely to have 'vetted' any applicant for such a crucial post thoroughly. If the post-plot confessions were to be believed, Astwood and Claymound talked to Warwick and later to Warbeck of escape, seizing the Tower, and killing the king, thus cozening both (Warwick being innocent of any crime so far) into committing treason. Which 'rebel' was to have the crown after the regicide was unclear, with both mentioned in different versions of the story.[73] Henry himself first blamed the treacherous group of Tower gaolers for commencing the plot, but later shifted the blame to Warbeck and Warwick in a letter to the new French king Louis XII that autumn.[74] Warwick, possibly simple-minded and certainly naïve after fourteen years in custody, was clearly entrapped and was prompted into treasonable words by Claymound, and probably the desperate Warbeck was equally gullible and clutched at a chance of escape. He does not appear to have done anything positive apart from exchange tokens and letters, but his participation was enough to condemn him. Claymound was either the main instigator, for unknown reasons, or a government 'provocateur' put in place to entrap Warbeck into doing something treasonable – to ease Henry's conscience about going back on his earlier leniency? The plot was 'exposed', whether it was a genuine threat to Henry or not, and the prisoners were indicted for treason in November. Warbeck was hanged at Tyburn as a low-born criminal and Warwick allowed the dignity of the axe, and the Spanish marriage duly followed. It is alleged that Henry had a guilty conscience over entrapping the harmless Warwick for reasons of state,[75] which argues for his lack of that cold-blooded ruthlessness which was to characterise his son Henry VIII.

Overview

The king had been merciful to the earlier pretender Simnel who survived in the royal household as a harmless retainer for decades. Legendarily made a kitchen-boy and probably paraded in front of sheepish Irish lords who had once hailed him as king at court in the early 1490s ('My lords, you will crown apes next') he ended up as a falconer. He had been younger and more obviously a puppet of his backers, and Warbeck had been an adult active in leading his attempt to take over the throne. Even when captured, Warbeck had been treated leniently at first, though he may have been induced to escape in 1498 to excuse a harsher fate and he was certainly tricked into condemning himself in 1499. The mistakes and inconsistencies in his confession(s) cannot be written off as slipshod and hasty state construction of his 'real' identity, given that Henry was too careful and methodical to make such errors. His whole confession that he was not Richard of York could be discounted as forced, due to Henry's threats of torture and/or execution if he did not co-operate in September 1497, and the evidence of Clifford for his real identity is inadmissible given that character's untrustworthiness as a witness. It is more telling that Margaret also admitted after his capture that he was an impostor, as she might have been expected to reassert his royal birth – or even accept that he was her own son – in order to save his life and negotiate his decent treatment, if not his safe return. His Plantagenet looks are testified by all accounts from the 'mistake' made by the Cork onlookers in 1490 onwards, including by foreign diplomats who had known Edward IV.

The number of European rulers that he was able to persuade of his veracity may suggest that he was more than a clever actor carefully coached by Margaret, even if Maximilian had powerful reasons to turn on the pro-French Henry in 1493–4 and shamelessly forced Warbeck to make him his heir to England. Warbeck's apparent age – around 23 in 1497 – would indicate that he was too old to have been an illegitimate son born after Margaret was widowed. If she had had a son while still married, this is unlikely to have been able to be kept secret and political enemies would have reported it to endeavour to ruin her and the Anglo-Burgundian alliance that she represented. Some modern writers have sought to explain Warbeck's appearance and Yorkist connections by suggesting that he was an illegitimate son of Edward IV's, sired during his exile in Flanders and Holland in winter 1470–1. But this obvious solution was never raised at the time and would also make Warbeck older than was generally assumed. If he had been a son of Edward – or of Richard III or the Duke of Clarence – born around 1473 and smuggled out to Flanders at a later date, why did witnesses interviewed ovserseas in 1496 with no reason to want to please Henry (e.g. Brampton, a Yorkist stalwart) allege that Warbeck could not speak English in 1490? Warbeck's linguistic situation might be explicable if he had been sent out of England as a baby or small child and forgotten any English he had learnt, which would fit a son of Clarence sent away at the duke's arrest (late 1477) better than a son of Edward or Richard sent away in 1483–5. Margaret could have found a safe home for Clarence's illegitimate son in Tournai in 1478 as easily as for a son of Edward or Richard in 1483, or kept him near her until 1480 when the new Bishop of Cambrai took the boy to the Warbecks' home.

Brampton could have been responsible for taking the boy abroad, and kept in touch with him so that he could be used as a Yorkist pretender if the possibility arose – or have had no idea that the boy might be useful as a pretender at the time (pre-1483?) and just 'looked him up' later after the overthrow of Richard III and the failure of 'Simnel'. In that case, did he tell Margaret about a son of one of her brothers being in Tournai pre-1485 and she then took the boy up after 'Simnel' failed, telling Brampton to take him to Portugal for a courtly education? Hence he took Warbeck to Portugal c.1488 to accustom him to noble company and have him trained in moving around courts, and in 1490 had him paraded in Cork to see if it would spark off a Yorkist revolt. John Taylor, as a former servant of Clarence, would have been a crucial figure who perhaps knew the boy's true identity – and was the story of Taylor planning to take Clarence's legitimate son abroad in 1477/8 a garbled version of what he did with the duke's illegitimate son? Or did Taylor have no idea who Warbeck really was in 1490 (hence trying him out as a son of Richard III's rather than as 'Richard,Duke of York')? Did Warbeck just happen to be a Flemish boy who had a coincidental resemblance to Edward IV and was taken up as such by Brampton in c. 1488 and pointed out to Duchess Margaret as a useful participant in a plot against Henry? Fake, fantasist, 'chancer', or genuine Yorkist scion (but illegitimate?), the unsolved enigma of Perkin Warbeck continues.

Chapter Two

Anne Boleyn – Martyred Reformist Queen or Murderous Strumpet?

The execution of Anne Boleyn – probably 'framed', but why the unprecedented and unlikely charges like incest? Was her downfall planned (by Henry VIII or Cromwell?) or was it a mixture of bad luck and opportunism?

The saga of the rise and fall of Anne Boleyn has been a major object of interest to the visual as well as written media for many decades, with the compulsive story of how a seemingly minor court 'player', the younger daughter of a middle-ranking nobleman, ended up replacing the long-established queen who had failed to give her husband a male heir. Failed in the same 'task' herself, and ended up executed for supposed mass-adultery – and incest with her brother. Kings in search of an heir had rid themselves of unwanted wives in favour of hopefully more fertile replacements in the face of church which bans divorce, for centuries, usually by finding (or inventing) some legal problem in their first marriage that could lead to complaisant lawyers agreeing that it had been illegal and cancelling it – which made its (female) offspring bastards. Usually the church looked the other way, or even helped the process by arguing that the royal couple had been within the 'illegal' limits to cousins marrying, or any church permit that they had acquired had been faulty or fraudulent. Even if the king in question defied the church he could usually ride out the wave of papal disapproval until the Pope needed his political help and had to accept the new marriage – as King Philip Augustus of France (ruled 1180–1223) had done in the 1190s. Getting round the threat of papal sanctions by cutting the country's church off from the jurisdiction of the central Catholic church courts in Rome – a sort of early version of 'Taking back Control' from European bureaucracy, as with Brexit – had been threatened before but never actually done.

Typically, the bold and brash egotist Henry VIII pushed this threat as far as actually going ahead with the 'Break With Rome' and declaring himself the head of a (still Catholic at this stage) Church of England – though this saga has an air of inevitability in most accounts of it and people tend to forget that if Pope Clement VII had not been at the mercy of Catherine of Aragon's nephew and ally Emperor Charles V in Italy at the time he might have given in to Henry. Alternatively, the pious and normally dutiful Catherine could have agreed to go into a convent and let Henry have the marriage annulled rather than setting up a legal team and an appeal to Rome to challenge it. Or Henry's 'master-fixer' Cardinal Wolsey could have used the current occupation of Rome in 1527 by the Emperor's troops to declare that the Pope was unable to exercise his jurisdiction by being 'under duress' so a temporary committee of (anti-Imperial, probably French) cardinals should so do outside Italy, led by himself. Indeed, a less nervous, cautious, and Italocentric pope than Clement (who was a Medici from Florence and put his family's political interests first) could well have fled from the Emperor to France, as popes had done in the Middle Ages (they had a refuge there at the papally-owned city of Avignon), and agreed to Henry's divorce under an alliance with Henry and with Charles' long-term rival King Francis I of France. The 'ins and outs' of why and how the 'King's Great Matter', the annulment of Henry's first marriage (which was technically not quite a 'divorce' as the latter implied that the marriage had been legal while it lasted and an annulment implied that it had always been illegal), led to Henry marrying Anne are not quite a 'Royal Mystery' as a careful study can show why things happened and the probable motives of those involved. (Also, what did not happen and why it did not, bears examining.)

There are still disputes over crucial details where witnesses 'remembered' facts differently, such as the question of whether Catherine and her first husband – Henry's deceased elder brother Prince Arthur, who died within months of the marriage in 1502 – consummated their marriage during its brief duration. Nor was it ever made clear whether the legal decision by Pope Julius to allow the late Arthur's younger brother Henry to marry his widow – which was in contravention of Old Testament bans on this form of marriage – in 1506, formally requested by Henry VII in his under-age younger son's name, was 'water-tight' and so their marriage in 1509 was fully legal. Politics tended to determine international decision-making and legal decisions in the sixteenth-century as well as in recent times, not least in the papal courts, and the marriage of Henry and Catherine (seen as so dubious in 1506–9 that Catherine and the Spanish ambassador in London were both considering her return home as a probable option) could well have been avoided if events had occurred slightly differently. A longer-surviving Henry VII, who died aged 52 probably of TB, could easily have carried out his original plan to prefer the Holy Roman Emperor Maximilian to Catherine's father King Ferdinand of Aragon as his ally, and marry off his son to Maximilian's grand-daughter Eleanor instead. But these issues are minor compared to the issue of what happened and why in the next stage in the 'Tudor royal soap opera', the collapse of Henry's marriage to Anne Boleyn.

The basic facts (or at least those events that took place in public) are not in dispute – but the question of motives and that of what took place behind closed doors are still very much in debate. With them is the whole issue of whether Anne did commit adultery with a series of courtiers (the incest with her brother George Boleyn is far less likely but the allegation still has importance), and why this series of supposed shocking crimes was put out – almost unique for any European royal court over many centuries. Was there any truth in them, if not why were they invented, who was the mastermind behind their use (Henry or his chief minister Thomas Cromwell?), and what can be deduced about the state of court politics and the King's evidently growing paranoia from them? And was Anne a villain – or at any rate a major political actor with her own agenda who her enemies needed to silence permanently – or a victim? Which pieces of the 'evidence' can be reckoned as probably true, which were probably invented and why, and is there truth in the (still an issue interpreted anew by modern novels and films) 'feminist' argument that a powerful and independent-minded woman 'had to' be silenced by her misogynist male rivals?

Henry VIII gambled that Anne Boleyn would give him a son where Catherine had failed, and had appropriate hopes that their first child would be a boy. A rash astrologer predicted that the child expected at the time of their marriage would be a son,[1] no doubt hoping for due reward and prestige if he was proved right. Taking no chances about arguments concerning the baby's legitimacy, Henry arranged for his marriage to Anne (January 1533) and her coronation to be sped up, probably carrying the former out as soon as he heard she was pregnant. Arguably the dating of this pregnancy had major repercussions on English history and on the character and policies of the child in question (Queen Elizabeth I), as it occurred when the annulment proceedings for Henry's first marriage, to Catherine of Aragon, were at a crucial stage and so rushed the king into precipitate action. The blocked papal annulment which would legitimise his planned next (or as he saw it, 'first lawful') marriage could not be hurried up, and even though the timid Pope Clement VII was now in a stronger position regarding the militarily dominant Emperor Charles V (nephew and supporter of Catherine) than he had been earlier he was still delaying a decision. Catherine famously refused to co-operate with her husband's plans to divorce her, and at the delayed church legal hearing into the case in London in 1529, appealed to the papal court in Rome. Also, accepting what Henry wanted could renew that Imperial hostility to the Papacy which had led in 1527 to Charles' unruly and unpaid army sacking Rome and making Clement a virtual prisoner. Henry's best – though diminishing – hope after those debacles was that the Pope would be persuaded to accept the divorce/annulment by the other great regional military power, Henry's sporadic and current ally Francis I of France, and would so defy Charles' wishes. In 1529–31 Henry seems to have turned away from this possibility, spurred on by anti-papal advisers at court including the dukes of Norfolk (Anne Boleyn's uncle) and Suffolk, as symbolised by the disgrace and later death under arrest of his chief minister Cardinal Wolsey, who had failed to win him an annulment despite his supposed diplomatic leverage in Rome. Instead Henry arranged for English constitutional law to take precedent over Roman canon law, bringing about the threat of a formal 'Break with Rome' to (in modern parlance) 'take back control from Europe'.

It was now the king and his clergy within the realm who decided such matters as royal divorces, not Rome, and a patriotic and obedient Parliament duly carried all the necessary legislation into effect. Thus once the Archbishop of Canterbury, now his ally, Thomas Cranmer who as a Cambridge theologian had backed the rights of English over Roman canon law, ruled in Henry's favour the king's first marriage could be counted as dissolved. It would have been more questionable if the elderly Archbishop Warham, who backed Catherine, had not conveniently died in 1532 but had had to be dismissed; the last archbishops to be removed had been Thomas Fitzalan (Arundel) and Roger Waldby, for political reasons as the opponents of the current kings, in 1397–9.[2] Warham had been holding up the annulment within England in 1531–2, and could have been expected to keep up his opposition; and there was strong council opposition to proceeding with the marriage to Anne, led by the Duke of Suffolk, Henry's long-term closest friend and jousting-companion Charles Brandon (married to Henry's sister Mary, with their son and two daughters available as alternative heirs to the throne). Conservative peers such as Lord Dacre (future leader of the Pilgrimage of Grace in 1536) made threats in the Lords, though these were less likely than court pressure to influence Henry.

There was a reason for delay in 1532–3, which Anne's pregnancy ended. There were chances that Henry's foreign ally Francis I might yet prevail on the dithering Pope Clement to grant the annulment at that point; these seem to have caused Henry to delay the legal procedure within England where the Parliamentary actions of autumn 1531 had cleared the way to proceed. Had this occurred – or had Francis accepted that Henry had overwhelming political reason if not proper legal permission to re-marry and had backed the Boleyn marriage as a personal favour, Anne having spent some years of her youth at the French court and probably knowing him from then – Anne's marriage and her baby's legitimacy would have received official French support. In that case, Francis' son Henri II could hardly have refused to accept Elizabeth's accession in 1558 and backed her cousin Mary Queen of Scots instead; Anglo-Scots relations in 1558–67 would have been on a smoother path and Elizabeth would have been less legally insecure and so hostile to her 'fully legitimate' cousin and self-claimed heiress Mary. Instead of a smooth, continuing legal procedure to put the power of annulment in Henry's hands in 1531–3 and then a grand marriage to Anne once the legal mechanism was in place, Henry had to rush it through and marry in secret once Anne became pregnant. But the situation had not been straightforward for her before the pregnancy expedited matters, as in spring 1532 her father Thomas Boleyn, Earl of Wiltshire, and her uncle Norfolk were said to have been opposed to a quick marriage.[3] Indeed, one incident in July 1532 had implications for the chances and the course of Anne's eventual downfall and the possibility of Elizabeth's legitimacy being questioned in later decades.

There was a brief panic over a story (leaked to Catherine's partisans) that Anne's previous admirer, Henry Percy, Earl of Northumberland,[4] had been secretly but legally contracted to marry her – as with Edward IV and Eleanor Butler's arrangement, this could be regarded as invalidating any subsequent marriage to another party. Fortunately for Henry, this scion of the once-formidable clan of northern warlords was a timid and submissive character who obediently swore to Henry's investigators that there had been no such contract. (He later attended Anne's trial and voted to condemn her as the king wished, allegedly at the cost of a fatal breakdown afterwards.) Had he held out that Anne had been his legally contracted fiancée, had Warham been alive to back him in 1532–3, and had Suffolk and Princess Mary had more court support the Boleyn marriage would have been in serious trouble – at least until Anne became pregnant. Ominously, she and Henry had already been quarrelling in 1531 over her determined attitude to the obstructive Princess Mary, Henry's fifteen-year-old daughter, who refused to accept her bastardisation. Henry, always touchy of his dignity, complained that Catherine had never dared to shout at him like Anne did.[5] He was still, however, in love with Anne, and prepared to acknowledge her future role as his queen in the decorative scheme for Whitehall Palace (as extended after its confiscation from Wolsey) in 1531–2; all these problems were unlikely to have halted his second marriage.

Anne becoming pregnant in late November/December 1532 was the clinching factor in the rushed and legally dubious marriage. Had she not been pregnant in early 1533, Henry could have proceeded with less haste then and had the marriage carried out formally by Cranmer as Archbishop of Canterbury once his papal recognition had arrived in late March. The fact that his marriage was not in public – it was probably carried out in Whitehall Palace c.25 January – would lead to rumours that it had not taken place at all and even the ever-vigilant foreign ambassadors did not hear of it for some weeks. Indeed, one remaining 'Royal Mystery' of the Tudor era is where and when the crucial Henry/Anne marriage took place; the secret remains 490 years later so 'public' Tudor court life and its rampant gossip was evidently capable of keeping some secrets. For that matter, a few decades before it had been accepted church law that a private marriage (especially one that was not in a church) with no or few witnesses was not fully legal, and Edward IV's marriage to Elizabeth

Woodville in secret in May 1464 had been attacked on that account. This was not just legal semantics – if the marriage was illegal, Henry's mother Elizabeth of York (1466–1503) was a bastard and the Yorkist claim to the English throne had not descended legally to him but was presumably vested in Edward IV's next brother Duke George of Clarence's daughter, Lady Margaret Pole (ironically, now Princess Mary's governess). Indeed, there were still stories going around in the mid-1530s and reaching Emperor Charles V's ambassador Chapuys, that due to the 'invalid' Edward IV/Elizabeth Woodville marriage, Lady Margaret or her son Lord Montague were the rightful sovereigns – and Henry was to have both arrested for alleged treason and executed. Henry himself originally preferred to carry his marriage to Anne out publicly in the presence of his ally Francis in Calais during the 'summit' that he, Anne, and the French king held there in October 1532 – thus binding Francis to support it in the face of probable papal and Imperial fury. Tying the French king to being complicit in the marriage would have improved Henry's international position and reduced the risk of the Pope retaliating as now Clement could hardly condemn Henry for defying him without punishing his ally too. It would also keep the ceremony public and undeniable but avoid the likely riots against the widely detested 'whore Nan Bullen' if it was carried out in England, which would humiliate the always touchy and vindictive Henry and encourage the Emperor and Catherine, plus their English supporters. The Papacy needed France (a valuable political force in Italy even after it finally lost control of Milan to Charles V at the battle of Pavia in 1525) as an ally against the Empire more than it needed Henry. Thus in 1533 the Papal-French alliance was to be cemented by the marriage of the Pope's niece Catherine de' Medici to Francis' second son Henri, at Marseilles.

The formal Parliamentary legalisation of the ban on church court appeals (such as Catherine's) to Rome and the arrival of papal recognition of Cranmer as archbishop both took place late in March 1533, and court rumours reaching the Imperial ambassador Chapuys and others spoke of Henry marrying Anne later that spring.[6] There was no confirmation for weeks that the marriage had already taken place. Indeed, once the news did emerge there was confusion over who had been the celebrant – possibly Rowland Lee, Bishop of Lichfield, or an Augustinian friar called George Brown as Chapuys heard- and who had attended. It was supposed to have taken place in a chamber over the Holbein Gate, not a consecrated chapel, which would have been dubiously legal. Catherine's partisans plausibly claimed that the conscientious priest had asked if Henry had received papal approval and the king gave an evasive or lying answer.[7] To Catholic partisans for decades to come, the marriage was a fraud and Elizabeth a bastard – which was to be an important political weapon against her during Mary I's reign and into the 1570s. A public marriage at Calais, reluctantly recognised by the unimpeachably orthodox French king, or in a chapel/cathedral in England and performed by Cranmer as Archbishop, would have been less easy to attack. Elizabeth's detractors would have had to fall back on the argument that the legal breach with Rome was illegal and the King of England and his clerical appointees had no right to be supreme in canon law matters – and the less scrupulous Catholics would have had to rely on the possible implications for her legitimacy of Elizabeth's mother's alleged adultery (revealed in 1536).

The birth of Elizabeth at Greenwich on 7 September 1533 was an embarrassment for the king, though he put a brave face on it, paraded the baby, and claimed that he was satisfied that with God's help, and that sons would follow.[8] At least it showed that Anne was fertile and could carry a healthy child to full term, as Catherine had failed to do ever since the birth of Mary Tudor in February 1516. (She had been aged thirty then; Anne was now aged somewhere between twenty-six and thirty-one.) To Henry's opponents, the birth of another daughter after all his efforts showed that God had punished him for his unjust and illegal treatment of Catherine.[9] If Elizabeth had been a boy as her parents had hoped, the arguments for accepting the '*fait accompli*' of Henry's second marriage and the security implied by a male heir would have been overwhelming for most domestic and foreign critics. Henry's daughter Mary would have found it hard to hold out against recognising the claims of her half-brother as heir at the time, even if she still maintained that he was a bastard, due to the circumstances of his birth, and would have had reduced support from the English nobility and from Emperor Charles out of '*realpolitik*'. It was easier to deny the claims of a new female heir in 1533–6, particularly as she was an infant and her succession ahead of a near-adult rival would mean a long regency under Boleyn control.

As it was, Henry had already taken the politically necessary but legally contentious steps to declare himself as the supreme authority in the church within England – which did not yet entail any shift away from Catholic theology on other matters towards the beliefs of the Continental anti-Catholic reformers. Either Martin Luther or his Swiss and German successors and rivals, though he held similarly dismissive views to theirs on the 'unchristian' decadence and amorality of the Papacy which invalidated its claims to authority. He also had some lukewarm sympathy for assorted early sixteenth-century calls to reform the 'corrupt' ways of the current church and remove such excesses as the sale of 'indulgences' to save people from Purgatory and the commercialised cults of the saints at their shrines, but this was going no further than some loyal but questioning reformist Catholic thinkers of the era such as Erasmus. The use of the secular prince as a 'godly magistrate' to enforce reform if the lazy and corrupt church authorities would not act was what chiefly appealed to him, especially to his vanity, and he could now use these arguments to excuse his seizure of authority over the English church. However, coupling this with an assault on the long-established primacy of Rome-directed international Catholic canon law, and using it to rid himself of his unwanted and ageing wife in favour of his supposed mistress, were two steps too far for many devout Catholics, including leading 'activists' within the church (such as Bishop Fisher and assorted reformist monastic personnel in the new Carthusian Order) and lay thinkers such as his ex-Chancellor Sir Thomas More, a critic of corrupt practices among the church's personnel but a scourge of doctrinal heretics. Their refusals to swear the new oath of allegiance to Henry's control of the church required of all male citizens – itself a very rare State intrusion into people's consciences – led to a round of arrests, judicial prosecution, and executions, and enraged the Papacy further, and Anne and her faction became by default allied to the cause of reform for mutual survival.

Supporters of reform of the new independent English church and supporters of Anne's marriage and thus Elizabeth's legitimacy as the new heir to the throne were flung together, though Anne's own interest in church reform had at best been sporadic and 'low-key' before 1533/4, and the new 'strongman' organising and systemising the king's control of the church, the 'Vicar-General' and rising self-made bureaucrat Thomas Cromwell, became Anne's (unreliable) political ally. To what extent their temporary coincidence of interests ever became a serious, let alone idealistic, political alliance is one of the mysteries of 1530s history, and historians since then have diverged widely on this question – not least as Anne was presented in strongly reformist tones as a proto-Protestant and cheerleader for radical reform under the reign of her daughter Elizabeth after 1558. After the traumas and widespread executions of Protestants under Mary Tudor in 1554–8 (not least Anne's ally Archbishop Cranmer, who had baptised Elizabeth and from 1547 been a theological Protestant but had not in fact held the same views under the firmly Catholic Henry in the 1530s) it seemed as if Anne and her allies had been the 'godly' harbingers of the Protestant Reformation that had occurred under Edward VI after 1547 and therefore Mary, her mother Catherine, and their allies in the early-mid 1530s had represented the forces of old-fashioned and unholy 'reaction'. In reality the situation of the years 1533–6 had been far less simple, and despite the undoubted easing of official state persecution of those few Protestants who were active in England in this period (probably due to Cromwell's sympathies not Anne's) the queenship of Anne Boleyn had not been a period of steady Protestant advances directed by her. It is unclear even if she was in theological terms a Protestant, though she did want to see drastic reform of the church and the abolition of many or all the monasteries – and their resources' use for education, hospitals, and other good works with which her husband did not bother after 1536. By the same definition, her fall cannot be written off as a 'Catholic plot' organised due to her religious attitudes and her influence on her husband's policies in that direction – and it was organised and orchestrated by the rather more obviously pro-Protestant Cromwell, who to complicate matters had his own political agenda rather than religious reasons to embolden the international Protestant movement and so weaken his master's rival Charles V.

Anne was pregnant again late in 1535, at a time when the renewed Imperial-French clash over Milan (whose duke died in November) led to a military distraction for Charles V from any possible invasion of England. The Pope's excommunication of Henry for executing Bishop Fisher of Rochester, who had refused to accept the 'Break with Rome' as legal, was thus not the legal prelude to invasion by Charles on Mary Tudor's behalf. Francis, who invaded Milan in January 1536, needed Henry as an ally rather than being able to join the Imperial-Papal alliance. In the next major English/Imperial crisis of 1539, Charles and Francis were not at odds and temporarily allied against England under papal auspices; had this occurred in early 1536 the public anger over Catherine's and Mary's treatment would have added inducements for them (or Charles, with Francis standing aside) to invade.

On 24 January 1536 Henry had a serious accident in the tilting-yard at Greenwich, was knocked off his horse, and was unconscious for several hours, and on 29 January Anne miscarried. The child was a boy, as her detractors gleefully reported; and Henry's immediate reaction was reported as being superstitious fear that God was punishing him for his sinful second marriage.[10] This detail was reported by Chapuys in his first letter to the Emperor after the accident, before he even referred to the miscarriage, and was delivered to him in a letter sent on the day of the miscarriage by Anne's enemies, the Marquis of Exeter (the son of Elizabeth of York's next sister, so with his own claim to the throne) and his wife, both partisans of Catherine of Aragon. Therefore, it was clearly Henry's immediate and public reaction and the current queen's enemies were duly jubilant at it. The miscarriage did not immediately follow the accident so it may have been gossip or guesswork that it was the direct cause, but Anne's uncle the Duke of Norfolk was blamed by her for his over-dramatic announcement of the incident to her, as reported by Chapuys, so presumably told to him by the Exeters. As Anne would have realised, if the king had died the nineteen-year-old 'Lady' Mary would have been more likely to rally support in a struggle for the throne than the two-year-old Princess Elizabeth, whatever her legal situation, and a civil war might easily have followed, even if Mary had been arrested as a result of Henry's senior ministers (most crucially Cromwell) rallying to the Boleyns. Anne was more resilient and was sure of conceiving again, and seems to have mishandled her first encounter with Henry after the miscarriage as it ended with harsh words about his fidelity to her. The story that she blamed the king for upsetting her by paying recent attention to other women (Jane Seymour?) may have been exaggerated, and the version which Chapuys reported on 10 February[11] owed much to wishful thinking; he was already making the most of stories that the couple had not been seen much together for the past three months. Anne and Henry had long had a stormy relationship without it affecting their determination to conceive another child or their underlying closeness, and the king had paid attentions to other women during his marriage to Catherine without it triggering any attempts to annul his marriage – even after one of them, Elizabeth Blount, had given him a son in 1519. The story that Anne's stillborn baby was deformed – and hence superstitious alarm at this could have caused Henry and others to think that Anne had caused Divine punishment – only emerged several decades later in unreliable, Catholic sources hostile to her along with the equally dubious story that she had a sixth finger on one hand. (Both could imply that she was a witch, so this was useful propaganda; but they did not appear at her trial in May 1536 when this sort of scandal would have added to the useful blackening of her reputation to ward off any public sympathy.) But the episode of the accident and miscarriage seems to have been a turning-point, at least as seen in retrospect, when the royal marriage did break down late in April. It was exploited by the partisans of Catherine and Mary, who were now safe from the logical argument that repudiating Anne made her predecessor the rightful queen again – now that Catherine was dead Henry could even proclaim Mary (aged 20 so old enough to reign in an emergency) his heiress instead of the two-year-old Elizabeth without having to restore his ex-wife too.

An alliance seems to have followed between the conservative partisans of Mary and the Seymour family, with Jane's brother Edward Seymour (the future Duke of Somerset and Protector, and not yet identifiable as a religious radical) usefully a Gentleman of the Privy Chamber as of March 1536. Jane was the object of love-letters and gifts from the smitten king, and was encouraged to hold out for marriage as the price of submission to his advances as Anne had done effectively in the mid-1520s. Indeed, it is still a matter of mystery what role Jane herself played in ensnaring Henry and if this was calculated by herself as well as by her politically ambitious and wily brother Edward Seymour – traditionally she has been regarded as more unworldly and submissive than the feisty Anne, and as attracting Henry on this account. Some modern writers have conversely argued that this was an 'act' and she knew very well what she was doing even if her brother and her father coached her in how to attract Henry – probably starting with his famous visit to their family home, Wolf Hall in Wiltshire, in autumn 1535. (This provided the title of the first of Hilary Mantel's trilogy on the career of Thomas Cromwell, as highlighting its importance as well as being an appropriate pun for the 'wolfish' behaviour of Tudor politicians.) Henry Courtenay, Marquis of Exeter, conservative son of Henry's aunt Princess Catherine Plantagenet,

Lord Montague (son of Mary's ex-governess Lady Margaret Pole) who was also a royal cousin with Yorkist ancestry and a claim on the throne, and Sir Nicholas Carew aided the plot at court and set up a link via Chapuys to Charles V,[12] and Anne was outmanoeuvred. In desperation, Anne and her allies seemed to have suggested that they back the Imperial alliance too and abandon France, in order to undercut Mary's overseas support and reassure the emperor that he did not have to insist on Anne's removal for Mary's security.[13] This 'me too' shift was a clever move to keep Anne as queen even if Mary returned to her role as heir, though given the toxic mutual mistrust of the various factions that would now pretend to unite it was unstable long-term. Exeter and Montague's claims to the throne were to make them the next victims of the paranoid king in 1538 and Anne could logically have used this threat to work on her husband's mistrustful nature. (This personal interest in the succession did not imply that they were genuinely trying to sabotage the succession of Elizabeth on their own behalf; presumably they regarded themselves as 'old' nobility opposing the 'upstart' Boleyns in the cause of honest English traditionalism, as on lower social level rural peasantry attacked the self-made minister 'Crummel'/Cromwell for trying to wreck the monasteries). The tradition of the royal kin resenting any 'low-born' intruders on their right to counsel the king was a long-standing one in late medieval England; it lay behind similar grudges against unwanted 'upstart' advisers and 'favourites' under Edward II, Richard II, Henry VI, and Edward IV.

Crucially, the international crisis between the Empire and France in early 1536 altered Henry's allies' attitudes to the annulment – and to Anne. Often overlooked in Anglocentric narratives of the fall of Anne, the Milan crisis meant that Charles V, as well as Francis needed Henry's goodwill and his intense hostility to the new queen – and potential to assist attempts to remove her – was abated just at the time that Anne was supposedly threatened by the loss of her unborn child at the end of January. As a result Charles was temporarily less hostile to the Boleyn marriage and the Boleyn faction – and Anne's astute brother Lord Rochford endeavoured to exploit it with an approach to Chapuys. The latter's dislike of Anne was undiminished and he continued to feed negative stories about Anne to his master (and to provide plenty of evidence for later historians of anti-Anne machinations in the Tudor court elite), but he would have had to obey had Charles instructed him to respond favourably. And was Chapuys, a prejudiced witness, too willing to play up all instances of anti-Boleyn gossip, which were really less significant than they appeared? Have modern interpreters of the crisis placed too much reliance on his 'unbiased' word? In March 1536 Charles even made an offer to the English ambassador in Rome to back the Boleyn marriage provided that Henry re-legitimated Princess Mary ahead of Elizabeth, which made practical sense as she was adult and intelligent, and thus able to rule the kingdom should Henry succumb to another accident. Also, now Catherine was dead, restoring Mary as heir would not risk the fallout of rehabilitating her mother and the resultant purge of 'reformists' – even Cromwell might be retained in power with his enemy Norfolk damaged by his niece Anne's fall. An English king and his Parliament could legally legitimise his bastard children without having to declare his marriage to their mother legal, and in 1396 Henry's Beaufort ancestors (the children of Edward III's third surviving son, John 'of Gaunt') had been legitimated by their cousin Richard II without prejudice to the fact that John had been legally married to another woman when their mother bore them. The possibility that Henry would divorce Anne also now meant that the king would be free to marry a European princess, and given Francis' need of English goodwill he might offer him a French princess. Charles had no daughter available to offer Henry, so he had reasons to block Henry's divorce from Anne for the moment. This meant that as of March-April 1536 Charles was not definitely committed to aiding any plot to remove Anne, and had Henry gone along with re-legitimating Mary he could have backed away from supporting the plans of Anne's enemies at court to get her disgraced. The legitimacy of Mary was more important to Charles than removing Anne – and when Catherine was dead it was easier for Henry to grant this demand of his. To that extent, Catherine's death helped rather than hindered Anne – as did the often forgotten Milan crisis.

Anne had done her best to humiliate and intimidate Mary throughout 1533–6 and would have opposed any legitimation of Mary (let alone putting her first in the line of succession) as affecting her own daughter Elizabeth's rights. But the king always did as he wished and resented open challenges to his will. No doubt Mary hated Anne as the 'slut' who had ruined her parents' marriage and any chance of reconciliation between them that Henry might have harboured was hopeless, not least due to her insistence in 1533 that Mary serve in Elizabeth's household. But this arrangement was the norm for a royal bastard, e.g. Edward IV's daughter Grace to her half-sisters – and it was as much a security-measure to keep Mary safe from plotters as a spiteful humiliation. The ex-princess could less easily be kidnapped by her partisans while in a household headed by Anne's friend Lady Bryan and dominated by Boleyn partisans, all of whom could keep her under surveillance and frustrate any kidnap-attempts by Catherine's partisans (or even men sent by Chapuys on Charles' orders to get her out of the country). But would Anne have dared to risk her marriage by making a stand if Henry ignored her demands to keep Mary illegitimate? Nor could Anne rely on Francis as a counter to Chapuys and the court conservatives in influencing Henry; thanks to the Milan war he needed Henry's aid in spring 1536 too much to risk annoying him. Anne was in a weak position to prevent Henry doing exactly what he liked about the succession, and his accident in Janaury had clearly made him aware of his insecure position and potential Divine disfavour as seen by his comments to his intimates at the time. But it appears from Henry's subsequent insistence that Mary had to acknowledge her illegitimacy before he would rehabilitate her that in 1536 he was determined to teach his elder daughter a lesson. Now Catherine was dead he seems to have transferred his anger at her defiance in 1527–36 to their daughter, though in legal terms all English subjects had to swear allegiance to the king's new marriage's legality as of 1534, so Mary could not be allowed an exemption. Mary was to give in and accept her bastardy, but only reluctantly and no doubt at immense psychological cost – and her obstinacy over submission to her father would have similarly soured any attempt from him to offer her re-legitimisation (on his, not Rome's, authority) as the reward for submission over his right to annul her parents' marriage.

The situation at court thus seemed momentarily to hold out hopes of stability as of early spring 1536, rather than being one of an 'inevitable' loss of influence by Anne, who had lost yet another child, ahead of her ruin. So what went wrong and why? The king's brooding character and extreme mistrust made any 'stability' at court dubious; like modern autocrats like Stalin and Mao, he could turn on any of his intimates with minimal warning and their enemies duly made the most of this. During the delicate negotiations to persuade him to reconcile with Charles and put Mary back in the line of succession, there was one ominous incident where senior ministers (led by Cromwell) were trying to coax the king into accepting Charles' terms in a private consultation during a 'break' in a royal audience with Chapuys. The latter saw the king have heated words with Cromwell who retreated out of harm's way, and then Henry came up to Chapuys and demanded that Charles put his offer in writing which Chapuys (as per Charles' instructions) refused. The Emperor wanted to keep this delicate diplomatic 'quid pro quo' unofficial, but Henry refused to 'play ball', snapped that he was not a child to be alternately coaxed and whipped, and started to rake up ten years' worth of reasons why he mistrusted Charles – which he had evidently been brooding over. This mixture of paranoia and petulant outbursts was thus well in evidence years before his alleged 'character deterioration' in his later years, which various modern writers have linked to the injuries he suffered in his jousting fall in January 1536 or a medical condition (even syphilis, which is now discounted). The courtiers could duly work on this, and it had to be a subtle and trusted adviser – Cromwell until July 1540 – who could fend it off or win Henry round. Allegedly the king was enamoured of Jane Seymour by this point, providing a major new reason why he should be thinking of getting rid of Anne, and be seeking for logical and sympathetic reasons for doing this in his mind – where his self-interest was intimately bound up with his 'duty' or a plot' as he chose to interpret matters. The king's interest in Jane may have dated back to his famous visit to her family at Wolf Hall in Wiltshire in late summer 1535, or at any rate been latent as he toyed with the idea of making her his mistress – though the vigilant Chapuys did not hear her name mentioned until weeks after Anne's miscarriage. At least according to the Countess of Exeter, not an unbiased witness as she and her husband were deep in the plot against Anne, in early spring 1536 the smitten king was sending love-letters to Jane and she was coyly insisting that as a modest and virtuous gentlewoman she could not in honour respond to such offers. Nor could she see him in private in case gossip emerged that ruined her spotless reputation, which was her pride – and so by implication the only way that Henry could have her was as his wife and he must get rid of Anne to win her. The countess also alleged that Jane's backers, led by her brother Edward Seymour who had just been appointed a gentleman of the Privy Chamber, persuaded her to not only toy with Henry flirtatiously and inflame his desire by seeming modest and honourable but to undermine his current wife by stressing the illegality of his marriage. The conservative allies of Mary who would be in attendance at these meetings with Jane would duly back her up and promote her cause to the king.[14] This ongoing plot, probably led by senior courtier Sir Nicholas Carew and aided by Chapuys (who also saw it as a holy duty to undermine heresy by aiding Mary and the chances of the king reconciling with Rome once Anne was removed), led to quiet enquiries to the English church leadership about the legality of a new royal divorce.[15]

The king's agreement to the new alliance with Charles and the probable effects of this on his current marriage was not certain at this point however, and Henry was notoriously moody and liable to change tack on a whim. The day after his confrontations with Cromwell and Chapuys, his entire council reportedly begged him on their knees to go ahead with the alliance – the sort of dramatic gesture that would appeal to him but which would also imply their heightened worries about it.[16] In typically teasing and mischievous manner, the king now tricked Chapuys on his 18 April visit to court into coming face to face with Anne at close quarters for the first time and having to politely bow to her – implying that he recognised 'the whore' as legally queen. This duly infuriated and worried Mary's supporters,[17] presumably as Henry intended – his acquiescence in any dramatic change of policy (or wife) was not to be taken for granted. The king now dangled his potential as an ally to both Charles and Francis at the same time – and on both sides on his terms, without concessions, which in Charles' case meant him accepting that Henry could keep Anne as queen and settle church affairs as he pleased whatever the pope said. The danger of this was that one or both of the great potentates would call his bluff due to his excessive confidence, and indeed Francis was now supposed to have got hold of a copy of the papal decree declaring Henry deposed and to be planning to publish it to undermine him.[18] As of the last week in April, the Council were meeting every day to decide what to do and try to push or coax Henry into a firm decision, with Cromwell reportedly taking to his bed with exhaustion or to keep out of the king's way (according to Chapuys).[19] At this point there was no hint that Anne's position was in serious or immanent danger, let alone an 'arc' of events leading to her disgrace and arrest – though her apparently manic and reckless behaviour in the next week or so indicates that she was under considerable emotional strain. Possibly the reported transfer of one of Cromwell's rooms to Jane Seymour on the king's orders – no doubt intended to facilitate private meetings that hopefully would not be reported to Anne and cause scenes – made her fear a king/Cromwell plot that could lead to Jane becoming even more indispensable. As far as Chapuys was aware, the breach of trust between the queen and Cromwell only occurred at the end of March, around this time – or so Cromwell told him on 1 April, confirming rumours.[20]

According to Chapuys, the 'mastermind' of Anne's fall – or at least the facilitating agent – was Cromwell, and the latter told him that he had felt in April that he had to act because of Henry's unrealistic hopes of the Imperial negotiations. Henry wanted Charles to 'climb down' and accept the Boleyn marriage in writing rather than the verbal and vague assurances that were all that Chapuys would give – and which had sparked off his irritation with Cromwell and Chapuys on 18 April.[21] By implication, Henry was fond of demanding the politically impossible from his ministers, as with requiring Wolsey to push the timid Pope Clement into granting the annulment from Catherine of Aragon, despite her and Charles' express wishes – and if the minister failed, as Wolsey had done in 1529, their career would be finished and the circling court vultures would move in. Wolsey had escaped initial prosecution thanks to his circumspect grovelling and Henry's respect for his long and faithful service, but his absence from court (on Henry's orders) and his rivals' intrigues had led to his arrest and death while under investigation for treason. Would Cromwell go the same way if he was seen by the king to 'let him down'? Accordingly, from what Cromwell told Chapuys, he had to alienate Henry from Anne and 'move on' the king to wanting to marry Jane Seymour instead, so that there were no more impossible demands to get Charles to openly recognise the Boleyn marriage. Therefore, Cromwell now appears to have moved to secure the backing of the conservative courtiers, such as Exeter and his wife and Sir Nicholas Carew, who had long backed Catherine and Mary and were now encouraging Henry to reconcile with the latter. Chapuys made some sort of approach to Mary in these weeks, given the context (i.e. following Cromwell seeking him out) presumably on Cromwell's behalf, and received her agreement. This followed various minor but significant examples of goodwill from Cromwell to Mary, e.g. handing over a cross which had used to belong to her mother, which can also be seen as winning her as an ally.[22] These manoeuvures would suggest that Cromwell was not putting a long-planned attack on Anne into action but reacting to his difficulties with Henry over the terms of reconciliation with Charles – though he may have been keeping Anne's court under quiet surveillance in recent weeks, in case he needed to produce evidence in a royal divorce-plan. Cromwell's words to Chapuys may not tell the full story, given the deviousness and ulterior motives of both men – but it is logical that Cromwell did not want to go the same way as Wolsey had done. (He did in the end, in 1540.) At this point it seems to have been assumed that Henry would just divorce and send Anne away, with no talk of her having committed any treasonable or otherwise capital crimes – though this could bring up legal difficulties about whether Henry's annulment from Catherine had been legal depending on what grounds the Boleyn marriage was ruled to be illegal. This 'Cromwell/Mary' alliance does not mean that Cromwell had agreed to a long-term alliance with Mary's faction, who had after all opposed the 'Break with Rome' and argued that his annulment from Catherine and marriage to Anne were illegal, so they had defied Cromwell's own religious legislation of 1531–6. Their alliance was merely tactical, and was probably bound to break down over Cromwell's leadership of the current moves to shut down and sell off the monasteries. (One of Mary's loudest supports, Lord Darcy who was supposed to have considered 'rescuing' her from Anne's household to restore her position in the succession by force, was later that year to lead the 'Pilgrimage of Grace' in defence of the monasteries.) The issue of the monasteries, which had just been brought under full royal control ahead of 'reform' /dissolution by Parliament as directed by Henry and Cromwell, may also have had something to do with Cromwell's breach with Anne. Historian Diarmaid MacCulloch, in his recent biography of Cromwell, suggests that the timing of Anne's recent support for reformist preachers who wanted the monasteries turned into charitable institutions, means that Cromwell would have perceived this as a threat to his master-plan to raise large amounts of cash for Henry by selling them all off – though even if some were kept as schools and hospitals as Anne wanted he could have sold their lands and contents. Perhaps we can also see Cromwell's hand in the subsequent insistence by Henry that Mary must accept that the 'Break with Rome', the annulment, and her bastardisation were legal before she would be allowed back to court. That way, the Royal Supremacy and independence of the English church would be legally reaffirmed – and its opponents such as the Exeters and Montagues could yet be arrested for subversive words about them.

Cromwell's plan to amass evidence against Anne that could make divorcing her easier now proceeded, though as yet there was no talk of her committing any capital crimes. Was the latter in Cromwell's mind as a way to silence her permanently – or was it thought up by him or the supposedly 'cuckolded' king as the stories of what had been said and done at her apartments came in? Events indeed proceeded shockingly fast – Anne was reluctantly recognised as queen by Chapuys as a result of a trick by the king on 18 April 1536, the first arrest of a suspect in the case (Anne's devoted musician Mark Smeaton) was made by Cromwell on 30 April, the famous incident of 'courtly admiration' by Anne's admirer Sir Henry Norris at the May Day tournament at Greenwich on 1 May was followed by his arrest and interrogation, the king then left the queen for Whitehall and had her restricted to her apartments later that day, she was sent to the Tower on 2 May, and she was put on trial on 10 May and executed on the 19th. The king's long-term close friend Norris (Anne's 'Groom of the Stool' so in constant attendance on her), her brother Lord Rochford, the unfortunate musician Smeaton, and Privy Chamber stalwarts Francis Weston and William Brereton were all executed too and several other people's careers were ruined, amidst lurid and unprecedented accusations of royal mass-adultery and incest that were bound to cause gossip and incredulity all over Europe. Indeed, there was a long gap between the first signs of Cromwell presumably needing, as a matter of political security, to destroy Anne and the first arrests. This was indicated to him by the king's impatient attitude to the Imperial talks on 21 April, and the arrest of key witness and alleged adulterer Norris on 30 April. Indeed, modern investigation of the first apparent sign of preparations for a typical Tudor 'purge' – the issuing of a legal patent on 24 April to set up a commission of 'oyer and terminer' in the county of Middlesex, which included Westminster, to investigate assorted cases of possible treason[23] – suggests to experts such as Anne's biographer Eric Ives that this may not refer to the Boleyn investigation at all. It may be either coincidence or just a sign that possible action against certain people among Anne's faction at court were being considered by Cromwell –

'silencing'them by severe charges so they could not interfere in a divorce, but not necessarily by accusing them of adultery with the queen. The first man to be investigated for the latter, i.e. Smeaton who was in constant attendance on her, known to be devoted to her, and a highly-strung and romantic 'type' open to blackmail or being 'lent on', did not occur until six days later – surely he should have been under investigation already if Cromwell was looking for evidence for a case? Indeed, on 25 April the king wrote to his ambassador in Rome, Richard Pate, recounting his recent sharp words with Chapuys and asking him to continue to press the Imperial envoys in Rome to get Charles to accept his full terms on the legality of the Boleyn marriage. He also referred to the probability of duly having a son by Anne, his 'dearly beloved' wife[24] – so as of the 25th he had no notion of removing her. On the 27th the summoning of a new Parliament was ordered, but that might have been to confirm the restoration of Mary in the succession, not the fall of Anne. As of the end of April all Chapuys had heard was a plan to revive the allegation that Anne had been 'pre-contracted' to marry the Earl of Northumberland years before so her marriage to Henry was illegal – which sounds like the 'royal divorce' rumours circulating recently. None of this suggests that any inkling of the seriousness of the charges to be made against Anne and her 'lovers' in the charges laid against them in the second week of May was known at this date.

Cromwell may indeed have been 'fishing' for evidence from 24 April, or even the 21st, but as of the 25th the king clearly knew mothing of it and had no serious thought of a divorce. His explosion of rage at the May Day tournament at Greenwich (if this has not been exaggerated) and his undoubted emotional state as he departed unexpectedly for London later that day – he was supposed to be heading for Calais for a 'summit' with King Francis as of 30 April and its cancellation was not known or even rumoured – suggest that he was taken by surprise by the events. Indeed, such a public 'scene' was unusual for Henry, a man touchy about his dignity. He may not even have known about Smeaton's arrest on the 30th and his subsequent interrogation, which was carried out in private at Cromwell's house at Stepney not in London or Greenwich. The low-born, young, and probably rather gauche musician Smeaton, possibly son of a carpenter and certainly not one of the noble elite household officials around Anne accustomed to witty exchanges with the queen but a 'menial' person, was apparently 'hauled in' after a report reached Cromwell of some injudicious and possibly lovelorn words which he had said to Anne. These referred to his role in her household as her 'servant' (which could mean her courtly admirer rather than just an employee) and his humble satisfaction in looking on her face regularly, and he was at least questioned closely as to what had been going on between them and may well have been tortured. (This was first alleged some years later, however; the anti-Henry Spanish *Cronica del Rey Enrico* alleged Cromwell had a cord twisted round Smeaton's head.) He held out until well into the 1st May and then confessed,[25] presumably to a 'made-up' case of adultery, and Cromwell then took this evidence to Greenwich; in the next few days during the 'news blackout' about the ongoing investigations it was supposed at court that Smeaton was the only person who had actually alleged that he had committed adultery with the queen. Until the gossip about his words with Anne (occurring in her Presence Chamber at Greenwich on the 29th) had been relayed to Cromwell he may not even have been 'in the frame'.

Similar confusion surrounds the course of the concurrent investigation into the more serious and incriminating exchanges made between Anne and Norris on or soon before the 28th, when Anne enquired of Norris why he had been delaying his marriage to his fiancée Margaret Shelton. She teasingly told him that 'You look for dead men's shoes; for if aught came to the king but good you would mean to have me'. 'Imagining the king's death' amounted to treason quite apart from the court being full of malevolent gossips and Anne already under threat from the king's interest in Jane Seymour (in her own mind at least), and the horrified Norris denied it hastily and assured that if he had ever had such thoughts he would wish that his head was off. Anne pursued it and said that she could ruin him if she so wanted, which implied that he had said or done some injudicious things earlier – flirtation? – and she could bear witness to them, as he would know. Norris later made a hurried visit to the queen's (clerical) almoner to take an oath that he believed the queen to be a good woman, apparently on Anne's instructions; he was clearly terrified, and with good reason.[26] Word of this got to Cromwell as well as around the court although the occasional verbal excesses of 'knightly devotion' towards the queen would not have been unprecedented, and this was presumably the reason for a heated quarrel between Henry and

Anne witnessed by the visiting Scots cleric Alexander Ales, probably on 1 May as it was shortly before the king left Greenwich for London. After the king had walked out Ales saw Anne hold up their daughter Elizabeth at the window in a final vain appeal to him, and as Ales was not involved in current English politics and only recalled this on a visit to the latter's court over twenty years later his word can be trusted.[27] The events of 1 May also saw the famous joust at Greenwich where the king was allegedly furious at one of Anne's knightly admirers wiping the sweat off his brow with her handkerchief which she passed to him as a 'favour' to wear as her champion, but the evidence for this is uncertain. More clear is that after the jousts the king departed unexpectedly for London with only a small group of companions, only six or seven, and that he summoned Norris to be one of them and *en route* questioned him closely about his relationship with the queen. Norris was promised his pardon if he told the truth and Henry may even have meant it (then), but next day Norris was sent to the Tower.[28] The 'round-up' of other suspects then proceeded – but clearly it was only initiated after Cromwell had investigated a report of Smeaton's injudicious (but probably innocent) behaviour and the king had investigated what Cromwell had told him of the exchanges between the queen and Norris. The 'timeline' of events suggests that at best Cromwell was 'fishing for' evidence but until Smeaton confessed had none worth proceeding with, and that Henry was taken by surprise by what he heard about or from Norris and reacted with instinctive fury.

The royal mistrust and jealousy of Anne's alleged admirers at court and the resulting explosion of rage by the king at the May Day tournament is the traditional story of events used for novel, film and TV reconstructions, though the traditional narrative of events owes much to hindsight. The 'evidence' amassed against Anne by Cromwell once the king seemed to be willing to be rid of her were bound to be exaggerated, both by him to obtain convictions and an overwhelming case to put before the judges, blackening the names of Anne and senior allies of hers with the king's ear like Norris, and by the accused in an attempt to save their lives by co-operating and blaming Anne for everything. Anne had possibly over-acted (manically?) the role of queenly patron of love-smitten courtly admirers, an accepted contemporary role as played up in literature, to put a brave face on her fears. Given that the sort of semi-flirtatious and charged exchange she had with Norris at the end of April was only an exaggerated version of normal 'courtly' interchanges between a queenly 'Lady' and her devoted knight but it clearly scared Norris as 'crossing the line', until this point Anne had not used this sort of wordage. Similarly, until now he and others had not been afraid of a violent and jealous reaction from the king – if the latter had heard any rumours of flirtation (which troublemakers would have been only too glad to report to him or Cromwell) he had passed it off without more than mild irritation. Anne was already under threat if what the Countess of Essex recalled was true, and the Countess' account more or less ties in with what Chapuys wrote to Charles V – though both of them disliked Anne and would probably exaggerate the danger to her in February-April 1536 out of wish-fulfilment. Clearly Norris was aware that his exchange with Anne could be reported to Henry or Cromwell quickly and lead to his ruin, as shown by his panicking reaction, and as Anne backed him up in going to her almoner she knew this too. So did she just make 'off-the-cuff' remarks due to stress, or plan to make Henry jealous and win him back? If she hoped to tease Henry into feeling jealous and hastening to reassure her of his devotion, this was a fatal miscalculation. Once he had given the 'go-ahead' for a legal investigation the queen's enemies were able to manufacture the evidence that they needed to ruin her.

Harmless if possibly sexually charged flirtation, injudicious dramatic flourishes of devotion from the 'courtly knights' in her entourage to their lady, and the king's brooding paranoia were turned into a lethal cocktail – clearly by Cromwell. It was aided by Cromwell already having spies in the queen's household, and thus being able to pinpoint a 'weak link' and set to work on Mark Smeaton to investigate and exaggerate probably innocent but potentially 'improper' exchanges between him and the queen overheard at court at the end of April. More serious was the exchange between the queen and her more well-born courtier admirer Norris, given that Norris was a 'senior gentry' figure of long standing at court and a personal friend of the king's. If Cromwell wanted to destroy Anne's faction as well as her, Norris was a key figure and bringing him down – to the block or just driving him into disgrace and exile – should terrorise his allies into silence. The king duly postponed his intended trip to Calais, a major 'summit' that could keep Francis from allying to Charles and attacking England, and was unsatisfied with his personal questioning of Norris and ordered his arrest. This may have been more important than the dubiously accurate accounts of Henry storming off from the May Day tournament after a knightly admirer was allowed to wipe the sweat off his face with Anne's handkerchief, which first appears in a later partisan account of the crisis by the Catholic writer Nicholas Sander. In any case the king went into seclusion, immune to appeals from the most highly-placed Boleyn partisans. This enabled Cromwell to isolate and pick them off one by one, and was Henry's choice not Cromwell's – Henry did not like confrontation and was to avoid it with Cromwell himself and with Queen Katherine Howard when these two were arrested in 1540 and 1542, so his confrontation with Norris showed that he valued the latter – but was used by Cromwell. Anne's brother and close adviser Lord Rochford, still at large on 1 May, was prevented from seeing Henry by Cromwell and arrested next day at Whitehall.[29] Had he been under serious suspicion on the 1st, it would have made sense for Cromwell to have him accused and arrested then at Greenwich to prevent him asking the king for help and denying the allegations concerning Smeaton and/or Norris; instead Rochford seems to have been able – and willing – to go to Whitehall and try to see the king there. By this reckoning, any gossip about his supposed intimacy with Anne or his rude remarks about the king's sexual inadequacy were unknown to Cromwell and his queen's household informant(s) as of 1 May – suggesting that they were either secret or (partly?) invented. Most Boleyn allies, led by Anne's father Sir Thomas Boleyn (earl of Wiltshire) and Sir Francis Bryan, made haste to abandon her and to deny that they knew anything about her alleged misdemeanours, let alone try to defend her (at least once the cause was hopeless). Bryan was only allowed to see the king after interceding with Cromwell, who no doubt checked what he was going to say and warned him not to defend the queen to Henry or he would be arrested too; even the highly trusted Archbishop Cranmer was reduced to appearing before the council's special judicial committee (the 'Star Chamber') to relate what little he knew and writing a grovelling letter to Henry assuring his shock at the allegations, not questioning their accuracy, and distancing his reformed religious cause from the queen.[30]

Worse, Anne's injudicious conversation to her attendants after her transfer to the Tower – probably letting dangerous details out due to sheer relief that she was in the royal apartments not the dungeons – apparently revealed new 'leads' for Cromwell to back up the Norris allegations, namely the fact that her household courtier Francis Weston had known about Norris' long-term devotion to the queen for a year or so and had once told Anne that the other man was coming to her apartments to feast his eyes on her and not on his betrothed, Margaret Shelton. An exchange between Anne and Weston in 1535 had centred on Anne teasing the latter for being devoted to her himself, so he could be and was arrested and blackmailed by Cromwell into saving himself from trial for adultery with the queen by 'dropping Norris in it' instead.[31] Cromwell had carefully placed informants hostile to Anne in her Tower retinue to record and report all that she said, and if she had had more sense she would have realised that and acted innocent – and Cromwell had no means of knowing in advance that she would incriminate herself. Less certain is the later allegation by the Scots observer Alexander Ales that Anne's ruthless anti-reformist foe Stephen Gardiner, currently ambassador to France and later to betray Cromwell in 1540, sent reports from Paris that stories about Anne committing adultery were flying around the French court due to gossip leaking out of her household.[32] Another French source, Lancelot de Cales, alleged that a somewhat puritanical Henrican councillor who was horrified at the emerging scandal tasked his queen's household member sister with involvement in tawdry goings-on and she told him that Anne had been carrying on not only with Smeaton but with her own brother.[33] This led to the crucial investigation of Lord Rochford and the 'incest' charge. Another French account – later, in Elizabeth's reign – alleged that it was a former royal mistress (unnamed) who revealed the 'Rochford incest' story, and this was reported by her brother 'Doctor Brun' – presumably a garbled reference to Henry's senior Gentleman of the Privy Chamber and intimate Sir Anthony Browne.[34] But all these stories are overseas in origin and seem to reflect gossip not specific details traceable to contemporary accounts in May 1536.

Henry in a rage was always difficult to reason with, and in a deferential court and age few people would have dared to do so even if they had the opportunity – which Cromwell denied them. Only Rochford might have dared, and he was speedily neutralised with Cromwell including him in the indictment against his sister and securing supposedly damning evidence that he had been discussing Henry's sexual inadequacies with Anne (which was guaranteed to enrage the king). The confessions of Rochford's wife Jane, to his alleged indiscretions, on which the 'incest' charge was built, are undoubtably of contemporary and reliable origin, as they were reported by Chapuys in his account of what happened at the ('closed session') trial in the Tower of London, based on what witnesses had told him.[35] Some unknown or lost contemporary evidence, including the lost journal of Antony Anthony, also named Lady Rochford as the source of the 'incest' allegations, and were accepted as reliable by the late seventeenth-century Scots Presbyterian (i.e. Protestant so pro-reformist) historian Bishop Gilbert Burnet.[36] They have long been taken as damning to Lady Rochford's reputation, and possibly due to spite rather than stupidity or fear – Burnet accused her of jealousy at Anne usurping her intimacy with Lord Rochford, and others have assumed that evidence of her new friendship with Princess Mary in 1536 hints that she was spying on Anne on behalf of the 'Marian' anti-reformist conservatives.[37] Attempts have been made to rehabilitate her, including a recent biography, and certainly accounts of her alleged spite and jealousy are gossip not fact. Possibly, Cromwell blackmailed her so that she could save her own life by sending her husband and sister-in-law to the block. Other evidence may have come from writings by the late Lady Wingfield, a former member of Catherine of Aragon's household who was in Anne's service around 1530 (and was linked to fears of her indiscretion by Anne), who was named as a major source of detail by one of the judges at Anne's trial, John Spelman, in a later account examined by Bishop Burnet.[38] Three court ladies (Anne Cobham, Lady Worcester, and an unnamed person) were cited as the witnesses for the charge at the trial by the king's uncle Lord Lisle's agent John Hussey, as preserved in the famous contemporary source the *Lisle Letters*.[39] Lady Worcester was Sir Anthony Browne's daughter – so was she the origin of the French stories linking Browne and his female kin to the allegations? The number of names, however, may only indicate that Cromwell was casting his net wide and trawling up any information that he could acquire or exaggerate about what Anne and her brother might have been up to in private – and that both Anne and her brother did not care for convention about 'seemly' behaviour and were as of c.1531–5 relaxed about gossip. The details may well have been twisted out of recognition by threatening the witnesses with being charged as collaborators with their adulterous queen – and even if well-connected figures who Henry trusted might escape execution (as did accused courtier poet Sir Thomas Wyatt senior) they could still be ruined and lose all their valuable sources of income from the king and his officials unless they did what Cromwell told them.

This escalation of the charges against Anne of adultery, with Smeaton and Norris to incest, was unprecedented for a contemporary royal scandal and was far less easy to believe – and as Anne could have been divorced for adultery and left Henry free to marry Jane Seymour without it the crucial question must be 'why?' On the issue of '*cui bono*' ('who benefits?'), the answer to that hints at the reason for the lurid and seemingly bizarre charges. Cromwell was the man who laid the charges and the interrogations were organised and mostly conducted by him, so he was clearly their main motivator. Anne's fall was guaranteed if she could be convicted of adultery, but Henry was a man of changeable moods and he might have a 'mood-swing' before the trial and decide not to go ahead – or Anne could be left alive and in disgrace and the conviction turn out to be unsafe later once he tired of Jane Seymour (or she died as in real life). The only way of preventing that was to make sure Anne was firstly tried and then executed – and the more lurid the charges, the greater chances of the latter. The accusation of incest should be capable of making the king so horrified and disgusted that he would recoil from Anne and refuse any notion of reconciliation, thus ruining her and preserving Cromwell from a later Boleyn 'come-back' – and if Lord Rochford could be ruined and executed too that would exclude him, the uncle and close male kin of Princess Elizabeth, ever serving as a regent or senior minister should Henry and Mary both die and Elizabeth become queen. Cromwell was a shrewd man who was capable of thinking far ahead, and he had reason to make the fall of the Boleyns as complete and as scandalous as possible.

The charge that Anne had committed incest with Rochford, with the intention of getting herself pregnant again so she could pass off the baby as the king's, was almost certainly an ingenious but twisted invention of Cromwell's – probably to rouse up opinion at their carefully-vetted trials as well as to disgust the king. If Anne could be condemned for incest she could be executed whether the rest of the accusations of adultery were proved or not. Moreover, it is quite possible that Henry and Cromwell feared that she would falsely claim to be pregnant at her trial, in order to hold up her condemnation and give the king time to have second thoughts. Holding the trial in secret within the Tower would diminish the impact of such a claim, but news of it could still leak out. Thus, alleging that any child Anne was carrying was her brother's would warn her off making such a claim. If she tried to claim she was pregnant, the king could deny that the baby was his and her admission would therefore be 'proof' of incest.

A mixture of threats and blandishments produced the evidence that Cromwell and the conservatives needed from the accused aristocratic figures who had paid extravagant court to Anne, and the advantages that the interrogators had in working on their targets in the Tower meant that however innocent all such relationships had been, someone was bound to 'confess' to what the government wanted them to say in the hope of clemency. As in Soviet-era Eastern Europe, once the state had decided on its course of action and determined the result any judicial investigation and trial was a foregone conclusion – though using the legal process as an 'arm' of state power not an independent force was not an invention of Henry VIII's (or Henry VII's) and was a 'given' of late medieval court politics too, as seen by the 'show trials' of opponents of the current regimes (or the partisans of overthrown regimes) in 1322, 1326, 1387–8, and 1450 in England. Once Henry had been isolated from appeals by Anne's supporters she was doomed, barring a last-minute change of mind by a man who was never known for his emotional generosity. But the importance of the king's outburst of anger at and physical abandonment of her on 30 April – 1 May cannot be denied, and it is probable that Cromwell made the most of this unexpected quarrel to hastily round up suspects and build up a dossier of the most incriminating evidence (or inventions) possible rather than putting a long-planned scheme into effect on schedule. A master of politics and 'spin' like him may well have already had a basic scenario and list of potential suspects and charges sketched out, but what was actually done would have depended on how events developed day by day – and like Stalin's police-chiefs, the varying moods of 'the boss' had to be kept in mind throughout for fear that he would change his mind. Without the chances provided by Anne's (and Henry Norris') reckless words, the devotion of Mark Smeaton being ferreted out, and the episode of the May Day tournament the alienation of king and queen could have built up for months more before causing a fatal clash, though Anne's character was such that she was likelier to confront him than play for time if she felt her influence slipping away. Once Catherine of Aragon was dead and the king was infatuated with

Jane Seymour her position was under threat, at least in the long term. Indeed, now Henry could name his own heir at will – without having to be married to the heir's mother – he could even have kept a son by Anne as heir and removed the baby's mother in case of a serious quarrel or another infatuation.

This all shows that the usual narrative of Anne's fall suffers from several serious misconceptions. The loss of Henry and Anne's child in January 1536 was not fatal to their marriage, even if the couple had a serious row afterwards; nor was the death of Catherine of Aragon; nor was the international situation. Temporarily Imperial hostility was reduced over Charles fearing that Henry would marry a French candidate next – provided that the king re-legitimated Mary. But the king's new ability to nominate heirs at will gave him a wider range of options, and meant that he was less tied to Anne as his wife; even if they had a son he could safely remove her. This could have happened in the next few years, whether or not the crisis of April-May 1536 had been avoided, and Henry's emotional stability was precarious as was his conscience – and his always flexible interpretation of what God seemed to intend or want of him. Given the tempestuous nature of his relationship with Anne and his growing ruthlessness, his need of foreign allies (as in real-life 1538–9) could have impelled him to seek a 'respectable', legal foreign wife as part of a renewed alliance with either Charles or Francis then. In real life his next wife Jane Seymour had died; but he had the legal power to rid himself of Anne at will and the diplomatic imperative could have made it seem attractive. All the evidence suggests that though Jane was the catalyst for the collapse of his marriage he was capable of finding others – another woman at court, or another valuable foreign princess – whenever he wished. His frequent complaints at Anne's temper and lack of respect for her sovereign make it evident that he could weary of her attractions, and decide in favour of a more acquiescent wife. Their sexual attraction was not going to be overwhelming indefinitely. Moreover, although he had shown himself capable of managing relationships with two women at once, and Catherine had not shown any anger about his mistresses (e.g. Bessie Blount and Mary Boleyn) or insecurity about him favouring his illegitimate children, Anne's anger at Jane's alleged role in spring 1536 shows that she was not capable of putting up with a rival as royal mistress.

Anne's indiscretions to her intimates at court and flashes of temper were likely to be reported by her rivals and worked upon with the king, although it cannot be taken as certain that her brother Rochford's wife Jane (the main source of some of the most damaging allegations about her in May 1536) was actively plotting a spiteful revenge on her or 'spying' for her enemies (Cromwell?) as opposed to 'confessing' what was wanted by her interrogators when her own life was under threat. The role and character of Jane Boleyn in this snakepit of intrigue and rumour are among the many unanswered questions of this mystery, though nowadays the general opinion of commentators has been more sympathetic than in the times of the early, disapproving and sensationalist ninteenth-century 'romantic' writers. Nor is it clear that the alleged rake Rochford had so annoyed his wife Jane by his infidelities that she was eager – or at any rate persuadable with promises or threats – to 'drop him in it' and ruin him, and Anne by association. The idea that she was specifically humiliated and furious at his close – suspiciously so? – and flirtatious relationship with Anne is even less proveable or likely, despite its appeal to later writers and usefulness in winning them more readers. The fact of her recall to serve in the royal household for later queens a few years after her 1536 interrogation and disgrace suggests not so much that her case for a second chance was 'pushed' by her late husband's uncle Norfolk or another ally – the king was notoriously unforgiving and fond of grudges, and her husband George Boleyn had humiliatingly suggested that he was impotent – as that she was seen as personally or politically 'harmless'. She thus did not have a reputation for betrayal or spite, which opponents of the Boleyns would have been keen to remind the king of in 1539–40 to keep her away from any role of importance – instead she was given a key role close to the new queen, the naïve and sheltered German Anne of Cleves, who would need wise guidance. After Anne had been married to the king for a few weeks and was hoping that she was pregnant, Jane and her fellow senior (all aristocratic and titled) ladies of the household then took it upon themselves as experienced married women to check up that Anne had in fact been having sexual relations with Henry, not just sharing a bed which was what Anne had implied – and when the truth about his abstention emerged, it gave the naïve queen some 'no holds barred' information on what full sexual relations entailed, which she evidently did not know.[40] Jane's role under Queen Anne was that of a fully trusted and helpful, not 'meddling' or intriguing, royal confidante and she was reappointed to serve the (actually far more worldly and sexually experienced though younger) next Queen Catherine Howard, in the same role. This led to disaster as she ended up as the queen's confidante and 'go-between' in her secret affair with Thomas Culpeper behind the king's back, right from the pair's first meeting at court since the royal marriage when Catherine sent her former admirer Culpeper (now a junior member of the king's 'Privy Chamber' staff) a cap as a gift in Lent 1541 and Jane was the person chosen by the queen to arrange a private encounter and see how he had taken this gift.[41] (Note, it was the queen not Culpeper who made the first advances – so this makes the modern theory that 'sex pest' Culpeper was blackmailing the queen into an affair by threatening to reveal their past indiscretions unlikely). The increasingly bold – and probably bored – teenage queen found Jane a reliable and discreet 'go-between', and continued to use her to arrange ever more daring meetings behind the king's back for months to come, including on the (rare) royal tour of the east midlands up as far as recently rebellion-affected York that summer. The way that Jane, who seems to have attracted dislike from some of her fellow-ladies of the bedchamber for her unusually intimate relationship with the queen, helped the latter and Culpeper to commit adultery behind the king's back was not only treason (which she had barely escaped execution for once already) but foolish in the extreme, and her frank sexual talk back in 1536 and 1540 suggests that she was unusually daring, indiscreet, and fond of gossip. But this is not enough to imply that she was the 'evil genius' and 'arch-betrayer' to both George Boleyn and Catherine Howard, though in both cases her conduct was risky and the latter case ended up with her being executed along with her mistress. It is noticeable that after she was condemned in 1541 but was ruled as being 'insane' (genuinely or an attempt to save her from execution on a technicality?) the king had the law changed so that insane persons could be executed and applied it quickly to her – he was evidently keen to see her meet what he saw as her 'just deserts'.

The question of Anne's real religious opinions (conventional Catholic, reformist 'Erasmian' Catholic within the limits of 'progressive' opinions by respected international scholars such as Erasmus, or proto-Protestant?) have been hopelessly muddled by the abuse heaped on her after her fall, the rehabilitation of her under her daughter Queen Elizabeth as a supposed progenitor for the latter's 'moderate' Protestantism, and the hatred of Counter-Reformationary English Catholics for her as the origin of the 'Break With Rome.' She was certainly seen with nostalgia after the 'reaction' (in English religious policy, appointments, and judicial proceedings and in foreign alignments) commenced with the fall of Thomas Cromwell in July 1540 – in the 1560s Alexander Ales, her former supporter who was now reviving her standing under her daughter's regime, told Elizabeth that 'true religion in England had its commencement and its end with your mother'[42] and the master propagandist and Protestant biographer John Foxe ranked her with Cromwell and Cranmer in its leadership.[43] She undoubtably patronised leading, idealistic, and 'risk-taking' theologians such as new bishops Hugh Latimer (her chaplain and later a Marian 'martyr') and Nicholas Shaxton, and used the king's reformist physician Dr William Butts to recruit such men for her household from the ranks of promising young academics at Cambridge University – a sort of 'brains trust'? She was also recalled by Latimer as using him to advise the king in a sermon to use the dissolution of the monasteries to convert these institutions to useful charitable purposes rather than to just sell them off[45] – an imaginative and idealistically Christian purpose that might have alleviated a lot of suffering at a time of damaging economic and social change. Her support for the Lutheran cause in Germany in the 1530s – politically risky given the king's continuing orthodox views on theology, e.g. the transformation of the Sacrament into the 'Body and Blood of Christ' – was another useful weapon if and when the king turned against these attitudes and Cromwell (as he was to do in 1540). It need not imply her sharing their opinions on theology, merely a shrewd 'political' desire to use these potentially rebellious German princes and theologians as a way to keep her foe Emperor Charles V too busy at home to dare to intervene in England – and the staunchly Catholic monarchs of France were to do this for decades to come to outwit their Habsburg rivals, the rulers of Spain and Germany.

The 'Anne the proto-Protestant reformist' theory is less certain to recent investigators of her beliefs, e.g. Eric Ives and Diarmaid MacCullough, than it was in earlier times. Within the limits of 1530s religious politics she was probably less adventurous in 'reformist' experimentation than her subsequent admirers proclaimed; much was written in hindsight when she could be portrayed as the forerunner of her Protestant daughter.

Those of her protégés who were earnest reformers in the 1540s and 1550s, from Thomas Cranmer to Nicholas Hooper, were not necessarily known as such at the time and whatever they believed privately they had to be cautious as unorthodox theological views were still illegal. The medieval statutes on heresy had not all been repealed, although under Cromwell's 'Vicar-Generalship' they were generally not enforced and illegal Continental Protestant writings appear to have been circulating in London. But Anne was undeniably interested in religion and active in religious thought and patronage as her successor Jane Seymour was not – and Henry preferred the latter. He is reliably supposed to have told Jane not to meddle when she spoke up for the conservative victims of his post-rebellion punishments in 1537, and by 1546 he was capable of toying with the idea of arresting Catherine Parr for her reformist religious activities. She had to grovel and assure him that she had only sought to aid his studies and learn from his superior wisdom, which Anne would have found impossible to admit. The ailing, ageing, anti-reformist Henry in 1545–6 would hardly have tolerated Anne's outspokenness, and his attitudes and increasing paranoia argue against her chances of survival after the late 1530s, unless she had become indispensable (with three or four children?) or much more cautious. But the sudden fall of Anne Boleyn in 1536 – and behind that her failure to give the king a son – was clearly a major tragedy for the chances of a relatively smooth pathway to a reformed Church of England as well as a disaster for the Boleyns and their allies, and Anne was a more talented and multi-faceted figure than the scheming adventuress that still appears in some modern media interpretations of her.

Chapter Three

Was Elizabeth I's Marriage to Robert Dudley Sabotaged by his Wife's Supposed 'Suicide'? And Who Sabotaged It?

Elizabeth I: did she seriously consider marriage? The missed – or sabotaged? – opportunity with Robert Dudley.

'The Virgin Queen' stands as Elizabeth I's proud motto – the English sovereign who never married and told her Parliament that she was married to her realm, not to a person. Her opposition to the expected marriage, or at least rushing into one, was made clear to her first parliament on 10 February 1559 as the first wave of pressure for her to marry and feverish controversy over who would be the best choice mounted. In contrast to the expectations of the period for women in general and for women rulers (still a rare species, and regarded by suspicious cultural conservatives such as the Scots preacher John Knox as an abomination), she did not accept that women naturally needed male guidance and were too emotional and inconstant ever to shoulder the burden of rule alone. The much-vaunted 'natural order of things' played up in contemporary culture and lauded as God's will in the Bible stated that women were to obey and be directed by men, and a wife should obey her husband as stated in the marriage-service. That applied to women rulers too – and in practical terms a woman ruler needed children to keep her dynasty going and her husband should be her social equal in birth as well as her political and marital partner. This of course provided the problem that if he was of royal blood he would come either from her own extended family – which was impractical for the small and mostly unhealthy Tudor dynasty, many of whose males had died young like Henry VIII's elder brother and both his sons or abroad – and if he came from a foreign dynasty he would thus entail a close political link to this family and the country it ruled. How could it be certain that this link would be in England's long-term political interests, and if the Queen Regnant was to obey her husband would she not be tied down to backing the interests of the latter's country? Moreover, if her husband was designated as (or became by reason of early deaths among his relatives) the ruler of his dynasty's country, would he not put that state's interests first, neglect England, and use its resources for his own dynasty's interests? This dilemma was particularly acute in sixteenth-century England, as the power-politics of Europe involved a long-term struggle between the rival dynasties of Habsburg (as of 1452 usually ruling the Holy Roman Empire in Germany to add to its hereditary lands in what is now Austria, plus as of 1482 the Netherlands and as of 1516 Spain and its expanding American empire) and Valois (since 1328 ruling France). The two were engaged in a series of major wars plus a constant 'cold war' struggle for influence, and England had to choose who to back; if either came to or threatened to dominate Europe it usually behoved England to back their rival. But how could England do that and avoid being swallowed up as a minor part of its queen's husband's realm if it was tied down to one of the two 'Great Powers' by reason of a long-term marital alliance?

The long-term diplomatic and military 'fencing' between Charles V of Habsburg (King of Spain from 1516–56 and Emperor from 1519–55, plus ruler of the Netherlands and from 1526 brother of the King of Hungary and Bohemia) and Francis I of France (ruled 1515–47), succeeded by his son Henri II (ruled 1547–59), saw Henry VIII shift his alliances from one side to the other as occasion demanded. Accordingly his eldest daughter and original heiress Mary was betrothed in turn into the Habsburg and Valois families as the current position of English diplomacy demanded. To firmly ally with one 'Power' would ensure the other's enmity, and in due course the regency for Edward VI allied firmly with France, Henry's foe in the mid-1540s, in 1551–3 and Edward was engaged to Henri II's daughter Elizabeth (who as events turned out ended up after Edward died married off to Charles V's son and heir Philip II of Spain in the Franco-Habsburg treaty of Cateau- Cambresis in 1559). Ironically, at this stage England was vehemently Protestant under the 'Edwardian Reformation' and France was staunchly Catholic and was also propping up the Catholic regency of Marie de Guise in Scotland – but great power politics came first. Edward's death aged fifteen saw his shaky and reluctant successor Jane Grey's regime, led by her father-in-law the Duke of Northumberland, frantically seeking French help to stave off a rebellion by the 'cheated' rightful queen, Mary Tudor – and offering Henri II the handover of England's last possession in France, Calais, plus Ireland to no avail. Mary evicted Jane's crumbling regime (apparently to the embarrassed 'Nine Days' queen's personal relief), restored England to Catholicism and the obedience of Rome in reversal of her father's policies, and duly allied with her long-term backer of over twenty years, the ultra-Catholic Charles V. She then married his son Philip, who was eleven years younger than her, and as the ageing Charles started to divest himself of his dominions, was due to take over rule of the Netherlands and then Spain and its empire (plus satellite states in Italy such as Milan and Naples).

The marriage was deeply unpopular in England as threatening to turn England into a Habsburg satellite and led in 1554 to a major revolt, the Wyatt Rebellion, that nearly succeeded and led to fighting in the streets of London and within yards of Whitehall Palace. Once Mary was married to Philip and pushing England back into obedience to the pope – who in fact was a harsh critic of Spanish rule in Italy and as a result ended up at odds with, not supporting her – she duly joined in Philip's war with France in 1555–8, but only ended up losing Calais to a surprise French attack. This, plus her humiliating failure to have a child despite a public announced and much-lauded (phantom) pregnancy in 1555, made Mary's reign seem a disaster. However, the amount of actual open dissent to her dramatic reversal of Edwardian policies in religion and diplomacy was small and the majority of the English people were almost certainly still Catholic or at least not violently opposed to Catholics in her reign. The Edwardian Reformation had largely been a 'top-down' affair ordered by a small and determined governing elite in Privy Council and church, with a substantial faction of conservative councillors able and willing to rally to Mary in 1553, though it would inevitably mean becoming Catholic again. The majority of Protestant 'martyrs' in 1555–8 were in the south-east of England, especially London, Kent and East Anglia and of the lower social classes – the higher classes either conformed quietly or if sufficiently strong-willed to refuse emigrated – and there were always plenty of informers willing to 'turn in' defiant Protestants to the government; there was no mass-revolt in favour of the suppressed religion as with Catholic northern England in 1536 and Cornwall in 1549. (The Wyatt Rebellion was chiefly aimed at the danger of political subservience to Spanish interests by Mary marrying Philip, though her expected return to allegiance to Rome was already being signalled.) Much of the north of England was indeed still Catholic in the 1560s and only slowly converted under pressure from Elizabeth's government, with the strength of enthusiasts for the two religions probably evenly balanced in 1558 – and Elizabeth did not hurry to abandon Mary's legislation or arrest her persecutory zealots in 1558–9 so she was not the eager leader of an inevitable 'Protestant triumph' over a deeply unpopular 'reactionary' policy.

Arguably, had almost all Mary's hard-line (or just principled) bishops not refused to crown Elizabeth as a 'bastard' in 1558 so she had to turn to the Protestant religious elite for support, it is possible that the famously 'fence-sitting' Elizabeth, who was annoyed at the new Parliament of spring 1559 rushing to cancel Mary's religious legislation at the risk of offending England's ally Philip, might not have moved back towards Edwardian Protestantism so quickly or fully. The events of 1558–9 were not a simplistic case of a firmly Protestant Elizabeth, the devout heiress of the late reformist heroine Anne Boleyn, leading a thankful and united nation back to Protestantism, as might seem from the accounts in 'heroic' and determinist later Protestant history-books written with a mind to blackening the Catholic faith as bloody, persecutory, 'Popish', and foreign. (This bias was evident as late as Victorian accounts of the period and had a tendency to reflect contemporary fear of the revival of English Catholicism from the 1840s as much as genuine sixteenth-century history.) Subsequent modern analysis has been kinder than the contemporary verdict of Mary as a failure who had ended her reign with Calais lost, and her administrative and economic policies have been praised as being broadly in line with – and even inspiring – Elizabeth's policies, which were partly directed by the same councillors. (Some regime stalwarts with elastic religious consciences indeed survived in government under Henry VIII, Edward, Mary, and Elizabeth and changed religion as and when required, e.g. Lord Treasurer William Paulet, marquis of Winchester.) The long memories of 'Bloody Mary' and her unprecedented mass-burnings of (mainly lower-class) Protestants have affected subsequent interpretations of her reign and the situation in and after 1558, but at the time the reality of politics was rather more ambiguous.

But, faced with that recent memory from 1554–8 of what a foreign marriage could do to a ruling queen and her reputation, Elizabeth had no reason to look on another marriage to a ruler or his near-relative of a major European power with favour, quite apart from any 'hang-ups' about close personal relationships based on her parents' tempestuous marriage and its bloody end. Some hesitation when Elizabeth took the throne was inevitable. As for one thing France and Spain were still at war so alliance to one would mean the hostility of the other – and Henri II 'threw down the gauntlet' at once by recognising Mary Queen of Scots, Elizabeth's cousin, as rightful queen of England on account of Henry VIII and Anne Boleyn's marriage being illegal. If neither Habsburgs nor Valois were a wise source of marital partners, there were other less important states – but Catholic Portugal, an English ally, was a Habsburg ally (so a Valois foe) and currently had no princes available and choosing a Protestant northern European prince (Danish or Swedish?) could alienate the ultra-Catholic Philip II. If Elizabeth was to choose an English nobleman instead of a foreign royal, the chances were that his rivals would turn against her and the new regime was short of men, money, or stability. A delay in choosing a husband was logical. But nobody in 1558–9 could have expected that this would go on throughout Elizabeth's forty-four-and-a-third-years reign. Did she in fact come close to a decision in 1559–60, and if so what stopped her? Was it yet more court intrigue – or murder?

Elizabeth's reasons for her choice seem to have been partly personal, partly political, and acres of academic study, psychological analysis, and historical fiction have been expended on them. As with the equally popular subject for the printed and visual media Anne Boleyn, some are more unlikely or sensational than others, but many modern theories – especially in commercially-orientated media – do not go into the context in detail and so miss explanations that are more likely if less attractive to the public. Nor are the 'public access' and 'prone to leaking gossip' aspects of court life given enough consideration – most notably with the theories of Elizabeth having a secret baby without any of her court ladies who attended her every minute of the day having told anyone about this in an era when 'interested parties' would pay well for damaging information. Elizabeth clearly did not want to become eclipsed by her husband and tied to his country or political faction as her sister had been, her sister's and father's marriages had been a succession of traumatic disasters, and if she chose one candidate in the 'marriage stakes' it would upset the delicate political balance of her realm and foreign policy by alienating their rivals.

As of her accession in November 1558 it was assumed that she undoubtably would marry, as had been the case with Mary, and an unmarried woman exercising authority as Queen Regnant without a husband was unnatural by the standards of universal custom. Women were subject to men – husbands then fathers – in law and by Biblical authority her husband would have a right to exercise authority over her, though Mary had specifically limited her husband's legal rights in England by statute and this could be repeated. Elizabeth's choice of husband was also bound to be contentious if not, as some pessimists assumed, inevitably ruinous – and her past record of flirting with Thomas Seymour meant that as of 1558 her 'wisdom' and 'shrewd playing off of factions' (which we can now see in hindsight) was not the attitude of contemporary political 'actors' to this new and untried sovereign. A foreign prince or king, of equal rank to the queen as was socially seemly, would subject England's interests to his own state's – the dilemma which had faced her father as he sought to marry off Mary, as his heiress, to the heirs of the Empire/Spain or France from 1516–27. A domestic husband of high social standing from the nobility would arouse jealousy from his rivals – by one gloomy contemporary estimate half the kingdom's great men would oppose any noble who was so chosen, presumably in arms.[1] A domestic choice of queen also had a bad history in England, given the controversy surrounding the alleged greed and hunger for power of Edward IV's controversial wife Elizabeth Woodville's relatives in the mid-late 1460s and the part which this had played in the temporary overthrows of Edward by his cousin Warwick 'the Kingmaker' in 1469 and 1470. This had inhibited Henry from choosing an English noble as husband to Mary, and faction was as fierce and the monarch as paranoid in 1558–68 as in the 1520s. If Elizabeth chose someone of lower social rank who did not have this list of noble enemies, the 'insult' to the nobility of their having to defer to a man of lower rank would allegedly cause them to rise as one and murder both Elizabeth and her husband.[2] This panic was probably exacerbated by fresh memories of the two unpopular and contentious consorts of 1553–8 – Guildford Dudley, an inexperienced teenager chosen for Jane Grey by her and his power-hungry parents, and the foreign Catholic Philip of Spain.

The new queen's cautious and canny personality made a swift decision on finding a husband (and thus creating a number of disappointed and possibly violent defeated candidates with a stake in removing her) unlikely, as she was better able to stand up for herself than the naïve and inexperienced Jane had been and more cool-headed than and just as ruthless as Mary. Possibly she was assumed by those who did not know her – most of the elite, as Henry VIII had often kept her away from court and she had been secluded at Woodstock in Oxfordshire as an interned political suspect in 1554–5, then usually away from court at Hatfield House in Hertfordshire – to be like her mother Anne Boleyn, whose alleged sexual impropriety had ruined her. Unlike Mary she had maternal kin in England, from Anne's sister Mary Boleyn's Carey/Knollys children and grandchildren (led by her chamberlain Sir Henry Carey) to her noble cousins the Howards, and so had a considerable faction with wealth and political experience behind her – but her sister Mary had also had this, in the form of the 'conservatives' (political and religious) who had defended her mother's rights as Henry VIII's legitimate wife in the 1530s and she had struck out on her own in the risky and increasingly bloody religious purge of 1554–8 which had cost her much goodwill. Elizabeth did not however have strong political allies in the Marian administration, having inherited most of her ministers from Mary and some of them from her father's time – men who had backed either Edward's Protestant or Mary's Catholic religious policies (and sometimes both in turn) and who had never had occasion to look to her, 'third in line' for the throne and of dubious legitimacy as of 1537–47, as their choice of sovereign. Her most experienced adviser was Edward VI's former Secretary of State in the late 1540s, William Cecil, and not all of the Protestant clerical and lay 'reformists', who had either kept their heads down or had fled abroad in 1553–8 and who now looked to her to restore Protestantism, had the same (cautious and non-Calvinist) attitude to it that she did.

The suspicion of her unknown political skills and what would now be called her 'flightiness' from the 1548–9 crisis ignored one powerful argument that suggested that Elizabeth either would not marry (at least yet) or would stand up to her husband as the doting Mary had not stood up to the neglectful and often absent Philip. This was the effects of the trauma of Elizabeth's investigation by the Edwardian regency council for alleged dalliance with the then Protector Somerset's ambitious brother

Thomas Seymour in 1548, in which the latter had seemingly hoped to marry her and become closer to the crown once his wife Katherine Parr died in childbirth – and had been flirting with her and paying 'improper' visits to her in her bedchamber before she was dressed in the mornings in his wife's lifetime. Katherine was supposed to have witnessed and not minded one such incident, according to Elizabeth's governess Kat Ashley's account in the records of the later council investigation into Seymour's behaviour – presumably thinking this was just another of his well-known rakish but harmless 'gallantries' to young women. However, she had ended up telling Elizabeth off for encouraging him and sending her away from her then residence, Chelsea 'Palace' (manor-house) near the modern Chelsea Embankment in London, so the princess had not been 'above reproach' in contemporary terms. It is probable, though that Elizabeth was unaware that Seymour was also using his position as 'Master of the Mint' to siphon off official money for his own use and was hiring mercenaries and stockpiling weapons at isolated Holt Castle in the Welsh Marches, allegedly aided by his supporter Sir William Sharington – was this just a precaution against his rivals or was he planning a coup to depose his brother as chief regent?

Having been baulked of his ambitions with Elizabeth, not least due to the intervention of members of his alarmed elder brother Somerset's Protectoral Council who warned him not to go any further with such a stupid and ruinous idea (presumably fearing that he would be forbidden to marry the princess, defy this, and be arrested), Seymour tried to win over the boy-king to back him up. Denied access to him, in January 1549 he attempted to gain entrance to his bedchamber at Whitehall Palace late at night behind the council's back using a key while the guards were briefly out of earshot. He was stopped by the king's barking spaniel, which Edward had apparently put outside the door after noticing that the guards had wandered off – and he then shot the dog. He was promptly arrested by the alarmed guards, thrown in the Tower for treason, and later executed – with the council having Elizabeth questioned as to just how far she had gone with Seymour when they were alone together. Elizabeth denied any impropriety and so did her governess Kat Ashley, and she was cleared – but the time that she spent away from court at isolated home counties houses in semi-disgrace in early 1549 has led to wild allegations from conspiracy theories in recent centuries that she had been pregnant and had secretly had a child. (In fact Edward' sisters Elizabeth and Mary were both only rarely at court, but this was politically logical rather than sinister – Elizabeth's status as Henry VIII's legal daughter was seen as dubious in religiously conservative quarters due to her parents marrying in Catherine of Aragon's lifetime and Mary was a Catholic who was hostile to the regency's religious policies.) One theory even had it that Elizabeth's 'secret baby' was adopted by a complaisant courtier and was the later Edward de Vere, seventeenth Earl of Oxford (1550 – 1604), one of the men alleged to have really written the works of William Shakespeare – though the dates were wrong for a start and the baby would have had to be born in early or mid-1549. At the time, the Council records of the investigation show that current London rumours did speak of Seymour plotting to marry Elizabeth well before his arrest, which Kat Ashley warned Elizabeth about in a vain effort to get her to be more decorous in her relations with him, so this had leaked out – but no story about pregnancy was mentioned. At the most, the shrewd but rash princess was said to have commented when Seymour's envoy told her that her stepmother Katherine Parr had died that she was not going to write him a letter of condolence (as would be expected) as he was not in need of it – i.e. he was really in love with her not his wife? The scandal thus suggested that she might be emotionally manipulated by another flattering courtier with his own agenda or governed by her passions – which was the normal contemporary social view of women anyway, added to by the attitude of the church to Eve luring Adam into 'sin' – but a closer look would suggest that in fact she was clearer-headed towards Seymour than at first appeared.

Later, her imprisonment and near-execution for supposed dealings with the Wyatt rebels in 1554–5 created more scandal, with the hard-headed Lord Chancellor, Bishop Stephen Gardiner of Winchester, reported as being keen to have her executed so this potential 'Protestant hope' would never replace his Catholic sovereign.[3] As with the case of the wilder rumours about Anne Boleyn's lovers and the supposed 'real father' of Elizabeth being Anne's low-class musician admirer Mark Smeaton, the stories about Elizabeth then and during her reign usually emanated from hostile Catholic sources and were designed to discredit the Protestant cause in England – which has to be borne in mind regarding the question of the Amy Robsart 'suicide/murder' theories too. There were serious enough doubts of Elizabeth's legitimacy as of her accession for almost all of her sister's bishops to refuse to crown her, though at that point she was a Catholic and not definitely hostile to their religion – and in 1553 Edward VI had passed over her claims in the succession and preferred her cousin Jane Grey, grand-daughter of Henry VIII's younger sister Mary (died 1533). This exclusion by the teenage king of both the half-sisters – who his father had specifically named as in the line of succession after him in his own 1544 will – is one minor 'Royal Mystery' as Elizabeth, unlike Mary, was seen as a Protestant and so could protect Edward's religious legacy. But it was probably not some deep-seated 'plot' by the Dudley family to make current chief minister John Dudley, Duke of Northumberland's daughter-in-law Jane Grey Queen; more likely is that Edward was worrying about the still potent claims that his father and Anne Boleyn had not been legally married so Elizabeth was seen by many as illegitimate. This might well put off conservative councillors from backing her as queen; Jane Grey was less controversial on that count. But it illustrates the precarious legal position and dubious reputation that Elizabeth had for 'legitimists' in the 1550s, which King Henri II of France was to exploit when her half-sister Queen Mary died by recognising another 'legitimate' Tudor cousin – Mary Stuart – as queen instead. As of her accession Elizabeth had the 'unreliable' and slightly strained reputation for sexual dalliance and unwise political gambles that later settled to an even worse degree on her cousin Mary Queen of Scots, particularly among Catholics and Marian loyalists who had been dubious about her as the daughter of the 'notorious whore' Anne Boleyn and had conspicuously failed to hurry to Mary's side as the Wyatt Rebellion broke out. Her judgement may have been rashly incautious then and her real intentions towards Wyatt remains unclear, but her 'mysterious dalliance' with Thomas Seymour had more clearly been a case of her being taken advantage of by a power-hungry and unscrupulous older man even if she had rashly encouraged Seymour at times, no doubt flattered by his attentions.

Mary Queen of Scots had an unsullied reputation as she came to power in Edinburgh on her return home from France in 1561 aged nineteen, and unlike her subsequent reputation, was at the time seen as above scandal. In contrast, Elizabeth's half-sister Mary had to put her in the Tower for suspected links to rebels aged twenty, and was encouraged by veteran hard-line Catholic Lord Chancellor Stephen Gardiner and others to execute her. Elizabeth however had advantages of character over Mary Stuart in terms of shrewdness and an ability to calculate her own advantage – and was said to have remarked when Thomas Seymour was executed in 1549 that he had been a man of very little judgement. At the age of fifteen she had (eventually) shown a more 'adult' reaction to a charming but reckless and ruthless man's real character than Mary Stuart was to show aged twenty-four to the similarly rakish and violent Lord Bothwell in 1567 when the latter was accused of involvement in Mary's then husband Lord Darnley's murder. Elizabeth had stayed calm (openly at any rate) and not admitted any guilt on either occasion when she was under suspicion in 1548–54, either to any sexual entanglement with the widower Seymour or to flirting with the idea of joining the Wyatt rebels and so deliberately keeping away from Mary's court as they marched on London. Procrastination had helped to save Elizabeth on these occasions, as nothing could be proved against her, and neither Seymour's furious brother Somerset in 1548–9 nor Mary's aggressively mistrustful minister Gardiner (Thomas Cromwell's old foe) in 1554–5, managed to compile enough evidence to send her to the block. So would she delay a choice again on this occasion of considering marriage in 1558–68 and trust to events to keep the rival factions backing different candidates as her consort from ever forcing her to make a choice? Once she decided, she would probably acquire the enmity of the defeated candidate. As was to be the case throughout her life, Elizabeth chose the wisest course in 1558–68 of never alienating one powerful party or faction – domestic or foreign – by throwing her lot in with their rivals unless absolutely driven to it. This was visible even in her first months in power, as she did not hurry to restore Protestantism or to evict the resented persecuting Marian bishops, or even to prosecute particular abuses of authority in the recent religious persecutions.[4] Even the loathed Bishop Bonner of London initially kept his seat despite his mass-executions of Protestants and reputed sadism towards his victims, though Elizabeth refused to let him kiss her hand as she arrived in London to assume power.[5] Her caution was thus present even in winter 1558–9, not learnt with experience on the throne – and choosing one candidate for her hand would risk an unnecessary crisis. At this point, even her closest ally William Cecil, her new Secretary of State – no fan of a marriage to a Catholic prince, or to her close friend Robert Dudley, Northumberland's 'flashy' and ambitious third son – was assuming that she would marry and provide an heir.

England faced Mary Stuart's sponsor France as its major potential opponent in 1558–9 – thus the need for Elizabeth to keep in with Philip of Spain as a matter of political urgency and even go along with the rumours that he might want to marry her. This ended with French King Henri II's unexpected death in a tournament-accident in July 1559, as a splinter went through his visor as he took part in combat to celebrate the Treaty of Cateau-Cambresis ending the Franco-Spanish war – which provided the widower Philip of Spain with Henri's daughter Elizabeth (Edward VI's ex-betrothed) as his new wife so he lost interest in the Tudor queen. Henri's son's fiancée Mary Stuart was now queen of both France (by marriage to Henri's son Francis II) and Scotland. Her feeble and ailing young husband Francis II was to die in December 1560, but military action to put her on the English throne might still be taken by her maternal Guise relatives, the aggressive mainstays of the French Catholic cause against the Protestant 'Huguenots'. Luckily, any notion of French aid to Mary Stuart to take over England would boost the Guise faction's power in France, so it was opposed by the new French King's mother, Henri's Italian widow Catherine de' Medicis. This Guise threat ended with the French religious civil wars that broke out in 1562, which Henri's repression of the rapidly spreading Huguenot sects had made more likely but which immediately resulted from the willingness of senior Huguenot nobles (led by the Prince de Conde and Admiral Coligny) to take up arms against the French state. The latter arose directly from their perception that the government – now a regency for Francis' next brother, Charles IX – was hopelessly under the control of the Guise dynasty and their allies. Arguably the replacement of the older but ailing and vulnerable Francis, sixteen at his death in December 1560, by the nine-year-old Charles could well have ended the Guises' power, given that they were no longer the king's 'in-laws' and could not control Charles through Mary as they had done Francis; while Francis was still alive the Huguenot nobles had been reduced to a Scots-style plot to abduct the king at Amboise to seize power.[13] But the existence of a need for long-term regency for the new king meant that faction-struggles intensified and combined with the 'grass-roots' sporadic provincial violence between

Catholics and Protestants to overwhelm the governance of the queen-mother, Catherine de Medici, in civil war from spring 1562. The latter was reckoned politically and religiously untrustworthy by the Guises and their ally Philip II, and indeed the subterranean political manoeuvures of 1561 led to the Guises seeking to betroth the widowed Mary Stuart to their Spanish ally's sixteen-year-old son Don Carlos. Had this been carried out Mary would have been heading for Spain in 1561, and as she would be wife of Philip's heir, the main threat to England would have been a Spanish-Scots union; Philip could not have been expected to tolerate the recent (1560) takeover of Scotland by the rebellious Protestant nobles and their enforced 'Reformation'. Nor would Elizabeth's government, which had encouraged and militarily aided the 1560 rebels in order to destroy the pro-French Guise regency government in Edinburgh, have accepted Spanish troops and clerics restoring Catholicism across the Border. The chances would have been that Elizabeth, prodded by the more militantly Protestant Cecil, would have sponsored a Scots noble revolt against Mary, with the latter's Protestant half-brother the Earl of Moray as the likeliest leader.

The fall of the Catholic regime in Scotland, a major bonus to the embattled English government, via the Scottish revolt against the Francophile regency in 1559 to Elizabeth's benefit. This was a bonus to England but was not a deliberate plan by the ever-cautious English queen, who did not want to provoke France. The outbreak of a Protestant rebellion in Scotland was due as much to growing 'grass-roots' anger among the Lowlands laity, lairds and peasantry alike, at perceived 'Popish idolatry' (stirred up by preachers such as John Knox) as to the desire of greedy nobles to seize the estates of the church and the monastic orders. Hatred of the church and its wealth and power had been spreading in major towns such as St Andrews, Dundee, Perth and Edinburgh since the 1540s, when a mob of urban zealots had assisted the self-appointed task force of 'godly' conspirators who murdered the Francophile chief minister Cardinal Beaton (in bed with his mistress) at St Andrews in 1546 and held out in its castle for months. This combined in the 1550s with dislike of the French domination of the regency and its foreign policy (and large demands for money), though in fact regent Marie de Guise's government was one of the less partisan or self-seeking of recent decades and it had temporarily halted the usual inter-noble feuds and coups.

Excluded nobles resenting French control of power and appointments, plus spreading Protestant preaching which these men were promoting, meant that anger was 'coming to the boil' for domestic reasons in the late 1550s, independently of any support from England (which was Catholic anyway until 1559). The aid came from England for this was strictly unofficial and unconnected to the government. This then exploded into action after the death of Mary Tudor, as large-scale petitioning of the Marie de Guise regency in favour of religious reform led to urban disturbances and iconoclastic vandalism. The anti-French nobles raised their tenants to join the rising, and a civil war followed with the regent 'holed up' in Edinburgh Castle and her Scots/French forces struggling to hold onto the vital port of Leith. The replacement of Mary Tudor by Elizabeth, and the first moves to reform in England in spring 1559, gave the petitioners and the land-hungry nobles more confidence to act. But the turbulence of Scots politics was such that some sort of armed rising against the regency was probable as soon as French attention and military commitment wavered – which would have been likely once Henri II died, even if Mary Tudor was still queen of England. The fall of the regency regime was a mixture of armed aristocratic coup (normal for Scotland), populist Protestant revolution led by radical preachers, and later English armed intervention to drive out the regency's French troops. When the English army arrived – after initial hesitation from Elizabeth and greater enthusiasm than Cecil – the French were blockaded into evacuating Leith and returning home. Marie de Guise opportunely died of dropsy (some said aided by English poison), and a Protestant noble junta, the 'Lords of the Congregation', took control and imposed the secularization of monastic property in the Reformation.

Mary Stuart had to recognise this *fait accompli* on her return home in 1561. But it was lucky for the Protestant rebels of 1559–60 that Mary Tudor had died and Elizabeth was willing to help them with troops (eventually, when prodded by Cecil) in order to bring an end to French influence north of the Border – and that Henri II died and his sons' government had other priorities. As a result, Mary Stuart returned home to be constitutionally and religiously constrained in a manner foreign to her ancestors, and was unable to act in the interests of the Guises against England even had she wished to; her Protestant half-brother Moray and other great nobles on her council were aligned to England as guarantor of their new Protestant faith. The political and personal isolation of the Catholic queen, brought up since she was five at a genteel court in France not in the rough-and-ready world of Scotland, was shown by her experiences as a new sovereign in fiercely Protestant Edinburgh. She politely attended the popular and charismatic John Knox's sermons at first to win support, only to have him uncompromisingly denounce her religion and her foreign entourage. The first time her priest celebrated mass privately in the Chapel Royal at Holyrood, as he was legally entitled to do, an indignant mob gathered outside and tried to storm in and lynch him; the Earl of Moray had to bar the door to them.

Elizabeth now had a breathing-space free from the combined threat of Catholic France and its ally Catholic Scotland, and did not need a foreign marriage and military aid from her husband's country as she had seemed likely to do in the critical first months of her regime in 1558–9. But was her decision not to marry inevitable, and a fixed policy throughout her reign? Would personal feelings ever have caused her to throw caution to the minds, or a desire for one particular alliance abroad have caused her to risk alienating their enemies by marrying their candidate? As of 1558–9, the latter possibility centred on Spain as England's current ally under Mary, and the near-bankrupt English state – as gloomily estimated by Cecil in one of his famous memorandums of the 'state of play' in November 1558[6] – seemed in need of Spanish help against France under its aggressive ruler Henri II, recently conqueror of Calais in a move against the then Anglo-Spanish alliance under Mary Tudor. He had claimed when Mary Tudor died that Mary Queen of Scots, wife of his semi-invalid teenage heir the Dauphin, was rightful queen of England and made her assume its royal heraldic arms – so would he invade England next to control it as he controlled the fractious Scots regime of Mary's mother and regent, his cousin Marie de Guise? To stop this, might Elizabeth even marry her sister's widower King Philip, who had been of good service to her in 1555–8 though he had tried to marry her off to his junior ally Duke Emmanuel Philibert of Savoy and pack her off to Italy? Philip was apparently interested in her early in 1559, unless this was just a diplomatic ploy to keep England in the war with France[7] until the latter had signed up to a peace-treaty on Philip's terms at Cateau-Cambresis. Or was he trying to alarm France into hurrying to agree to peace on his terms or he would set up a permanent Anglo-

Spanish alliance by marrying Elizabeth? He then agreed to marry Henri II's daughter Elizabeth, formerly Edward VI's fiancée, instead in the peace-treaty with France. His engagement to Elizabeth led to Philip proposing the candidacy of his cousin the Archduke Charles (a younger son of Emperor Ferdinand, Charles V's brother and successor, so not in line for the Imperial throne). Charles was seven years Elizabeth's junior, and Elizabeth was to keep dangling the possibility of her acceptance of him into the mid-1560s to ensure Spanish goodwill – though this did not stop agile Spanish ambassadors considering favourably the alternative (more palatable personally to Elizabeth) of her marrying Robert Dudley.

She certainly seems to have considered marrying her long-time admirer, friend, and contemporary Robert Dudley in 1559–60, despite the bad reputation and many senior aristocratic enemies that the '*parvenu*' Dudleys had acquired during the 1550s. Dudley's father John, earl of Warwick and later duke of Northumberland, had outmanoeuvred his rival Edward Seymour (Duke of Somerset and 'Lord Protector' i.e. regent) in the vicious 'in-fighting' among Edward VI's council in autumn 1549, leading discontented Councillors to stage a coup and depose him, and had thereafter led Edward's council but carefully not assumed such a controversial mass of powers as Somerset had done. The latter had tried to stage a 'come-back' with an incompetent and unsuccessful plot in 1551 and ended up executed – with opinion then and since divided as to whether this was at least partly a trap by the devious Northumberland to find an excuse to ruin and execute him as a rival. When Edward VI, a fanatical and dogmatic Protestant, had died unexpectedly young in July 1553 he had designated his teenage, reliably Protestant cousin Jane Grey as heir rather than either of his sisters (both of whom Henry VIII had had bastardised so their legitimacy could be questioned), and as Jane had recently been married off to Northumberland's younger son Guildford Dudley, the duke had been the power behind the shaky throne. At the time of the marriage, however, it is unlikely that the supposedly 'power-mad schemer' John Dudley arranged it in order to put Jane on the throne with himself as the real ruler, despite the 'Black Legend' of his family's insatiable greed and plotting for power. The ailing Edward VI's first choice of heir at this point was an as yet unborn son of Jane and Guildford Dudley, as seen in the first draft of his 'Device' for the succession – so he presumably thought that he would live to see the baby being born, i.e. for another year or two. Nor was Dudley/Northumberland alert for Edward's death and ready to take over, as he spent a considerable time away from court in spring 1553, when if he had been the master-villain of legend, he should have been busy preparing his coup. Nor did he require his likely challenger if he installed a new Protestant sovereign, i.e. Mary Tudor, summoned to court or to a residence near London ready to be arrested as soon as Edward died. The sudden switch of the name of Edward's heir to Jane was done in Edward's hand and was probably his own choice as his decline took an unexpectedly sharp and sudden new turn, and Dudley seems to have been caught by surprise that he died as soon as 6 July – for a start, he did not alert his ally the French ambassador that he might need military help to fend off a challenge by Mary.

The subsequent July 1553 coup naming Jane as the new queen, unwelcome to the vast majority of Englishmen (Catholic and Protestant alike) as seen by the wide variety of provincial nobles and gentry who had risen in Mary's name, was defeated by a major revolt which Mary led. Dudley ended on the execution-block and his sons in the Tower of London for treason. Partly to save themselves from being implicated in the Jane Grey 'usurpation', the Councillors who had initially backed the duke in making her queen then deserted her, as her regime unravelled and had blamed him for it all, and Mary chose to accept this 'narrative' to keep a broad base for her regime and avoid more executions. (The execution of Jane, much sentimentalised in later centuries as the vindictive judicial murder of an innocent Protestant teenager by 'Bloody Mary', only followed the Wyatt Rebellion which Jane's scheming father the Marquis of Dorset had joined.) As a result of the events of 1553, the 'Black Legend' of the Dudleys as power-crazed and ruthless political operatives had emerged among their many rivals and detractors – Northumberland had even abandoned Protestantism before he was executed so he could not be hailed as a martyr for his religion. For those who had long memories there was also the fact that his father Edmund Dudley, a '*nouveau riche*' and unpopular minister of Henry VII who specialised in financial extortion of the nobility, had been executed by Henry VIII in 1510. Northumberland's eldest son John had died in 1554 shortly after his release from the Tower, and Guildford had been executed along with his wife Jane Grey, but the other Dudley sons – including Robert who had vainly chased the escaping Mary Tudor across the Fens on his father's behalf in the 1553 showdown – were back in favour as of Elizabeth's accession after a few years loyally fighting for Mary in the Franco-Spanish war. Their rivals feared that Elizabeth's reign would see their return to favour and so sought to stop this by all means possible, and as Elizabeth was an old friend and admirer of Robert Dudley (who was the same age as her and had shared her imprisonment in the Tower in 1554) attention focussed on him, the new queen's 'Master of the Horse'. (This was not an unusual or unfitting appointment, given that he was one of the best horsemen in the country, an expert judge of horseflesh, and a veteran of the sort of royal pageants and tournaments that this official would be organizing, and his late brother John had held the office under Edward VI.) Robert's older brother Ambrose, now Earl of Warwick, became Master of the Ordnance, i.e. in command of the royal artillery stores, and their sister's husband Sir Henry Sidney – father of the later poet Sir Philip Sidney, King Philip's godson – became President of the Council in the Marches of Wales.

Fortunately for those fearing the effects of Robert's rakish charms on the queen, he was already married – in 1550, to Amy Robsart (born 1532 so his exact contemporary) from a leading Norfolk gentry dynasty near Norwich. Ironically, they had met while Robert was helping his father to put down the major socio-economic disturbances of the 'Kett Revolt' in Norfolk in summer 1549, and the Robsarts were related to Kett but prudently backed the government against that disturbingly anti-elite populist rabble-rouser and his efforts to destroy the enclosures of common land used by the rural public by encroaching farmers and landlords. But the Elizabethan court was a hotbed of intrigue and romantic assignments, and the probably shy and awkward, and possibly already ailing Amy kept away from it though rumour, said that she was being kept away by her husband so he could carry on with the queen without interference. Tongues were soon wagging about what Lord Robert and the queen were getting up to, and Elizabeth was enjoying herself too much with Robert at the round of court entertainments to follow the prudent course and either send him abroad on some long diplomatic mission or summon his wife to court. Nor did Robert bother to invite his wife to the grand ceremonial visit that the court paid to the current home of the Earl of Arundel, a leading conservative Councillor who had uncomfortably supported Northumberland in 1549–53 and the Jane Grey coup in July

1553 but then led the desertions to Mary and been a stalwart of her regime, at the former royal country palace of Nonsuch at Ewell in Surrey in summer 1559. Most of the nobility were there with their wives and the ambitious earl was 'casting his cap at' the queen (nineteen years his junior) and endeavouring to persuade her to marry him, but Amy Dudley did not get invited to the lavish displays and other entertainments and as usual had to stay at her remote and not exactly grand country residences where Robert now rarely visited her. Notably, her main residences were her own family's country manors and a family friend's home at Denchworth near Abingdon in Oxfordshire – Robert did not bother to spend money on acquiring or improving a suitable country estate fit for his new elevated social status and as a present for his wife (though he was rumoured in 1559 to be considering buying his ancestors' Dudley Castle in the west midlands), but spent most of his time at court with Elizabeth on the excuse of his official duties. Parsimony was not the reason for this, as his conspicuous consumption – on clothes, jewellery, hangings for his apartments, furniture, silverware, horses, and so on for court life – was notorious. Elizabeth did not respond to Arundel's wooing, and besides being much older, his religious conservatism made him a problematic consort when she was encouraging the radical Protestants to see her as their 'godly' patron. But neither did she seek to hide her reliance on having Robert by her side – and Councillors like Arundel who had deserted Robert's father in July 1553 and helped his downfall had no reason to want his hot-tempered son as their new royal consort.

The queen's and Robert's intimate relationship was obvious to Spanish ambassador De Feria who wrote in April 1559 that 'the queen is in love with Lord Robert and never lets him leave her'. Robert was also supposed to be in her private chambers at all hours of the day and night and hoping to marry her if Amy died.[8] Their indiscreet conduct gave despair to the prudent William Cecil, who feared that the queen would disregard his pleas to keep away from Robert and the two of them would contrive a way to get married – though there were no obvious grounds for Robert and Amy to divorce. Such an indiscreet royal marriage to one of a race of traitors would cause rebellion.[9] The queen's closest female confidante and 'mother-figure' Kat Ashley, who had been in charge of her domestic attendants since her early years,was driven to beg her on her knees not to marry Robert and thus cause civil war, citing the fact that she would have to answer to God for ruining the country if that happened. Mistress Ashley was not, however, known for her political acumen; she had been arrested by the Somerset regency in 1548 for encouraging Thomas Seymour's near-treasonable flirting with the princess.[10] Elizabeth was able to operate on a separate personal and political 'level' and to enjoy flirting and showing off her new power without closing her eyes to the consequences of acting on her emotions – unlike Mary Stuart. She showed her attentions to a number of handsome young(-ish) admirers in her first years as queen, not just Dudley – and in spring 1559 rumours about an engagement also centred on the gallant and good-looking Protestant courtier Sir William Pickering, recently returned from 'godly' European exile (which showed his staunch refusal to convert under Mary), of gentry not noble blood and with no political 'past' either, so with no aristocratic enemies unlike the Dudleys, and in his mid-thirties.[11] She was to continue to 'play the field' and lap up admiration from admirers into late middle age, as was notorious, and her susceptibility to a handsome and accomplished flatterer was supposed to have been behind the rise to influence later of her Lord Chancellor Sir Christopher Hatton and her Captain of the Guard and naval adventurer protégé Sir Walter Raleigh. In the meantime she was already taking her lifetime 'line' that she considered herself married to her country, not to a man, and was content for this to remain so, as she addressed a Parliamentary delegation asking her to marry in February 1559.[12]

The Spanish diplomats in London reported to their masters at home that the domestic candidate to watch out for was Robert Dudley. He was evidently seen as an acceptable compromise if the match that Philip proposed for his ex-sister-in-law with the Archduke Charles did not succeed – and neither Philip II nor the archduke's father, Emperor Ferdinand, thought fit in 1559–61 to nudge the archduke into paying suit to Elizabeth in person to speed up matters, though they would have had to find the money to equip this impecunious minor Habsburg suitably to impress the 'showy' and fashion-admiring Elizabeth. Indeed, at one Thames river-party on a barge in 1561 Bishop de Quadra, the Spanish ambassador, is said to have offered to marry Elizabeth and Robert on the spot.[13] This would have given Elizabeth the diplomatic bonus of tying the military might and Catholic zeal of Spain to supporting her choice of husband, but she did not accept the offer. Would this have conceivably given Elizabeth the reassurance that she could get away with marrying Robert, with Spanish troops in the Netherlands at hand to aid her if her husband's domestic enemies revolted? Or was the memory of the indignant popular reaction to the last unpopular royal marriage (Mary and Philip) in 1554, the Wyatt revolt in Kent, too vivid? A similar proposal had been made by Henry VIII to marry Anne Boleyn in Calais in 1532 with Francis of France as witness and supporter. In both cases, there were advantages for a politically isolated Tudor ruler in having a major international ally visibly associated with their controversial marriage, and with the half-French Mary Stuart by now back home in Scotland (though politically reined in by the Protestant 'Lords of the Congregation' thanks to the anti-Catholic rebellion there fostered by Elizabeth's minsters in 1559–60) Philip was a counter-balance to her French links.

Certainly, Elizabeth was not serious about considering other, more appropriately 'old nobility' and 'respectable' suitors of distant royal blood such as her own cousin Thomas Howard, (nominally Protestant but Catholic-sympathising) widower duke of Norfolk (born 1536), whose wife Mary Fitzalan (heiress of the earldom of Arundel and Arundel castle) had died in 1557, and the older and more conservative council veteran Henry Fitzalan, Earl of Arundel, Mary's father. Neither was a '*parvenu*' like Dudley; Norfolk was descended from Edward I's second marriage and Arundel was descended from the second wife of King Henry I in the twelfth century, and both were major landowners whose ancestors had built up local networks of clients over centuries. Her personal approval lay with her contemporary and fellow-ex-prisoner of 1554, Robert Dudley, despite the dislike of most of the council for him and his ambition and arrogance. Even William Cecil, former protégé of Robert's father Northumberland who had given him his first major role in government under Edward VI, had his doubts about Robert – who at this stage was not as firmly tied to the Protestant cause as Cecil and had been serving Mary Tudor and Philip of Spain on the battlefields of Flanders in 1557 when Cecil was living in principled 'retreat' from the 'Papist' Marian court and government. The Seymours, kin of the executed Duke of Somerset, disliked the Dudleys due to Northumberland's role in ending Somerset's ill-fated Protectorate for Edward VI in 1549, then entrapping and executing him in 1551–2. There were also hereditary fears of or distaste for the 'low-born' Dudleys as '*arrivistes*' by great nobles of ancient birth, in particular those with partial royal descent such as the queen's cousins the Howards (descended from Thomas of Brotherton, younger son of Edward I) and the Fitzalans. In addition to the aristocratic disdain which Norfolk's grandfather had shown for Wolsey and a variety of nobles forced to pay up extortionate bonds for good behaviour had shown to Robert Dudley's grasping ministerial grandfather Edmund Dudley in the 1500s, there was the matter of feuds left over from Edward VI's minority and the 1553 coup. Conservative Arundel, more comfortable with Mary Tudor's Catholic regime than with the radical Protestant tone of Edward VI's government (which Robert Dudley's father Northumberland had led), had backed Northumberland against the duke of Somerset in 1549–53 but then abandoned him – literally – as Northumberland left Arundel in charge at the Tower and tried to attack Mary Tudor in Norfolk in July 1553. This gave rise to fears on Arundel's part that Robert might seek revenge for this betrayal, which had ended with Northumberland being arrested and executed by Mary – and other councillors who had abandoned the Dudleys in 1553 were still in office too, led by Lord Treasurer William Paulet, marquis of Winchester.

Council alarm at Robert's power and capacity for revenge would have worsened significantly had he married Elizabeth and so become 'Consort' as well as a personal intimate of the queen's – though the shrewd Elizabeth was unlikely to have given Robert the 'Crown Matrimonial' and thus legal authority which her cousin Mary Stuart was to give to her immature and greedy young husband Darnley in Scotland in 1565. Potentially alarmed nobles did not have a rival candidate lined up to replace an Elizabeth/Dudley alliance in an armed revolt, however. The heir under Henry VIII's will, Jane Grey's sister Lady Katherine Grey (born 1539), was young, impulsive and malleable – and Protestant – but caused a scandal and was imprisoned in early 1561 for secretly marrying Edward Seymour, earl of Hertford – the son of the duke of Somerset, a man who Arundel and his allies had also abandoned (in 1549). It would have made no sense to overthrow a 'Dudley puppet' Elizabeth in favour of the wife of another heir of an executed rival of theirs who could seek revenge.

The strange death of Amy Robsart: convenient or inconvenient? Did she fall or was she pushed? Elizabeth's embarrassing position in 1560 foreshadows Mary's in 1567.

As of 1559–60 the political odds in England were that Elizabeth would marry Robert Dudley, who was showered with gifts and was constantly in her company. He was after all the new candidate that she both knew personally and trusted, her royal blood (and swift changes in status from legitimate to illegitimate and back again depending on her father's whims or attitude to her mother) having kept her isolated both in court and at the various country houses around London where the royal children were usually stationed to keep infection at bay. She had probably depended on King Philip for her life at one point in 1554 if Mary was genuinely considering executing her to follow Jane Grey's fate, and at other points her projected overseas marriage had been to one of his and his father's rather than Mary's allies – with none of this giving her any reason to want him near her permanently. Her cousin Norfolk was younger than her and known for his high pretensions as semi-royal and his demanding nature, and as 'Consort' he would probably be even more arrogant and likely to cause feuds with his old rivals at court. (His attitude to Robert Dudley as of late 1558 is unknown, but his father and grandfather had not been friendly to Robert's '*parvenu*' family in the 1540s so trouble could be expected.) Arundel seems to have been less petulant than Norfolk and was older and wiser and a councillor of some years' standing, but he seems to have been smugly confident in 1559 that his courtly entertainments would woo Elizabeth successfully – so was he also at risk of provoking personal feuds with his old rivals as consort? As for Archduke Charles of Austria, he was an unknown quantity and as one of the Habsburgs (though not in line to receive a major realm to rule) would be regarded as a Spanish proxy by the French and so threaten any Anglo-French rapprochement. The Spanish ambassador, Count Feria, was keeping a close eye on Robert Dudley and kept King Philip up to date with all the court rumours – which no doubt Sir William Cecil's intelligencers were aware of. (By the same reckoning, the queen would have known this and steered clear of any risk of being 'trapped' by getting pregnant by Robert – the political 'balancing-act' which she was engaged in in 1559–60 is at odds with the theories that she ever had a 'love-child', let alone then.)

Feria wrote that Robert was in Elizabeth's apartments at night and people said that when his wife Amy, already ill (probably terminally) with a malady in one of her breasts, died they would marry.[14] In these circumstances, Feria asked if it would be wise to accept the inevitable and cultivate Robert's goodwill. The timing of these stories has also given credence among some conspiracy theorists for the – much later, not contemporary – allegation that Elizabeth did really have a child at this time and he was secretly adopted to avoid scandal – the baby in question being the later polymath, scientist, and writer Sir Francis Bacon, no less. Bacon (born January 1561), who was also claimed to be the 'real William Shakespeare' and who wrote the 'Bard's plays under an assumed name, as it would be socially ruinous for a respectable elite figure to be seen as writing crowd-pleasing comedies for the masses, using the impecunious Warwickshire theatrical manager as his 'stand-in'. For good measure, the eccentric American literary theorist and cryptography enthusiast Orville Ward Owen (1854–1924) alleged in *Sir Francis Bacon's Cipher Story* (published 1893–5) that Bacon had then 'hidden' the true story of his origins in various of Shakespeare's plays, using a complicated cipher to avoid detection. The cipher which he laid out was examined by William and Elizabeth Friedman and declared in their careful published analysis of it in 1957 to be non-existent, and in any case the assumption that even a genius like Bacon could write both his acknowledged works and all of Shakespeare's (the latter with a separate and distinctive style) and then put the 'truth' into the latter in a time-consuming code worthy of a twentieth-century 'Enigma' machine was highly improbable. But the story has persisted despite the lack of any sixteenth-century reference to Elizabeth's supposed pregnancy (which would have been bound to leak out at a faction-ridden court with not all her great nobles or the foreign ambassadors unswervingly loyal to her cause let alone to Dudley). Nor did any rumour ever emerge that Bacon was only the adopted son of her Lord Keeper, Sir Nicholas Bacon, or that she had ever had any child, even in the fevered atmosphere of Catholic attempts to undermine her in the latter decades of her reign. The 'Baconian' story became ever more unlikely, ignoring her real-life lack of any serious attempt to advance the career of her 'son' and blaming this on the hostility of the powerful Cecil dynasty to him, and was mixed up with the theories that either he or the seventeenth Earl of Oxford (as mentioned, another candidate to be her 'love-child') was the author of Shakespeare's works.

In April 1559 Feria reckoned that Elizabeth was in love with Robert Dudley; and marrying him would end the loudly-proclaimed expectations of the main English Catholic conservative claimant, the arrogant Earl of Arundel. Moreover, at this point Robert, the future anti-Spanish leader of the 1580s, was friendly to the interests of Spain as in January 1561 the new ambassador Bishop de Quadra reported that Robert had sent his brother-in-law Sir Henry Sidney (father of the future poet Sir Philip Sidney, who was King Philip II's godson) to propose that if Spain backed the Dudley/Elizabeth marriage Robert would help their interests.[15] He might even favour a return to Catholicism.[16] Robert also suggested to De Quadra that he could be sent to the reforming Catholic church Council of Trent in northern Italy as the English ambassador – an observer rather than a participant as England was now Protestant again, but still a sign of his goodwill.[17] The fervently anti-Catholic English ambassador to France, Sir Nicholas Throckmorton, was writing to his employer Secretary Cecil speaking of Robert as a threat to England's Protestant alignment, on account of the emerging hard-line opposition of Philip to Protestantism across Europe (including the Huguenots in France) and his repression of his Protestant subjects in the Netherlands. Throckmorton, a pioneer of the new concept of a foreign policy based on ideology rather than cold diplomatic pragmatism, could see Protestant England as a patron of the Continent's 'godly' believers against the persecutory alliance of Spain and the Catholic zealots in France, and this could also serve a practical purpose in neutering the expansionist threat of the Habsburgs (or the ultra-Catholic Guises in France) to England.

Religious revolution aided by England had sapped the strength of the Catholic nobility and politically hamstringed the pro-French Catholic queen in Scotland – could the same be done in France by arming the Huguenots? This was precisely Cecil's reckoning, and when a religious civil war broke out between Protestants and Catholics in France in 1562–3 these ideologues were to successfully persuade Elizabeth to send a (small due to her caution and parsimony) expeditionary force to Normandy to aid the Huguenots against the unfriendly anti-English regency of Catherine de Medici for Charles IX – led by Robert Dudley's elder brother Ambrose. But was an alliance between Robert, as potential or actual 'King Consort' of England, and Philip to induce Elizabeth to back the Catholic cause – in return for papal recognition of her as legal queen? – would prevent this, so Throckmorton called for Robert to be stopped as a matter of national security.[18] As of 1560–2 the traditional enmity between the Dudleys and the older nobility was what was important at the Elizabethan Court – ironically, within a decade a changed 'religious' alignment was to see Robert allied to other Protestant nobles in opposition to the pro-Catholic

Howards. The earls of Arundel and Pembroke were hostile to him through the 1560s due to his potential for seeking revenge on them over their abandonment of his father Northumberland in July 1553.[19] The potential thus existed for an alliance of the precariously powerful Robert with the Spanish ambassadors against other great nobles, with Cecil allied to the latter due to his fears of Catholic influence. However, this was not going to translate into action without the queen's approval, and Elizabeth's refusal to send any 'observers' to the Council of Trent in 1561–2 showed that she would keep to the Protestant alignment.[20] Meanwhile the continued prominence of Robert at court in summer 1560 and the queen's shutting her ears to the pleas to send him away led to Cecil even contemplating giving up his role as secretary in despair at the queen's ignoring his pleas. He complained that the unreasonable queen was continuing to harp on about his failures to achieve the impossible (e.g. in securing better terms of alliance with the 'Lords of the Congregation', the new Scots Protestant regime which had been aided in its triumph by an English army after Cecil prodded the queen into reluctantly intervening). He wrote to his ally the earl of Bedford of his desire of retiring to the country as soon as he could persuade Elizabeth to let his equally Protestant protégé Nicholas Throckmorton return from his ambassadorial post in Paris and succeed him.[21]

This all has a bearing on the question of the scandal of Amy's death that was now to afflict Robert's reputation. Not only the frustrated Cecil, but traditional aristocratic foes of the 'jumped-up' Dudleys (e.g. Arundel and Winchester, who had quickly deserted Robert's father during Jane Grey's short reign in order to save their chances with Mary Tudor) had something to gain if Robert was disgraced and expelled from court – or at least 'smeared' enough to make the queen wary of marrying him. A scandal would give even a lovesick Elizabeth pause for thought about continuing with her presumed affair as far as marriage – and these were rich and successful men who had already abandoned one queen (Jane) and two religions (Edward VI's Protestantism in 1553 and Mary's Catholicism in 1558–9), politically if not in all cases personally yet, to keep their heads, their jobs, and their estates. Forcing Elizabeth's hand and in the process thwarting Robert was quite a plausible course to follow, even if it entailed murder – and if Amy Dudley was rumoured to be dying anyway it was only hastening the inevitable. In this context, Robert's wife's death can bear different interpretations. Did Robert rid himself of her out of impatience with her survival, or his foes kill her to ruin his eligibility as a royal consort? Was she so distraught at the rumours about Robert and her own fears that he would abandon her that she had a lapse of concentration and fell down the unfamiliar Cumnor Place stairs, or did she kill herself? Did the councillors exploit a genuine accident to hint to the queen that it was deliberate, or at least that the public would think that? Amy was kept from court, whether by her own ill-health or by Robert's wishes is unclear, and when Arundel was staging elaborate pageants for the queen at Nonsuch Palace in Surrey in June 1559 to woo her, Robert deserted his wife to accompany the queen there. Elizabeth's totally loyal ex-governess Kat Ashley, who had been with her since her girlhood and had been the principal target of angry Council interrogation in 1548 about her charge flirting with Thomas Seymour, unsuccessfully begged the queen on bended knee to abandon Robert and find a suitable husband elsewhere. Late in 1559 the favourite's aristocratic arch-enemy Thomas Howard, Duke of Norfolk and Elizabeth's cousin, nearly came to blows with him and was reported as saying that Robert would not die in his bed.[22] Was he intending to see that that was the case or was this just a momentary burst of petulence? Elizabeth now sent Norfolk off to northern England as its commander-in-chief in what amounted to exile from court.

Elizabeth now became embroiled in the same sort of scandal that was to – rather more permanently – damage Mary Queen of Scots' reputation, involving the unexpected and violent death of the current obstacle to her marrying her ruthless admirer. In Mary's case it was to cause her overthrow and centuries of mystery as to how much she knew of the murder-plot – did she just 'look through her fingers' at what was going on, was she fully aware of it, or was she entirely innocent? – and in Elizabeth's case the same questions were raised at the time. Her reputation survived better, but at the time her role as the potential beneficiary seemed evident to hostile observers and her survival as queen was seen as being in doubt. But unlike Mary she had fewer powerful enemies in her own country and was both more canny – especially in distancing herself from the other main accused not marrying him as Mary did – and more lucky. Indeed, the sheer scale of the scandal that now hit her and her 'lover' Robert Dudley was such that more thoughtful observers then and since could conclude that it would have been sheer folly to 'bump off' Amy so publicly – especially if the report De Quadra heard was true and Amy was supposed to be seriously ill, as then all Robert and Elizabeth had to do was to wait for her to die. Killing her so dramatically made the reaction to the incident so public and so hostile that if the alleged 'lovers' now married they would face outrage across Europe and the real possibility of a rebellion, given how hated Robert already was by great nobles with armed tenants at their call such as Norfolk. So could Amy have been killed by opponents of the Dudley/Tudor marriage threat, precisely to make it impossible by blackening Robert's name as a wife-killer and so scaring Elizabeth off marrying him?

Would Elizabeth gamble on a '*fait accompli*' and marry Robert then defy her enemies to do their worst? Cecil may well have feared this, but any chance of it was halted for the moment when Amy was found dead at the bottom of a staircase at Cumnor Place near Abingdon in Oxfordshire on 8 September 1560. (The convenience of the episode to Cecil's own wishes in thwarting Robert's alleged marital plans has in turn given rise to suspicion of his role in what happened). Amy did not own the house; as we have seen she usually resided at her family's own estates or at a friend's house near Abingdon, and Robert had not bothered to spend his money on acquiring a grand new home suitable for his inflated pretensions since his failure to persuade the owner of his ancestors' Dudley Castle to sell up in 1559 and had usually lived at court. Amy's recent move to Cumnor Place had been arranged by Robert, whose steward Anthony Forster had leased it from William Owen – son of the royal physician Dr Owen, who had bought this former country residence of the abbots of Abingdon at the Reformation. Some found Robert's acquisition of the house sinister due to what happened later, given that his own officials were involved in the household – had he called them in to get rid of his wife in private? In fact, this arrangement would have been perfectly normal for the time, in the case of a wife who did not normally live in her own establishment and a richer husband who had his own household and officials available to help out. Robert's close friend and protege Richard Verney, of Compton Verney House, who had deputised for Robert as Lord Lieutenant of Warwickshire in 1559, was also apparently involved with the household and was said to have been at Cumnor on the day of the 'accident' and to have been seen at Abingdon fair around the time of the accident/murder talking privately to a servant (who thus might have just come from the house and been up to no good). This was reported, albeit by a hostile writer (John Hales), in a document that has now been dated to 1563 so it was not just later embellishment. Amy had previously stayed at Verney's home until moving to Cumnor late in 1559, though we do not know her opinions of him, and as Robert had not been near her for months before her death, Verney was presumably acting as his proxy in keeping an eye on her. It is also clear that at the very least Elizabeth did not have the political sense to instruct Robert to invite or insist on Amy coming to court occasionally or go and see her, which would look better to observers – she preferred to flirt with him in his wife's absence.

Despite the stories of Amy's ill-health that reached the Spanish embassy (which as we shall see William Cecil apparently did not believe), her private accounts show that she was perfectly capable of, and vigorous in, transacting household business so she was not medically incapacitated. This would make a natural trip down the stairs possible, especially if she was not accustomed to navigating the house's floors and steps in a cumbersome long dress – or if she was weak or distracted (by misery about her husband's philandering with the queen?) she could have overbalanced. She had sent her servants out to Abingdon Fair, as shown at the inquest, and insisted on one who wanted to stay behind going; this was confirmed later by her personal maid. But there was no indication that she had got rid of them to facilitate a suicide-attempt, and her maid said that she was a very religious person who prayed daily which suggests that she was unlikely to commit the capital sin of killing herself. The maid also said that Amy had prayed daily for release from her suffering, but it is unclear if this refers to Robert's philandering or her illness and she fiercely denied that this implied suicide. There is some doubt over the question of whether the stairs at Cumnor were high enough for someone falling down them to kill herself or if the blows seen on Amy's head at the inquest could have been caused by hitting a stair or the bannister as opposed to her being attacked, and the house (said to have been haunted by Amy's ghost) has since been pulled down. From later accounts there was only one staircase of more than a few steps, i.e. one suitable for a fatal fall – that from the upper to lower floor, which was a 'dog-leg' with perhaps four or five stairs in each part and no more than fourteen overall. This was drawn by the topographer Richard Lysons for his guide-book

Magna Britannia in 1807 and so survived until then. It is uncertain how dangerous this was, but modern medical experts have claimed that if Amy's rumoured 'malady in one of her breasts' was cancer this could have weakened her bones, so a normally survivable fall could have broken her neck. Alternatively, she could have been strangled then pushed down the stairs to make it look like murder, and the staff been too scared of official reprisal to query a verdict of accidental death even if they suspected different.

The royal court was currently at Windsor, within a few hours' ride – which could imply to suspicious minds that Robert, with the best horses available to him, could have ridden over to Cumnor to push his wife down the stairs or else gone to a rendezvous *en route* to issue his orders to his minions (Forster who was in charge of the household, or Verney?) to do this. The stories circulating in anti-Robert Catholic circles by the 1580s, possibly based on Hale's report of 1563, alleged that Verney had been heard at Abingdon fair asking an arriving servant if he had done what he was told, but did not cite who had witnessed this and if they were reliable. Currently, as shown in De Quadra's letters from court to Philip II, Cecil was in despair and told the ambassador on the 6th that he feared 'impending ruin' (to his own influence as well as to his royal mistress' reputation and national political stability?) and 'the queen was going on so strangely that he was about to withdraw from her service'. This was as :

> 'the Lord Robert had made himself master of the business of the state and of the person of the queen, to the extreme injury of the realm, with the intention of marrying her, and she herself was shutting herself up in the palace to the peril of her health and her life, that the realm would tolerate the marriage he said her did not believe.... He implored me for the love of God to remonstrate with the queen, to persuade her not utterly to throw herself away as she was doing, and to remember what she owed to herself and to her subjects. Of Lord Robert he said twice that he would be better in Paradise than here... Last of all he said that they were thinking of destroying Lord Robert's wife. They had given out that she was ill, but she was not ill at all; she was very well and taking care not to be poisoned...'[23]

If this was not a 'smoking gun' it is evidence that Cecil was – or thought it politically useful to him for it to be thought that he was – in despair at Robert's current power over the queen and apparent plans, and that the latter were supposed to include poisoning his wife who was not actually ill at all. If 'they' means the queen and Robert, Elizabeth was so impatient to marry Robert that she was prepared to cover up murder – the usual charge made of Mary Queen of Scots over the Darnley murder in 1567. If Cecil was using De Quadra as a conduit to the queen who would not listen to Cecil himself (in contrast to her usual procedure over forty years) it would indicate that he feared that she was controlled by her passions for once, as manipulated by Robert, and could easily do something stupid that would cause disaster – killing, or turning a blind eye as Robert killed Amy and then marrying Robert? On the surface this seems like an exact parallel with the case of Mary Stuart, who has been remembered by history as an unwise and immature slave to her passions unlike the cool, collected and ultra-intelligent politician Elizabeth, marrying her hated lover Bothwell after being supposedly implicated in the murder of the main obstacle (in her case, her husband Darnley). De Quadra had no reason to invent the story and it fits with other reports of Cecil's despairing threats to retire from office unless Robert's influence was rapidly abated and the queen came to her senses, and it also fits that if Robert was monopolising the queen's time and persuading her not to listen to Cecil the latter would try to use De Quadra to send her a message about what he would do if this situation continued.

The rumours that Amy was not ill and Robert was planning to kill her are also extraordinary given what was about to happen, and much has been made of Elizabeth telling De Quadra that Amy was 'dead or nearly so'.[24] This encounter and De Quadra's written report of it was originally dated by ninteenth-century historians reading De Quadra's reports home to the day before the accident – so it seemed suspicious in retrospect as if the queen was anticipating Amy being killed and Robert being free to marry. If Amy was actually ill it may have related to Robert's latest (tastelessly anticipatory?) account of his wife's condition, whether or not he had exaggerated this and if so for what purposes. But more recent analysts have reckoned that the encounter could have taken place on the actual day of the accident, so in that case it is dubious 'evidence' of a plot to kill Amy by Robert that Elizabeth knew about. More likely is that

Elizabeth saw the ambassador a few hours after the incident (Cumnor being a couple of hours' ride from her then residence at Windsor) and the first report of it had just arrived there, apparently from Robert's staff at Cumnor. He would then have told Elizabeth, and she would be talking to De Quadra before she knew exactly what had happened but with no suspicious 'foreknowledge'.

The more damning evidence is what Cecil said to De Quadra. At the best, the devious Cecil found it useful to spread rumours abroad via De Quadra to England's current ally Philip (who he did not approve of as a persecuting Catholic conservative) and back to the queen that Amy was not really ill and if she died soon it would be by foul play. Had he heard rumours of a murder-plot and was determined to 'head it off' and save the queen from scandal by warning Robert that it was known about and he had better leave Amy alone? Was he just assuming that the rumours he had heard of an intended murder implied that Robert was the guilty party, and like other contemporary foes of Robert (e.g. the Emperor's ambassador) believed the worst possible rumours about him? Was he warning the queen that Amy was not really ill as Robert said, or gambling that if Elizabeth believed Amy not to be ill and she then died the queen would assume that Robert had killed her and recoil from marriage? Or was he gambling that by exposing the rumours of a plot (which he had clearly heard about), if Amy did die (naturally or by violence) it would be assumed in England and abroad that it was by foul play and thus Elizabeth would not dare to marry Robert? Some have even suggested that if Cecil hated Robert that much and was determined to stop him marrying the queen, he could have planned to kill Amy himself and have Robert blamed for it. Alison Weir has suggested that this is plausible. But given Cecil's careful concern over forty years for the queen's reputation and the realm's stability, other modern observers have reckoned that Cecil would never have invented stories about Amy not being ill (so that any sudden death would seem like murder) let alone had her killed, in case the situation spiralled out of control and Elizabeth ended up being overthrown. Would he have taken such a gamble?

Elizabeth cannot be acquitted of having a sense of anticipation about what Amy's (natural or not) death would mean for her, but her 'off the cuff' remark to De Quadra is not proof of anything – at least now that its date is unclear and it may well have followed, not preceded the accident.

Proving anything more against either her or Robert is impossible, though it was not beyond the ruthless Robert to tell the queen that Amy was seriously ill so that if she did die suddenly – with help from him? – Elizabeth would not blame him for it. It would be ironic if he was seriously considering murdering Amy to 'speed up' his hoped-for engagement to the queen but Amy had a genuine accident before he could do anything, which may be possible if there is any truth in the rumour that he or his associates had been trying to get her doctor to poison her. In any case, the scandal of Amy dying violently was to the detriment of the presumed lovers' future; it was a simple matter to wait for her to die naturally if she was ill. But given what Cecil said to De Quadra, was she actually ill at all or did she have a minor illness and her condition had improved by early September (disappointing Robert)? The chances would seem to be that the current court gossip about her illness did not just emanate from the devious Robert who wanted an excuse for her death to seem natural, and to reassure the queen if Amy did die that he was not involved, or from Cecil (who wanted any immanent demise of Amy to seem so scandalous that the queen would be scared off marrying Robert). But neither can be ruled out.

Amy had sent her servants off to Abingdon Fair a few hours before the 'accident', and had tried and failed to persuade her landlord Mr Owen's elderly mother Mrs Odingsells (currently staying at the house) to go too. This could be interpreted as her 'clearing the decks' so nobody would see her kill herself and try to stop it or give evidence that it was suicide (a major sin and/or something that could be blamed on Robert) not an accident. If Richard Verney was in the house that day as subsequently alleged, Amy did not apparently try to get him out of the way – though he may have been in his own rooms preoccupied with estate or Dudley business and would have been no problem as a potential hindrance if Amy was planning to kill herself some distance away, out of earshot. If he did go to the fair and was seen there (as seems to have been heard c. 1563 by the anti-Robert pamphleteer John Hales), does this prove his innocence or was he really giving himself an alibi while his henchmen disposed of Amy? Is the unattributable story of his 'suspicious' conversation with a servant reliable, was it invented, or did it refer to another matter entirely? Amy was discovered at the foot of the stairs up to her first-floor rooms a few hours after the servants had returned for their evening meal. The cause was unclear, and when Robert was informed he wrote to his chief household officer Thomas Blount asking him urgently to find out the truth without regard for anyone (ie their feelings or reputation) as he knew what the world would say.[25] Blount was then the person who questioned the deceased's personal maid and found out about Amy sending the staff off to the fair, according to the inquest. He also wrote to Robert in his initial report of his questioning that the servants' evidence suggested that Amy had been in a 'strange mind', which could indicate a planned suicide – though Robert's detractors could suppose that he was either part of the cover-up or was offering Robert a means to reassure the queen and others that all was 'above board' and cleared him of suspicion.

The shocked queen sent Robert off to a house she had given him at Kew and required him to stay there away from court, though she was soon quickly putting it out to the foreign ambassadors that Amy had broken her neck (i.e. in a fall). This was, however, a natural assumption given where she was found as the inquest would have heard this quickly. Blount seem to have been keeping Robert informed about what they were being told; the queen would not have known how high the stairs were. De Quadra estimated the situation as so volatile – Cecil might still resign – that Elizabeth could end up in the Tower and be replaced by one of her relatives, probably the adult, male, and competent Protestant peer Henry Hastings, earl of Huntingdon (descendant of Edward IV's brother George, duke of Clarence).[26] Henry was also to be considered a 'front-runner' for the throne by the Protestant Council of State when Elizabeth was seriously ill with smallpox in October 1562 – an occasion when she could easily have died and so been seen by posterity as a very minor, short-lived ruler subject to unstable passions for Dudley rather than as a great queen. But Elizabeth was more canny and politically aware that Mary was to be in 1567, and her elite were less hostile to her, therefore the regime survived, not least as unlike the case of Darnley there was no proof of murder.

The crisis also made the shrewd and ruthless Cecil indispensable; the queen called on him for help, and he ended up acting as a 'go-between' with the temporarily 'banished' Robert who duly thanked him for his support.[27] This was ironic if Cecil had in fact either had Amy killed or (more likely) had used a genuine accident to stop the Elizabeth/ Robert marriage. The affair certainly caused a mass of lurid speculation to Elizabeth's detriment abroad, e.g. in Paris whence ambassador Throckmorton retailed the gleeful gossip about 'murder' and encouraged Cecil to use it to put Elizabeth off the threatened marriage.[28] The queen's rival Mary Stuart gave voice to stories abroad in commenting maliciously that Elizabeth would marry her 'horse-keeper' (Robert was Master of the Horse) who had murdered his wife to make way for her. The question of 'murder or suicide' was to be resolved officially by the local coroner's jury, and although the latter returned a verdict of accidental death it is always possible that they were 'lent on' with the members being persuaded not to dare to offend the powerful Lord Robert and the queen. The head of the jury was one Richard Smith, presumably the Sir Richard Smith who was mayor of Abingdon in 1564–5 and had earlier been an official of the queen's household when she was a princess. Although this was not necessarily a 'fix' by her and Robert to make sure the latter was acquitted, as he was the sort of eminent local gentry 'bigwig' who would normally head a jury. (There has been suspicion about Smith and Robert's later friendly business transactions, but this was normal contemporary practice and seems to refer to buying supplies for the queen's state visit to nearby Oxford in 1565; Robert was by then the university's chancellor.) Other jury members were also apparently vetted before being appointed – but as Robert had many enemies, checking that none of the latter could get a henchman or suspected hireling onto the jury to cause trouble was normal procedure, and not necessarily sinister. Indeed, some of the steward Forster's detractors were allowed onto the jury, and Blount wrote to Robert that that would assure suspicious minds that there was no 'fix' – though Robert failed in his hint to the authorities that they should ask a separate panel of interested parties, including Amy's half-brothers, to sit separately later on to confirm that all the evidence was satisfactory and nothing was being hidden. (In the event, Amy's half-brother John Appleyard did raise angry queries several years later, so this would have been a wise move.)

The world of the Elizabethan elite in any county was small and interconnected, and most 'respectable' figures would have some connection and obligations to one or more of the nobility connected to court – though this did make 'rigging' verdicts easier. The court and queen took up their verdict in April 1561 with relief and declared that the jury had confirmed that none of Robert's men had been in or near Cumnor Place at the time of death and it was clearly an accident.[29] The story that Robert's close ally Sir Richard Verney had been in the house at Cumnor on the day of the 'accident' and might have killed Amy did not emerge publicly until the 1580s, although pamphleteer John Hales apparently heard it around 1563, and then it was circulated and embellished in the Catholic and virulently anti-Dudley polemic *Leicester's Commonwealth* – which probably relied mainly on Hales' story. At the time Robert had turned into one of the leaders of the anti-Spanish Protestant ideological faction at court, and was duly a subject of abuse from the militant Catholics who were hoping to overthrow Elizabeth and install Mary Queen of Scots on her throne, so this source, (which contains known falsehoods and exaggerations) and its suggestion that Robert arranged for Verney to murder Amy and/or push her down the stairs, cannot be trusted.

Robert was affirmed as 'innocent' by the jury and was recalled to court – but Elizabeth did not marry him, though the talk about this possibility continued so observers evidently did not notice any great 'cooling-off' in the queen's public attitude to him. It was probable that the sick (or mentally distracted) Amy had accidentally over-balanced, and given her condition a minor fall could have broken her neck. Less likely, she might have committed suicide in despair at the open nature of her husband's flirtation with the queen. But it was suspiciously convenient for Robert that many did not know Amy was seriously ill, and coincided with rumours that he would get a divorce. No question was raised by the jury about the story known by Hales in c.1563: that one of his closest henchmen, Verney, who Robert had charged with supervising his wife's household, had been the only person said to be in Cumnor Hall at the time of the accident. In the early 1580s Robert's detractors were to claim in the libellous '*Leicester's Commonwealth*' that Robert had asked Verney earlier to poison Amy,[30] which goes beyond the initial mention of Verney by Hales. The crisis of Amy's sudden 'accident' brought an end to the possibility that the worried Cecil, hopeless about his eclipse by the Dudleys and in despair at his capricious mistress' behaviour, would resign. It raises the possibility that Cecil's faction may have had Amy pushed down the stairs to cause a scandal and make it impossible for Elizabeth to marry Robert; though this can only be guesswork. Some historians have argued that Cecil, a protégé of Dudley's father Northumberland but a personal rival of Robert, was a ruthless enough operator to be capable of this.[31]

One generally assumed result of the incident was notable by its absence. It should be pointed out that the scandal did not immediately end attempts by Robert and his allies to create a 'ground-swell' of elite opinion to pressure the queen to marry him, as his ally the Earl of Sussex attempted (unsuccessfully) to organise a petition for this at the annual Garter ceremonies at Windsor Castle in April 1561.[32] This is on the surface, rather surprising given the sensation over the alleged murder/suicide, and shows that if someone (Cecil?) had arranged to have Amy killed to scare off the publicity-conscious queen marrying Robert, the latter was still trying to arrange the marriage once the initial scandal had faded a little. The petition implies that Robert was now trying to coax the queen to see that majority opinion among the elite, if not in the country, that the scandal had not put them off the marriage so it was safe to go ahead. The change in the queen's attitude to Robert – i.e. that it was now politically unsafe to marry a man suspected of murdering his wife – was presumably a more crucial result of the incident than the effect on Robert, given that the petition shows that he kept up his enthusiasm for the marriage into 1561. At the following year's Garter ceremonies feeling against Robert had abated, and for once his enemy the duke of Norfolk was prepared to back the proposal; in this case a majority of the Garter knights present agreed, but the queen's conservative ex-suitor Arundel and his ally the earl of Northampton (Queen Katherine Parr's brother) walked out in disgust.[33] If Robert had hoped that the size of the 'lobby' in favour of the marriage would reassure Elizabeth, he was disappointed – if she had not abandoned the idea permanently in summer 1560, the prospect of two senior councillors still being violently opposed to it would have warned her off marriage. Avoiding any open faction in her court or driving any major political figure into desperation – where they might think that their only option to save themselves from ruin or humiliation was a revolt – was a major strand of Elizabeth's coaxing approach to her ministers for decades, quite apart from the allegations of her chronic indecisiveness. Conversely, she was to carry on 'playing the field' with Robert by never quite rejecting his wooing well into the 1570s, as seen by his putting on a major entertainment for her at his country residence, ex-royal Kenilworth Castle, in the hope of winning her round in 1575. This grand public 'show' was the climax of that year's (regular) royal tour of the countryside. The tour was mainly for the shrewd and cost-cutting queen to stay with her richer subjects at their own expense, which included a famous display of fireworks – and may have been seen by local boy William Shakespeare as there was a literary reference in his 1594 play *A Midsummer Night's Dream* to one of its tableaux. Was Robert trying to 'play' her with his charms for his own advancement, not noticing that she was doing the same in order to keep him flattering and 'worshipping' her? The queen kept Robert 'dangling' in hopes of her eventually giving in to his charms for well over a decade – but eventually he gave up and married (secretly) his mistress, her widowed and younger cousin Lettice (nee Knollys), Countess of Essex. Predictably she was then furious and temporarily banned him from court.

There is also the question of the claims of Amy's half-brother John Appleyard, who spent several years trying to prove that the 1560 inquest was a cover-up though he had raised no complaints at the time. This does not, however, prove that he regarded Robert as the killer as he was quick to insist when the Privy Council questioned him, though if he suspected one of Robert's rivals of framing him the latter's name was never mentioned. Rather, he seems to have lobbied Robert to let him bring a private prosecution over Amy being murdered and thus require potential witnesses to give evidence, and Robert ignored this saying that it was not opportune. Appleyard was carefully ignored by the court and its supporters, but did not take the hint and shut up. When arrested for spreading slander he said that an anonymous Thames boatman had approached him with an offer of £1,000 from certain great lords to help his enquiries. These men were supposed to include Norfolk and Sussex, plus Sir Thomas Heneage, who if this was true were keen to see the marriage prevented – though this does not 'put them in the frame' for killing Amy, merely for exploiting the crisis and trying to use Appleyard to ruin Robert's reputation. The initial enquiry into what Appleyard knew was made in private on Robert's behalf by the ubiquitous Thomas Blount, who already knew all the details of what was said to or had occurred at Cumnor from his 1560 investigation – and as Robert's 'man of business' could be relied on to keep his mouth shut. But Robert was now angry or panicky enough to have the issue brought before the Privy Council, possibly hoping to 'smoke out' his enemies (who from Appleyard's names included some prominent councillors). Appleyard could not prove that the incident with the boatman had occurred let alone who the 'lords' had been, and was thrown in the Fleet Prison, interrogated by a council committee led by Cecil, and probably 'lent on' with a threat of severe punishment for malicious slander. The committee did, however, include Robert's current detractors Arundel and Northampton, so it was not totally 'fixed' in his favour; and Cecil's paperwork for it mentions assorted servants of Amy's testifying so if any of them had had any serious evidence they would presumably have been able to raise it. Appleyard was allowed to see the coroners' report, and found no fault with it so he did not think it suspicious that the fall should have killed Amy or argue that she could have been pushed rather than fallen. Browbeaten, 'boxed in', or genuinely persuaded that there was nothing worth pursuing, he grovellingly confessed that he had wickedly made up his story to slander the totally innocent Robert and other lords, and was effectively silenced.[34]

It is highly likely that he was telling the truth in alleging that Robert's enemies had paid him to investigate the case and so dig up some embarrassing questions – and he may still have thought the inquest a 'put-up job' that had deliberately kept some major questions unanswered but could not prove it. Once again, 'spin' and political machinations won the day at the Tudor court and in this murky world of high politics the only thing clear is that there was a great more going on behind the scenes than emerged into the open. At the least, the interest that people took in Appleyard's campaign to ruin Robert/get at the truth and the State's desire to shut him up as late as 1567 showed that the issue was still a dangerous one to investigate. From then on the story entered myth, with Robert's foes keen to point the finger at him as a murderer. The story of Robert's alleged disposal of his wife entered the world of high political 'spin' and vindictive polemic in *Leicester's Commonwealth*, and as the passions and intrigue that had been its real-life background were forgotten, later commentators did not note that both his supporters and his detractors had pressing political reasons to take up their views. By the time that the incident was referred to in the lurid popular play *A Yorkshire Tragedy* in 1608 (without naming Robert) as a classic example of a politician getting away with murdering his wife in a 'fall down the stairs' and pretending it was an accident, it was the drama in high places and not the truth that mattered. It was later taken up by the pioneering Romantic novelist Sir Walter Scott in his florid literary work *Kenilworth* in 1821, with Robert as the scheming murderer and Amy the tragic victim, although (as with his other works) Scott was not exactly known for strict historical accuracy. It was then investigated in the Victorian period by the historian J.A. Froude as a classic mystery of Tudor high politics. Having examined the Spanish diplomatic correspondence with De Quadra's tales of rumoured poison and anticipation of the victim's death in the 1860s, he concluded that Amy had been killed deliberately for political reasons and assumed that Robert was involved. Others, such as the Norfolk antiquarian Walter Rye (a pioneer of the sport of 'hare and hounds' aka cross-country running) in his book on the subject in 1885, also alleged murder by Robert. In more recent studies, an accident, suicide or murder by some rival trying to frame Robert (probably Cecil) have all been suggested, and murder by Robert is generally discounted as too obvious and too counter-productive for him to risk it. Seen in its context, it provides an intriguing counterpart to the contemporary and more famous Stuart 'whodunnit' of Lord Darnley's murder in 1567, and shows us Elizabethan high politics at their most murky.

Chapter Four

Mary Queen of Scots and the Murder of Lord Darnley. Who Killed Darnley, and was Mary's Fall a 'Stitch-Up'?

Mary in Scotland, 1561–5: the search for an Anglophile husband to control her.

The prospects for co-operation let alone trust between Mary Queen of Scots and her cousin Elizabeth I of England were always limited, given that when Elizabeth was born on 7 September 1533 her father Henry VIII's (secret and still not precisely dateable) marriage to her mother Anne Boleyn was not internationally recognised. Henry had not yet been granted a papal divorce from his first wife Catherine of Aragon by Pope Clement VII by this date and was thus still seen as married to her by internationally-accepted church canon law; the annulment of his first marriage was only granted by his 'tame', newly-created Church of England which had just broken away from the Catholic church by Act of Parliament. Henry had only given up on trying to get the church in Rome to accept that his son-less marriage to Catherine had been illegal and annul it, enabling him to marry Anne Boleyn and acquire male heirs, and turned to creating his own church that would do what he wished in 1531.

Catherine had been refusing to meekly give up her marriage, so she wrote for support to the pope and her nephew the Emperor Charles V (who since 1527 had been in effective control of Rome and central Italy), and had stymied the legal case in a church court in London in 1529 by appealing to Rome, where given Charles' power and the pope's timidity about offending him, the result would be a foregone conclusion. Henry duly took steps to declare his national church independent and prosecute any who opposed it as illegal – but he only hastened to marry Anne once she became pregnant in early 1533. As events turned out, the marriage was carried out privately, France did not recognise its legality, and the baby was another girl – Elizabeth – who could be called a bastard by her father's enemies and Catherine's supporters, as the latter did not die until January 1536. Ironically Anne was then executed for supposed adultery by her husband in May – enabling detractors of her and her daughter's causes for decades to claim that Elizabeth might not even be Henry's child given her mother's alleged promiscuity (usually citing Anne's musician admirer Mark Smeaton as a possible father).

As of November 1558, when Elizabeth's half-sister Mary Tudor (Henry's daughter by Catherine) died, France under King Henri II (Francis I's son) was at war with Mary and her husband King Philip of Spain, Charles V's son, and still did not recognise the legality of Henry's marriage to Anne – so Henri recognised his son and heir Francis' wife Mary Queen of Scots, as Henry VIII's older sister Margaret Tudor's grand-daughter, as the legal queen of England. She assumed the heraldic arms of the sovereign of England, and this duly poisoned her relations with her cousin Elizabeth – who most of the English (Catholic) episcopate refused to crown due to her supposed illegitimacy. The actual threat posed by Mary to Elizabeth as of 1558–9 was small, barring a French invasion which was unlikely given the toll that the current Franco-Spanish war was taking on Henri's regime and the fact that his general the Duke of Guise (Mary's maternal uncle) had just seized the main French goal of Calais, the last English bastion in France – which was seen thereafter as providing a fitting final humiliation for Mary Tudor's unpopular and persecutory rule of England. France and Spain were shortly to sign up to peace at Cateau-Cambresis in summer 1559 without England, but Elizabeth deliberately remained on good terms with her late sister's husband Philip of Spain and avoided the contentious (for devoutly Catholic France and Spain) act of returning England to Protestantism until well into 1559.

Then Henri II was killed jousting in the Paris tournament that celebrated the peace-treaty, a freak accident that 'up-ended' European politics and arguably set France on the road to a long religious civil war. The oppressed Protestant Huguenots would have been unlikely to dare to revolt against the adult and militarily successful, if harshly dogmatic, Henri but could challenge a series of unstable regencies easier. The loss of Henri also made Elizabeth's position in England easier, as removing one major enemy. Although the collapse of France into civil war in 1562 left the better-resourced Philip II, who had the treasures of the Spanish empire in the Americas to fund his armies, as a far stronger and just as anti-Protestant potential opponent. (In 1580 he was to inherit and annex Portugal and its empire and fleet as well.) Mary's immature and ailing husband Francis (II) succeeded to France aged just fifteen, and the subsequent weak governments of France under him and his brother Charles IX (ruled 1560–74) were too caught up in faction-feuds and Protestant revolts to contemplate any foreign adventures. Once Mary's unhealthy husband died aged sixteen and his nine-year-old brother succeeded under their mother Catherine de Medici's regency, she left for home in Scotland and had enough to do keeping hold of that throne to covet England. In any case, Henry VIII's will had barred the foreign-born (Scots)children of his elder sister Margaret and their offspring from the English throne in his will of 1544 and reiterated that in his plans of 1546, so Mary had had no support in England in the 1550s even under her fellow-Catholic Mary Tudor (who was luckily at war with France in 1555–8). When Mary Tudor was contemplating a 'safer' heir than Elizabeth, who had converted back to Catholicism but was not trusted and had been investigated in 1554 for contacts with the Protestant 'Wyatt Revolt' plotters, she had considered Margaret Tudor's younger child, the Catholic Lady Margaret Douglas (born 1515), who was the offspring of the Scots Queen by her second (Scots) husband the Earl of Angus, but had been born just over the English border in Northumberland so she was still qualified to succeed under Henry VIII's will.

Margaret had married Matthew Stewart, Earl of Lennox (born 1513), head of a major Lowlands dynasty based near Glasgow and of a junior branch of the Stewart dynasty who might well have a claim on the Scots throne if the main line died out. To complicate matters, Lennox was a controversial figure in Scotland for 'defecting' to Henry VIII after being captured at the battle of Solway Moss in 1542, turning Protestant, marrying Henry's niece Margaret, and acting as an English ally in his attempts of the mid-1540s to wrest control of the Regency for Queen Mary from the pro-French and Catholic Hamiltons. As a result he had been living in England with his wife for the following decade and a half, and despite a superficial reconciliation with the conservative Catholic nobles who had backed Marie de Guise to 1560 and warmer relations with his fellow-Protestants (in power since 1560), he was still widely disliked. Margaret was still a contender for the English crown as of 1559, distrusted by Elizabeth and her closest advisers for her role as a potential rival heir under Mary Tudor, and chose to live well away from court at Temple Newsam in Yorkshire, surrounded by like-minded Catholic gentry whose loyalty to Elizabeth was seen as equally dubious. Indeed, Margaret Douglas and her elder son Henry, Lord Darnley (born in 1545 and nearly three years Mary of Scots' junior), were seen as being as dangerous potential foci for Catholic plots as the Scots queen had been in the early 1560s – hence the attempt to bind them to the Elizabethan cause by finding Darnley a politically 'safe' and loyal wife. All such close royal relatives were supposed to follow their queen's wishes or face her hostility for possible plotting against her, and the seemingly docile and lazy Darnley's sudden 'capture' of Mary's heart, plus a probable 'Crown Matrimonial', was to revive Elizabeth's fears of his family's scheming.

Elizabeth's security within the British Isles was also improved by events early in her reign. The overthrow of the Catholic church (and the French military alliance) in Scotland by English-backed Protestant nobles against Queen Mary's mother and regent, Marie de Guise, in 1559–60 meant that Mary returned in 1561 to a firmly Protestant realm of Scotland, linked to an English alliance. The Protestant junta of great nobles who had driven out the regency and its French troops, the 'Lords of the Congregation', were now governing, headed by Mary's determinedly Protestant half-brother Earl James of Moray, the politically able and unscrupulous bastard son of her father King James V. Her Catholicism and her Guise family connections were thus less of a political threat than they would have been had the Reformation not been imposed on Scotland before her return, but she was still distrusted by the Protestant 'Lords of the Congregation' and their allies (most notably the most dominant preacher in Edinburgh, John Knox) as 'Papist' and by maternal descent a Frenchwoman connected to the overthrown regency and its 'idolatrous' church. On 19 August 1561 Mary landed at Leith, in a fog which the unwelcoming and distrustful Knox later saw as a metaphor for the sorrows and religious impiety which she brought with her. With a large French entourage including several of her Guise uncles, she was welcomed to her country by a posse of nobles headed by Moray and Argyll and was escourted to her new residence at Holyrood Palace. True to her and Moray's promises, she issued a proclamation that she would not seek to alter the (newly) established

Protestant religion but that she expected her foreign Catholic servants to be allowed to practice their religion unhindered too. But as she celebrated Mass at her palace chapel on her first Sabbath in Scotland a riot broke out, hotheads called for the priest to be lynched, and Moray had to guard the door and harangue those zealots who tried to storm it. The queen's seeming 'Papist' godlessness duly aroused the ire of the formidable Knox, who she invited to Holyrood and there he sternly warned her about the iniquity of her religion; he would concede her right to rule if she did not persecute the 'Saints' but he compared their positions to St Paul under the Emperor Nero.

Mary's tact, good humour, and failure to live up to rabid Calvinist expectations as a persecuting 'Papist' helped her to achieve the support of her lords for continuing to practice her religion in private, and this rare Reformation-era example of a sovereign worshipping in a different manner from their subjects survived. To modern interpreters, indeed, it has been the tolerant Mary not the militant zealot Knox who has moral approval; and in these first years Mary proved a competent and adroit sovereign. She even achieved Elizabeth's admission to her envoy Maitland at the end of 1561 that Mary had the most right to the English succession, and Elizabeth ratified the Treaty of Leith (the alliance between the 'Lords of the Congregation' and their English allies) without her original requirement that Mary should abdicate her right to the English crown, not only for Elizabeth's (and her children if she had any)'s lifetime but permanently. At this point it was Elizabeth not Mary who was seen as the over-emotional woman ruler too entangled with unsuitable paramours, namely her relationship with her close ally Robert Dudley (son of the co-victor of England's 1547 victory over Mary's regency at Pinkie, the Earl of Warwick). Dudley's ailing wife Amy Robsart had 'coincidentally' fallen down stairs and killed herself in 1560, arousing international scandal at a time when he and Elizabeth were rumoured to be planning marriage (see previous chapter), and by contrast Mary's reputation was intact.

The outbreak of religious war between Catholics and (Huguenot) Protestants halted plans for Elizabeth and Mary to meet at York in early autumn 1562, and the leadership of the 'ultra' Catholics by Mary's Guise uncles damaged her standing with Protestants in England if not in Scotland. But by this date, Philip of Spain, who had sought to 'control' her as wife to his son Don Carlos and was as much of an 'over-mighty and

Papist ally' threat to her regime and its reputation with Elizabeth, was concentrating on propping up his conservative Catholic allies in France against the Huguenot threat, and from the mid-1560s faced escalating armed defiance from autonomist nobles in the Netherlands (e.g. Egmont and Horn). The papacy – restrained by Philip – had not yet definitively broken with and legalised the deposition of Elizabeth, so Mary could be its loyal subject without arousing English fears. By the time Jesuits and Spanish agents were on the scene in the 1570s and seeking to use Scotland to undermine Elizabeth's regime, the Scots Catholic nobles had lost the advantage of a co-religionist on the throne, and the regency for Mary's young son James VI was determinedly Protestant.

All was not easy for her though, as her passion for music and dancing aroused the predictable ire of Knox and the rarified atmosphere of her culturally Francophile Court life was alien to almost all of the nobility. But such matters were of little immediate political import, the queen toured her country to show herself to her subjects and was keen on hunting, and for governance the queen wisely relied on the duo of Moray, closely linked to many of the aristocracy via his mother's Erskine relations. Mary also relied on the lesser-born 'new man' William Maitland of Leithington, her pro-English (but educated in France) and Protestant secretary, who was both a cultivated man of letters and a skilful and cunning court intriguer and had previously served her mother. Luckily the intolerant Knox alienated Moray and others by his rabid attacks on the 'ungodly' life at court, calling Mary 'Jezebel' after the murderous and idol-worshipping foreign-born Old Testament queen of Israel, and his support for illegal attacks on the queen's chapel in her absence. Knox's forthright and vituperative views on women rulers made him equally unwelcome to Queen Elizabeth, so he was unlikely to be useful as an English agent to coerce his queen's Catholic circle. His role as a loud and aggressive 'loose cannon' who had no respect for members of the elite (royals included) and who did not carry out what he regarded as the 'Will of God' – which had respectable Biblical precedents from the fulminating 'prophets' of the Old Testament, Elijah in particular – had been of long standing, and he had indeed commenced his career as the Protestant 'cheerleader' and resident preacher to the violent reformists who had assassinated the chief Catholic figure in Mary's regency, Cardinal David Beaton, when she was a small girl in 1546. (Beaton had been caught in bed with his mistress, a godsend for Protestant propaganda about 'decadent' Catholic cardinals.) Mary skilfully avoided giving any offence to her Protestant subjects or providing evidence of her hostility to their religion, though foolishly she did not sign the 1560 Scots Parliament acts ratifying the new Protestant religious order which suggested that she wanted to reverse it. Indeed, in August 1562 Mary's first tour of the north-east was used to demonstrate her even-handedness in taking on high-born Catholic malefactors – namely the fourth Earl of Huntly, chief of the Gordons, and his sons. Huntly's obstreperous son Sir John Gordon had been flouting the law by assaulting Lord Ogilvie and using dubious methods to steal lands that were rightfully those of Mary's 'Master of the Household', James Oglivy, and Mary's expedition sought to arrest him but were met with Gordon resistance. The Countess of Huntly interceded with Mary and persuaded her son to surrender, but sooner than face confinement and trial he escaped and raised an army without his father stopping him.

Later Huntly was accused of planning to kidnap Mary and murder Moray and Maitland if they had stayed at his castle of Strathbogie as invited – he had his own reasons for hating Moray as they were disputing over lands. Family pride was probably more at issue for Huntly (a grandson of James IV via his mother, like Arran was) than a coherent plan to overthrow the government and coerce the queen, though he had remonstrated with her for not backing the defiant Catholics in the north openly. The royal party proceeded north and found themselves denied entry to Inverness Castle, a royal possession, by its castellan on the orders of Huntly's heir; the Earl ordered her to be admitted and the offender was hanged over the battlements. Huntly now refused to come before the queen except with a large armed escourt to protect him and assembled an army to challenge the queen. His heir, Lord Gordon, was sent south to try to persuade the latter's father-in-law Chatelherault (head of the Catholic Hamiltons) to join the revolt, but failed. Refusing to appear before the Privy Council for which he was declared forfeit and outlawed, Huntly and his sons failed to intercept the royal party *en route* back south but then marched on Aberdeen. The queen and Moray marched out to confront him, and the resulting 'low-key' battle at Corrichie saw the royal artillery strafe the ill-armed host of 700–1000 or so Gordons, as Moray's men gradually wore them down. Huntly was captured, brought before Moray, and died on the spot of a probable heart-attack, and he was posthumously put on trial and had his titles and lands confiscated; two of his younger sons (including Sir John) were executed. The result left the northern Catholic magnates cowed and Moray's position enhanced, and Mary has been accused of unwisely striking down fundamentally loyal co-religionists and thus putting herself in the hands of the Protestant lords. Huntly's danger to her was, however, clear in her own mind, and kidnapping and coercing Stuart monarchs had a long history.

Given that Mary would not marry Elizabeth's 1564 nominee Robert Dudley, one solution might have been her cousin, James Hamilton, Earl of Arran – lineal next heir to Scotland behind his father the Duke of Chatelherault, head of the family, as senior descendant of James III's sister Mary, and five years older than Mary. (This was assuming that his parents' marriage was counted as legal, about which there was some doubt). His father was Catholic and pro-French and as such was suspected by the English government; but unlike Mary's chosen husband he had no claim on the English throne. His marriage to Mary would bring the hope – and the danger – of one major Scots noble faction, the Hamilton dynasty, being incontrovertibly linked to and thus protecting her security. Arran had already paid unsuccessful court to Elizabeth in 1559–60, hoping for success due to his usefulness to her as one of the senior noble Protestant leaders in Scotland and a means for her to exert influence on that country's elite and pull it away from French influence. Unfortunately Arran had been one of the 'Lords of the Congregation' who had revolted against and deposed Mary's mother as regent in 1560 and was a strong Protestant, neither of which would have endeared him to her, and she was uninterested in him in 1561–2. Worse, he was a mercurial character and increasingly mentally unstable and was mixed up in mysterious violent confrontations with his court rivals including Mary's future husband Bothwell, one of the more aggressive and mercurial Borders lords, and late in 1561 the latter brought an armed gang into Edinburgh twice to try to catch this supposedly moral 'godly' Protestant noble '*in flagrante*' with his middle-class mistress Alison Craig. They missed catching him but the attacks led to an armed demonstration by enraged Hamilton retainers in the city, a retaliatory parade by Bothwell's own large and thuggish force of tenantry, threats of clashes between them, and public scandal for both parties – but no serious punishment for Bothwell despite his breach of the royal peace, an ominous sign of Mary's indulgent favour for him.[1] Next spring Arran made wild but possibly believable claims to Mary that after reconciling with him (ironically, at the future Darnley murder site 'Kirk O'Field' outside Edinburgh) Bothwell had suggested that they should link up to abduct the queen. Then he suggested that Arran could do as he liked with her (presumably rape and/or marriage) and so drive her to become his political pawn to their mutual benefit.[2] Bothwell denied this, though it has similarities to what he actually did to her in 1567, and claimed Arran had been prompted in these fantasies by the earl of Moray in order to ruin him (i.e. Bothwell).

Both were arrested and put in custody in Edinburgh Castle, though allegedly Bothwell did later admit the eccentric earl's claim about his royal kidnap idea had been true. After he escaped down a rope from the castle battlements and fled to his Borders stronghold of Hermitage Castle he lurked around the Borders for a year or so but in early 1563 was shipwrecked in Northumberland while heading for France, detained by the English authorities at Mary's request, and imprisoned in Tynemouth castle. He was later sent to the Tower of London but soon released on parole, and by the time of his secret return to Scotland in December 1563 and subsequent 'under-cover' work for Mary as a secret diplomatic courier had built up allies in London as a possibly 'reliable' Protestant warlord who could keep Mary away from Catholic influence. (This was to have a favourable impact on his reputation there and English Council considerations of him as a replacement for Darnley as Mary's husband ahead of the 1567 crises.) Arran subsequently became paranoid and made even more wild allegations of plots to kill him by his rivals or by witches, and was soon to be placed in chains by his father at Dumbarton Castle and removed from serious consideration as a royal suitor or major political actor. He lived to 1609, reportedly insane, under constraint and the control of his relatives. Alternative – and usefully royal – Protestant candidates to Arran were suggested to Mary by Moray in 1561–2 without meeting any enthusiasm, namely the Protestant kings Frederick II of Denmark (born 1534 so eight years older than Mary) or Eric of Sweden (the latter was as unstable as Arran and ended up mad and under restraint too). These two also had two younger brothers each (Magnus and John of Denmark and John and Charles of Sweden), though some of these were considerably younger than Mary, so marrying one of these would not entail a problematic 'Union of Crowns'; the Vasas of Sweden were a '*parvenu*' line who had only gained their throne by revolt in 1523 so Mary might disregard them but the Danish line were her distant cousins.

The decline in Mary's fortunes commenced with her choice of husband, which was made despite Elizabeth's attempt to interest her in Robert Dudley (now made Earl of Leicester) in 1563–4. As of winter 1561–2 the most active English candidate to marry Mary – but not with Elizabeth's blessing – had been Margaret Douglas' and Lennox's son Darnley, with Margaret apparently writing letters from her Yorkshire base Temple Newsam to various Scots nobles to enlist their support. The possibility of Mary marrying Don Carlos, son of Philip II, had also alarmed the anti-Spanish (though equally 'hard-line' Catholic) regent of France, Catherine de Medici, into preferring a marriage between Mary and Darnley to block this. As of June 1562, when the Spanish ambassador in London Bishop De Quadra confirmed this, the latter also believed that Arran (insane though he was) was a serious enough contender for his father Chatelherault's foe Moray to be promoting the Mary/Darnley marriage idea as a way to stop this.[3] The meddling Margaret Douglas thus had useful and powerful allies, even if their reasons for helping her were not identical – but her plans and their backers also raised the alarm of the always vigilant (if not paranoid) Elizabeth. Moreover, it was the norm for that era for the court to place informants in a socially prominent suspect's household or at least pay servants and local retainers/tenants for news of what the suspect was up to, and even if Margaret had the intelligence to guess that this was going on she was not discreet enough to hide her activities successfully. Word of her canvassing support in Scotland got back via the English queen's spies to London, principally one of her husband's former servants called Thomas Bishop who was acting as a paid informant – and had already been thrown out of her household, which suggests that she or Lennox suspected what he was up to. (It may also suggest that he invented or exaggerated some details to get revenge.) Bishop's statements to the Privy Council in 1562 after the couple's arrest are the main source of detail on this activity and the similarity of what he and agents within their household (e.g. William Forbes) said suggest collusion to 'smear' the accused, but the international diplomatic letters agree that at least the Lennoxes were actively promoting Darnley's chances.

The 'lobbying' for Darnley also coincided with Mary's apparent fear of the hostile political intentions towards her of Chatelherault, as a possible and 'acceptable' male alternative sovereign, and her resultant interest in bringing Lennox back home to Scotland to help her frustrate this – which might entail marrying his son Darnley. This idea of hers was known to Maitland by 15 August 1561, when he warned his London ally Cecil of it.[4] Cecil and Elizabeth duly collected and mulled over reports sent by Bishop and others of what Margaret and her husband were up to, and in November 1561 Lennox was required to come from Yorkshire to London for investigation in the Tower. Margaret and her two sons were kept under watch in the north under the supervision of the young and semi-royal duke of Norfolk, Elizabeth's cousin (and ironically later another candidate to marry Mary), and in March 1562 were summoned to London. Darnley somehow evaded arrest and fled into hiding, which would have bolstered fears that he was intended as the figurehead for a plot against Elizabeth, but Margaret and her daughters arrived in London safely and were there placed under supervised house-arrest at the home of the queen's cousin and Chancellor of the Exchequer (i.e. deputy Treasurer), Sir Richard Sackville, at Sheen near Richmond Palace. According to the Spanish ambassador De Quadra, Margaret was claiming that in fact she had been doing her patriotic duty to help Elizabeth and ensure future stability for the succession, by tying her putative heiress Mary to England by marrying her to a loyal Englishman i.e. Darnley. Elizabeth was not convinced, and as usual talk of the English succession infuriated her.[5] Thomas Bishop and others made their detailed reports of alleged treasonous plots to marry off Darnley to Mary with an eye to the thrones of both Scotland and England, and of Margaret's alleged boasting that her son should end up with two thrones. Lennox was fiercely and repeatedly questioned but denied it all, the allegations made by Bishop (in a list of 'Articles' submitted on 7 May 1562) and others were pored over, and for good measure Margaret's alleged links to anti-English foreign princes and illegal performance of Catholic religious practices (and alleged possible witchcraft) were listed on the flimsiest of evidence.

Pressurised by these lurid and execution-worthy allegations and threatened with trial, Margaret was duly required to promise not to promote the marriage of Darnley to Mary again though – as Mary Tudor had done with Elizabeth in 1554 – the threat of trial and execution was not carried through. To undermine her claim to the English throne and supposed threat to Elizabeth, old allegations were revived (inaccurately) that her mother Margaret Tudor's divorce from her father the Earl of Angus had involved proof that their marriage had been illegal and void – so she had no claim on either the throne or any Angus wealth and was at Elizabeth's political and financial mercy. Before Lennox's belated release in November he was required to promise not to come to any agreements with other Scots nobles without English approval. In the complex and murky world of Elizabethan court politics, his formal submission to the queen's goodwill in August (which was at the time expected to lead to his quick release, or so Margaret claimed) was not followed by his actual release for months more for whatever reason. Lennox's actual release was supposed to be due to support by leading courtiers such as Robert Dudley, who wanted him and his wife as political 'counter-weights' to the claim to be English heir by Lady Jane Grey's younger sister Katherine, grand-daughter of Henry VIII's younger sister Mary. (The queen's recent near-fatal bout of smallpox would have made the succession issue crucial again.) Lennox was then returned to his wife at Sheen, and a few months later they were allowed to return to court free of constraint if not suspicion.

By June 1564 Darnley, now adult in body if not in emotional maturity and aged seventeen or eighteen, was in favour at court as a dashing young nobleman and was allowed to lead the official welcome to the new Spanish ambassador. By this point Elizabeth had decided to select her trusted and close friend Leicester, her 'Eyes', as her candidate to marry and so control Mary. As of 1560–1 he had indeed been seen as the favourite candidate to marry Elizabeth if she followed her own wishes and defied his numerous English enemies, as seen in the previous chapter, and even the suspicious death of his current wife Amy Robsart had not ended this possibility though it had added to his unsavoury reputation and may have headed off an engagement at the time of the crisis. Marrying him to Mary would defeat the risk of Mary marrying either one of the pro-Catholic Hamiltons (whose dynastic head James Hamilton, formerly second earl of Arran, held the French dukedom of Chatelherault), Philip of Spain's son and heir Don Carlos (the same age as Darnley so slightly younger than Mary) which Mary had herself suggested to the Spaniards, or the slightly older Archduke Charles, a younger son of Philip's uncle Emperor Ferdinand I and two years Mary's senior. Following Don Carlos' serious brain-injury falling downstairs and subsequent worsening mental state in autumn 1563, Mary seems to have veered towards Darnley for the first time in February 1564, with the approval and reportedly at the suggestion of Moray and Maitland – who as English allies were in turn responding to hints in London that Elizabeth had an English candidate in mind for Mary. Elizabeth had not named her candidate, and given Darnley's royal blood it was a reasonable assumption that he was the man she meant. On 15 April the English ambassador in Edinburgh, Thomas Randolph, wrote to Elizabeth's chief minister and secretary of state, William Cecil, that Mary had in mind to marry someone living between Berwick and Dover, i.e. in England, but not the person who Cecil probably hoped for – a hint that he knew Cecil wanted to get his rival Dudley packed off to Edinburgh as royal consort but Mary preferred Darnley. At this stage, Mary had not even met Darnley.

The ingenious idea of marrying Mary to Leicester was never likely to succeed, as quite apart from Mary considering Elizabeth's 'cast-off' lover beneath her, Leicester preferred to keep his power in England to an uncertain future in Scotland. He went along with his mistress' orders in going to Scotland and wooing Mary, but without enthusiasm or success.[6] Indeed, he may have found it useful to bring in Darnley as a 'rival' so that he did not have to go and live in Scotland himself but he could avoid blame by Elizabeth for his failure. There was still the problem of Elizabeth's fear of Darnley's parents' hostile intentions and the bonus that marrying Mary to Darnley would give them, but in June 1564 Elizabeth relented enough to write to Mary asking her to reverse the ban on Lennox entering Scotland created by his 1540s conviction for pro-English treason there, and to invite him back to take over his estates. This gave Mary the opportunity to invite Lennox to return home and so enlist his help for the marriage and/or get Darnley invited too, and on 19 September the Scots Protestant military commander Sir William Kirkcaldy of Grange informed Elizabeth's ambassador Randolph that the Scots would never accept Dudley as their queen's husband but they might accept Darnley if this was backed strongly by England. Changing her mind about Lennox, Elizabeth now asked Mary to ban him from Scotland instead to avoid her getting the blame for keeping him in England, but Mary refused and the earl's judicial condemnation was reversed (announced publicly on 9 October, confirmed by the Scots Parliament in December) enabling him to return. Mary now sent Sir James Melville to London that autumn as her ambassador to conduct arrangements for her marriage, without any warning to Elizabeth that Dudley was unacceptable. Elizabeth was using the embassy for one purpose (to promote Dudley's claims, for which purpose he was raised to the earldom of Leicester on 28 September) and Mary was using it for a contrary one, to link up to Darnley – and as well as that Melville visited the Spanish ambassador to see if there was still a chance in getting Philip in offering his heir Don Carlos. This threat of a Scots-Spanish link had already frightened her Guise uncles into proposing the Austrian Habsburg Archduke Charles instead, but Charles was however too poor, and the English opposed either a Spaniard or an Austrian having power in Scotland.[7]

Philip now had to drop the Don Carlos plan as his epileptic and erratic nineteen-year-old son's insanity became apparent. Elizabeth preferred a 'controllable' Englishman as Mary's husband, and in November 1564 Moray and Maitland met her envoys at Berwick to discuss Leicester's candidacy. Elizabeth seems to have been keener on this than Leicester, whose enemies backed the proposal as a way of removing him from the English court, and there were potential objections that Leicester's father and grandfather had both been executed and his first wife had died in suspicious circumstances. The Scots alleged that Elizabeth's envoys had also said that their queen's alternative candidates, if Mary did not want Leicester, were Darnley and the duke of Norfolk (the latter also being a cousin of the queen with a, much more remote claim to her throne) and that if Mary would marry as Elizabeth wanted she would then name the Scots queen as her heir – which does not fit in with Elizabeth's long-term attitude to not naming an heir and is more likely (if accurate) to be a ploy by her envoys to lure Mary into co-operating. But the Scots envoys turned down the Leicester idea and walked out of the talks rather than continue discussing it, and for good measure they also wrote demanding that Elizabeth recognise Mary as her heiress as a precondition for Mary letting her cousin help select her husband – logical given that if Mary was to end up queen of England her choice of husband would then affect England as well as Scotland. Elizabeth refused to do this, again. If the English envoys had indeed mentioned the possibility of Elizabeth naming Mary as her heir in return for co-operation over the marriage, then the Scots ones wanted it in writing, knowing how devious Elizabeth was, and that was a demand too far.

In January 1565 Elizabeth surprisingly allowed Darnley to visit Scotland and he quickly emerged in Mary's favour. Lennox had recently been allowed home in autumn 1564 by Elizabeth's belated permission, for the first time since his rebellion in 1544, with his first request for Darnley to be allowed to accompany him in November being refused. He apparently claimed that he legally needed his son and heir with him in Scotland to sign the necessary documentation for his estates' return to him, under Scots legal procedure – and Elizabeth found out that that was not strictly true and was angry at why he had being trying to trick her. The ambitious Margaret Douglas was probably behind the move to get Darnley to Scotland and secure his marriage without having to accept Elizabeth's interference and possible veto; she claimed in an appeal to Elizabeth to let him go and that of course he would return to England within a month, which was probably disingenuous. Also Leicester seems to have backed him in order to forestall Elizabeth packing him off to Scotland to woo Mary. Elizabeth eventually changed her mind and allowed his parents' requests to let him visit Scotland in January 1565, and although this was the homeland of both his parents, and he was heir to his father Lennox, so he might be mostly concerned with his meeting his future tenants there she must have been aware then that he might be trying to impress Mary and arrange an engagement. Or was she seeking to use him to distract Mary from marrying some foreign suitor (French or Spanish) and did not take his chances of marrying Mary himself seriously, as he had not made a good impression at the English court as young, gauche, spoilt and immature? She was shrewd enough to realise that what she regarded as faults in Darnley might well not appear the same to Mary, and that even if he was not fully 'signed up' to what his devious mother was planning he might fall for Mary and the lure of her crown, and woo her once he saw her. Sending him to Scotland was thus the sort of danger of things getting out of control that 'risk-averse' Elizabeth rarely took unless driven to it. 'Outside observers' with keen political 'antennae' were agreed that she knew what could happen when she let Darnley loose on Mary. The Spanish ambassador in London, De Silva, heard that Elizabeth had allowed Darnley to go to Scotland as she had accepted that Leicester refused to marry the Scots queen, so Darnley was the only viable alternative as a husband. A French diplomat in London, Michel De Castelnau, heard that Elizabeth had intended to make a 'present' of Darnley to Mary and had been persuading her that he was the best suitor available for her in Christendom – which fits in with the allegation that his name was mentioned as a possible suitor approved of by Elizabeth at the Berwick negotiations in late November. Although when De Castelnau discussed how the subsequent engagement was going with Elizabeth in early 1565 she feigned annoyance at it, he reckoned that she was in secret pleased.[8] De Silva heard that the match had been approved by some leading figures in London (Cecil or Leicester?), and Cecil himself told French ambassador Paul de Foix in March that the match was being arranged by Elizabeth – though this may have been making the best of a situation that had got out of control from his queen's point of view. Darnley turning up in Edinburgh 'under his own steam' and backed by his mother was more dangerous than Darnley being escourted there by and instructed in what to say and do by English diplomats – though in that case Elizabeth should have held him up in London for longer then sent him under 'expert' English courtiers' escourt.

There was also the possibility that the unstable and immature Darnley, unskilled in politics and never having been to Scotland (and also the heir to the contentious ex-'traitor' Henrican ally Lennox), might 'stumble' badly as a gauche and incompetent consort and cause civil strife – as astute English ambassador in Edinburgh Randolph warned Cecil by letter on 14 December 1564.[9] This accurate warning of what might happen was ignored – though Cecil had his own reasons for packing Leicester off to marry Mary instead, arguably he had now accepted that Leicester would not play along with that and he may even have reckoned that chaos in Scotland would keep a preoccupied Mary from having the time to claim Elizabeth's throne. Randolph also reported that the ultra-Protestant 'Lords of the Congregation', led by the ruthless and devious earl of Morton (head of a junior branch of the Douglases so with a complex family legal conflict with Lady Margaret and her Douglas kin), were dismayed at the prospect – and the religious threat – of Mary marrying a Catholic in general, and Darnley in particular. They knew how Lady Margaret had been a 'hard-line' Catholic enthusiast and expert intriguer at the court of her cousin Mary Tudor in London in the mid-1550s, and did not want her repeating that pattern as a 'power behind the throne' for her prospective daughter-in-law Mary Stuart. Given the later 'line-up' of the opposition lords who were to be implicated in Darnley's murder in

1567 and later in Mary's overthrow, Randolph's warning of who opposed the marriage and why was a sign of what was to happen two years later.

In January 1565 Elizabeth finally allowed Darnley to go to Scotland; he crossed the Border on 10th February and headed to Edinburgh to be greeted by Elizabeth's ambassador Randolph and assorted nobles. Meanwhile Margaret wrote ahead of him to Mary, advising her to marry Darnley as he would be a loyal, respectful and kind husband. On 17 February Mary met Darnley, young, handsome, charming, and well-turned-out, at Wemyss Castle, and despite Elizabeth's furious disapproval of the idea of him – another descendant of Henry VII and claimant to her throne – marrying their mutual cousin Mary took no notice. The relationship between the two quickly prospered, though Darnley also made a good initial impression on the Scots nobles, and Elizabeth pretended to De Silva in mid-March that she was pleased at the way things were going and that Lennox and Darnley would be returning to England in May – which fits in with Lennox's recent request to the queen in London for three months' more leave to stay in Scotland. Someone else – Margaret? – had told De Silva that they had no such intentions, and Margaret had asked De Silva to help promote the marriage to Elizabeth. She was supposed to have written to Mary that if she married Darnley they would have the allegiance of Catholics in England as well as Scotland. This would imply that Margaret was dangling the chances of Catholic help to gain the English crown in front of Mary to help her decide in Darnley's favour, and it fits with a gloomy English diplomatic 'aide memoire' of current regime thinking drawn up for envoy by Sir Nicholas Throckmorton early in 1565 (on behalf of and given the style probably written by Cecil) stating that once Lennox and/or Margaret were safe in Scotland they would work solely for their own advancement and could not be trusted to obey or be loyal to Elizabeth. There is, however, the possibility that this hostile report from Edinburgh about what Margaret was telling Mary is untrustworthy, given that Cecil's anti-Catholic spies in Edinburgh were implacably hostile to the Lennoxes and Darnley as 'Catholic agents' – and one of them was the mischief-making Thomas Bishop, their ex-employee and traducer in 1562, who was no doubt still out for revenge.

A bout of measles in early April that confined him to his rooms and caused anxiety about his health caused Darnley to receive frequent visits from Mary, who appears to have fallen in love with him around this point. English ambassador Randolph was duly scandalised both at the queen's 'improper' private visits to an unmarried man and at the rumours of an impending engagement, and warned London. Elizabeth's recent favour and invitations to important court events for Margaret abruptly ceased as Mary's secretary Maitland arrived in London on 18 April to gain her approval for the marriage.

Margaret now shrewdly called on Spanish ambassador De Silva for help, declaring that the Mary/Darnley marriage was possible though not finalised and assuring that she and Mary would appreciate Philip's backing for it as the queen-mother of France (Catherine de Medici) was very much against it, so the Catholic Scots queen relied on Spain as her only reliable Catholic ally.[10] Elizabeth was 'keeping in with' Philip for the moment as the regency in France (a country at war with England in 1555–9) was more hostile than Spain, but if Margaret thought that Spain could shield her family from Elizabeth's wrath, she miscalculated. Now the impending engagement of Mary and Darnley was known, Elizabeth denounced it and on the 22nd placed Margaret under house-arrest in disgrace for allegedly arranging it behind her queen's back and conducting correspondence with overseas heads of state without her permission. Darnley was clearly not seen as an 'official' and so controllable English choice, and the threat of matters proceeding without her control was probably as crucial in Elizabeth's panicked reaction as the fact of the engagement (which given Darnley's prolonged stay in Scotland and physical attractiveness, plus Catholic background was logically not that much of a surprise). Now Elizabeth instructed Randolph to find out how far things had gone between Mary and Darnley, hold up or if possible stop the marriage, and promote Leicester to Mary as a far more worthy choice. This attempt to put Elizabeth back in control was unlikely to succeed, and ignored the already known reactions of both Leicester and Mary to Elizabeth's alternative plan. Leicester had probably encouraged Darnley to go to Scotland as a way of stopping Elizabeth's plan to marry Mary to himself, and Elizabeth should have realised that by now and been more realistic. Indeed, Elizabeth had granted him permission to go there even if she later regretted it; as with her later reaction to the fall-out from her signing Mary's death-warrant in 1587, she finally made a decision under pressure with extreme unwillingness, faced the likely results, and then blamed everyone but herself.

Elizabeth now suspected Margaret (her own possible rival as heir to Mary Tudor in 1558) of not only securing Mary for her son against royal wishes but of improving her own chances of the succession in England, and reacted with the same anger that she had shown to her other cousin and potential rival Katherine Grey for marrying illegally in 1560. There was also the question of Catholic opinion in England and the effect marriage would have – De Silva heard that Elizabeth was furious as the marriage would bolster the English Catholics who wanted her to have a Catholic heir, by marrying the nation's two main Catholic candidates to each other, but conversely the pressure on Elizabeth to name an heir meant that by marrying Mary to an Englishman, and seeming to have them as Elizabeth's chosen successors, the queen could decrease the current pressure to explicitly name an heir. (This argument, however, assumed that Elizabeth would coolly follow logic.) Throckmorton was told to try to scare Mary off marrying Darnley by telling him there were (unnamed) reasons why he was unsuitable, and to warn her that her seeing him in private while he was ill had caused scandalous rumours to the detriment of their reputations.[11] This did not work, in the same way that Elizabeth's later warnings to Mary about marrying Darnley's reputed murderer Bothwell, a Borders ruffian with a scandalous past, failed – it was the wrong way to approach the impulsive Mary who did not care for her dignity like Elizabeth did. The possibility remains that Elizabeth intended to play the chances of Leicester or Darnley marrying Mary off against each other and keep Mary unwed for as long as possible, her usual policy in case of uncertainty in a crisis being delay. If so, she presumably now thought that Margaret and Lennox had deliberately outwitted her, with probable malevolent intent aimed at securing the English as well as the Scots throne, and as a result Lennox and Darnley were ordered by letters of 27 May to return to England at once. They refused, and on 16 June Margaret was arrested and thrown in the Tower – as Katherine Grey had been in 1560.[12] The fact that Margaret was lineal next heir to England after herself (and Mary if the latter's foreign birth did not invalidate her claim) and Darnley next after his mother added to the queen's sensitivity about implications for the English succession. Margaret and her ambitious, naïve son clearly had hopes of two crowns rather than one in due course. The timing was not coincidental either, as Scots secretary Maitland was due to arrive within a day or so to press for

Elizabeth to accept the marriage – the queen was showing her seemingly implacable hostility to it and threatening Darnley (probably already suspected of not being a strong character) through, his mother as well as placing his English estates under threat of seizure.

De Silva reported that popular opinion in London was in Margaret and Darnley's favour and there was dismay at the queen's reaction, which would have made her even more paranoid about their intentions and likely support.[12] Maitland tried to intercede for the disgraced Lennox family and speak up for the marriage when he met Elizabeth, but she flew into a rage and denounced it, and refused to let him see Margaret.[13] He had to return to Edinburgh empty-handed. Instead Mary and Margaret had to rely on the secret help of Spanish ambassador De Silva until Elizabeth's rage abated, and the ambassador established a secret line of communication to Margaret in the Tower (at the 'Lieutenant's Lodgings' on Tower Green where Henry VIII had imprisoned Anne Boleyn) to send her news and advise her what to say to her cousin and the latter's officials. The French embassy also offered her secret advice,[14] so Elizabeth's fears and anger about her cousin's private dealings with foreign powers behind her back were accurate – though Margaret's behaviour was logical if risky for someone in her position.

On 29 July Mary and Darnley were married (in a Catholic ceremony) at Holyrood Abbey, and Mary, clearly infatuated, proceeded to give her husband the 'Crown Matrimonial' as 'King Henry' the next day.[15] As Darnley and his mother were Catholic the marriage could be seen as boosting the Catholic faction, and both the major Protestant faction (Moray and the 'Lords of the Congregation' including Morton) and the major Catholic faction led by the Hamiltons now turned against the queen – with Moray seeking English aid to launch a revolt. In Darnley's favour, he was of royal blood so socially equal with his wife, he was also English so not linked to an overseas 'Great Power' who could dominate Scotland as France had done in 1548–60, young and potentially malleable, and with potential support in England provided by his dynastic position in the Tudor line of succession, he did not make Elizabeth determined to remove him as a threat. Nor was he particularly interested in religion, so he was open to Catholic and Protestant influence and had not yet irrevocably alienated all the power-hungry and violent Scots elite faction-leaders of either religion. His relationship with Mary's and his other cousins, the

Hamiltons – putatively the strongest advocates of Catholicism and based physically close to court in Clydeside, so with a double usefulness for him and Mary – was a problem, given his father Lennox's role in trying to overthrow the Hamilton-led regency for Mary in 1543–7 with English support. This could have been eased had he distanced himself from and sidelined his father, but this sort of political sublety was beyond him. His attraction to Mary seems to have been physical rather than political, he had no sense of decorum or skill at winning friends, and he soon proved himself to be vain, spoilt, drunken, and prone to jealousy – and open to suggestions from intriguing nobles.

Mary and Darnley did make an awkward diplomatic overture to Elizabeth for reconciliation and assured their goodwill to her and lack of desire to meddle in her country's affairs (or to change the national religion of either England or Scotland) in a letter to her on 13 August. Unfortunately, this also contained a request that she would formally name them in the succession in return for their continued goodwill and support, and this offer of a 'quid pro quo' was taken – as might have been expected given Elizabeth's sensitivity on the issue – as attempted blackmail.[16] The English queen was left even angrier than before, and this proved politically dangerous given the fact that she now had the ability to cause mischief in Scotland due to the alienation of the more extreme or anti-Lennox members of the 'Lords of the Congregation' – and most crucially Moray. The latter felt himself excluded from influence at court by the prominence of the returned and noisily triumphalist Lennox, and linked up with other alarmed Protestant foes of the queen and her Catholic husband and Douglas foes of their cousin Margaret (including Morton) while the Hamiltons – Catholics but enemies of Lennox and his family – were alarmed at their 1540s foe Lennox being back in power.

Moray now launched a rebellion in Ayrshire in August 1565 after withdrawing from court and refusing to return as summoned, backed by Chatelherault – and the earl of Argyll and several other Protestant peers. He claimed that the country was endangered by bad government and Catholic revival, as shown by the queen's marriage, but the lack of support he received shows that he mistimed his appeal. Darnley had not yet shown his spiteful dissoluteness and though he was Catholic he had attended Protestant services in both England and Scotland (including Knox's), and Mary was still popular. The queen acted with vigour and outlawed him on 6 August for refusing to obey her summons, confiscated his and some allies' estates on the 14th, and on the 22nd called a muster of troops to march against him in the south-west and reassured her subjects that no change of religion was planned. On 26 August she left Edinburgh for Glasgow with the armour-clad Darnley and a substantial force, heading for Chatelherault's estates, and in her absence Moray, Chatelherault (not yet forfeited), and the earls of Rothes and Glencairn led around 1,000 men into the city. Lord Erskine, now granted Mary's titles and estates, held the castle for the queen, the populace did not rise in defence of their allegedly endangered religion, and the rebels had to withdraw into Galloway in the hope of English aid. The queen waited at Stirling until her northern levies arrived and then rode after them, enthusiastic and apparently wielding a pistol, with the resulting 'non-contact' campaign being known as the 'Chaseabout Raid'.

Mary chased the evasive rebels across the south-west without any clash, and Moray and his men eventually had to withdraw into England (6 October), whence Elizabeth had sent only one half-hearted naval 'probe' into the Forth.[17] The refugee earl was summoned to Elizabeth's court, upbraided by the embarrassed queen for his pointless revolt, and interned, and among the other political casualties of the rebellion was Chatelherault who withdrew to his French estates in disgrace. Moray had thrown away his strong position as the queen's lieutenant in what appears to have been a mixture of pique and miscalculation, and it left Mary unchallenged – temporarily. She and Darnley took the opportunity to send an ambassador (Francis Yaxley) to Philip of Spain, assuring him of their goodwill for the Catholic cause and asking for his help via his envoy in London to get Queen Elizabeth to release Lady Margaret and to avoid assisting the fugitive rebels led by Moray.[18] Mary needed international help to combat both her own rebels and the threat that Elizabeth would back them, Philip was the strongest and most congenial (i.e. Catholic) ally and had already shown his goodwill, and France was slipping into civil war and was run by Mary's detractor Catherine de Medici, but a Spanish alliance would destabilise Scots politics further in the long run by seeming to make the Protestant radicals' worst fears correct. With the Hamiltons in disgrace, Mary could restore the late earl of Huntly's eldest son to his father's title and estates so that she had a strong new Catholic ally. Another beneficiary was the quarrelsome Border magnate

Bothwell, a notorious brawler and rake but a foe to the Hamiltons and Moray. Summoned back from exile by Mary and arriving by fishing-boat to elude the English navy, Bothwell (who she had first met in France during her first marriage) was to prove a personal and political disaster for Mary. In December Mary pardoned Chatelherault, decreasing the number of her active enemies but noticeably pardoning a major Catholic, not a major Protestant rebel, as the 'Lords of the Congregation' faction noted – and this action also led to her first major row with Darnley who had wanted his family's Hamilton foes ruined.

As of late 1565 Mary was pregnant, any aid or inspiration Elizabeth might have given to the Moray rebels to take over Scotland had been defeated, and her position seemed to be stronger than it had been for years. But the swift reversal of Mary's fortunes after autumn 1565 points to the mutability of elite politics in Scotland and to her own miscalculations, as well as bad luck. Like her predecessors Mary came to rely on a 'middle-class' secretariat of competent and personally loyal careerists, for company as well as transacting business, and her use of foreigners was not unprecedented either. Supposedly 'jumped-up' and acquisitive favourites had been a major source of discord under James III. But the fact that Scotland was now Protestant and most of her protégés were Catholic added to the usual disgruntlement of various nobles about these men. Their lack of social status not that much of a problem in itself – the Protestant lords' future ally Maitland, the queen's secretary, was a middle-class 'careerist' himself, though at least he was a Scott and from a minor landed family – but their religion and servile household roles adding to their alleged presumption. (The non-noble English ambassador Randolph wrote of them equally slightingly as 'crafty vile strangers').[19] The fact that the queen was a woman led to allegations of improper conduct by mischief-makers. These allegations came to centre on one of her attendants, a skilled but ugly Italian (Savoyard) musician called David Riccio (a.k.a. Rizzio) who succeeded her deceased French-born secretary Raullet at the end of 1564, and alienated ultra-Protestant nobles such as the earl of Morton, seem to have spread the rumours in order to damage the queen's reputation in retaliation for her failure to pardon their ally Moray. The nobles' attempt to get Moray and other exiles pardoned was backed up by Elizabeth who tried to insist on this as a condition for her releasing Margaret Douglas from the Tower, but

Mary would not agree – and there was every chance that if the exiles returned home unpunished they could stage another revolt, with more aid from the English this time after their sojourn in London inflaming Elizabeth and her ministers against their Catholic queen.

The combination of personal friends of Moray, mostly nobles, and the usual anti-Catholic clerical fanatics to blacken Mary's reputation as a dangerous Catholic stooge, even worked on Darnley as a useful ally at court, which was a cynical move given that as a Catholic he was technically one of their targets and he had been ostentatiously parading his religion by going to public mass at Christmas 1565 and later joining in a public procession for the Feast of the Purification. This would have been anathema to Knox and his allies, but apparently they were more concerned at inaccurate rumours that Mary would use the immanent Parliamentary meeting to join a supposed new international Catholic league (which did not exist). They were joined by Secretary Maitland who was alarmed at the failure of his efforts to tie Mary into a pro-English and anti-French policy. It was also around this time that Darnley, having already been egged on by his father to demand equal status as co-ruler of Scotland but denied this, had some sort of 'cooling off' with his wife – possibly linked to the mysterious affair of the withdrawal of the new silver 'ryal' coin (worth thirty shillings) struck earlier in 1565 to commemorate the royal wedding. The coin's lettering unusually placed Darnley's name not Mary's first ('HENRICUS & MARIA D GRA') though she, not he, was the ruling sovereign, and the withdrawal of this was rumoured to represent Mary's desire to reassert her position over that of her status-obsessed husband. Darnley was also said in the later memoirs of Mary's stalwart ally Lord Herries to have formed the erroneous idea that the Scots nobility rather than the queen's personal wishes had been the main reason why he had been chosen as her husband, and that they would follow him anywhere (e.g. in battle) and were uneasy at having a woman ruler.[20] This inflated idea of his importance and invulnerable popularity with the nobles on whom the crown rested, may well have induced both his anger at Mary seeking to reduce his role and his subsequent jealous vulnerability to gossip and the temptation to challenge her – in which case it may have doomed him by causing him to get involved in the plot against Riccio.

Once Mary was pregnant it was whispered that Riccio, not Darnley, was the father of her child, which English Ambassador Randolph passed on to Leicester and his sovereign in January 1566.[21] According to Randolph's lurid warnings to Leicester on 13 February, Queen Mary now hated her husband and in retaliation Darnley and his father Lennox planned to depose her (or worse?), with the possibility implicit that as Margaret Douglas' son Darnley could then claim the throne. In pursuit of this, Riccio would have his throat cut in the next ten days.[22] This was possibly just spiteful gossip, or the most extreme and rumoured plans of a few 'hard-line' plotters, and Mary was shortly to insist on Randolph leaving for England due to his hostility to her. But a drastic move to get Moray and his allies pardoned, not forfeited by the immanent Parliament by coercing Mary, was certainly planned and a 'bond' was now drawn up by the plotters, including Morton, lords Ruthven and Lindsay, and (in England) their allies Glencairn, Rothes, and Moray himself, though not Maitland.

Murder and deposition

Mary's second marriage now collapsed in a series of dramatic and bloody events, an ongoing crisis in which Mary's hitherto blameless reputation was to be fatally affected. This did not prevent her steadfast attitude to her religion continuing her appeal as a puppet-queen of England to Elizabeth's hard-headed 'Counter-Reformationary' European foes in the 1570s and 1580s, but it damaged her as potential heir in more fastidious people's opinions. It also fatally ruined her desirability as a sovereign to much of her nation, though perhaps not to the extent that is popularly assumed as she retained significant support within parts of the elite and her restoration to some degree of power remained a serious possibility into the early 1580s. The bloody feuding among her family and the elite also did wonders for the modern tourist trade, with Edinburgh the scene of two of the most spectacular events of the crisis. In the first twist of this series of violent political and personal showdowns, it seemed possible that Mary would be eliminated from the equation altogether, without a child. The sordid violence in her private chamber at Edinburgh Castle, when her secretary David Riccio was killed on 9 March 1566, could easily have caused her to miscarry the future James VI. The conspirators who deliberately set about to kill her favourite servant in her presence, power-hungry 'ultra' Protestants including Lord Ruthven and the future regent Morton, were allies of Mary's exiled half-brother Moray and their 'bond' of alliance was formally aimed at forcing his (Protestant) exile faction's restoration, coupled with the grant of the full royal powers ('crown matrimonial') to Darnley as he and his father Lennox had been desiring ever since the wedding. But the nature of the open murder of Riccio in front of the pregnant queen, which was chosen instead of an equally effective private stabbing or kidnapping, suggests that some of the organisers hoped or at least were willing to risk that it would cause the death of the pregnant – and undesirably Catholic – queen who was not allowed any medical attention afterwards. This would give the full crown to the weak and malleable Darnley, who would do as the rebel lords wished. The English ambassador Randolph's letter to Leicester on 13 February, mentioned above, hints that this was under consideration by Darnley, Lennox, and others. It cannot be thought likely that if Mary had died of a miscarriage the new 'King Henry', a weak and petulant character open to bad advice and no doubt seeking refuge in drink, would have lasted long as king in the hands of the circle of predatory nobles around him.

The coup took place on the evening of Saturday 9 March 1566, two days after Parliament had opened in Edinburgh. Mary was hosting a small private supper party in her apartments at Holyrood Palace, her advanced pregnancy and poor health having curtailed any more onerous public events, and this was interrupted by the arrival of firstly Darnley and a few minutes later Lord Ruthven, leader of the other conspirators. The account of events relies on evidence from both sides – one letter by Mary to archbishop James Beaton of Glasgow, currently ambassador to France, on 2 April after she had escaped from the attackers. Another one written by conspirator Lord Ruthven at the end of March with the help of his English ally, the earl of Bedford, to excuse his actions to an English elite audience. Mary also retold the story later in captivity to her secretary Claude Nau, who published it in his Memoirs of her, but this is less trustworthy as it owes more to hindsight and her desire to put a good 'spin' on the circumstances for her growing reputation as a noble and devout Catholic 'victim' – in which case, the sordid stories about her supposed sexual relations for her Italian secretary had to be dropped. But the accounts all agree that the arrival of Darnley and then the sick Ruthven – famously rising from his bed to lead the murderers, wearing armour over his nightgown – caught the queen and her attendants by surprise. Darnley kept out of the initial confrontation in the supper-chamber as Ruthven demanded that Riccio accompany him outside, and when Mary asked him if he was involved he returned an evasive answer. Ruthven then launched into a rambling attack on Riccio for his presumption and sinister influence over the queen and the latter for tolerating it and for not pardoning Moray and the others. At the end of this, Ruthven lunged at Riccio who had shrunk back into a corner, but Mary's attendants either grabbed at him or at least protested, trying to shield Riccio. Ruthven then called in the other plotters, who pushed the attendants – and possibly the queen, who Darnley may have grabbed aside and seized Riccio. The latter was clinging to Mary's skirts, but was prised free, dragged to the doorway out onto the privy stairs, and stabbed repeatedly – according to his wounds, around fifty-three times – as he was dragged downstairs and finished off. At least two of the murderers waved pistols around, and one was supposed to have been pointed at Mary's stomach. The likelihood of her having a miscarriage after seeing her secretary dragged away to his death and hearing his final screams from the stairs was obviously high and was deliberately risked by Ruthven and his allies, even if the situation got out of control, and quite possibly Darnley – who was badly shaken up and soon remorseful enough to be won round by Mary – had not expected his wife to be so close to the violence.[23] If Randolph was correct the unstable and jealous consort or his more experienced and cold-blooded father may have had thoughts of her as an adulteress who should be killed when planning the attack, but this is less likely.

Mary and Darnley were already at odds, but his agreement to his allies' insistence that he take part in the effective coup – they apparently left his dagger in Riccio's body to point out his guilt – inevitably caused their relations to deteriorate further once Mary had quick-wittedly charmed her unstable husband into helping her to escape from the plotters. Stories of Mary making pointed remarks during the escape about what she would do to her husband for his part in the murder may be hindsight or a fabrication by her enemies. In the aftermath of the attack on the evening of the 9th, the conspirators faced the arrival of a crowd of Edinburgh citizens alerted by the rumours of murder at the palace to rescue their queen and made Darnley call to them from the window to assure that all was in order and they should leave. Mary was told to keep quiet 'or else' and Lord Lindsay reputedly threatened to kill her if she did not obey. She allegedly had enough presence of mind and nerve to reproach Ruthven for his action as he sat down for a strong drink in her chamber after the murder, even if it was probably a later invention that she promised him that her baby would grow up to take vengeance on him. More practically, Ruthven's group's apparent other intended victims at the palace that evening as 'bad influences' on the queen – the Catholic Huntly and the Borders warlord Bothwell – had escaped the palace through the back windows during the murder and were available to flee Edinburgh, gather their men, and help the queen. Once the plotters had forced the queen to write a pardon for Moray and the others that had been ratified by Parliament next day (the 10th) their main political objective had been met, and from what Mary later told her 1580s secretary Nau they apparently intended to hold her captive at impregnable Stirling Castle until her baby had been born, and then put the latter on the throne. Darnley clearly felt remorse and/or severe shock, as he was allegedly (according to Mary) near-hysterical on the 10th as the conspirators' men kept a watchful eye on their royal captive(s) and was now won over by the quick-witted Mary to realise that his 'allies' were violent and untrustworthy thugs who had no obvious interest to make him king, and instead seizing power themselves and might well turn on him next. Moray was now recalled and arrived back in Edinburgh on Monday the 11th, and the queen gave him a welcome at Holyrood and seemed to be docilely submitting to the conspirators' direction. But Darnley then helped Mary to escape from Holyrood through an unguarded back door while the conspirators were celebrating Moray's group's return late on the evening of the 11th – and according to Mary they had to pass the freshly-dug grave where the murderers had dumped Riccio's body, at which Darnley expressed regret about how he had been tricked. Loyal courtiers, including Guard captain Lord Erskine, were waiting by the nearby abbey with horses on which they rode through the night to the safety of Dunbar Castle, twenty-five miles away. There Mary's allies including Bothwell assembled an army of their tenants to help her, and she was able to re-enter Edinburgh in triumph on 18 March and reassert her power. The conspirators fled – Morton, Lindsay, Ker and Ruthven to England – and were duly banished. Among those who had had some knowledge of the plot (presumably in advance) and approved of it even if they had not been involved and who now found it safer to retire

Piel Island, near Barrow in Furness, Cumbria. The Yorkist pretender 'Lambert Simnel' and his Irish-Swiss army landed here in 1487, and were joined by local rebel leader Sir Thomas Broughton. (© *David Dixon/Creative Commons*)

The battlefield of Stoke, 1487. The site of Simnel's defeat by Henry VII and the Earl of Oxford, at East Stoke near Newark on the River Trent. (© *Richard Croft/Creative Commons*)

The River Trent near the Stoke battlefield. This is where the Tudor army drove the fleeing Yorkists into the river, and Simnel's chief backer Lord Lovell was last seen swimming his horse across. But did he survive and hole up in Oxfordshire or not? (© *Trevor Rickard/Creative Commons*)

St. Michael's Mount. The second Yorkist pretender 'Perkin Warbeck' arrived here in 1497 to join in a Cornish tax-rebellion, but arrived too late and had to launch a separate one that had less support. He left his wife Lady Katherine Gordon here, but Henry VII captured them both and forced him to tell her he was a fake. (© *David Dixon/Creative Commons*)

Hever Castle,Kent. Childhood home of Anne Boleyn and her sister Mary, who both became entangled with their father's employer Henry VIII – Anne fatally. But was Anne a scheming manipulator or a sincere religious reformer? (© *Paul Gillett/Creative Commons*)

Great Hall, Hampton Court Palace. The main public room of the King's new 'showpiece' palace during Anne's reign, handed over by its owner Cardinal Wolsey. Henry lavished it with his and Anne's entwined heraldic emblems, which survive – an embarrassment for him after he had her executed for adultery. (© *Robert Lamb/Creative Commons*)

Tower Green and the Lieutenant's Lodgings, the Tower of London. The site of Anne's execution by an expert Calais swordsman – after she had watched her brother and other 'lovers' headless bodies being removed from nearby Tower Hill. (© *Pam Frey/Creative Commons*)

Church of St. Mary the Virgin, Oxford. Site of the burial of Queen Elizabeth's favourite Robert Dudley's wife Amy Robsart after she was found dead at the foot of some stairs in 1560. Robert was said to be impatient to be rid of her and she was in despair – but was it suicide or murder? (© *N Chadwick/ Creative Commons*)

The site of Cumnor Place, Oxfordshire , on the left next to the church. This is where Amy Robsart was found dead, with one of her husband's henchmen the only other person in the house – was the inquest a 'fix'? (© *Vieve Forward/Creative Commons*)

Temple Newsam house, Yorkshire – the childhood home of Mary Queen of Scots' second husband Lord Darnley. His mother Lady Margaret Douglas, Henry VIII's niece, brought him up as a staunch Catholic, but this spoilt rake was a less reliable enthusiast for the religion than his sponsors hoped. (© *Chris Heaton/Creative Commons*)

Holyrood Palace, Edinburgh. The site of the murder of Mary's Italian secretary David Rizzio in front of the pregnant Queen by a clique of embittered noblemen – but was her husband Darnley involved, and did this lead to his violent death? (© *David Dixon/Creative Commons*)

Hermitage Castle. A stronghold of Mary's thuggish third husband, the Borders ruffian Lord Bothwell. He and Mary holed up here after their shock marriage, and were besieged by an army of rebels which Darnley's family had organised. (© *David Gearing/Creative Commons*)

Lochleven Castle, on an island in Kinross. Mary escaped from here after her deposition to try to regain her throne – aided by the first of many romantic admirers, who had stolen the bungs from the bottom of her gaolers' boats. (© *Colin Park/Creative Commons*)

Tutbury Castle. One of Mary's main residences in northern England during her years of internment after her flight to seek Elizabeth's help in 1568. It was draughty and bleak and she complained about the smell of the drains. But was she plotting to overthrow Elizabeth herself, or was she still more interested in the Scots throne? (© *Richard Croft/Creative Commons*)

Wingfield Manor, Derbyshire. One of the more luxurious properties owned by Mary's gaolers, the earl and countess of Shrewsbury, where she resided under their guard from time to time. Mary found it like a palace – and her devoted admirer Anthony Babington stayed close by while he was drawing up his over-optimistic plan to rescue her. (© *Sam Styles/Creative Commons*)

The site of Mary's trial and execution in 1587, Fotheringay Castle, in the Fens. After her execution she was buried at nearby Peterborough Cathedral close to another royal Tudor victim, Catherine of Aragon. (© *Ian Simons/Creative Commons*)

to the country were Mary's devious secretary Maitland and the Catholic-hating Knox.[24]

Anyone with more sense than the vain, petulant, and not too intelligent Darnley would never have allowed themselves to become involved in this situation, whether jealous of the sophisticated if not handsome Italian secretary Riccio or not. The way he had helped his wife to escape was to his credit, but after this episode their relations deteriorated further. She had the sense to persuade the returned and pardoned Moray and his allies Glencairn and Argyll (head of the Campbells so with large number of armed Argyll tenantry) to reconcile with the young new Catholic leader Huntly (as lord of much of the north-east, in possession of an equally useful army of tenants) and the loyal and swashbuckingly daring Bothwell (in possession of a hardened Borders tenantry force). The only members of the March 1566 coup faction to be executed were insignificant junior thugs. (These were the under-sheriff of Perth, for taking charge of holding his queen captive in her palace on the rebels' orders so he had committed treason, and a retainer who had killed a Catholic priest during the attack.) But dealing with Darnley and his father Lennox was more difficult, and it appears that he may have denied agreeing an illegal 'bond' with his allies to use the coup to get him the 'Crown Matrimonial' – at any rate Mary did not mention this detail in her story of the coup sent to Archbishop Beaton on 2 April. Whether or not he confessed later – she told Nau in the 1580s that he had admitted it – the exiled plotters now sent her a copy of the 'bond' to make sure she knew how deeply he had been involved, and this may have revived her bitterness at his role in the murder. A story reached Ambassador Randolph in April that Mary's recent sending of an envoy to the pope was connected to her anger at her husband's role (implying that she may have been seeking a 'divorce' without affecting their child's legitimacy as an heir), but this may be gossip.

Birth of an heir: a 'game-changer' as now Darnley is expendable (and to a degree so is Mary)

The next crucial event was the birth of Mary's child which would secure the succession, though this had its own problems for Mary and for Darnley – with an heir available, her foes could plan to overthrow her and install the baby as a puppet-ruler and she could rid herself of Darnley as he had done his job as a 'stud'. The idea of her child being used to replace her and secure a controllable regency could appeal not only to her Protestant foes – now presumably led by the exiled Morton as Ruthven was too ill, but for the moment minus Moray who had had his lands and position at court restored – but to a concerned Elizabeth and her ultra-Protestant ministers led by Cecil. Mary's son and heir James (the future King James VI of Scotland and I of England) was duly born on 19 June 1566 at Edinburgh Castle, and proved to be healthy, despite the trauma his mother had suffered during the pregnancy. (There is however a possibility that the latter had affected the child, given his future extreme sense of insecurity.)

According to some accounts of the birth, Mary made references to the Riccio murder and how near she and her child had come to death as a group of important nobles and foreign ambassadors were shown the prince, mentioning Darnley's betraying her in a bitter manner to the English representative Sir William Stanley. Darnley protested that she had said she had forgiven him and she agreed to let it pass, but it clearly still rankled. She then notably presented the baby to his father in public proclaiming that she swore to God that he was the father, which reflected the continuing fear that the paranoid Darnley would not believe the latter.[25] Over the next few months, the husband and wife spent less and less time together, and Mary was supposed to be spending suspiciously large amounts of time with the demonstrably loyal and usefully militarily powerful – but reckless – Bothwell. The latter had recently married again – to Jean Gordon, the usefully rich sister of the queen's new ally the earl of Huntly – but was known to be a man of restless sexual appetites and few scruples who had many mistresses, and Mary's name was duly linked to his. At the time, the impropriety of her frequent private ventures out of her palace in ordinary clothes with minimal attendance by a few faithful servants to mingle with her friends was more clear than any sexual motives, though both were reported and the disapproving Bedford (not an unbiased witness) mentioned both.[26] Her father-in-law Lennox's subsequent account of events had it that her visit to Stirling a month after the prince's birth, to install him at the usual residence for the Scots heir in the impregnable castle, was a 'cover' for her unseemly lust for Bothwell and for planning her revenge on her husband, and he added for good measure that she behaved in an unseemly manner whilst there by taking part in public dancing in the marketplace. But he was not exactly unbiased, and was writing bitterly with hindsight after Darnley's death with a view to implicating her and Bothwell as luridly as possible in the murder. At the least he exaggerated and misinterpreted events with hostile intent, as indeed do most of our main sources for the forthcoming crises of 1566–7 (most to implicate and fewer to exonerate the queen). The truth is hidden in a fog of 'spin', hindsight, and self-justification by participants in the drama and their backers.

As with Mary's increasingly frequent 'holiday' ventures out of Edinburgh for private visits and hunting, a desire to escape the strictures of court life and get away from the scenes of her recent traumas are more probable than any supposed 'torrid affair with Bothwell'. Her political wisdom must, however, be doubted, given what often hostile observers were bound to say, and this is particularly the case with her sudden and 'out of the way' visit to see Bothwell at isolated Hermitage Castle in the Borders when he was very ill that October. She rode for many hours across rough country from Borthwick Castle to see him, though this may have been due to a practical desire to avoid an overnight stop in somewhere uncomfortable, and after checking that he was not in danger she rode back again in a equal hurry and collapsed at Jedburgh. A serious illness followed, centred on a pain in her side and high temperature, with no obvious cause, though extreme stress from her hard journey and her anxieties about her marriage and a possible coup are plausible. The Venetian ambassador heard that it was due to anxiety over her husband's suspicious withdrawal to a distance from her court and what he might be up to; her detractor Buchanan's later history put it down to sexual exertions with Bothwell – who was in fact bedridden and had to come to check on her condition at Jedburgh by litter. The most that Mary's exertions to see Bothwell at his remote castle in the hills and then to get back to 'civilization' without proper rest, suggests some degree of concern about his condition (and hence at least a degree of emotional attachment?) Plus a degree of stress and rashness, but in fact a contemporary French account as well as her own later defender Nau wrote that she had been advised by her councillors to check on the current state of the unruly Borders with Bothwell in case this mainstay of their defence died and left chaos behind. After her fall, her detractors Buchanan (her son's tutor and the era's main historian) and Knox both wrote that her action had been committed out of immoral lust for Bothwell, as usual seeking out the worst interpretation – and the further back Mary's 'adultery' could be traced, the stronger the case by her 1567 deposers (these books' sponsors) for alleging she had killed Darnley and removing her.[27] If anyone was causing her to over react and make unwise decisions at the time, it was her moody and erratic husband not a lover. Given her apparent bouts of ill-health and sudden and serious physical collapses, e.g. at Jedburgh, intermingled with manic energy and erratic decisions, it is possible that psychological strain from coping with the bloody and treacherous activities at the Scots court was exacerbated by a physical ailment. Suggestions have been made in recent decades that she suffered from porphyria or an allied complaint which was passed down through the Stuarts to the Georgian monarchs and even to the erratic and emotional Queen Victoria.

In the meantime, the evidently not fully reconciled Moray and other Protestant lords began to work on the anger and jealousy of the sidelined Darnley and, as with Riccio earlier, to use him for their own advancement by claiming that his adulterous wife was pursuing Bothwell and denying her husband his legal rights as co-ruler. Certainly, their mutual alienation was apparent by the time that Mary and her intimates took a holiday in rural Alloa without Darnley in August and he turned up to be snubbed and leave angrily. His increasing drinking and self-pitying outbursts to his entourage added to the problem, and enabled Mary's foes to work on his anger and possibly to encourage him to stage another coup – though at this stage it is unclear what they intended and whether England was involved too. Alternatively, he was reported by the French embassy to be considering leaving the country in secret, presumably given his 'contacts' for England and with the intention of causing his foreign supporters to invade Scotland on his behalf. At this point Darnley's anger was clearly unfocussed and capable of turning on anyone he fancied who was closer to his wife and/or undermining him, as he became violently jealous of Moray after Mary showed favour to the latter; he threatened to kill Moray and when he told his wife he would do this she told him not to be so stupid and showed him that his fears about the relationship were ridiculous. According to Lennox, Mary also suggested to Darnley that he find a mistress to amuse himself as she would not sleep with him.

When the ceremonial baptism of Prince James took place, Mary showed her loyalty to her faith and her long-term political aims – and her naivity? – by insisting on having a Catholic ceremony, which naturally aroused the hostility of the English ambassador, the Protestant earl of Bedford, and assorted invited Scots nobles who had to wait outside the church. The godfathers were the king of France (her teen-age 'hard-line' Catholic brother-in-law Charles IX, later perpetrator of the St Bartholomew's Day Massacre in 1572) and the duke of Savoy – and Darnley did not attend but spent the day sulking in his apartments. Worse, the Savoyard envoy De Croc (the deputy of the formal ambassador who had not yet arrived) refused to come and see him as requested, implying that as his wife was now treating him slightingly he was of no political use to him.[28] This shows that a publicly-known breach was evident well before Christmas 1566, and Darnley's friendliness to overseas Catholic ambassadors was not coincidental either – he was seeking foreign Catholic support. Accordingly, on 13 November the Spanish ambassador in London, De Silva, wrote to Philip II that Mary's arriving envoy Wilson had told him that Mary had heard that Darnley had written to Philip, Charles IX of France, Mary's ultra-Catholic uncle the Cardinal of Lorraine, and the pope, assuring that unlike his wife he was a solid and trustable defender of the faith.[29] This would logically have been with a coup in mind and shows that Mary was right to fear what he was up to, though given his mixture of laziness, fecklessness, recklessness, and ignorance he was far from a capable organiser so serious plans may be doubted.

The royal breach worsened, and on a visit to Craigmillar on 20 October, Mary was apparently advised by a cabal of trusted courtiers (including Bothwell, Moray, secretary Maitland, and Huntly) to divorce Darnley, but she refused. This episode shows that at this point both leading Protestant and leading Catholic peers regarded Darnley as a liability and now Mary had an heir they wanted to be rid of him, and that Mary – temporarily? – backed out of doing anything decisive about it.[30] From what Buchanan was told, around 1 November Mary received an alarming letter from or about Darnley that caused her to have an emotional outburst in which she told Moray, Maitland and Huntly that unless she could be rid of Darnley somehow, she regarded her life as not worth living and had a mind to kill herself.[31] Buchanan used this as 'evidence' that her resolution to this dilemma was to plan to kill Darnley instead, stimulated by her lust for Bothwell, but this interpretation was deliberately malicious, even assuming that the incident actually occurred – the three witnesses were all mixed up in the shady events of Darnley's murder and the first two of the three then joined in her overthrow. As ambassador Du Croc reckoned it, there was an impasse in late 1566 as she resented Darnley's mixture of arrogantly demanding respect and his rights – which he would not abate and so reassure her – and feared that any noble who visited him must be plotting with him, but she had not decided on any action. She was too depressed to offer the attendant nobles a 'lead' and arrange a way out of the problem, and this was the situation in which the latter began to plan ridding Scotland of Darnley themselves by the 'Craigmillar Bond' (see below).

Mary did not offer any degree of public reconciliation with Darnley either (however false this would have been) by resuming living with him and so keeping an eye on his activities, and so stoked up his own paranoia. Darnley turned up to see her at Craigmillar but was sent back to Stirling with her clearly unwilling to tolerate his presence. According to her long-term ally Lord Herries' later account, Moray was keen to see the breach widen as if Darnley was removed he, as the queen's nearest male kin, stood a better chance of being the power behind the throne if Mary was removed.[32] Conversely, if the breach continued amidst rumours that Mary's adulterous affair with Bothwell – a 'loose cannon' who Moray could not trust to work with him – was behind it the lords, the church and the public would call Mary a whore, which would make deposing her easier. Moray was duly backed up by his unscrupulous ally Morton, a family foe of Darnley's mother Lady Margaret, and the two of them encouraged the vain and ambitious Bothwell to think that if Darnley was removed then he would be Mary's natural choice as her next husband. In fact, they planned to betray him too. This explanation of events and presentation of Moray – as events turned out, the leader of the regency for James once Mary was deposed – as the mastermind of a sinister plot in winter 1566–7 to remove Darnley, Mary, and Bothwell in turn and seize power for himself is logical, but it must be asked how much it owes to hindsight.

Darnley, based at Stirling, had made a brief visit to his wife at Jedburgh at the end of October when he heard that she was ill – not as hastily and devotedly as Buchanan and Knox later claimed, but within a day or two of hearing of her condition. He did, however, leave Jedburgh quickly, and subsequent events suggest that he was at the least annoyed (at not being wanted there?) and possibly he was angry at how close Mary and Bothwell were. He now went to stay with his father Lennox in Glasgow, was detained there by illness (possibly exacerbated by the effects of his recent heavy drinking), and in the New Year had a bout of the 'pox' which delayed him further. Mary stayed in Stirling with her son until 20 January when she returned to Edinburgh, but on the 24th she set out for Glasgow to see and hopefully collect her husband. She took along a horse-litter, apparently so he could have a more comfortable journey back to Edinburgh than on horseback if he was still weak. He allegedly made some sardonic comments that he would rather it was Hermitage Castle and he was Bothwell as then she would have come quicker and with more enthusiasm, but agreed to go with her. They duly set out for Edinburgh on the 26th or 27th, arriving on the 30th or 31st. The fact that Darnley did agree to accompany her, and he suggested going straight to Edinburgh whereas she would have preferred him to stay at nearby Craigmillar Castle, argues for her innocence of any murderous intent and his lack of suspicion of such. Once the breach with Mary had occurred, and husband and wife started to live apart with the presence of an heir meaning that the husband was no longer vital to the succession, any senior Scots peer with a degree of self-preservation and suspicion who was in Darnley's position, would not have run the risk of returning to Edinburgh at all, or at least without an omnipresent armed guard. It might be beyond normal probability that his wife would kill him, but he had other enemies (including members of the Riccio murder-plot who he had betrayed, e.g. Morton) who in winter 1566–7 were intent on removing him from the political scene. Given the usual parameters of Scots politics, this meant a murder-plot was quite possible and the existence of a rival monarch in the person of Mary's son James meant that ambitious nobles who could not trust either Mary or Darnley to act as their puppets could remove both of them, crown James, and have the luxury of a long regency to govern the country. Even if Herries' later account of what Moray was up to is inaccurate or guesswork, other characters now had equal reason to destroy either Darnley or both him and Mary.

The nature of Mary's collusion with the plotting of Darnley's enemies at Craigmillar Castle at the end of November 1566 have been hopelessly muddied by the partisan accounts of all the 'witnesses', Mary's account being intended to acquit her of complicity in murder. Her allies Huntly and Argyll's 1569 'Protestation' account (drawn up in England at her residence for them to sign at her request to exonerate her conduct, but intercepted *en route* to Scotland by Cecil's spies) was similar in intent, and was also aimed at implicating their then foes Moray and Morton; the murderers' account of events was intended to incriminate her and justify her removal. Once she was deposed as queen the following summer, the accusation of her murdering Darnley served as an important part of the indictment and so all partisans of the new government had a reason to avoid exonerating her. All parties, it is agreed, wanted her to be rid of Darnley as consort. According to the 'Protestation', it was Moray and secretary Maitland who first suggested a divorce to Argyll and Huntly during a morning call on them in their bedchamber. Argyll did not know how they could be sure to succeed in ridding the queen of Darnley, and Maitland told him 'We shall find the means well enough to make her quit of him, so that you and my Lord of Huntly shall only behold the matter' i.e. not have to do anything. The pair agreed to the proposal without enquiring what exactly Maitland meant, and they all took the idea to Bothwell, as a means to win Mary's favour and so get her to pardon their allies the remaining March 1566 coup exiles. They all agreed on this; then the queen was asked to help. She agreed to a divorce, provided the terms of this did not affect her son's right to the throne – an annulment would make the entire marriage illegal and James a bastard. (If he was not to succeed, that would improve the chances of Moray, one of the Hamiltons, or even Darnley as Margaret Douglas' son taking the throne.) In canon law, the other legal means of rendering the marriage invalid would have been that the papal dispensation for Mary and Darnley, as cousins, to marry had not arrived until after the wedding – but in that case also, James would have been bastardised.

It seems likely that Mary was concerned with a divorce or, failing that, some 'other means' (a term first used by Maitland) that would be ratifiable by Parliament – which would not apply to killing Darnley unless he could be indicted for treason. She requested their help in acquiring this imprecisely named means of removing Darnley, and Maitland promised that if she left it to them the method used would be duly ratified. She did not enquire further beyond insisting that the methods must not reflect on her honour or conscience (which would seem to imply a veto on murder which they ignored), and granted the plotters' request to pardon Morton and other exiles from the Riccio murder-plot. Morton thus signed the 'Craigmillar Bond' later than the other plotters, on his return home; Moray did not sign and according to Maitland had said he would 'look through his fingers at' the method his colleagues chose to remove Darnley, not take part in it himself. If the above account of the meetings at Craigmillar are reliable, the plot – and the careful avoidance of mentioning what was actually to happen to Darnley – was the original brainchild of either Moray or Maitland, and the latter took the lead. (The unreliable account by Buchanan in 1569 has it that Mary suggested a divorce and someone told her that this would have to be an annulment that would bastardise James, causing her to drop the idea.) But so far any suggestion of murder was '*sotto voce*', and Argyll and Huntly might have suspected this as only as a last resort if divorce could not be achieved. Legally, a king could not be convicted of treason so Darnley's murder could not be legalised as execution for treason by Parliament later, and that implied that killing him would breach Mary's insistence on Parliamentary ratification of the method chosen. Bothwell was more ruthless (or practical) than those nobles who chose not to enquire too deeply into what was intended.

The 'Bond' and its full list of signatures has not survived, but according to Bothwell's arrested henchman John Hepburn of Bolton Bothwell had shown it to him (i.e. before his flight abroad after the battle of Carberry Hill) and fellow-henchman James Ormiston told a priest its contents as he was about to be executed. He named the signatories as Maitland, Huntly, Argyll, Bothwell, and Sir James Balfour, but these were all safely dead or in disgrace with the current regime at this point (1573) and he did not even name Moray, so his word must be doubted. In December 1567 Bothwell's retainer John Hepburn named Balfour as probably being behind the 'Bond' but not having signed it (a detail that was omitted from the published record of the accused's confessions), and Ormiston claimed that as a lawyer Balfour drew the document up. Mary later told Nau that Bothwell had handed her a document before he fled at Carberry Hill and told her that it contained the signatures of his fellow-conspirators in the murder which proved that he had not acted alone as they were claiming; this was presumably the 'Bond'. The likeliest explanation for its disappearance is that as it implicated so many leading nobles in the post-

1567 regime, and contradicted their planned 'narrative' of the murder. they took it from Mary when she was captured and destroyed it. Assuming that she knew of the plot to rid her of her husband – which fitted in with the divorce the Craigmillar group had been urging on her – but not of its violent intentions, she may well have expected that some legal device or kidnap was planned. What is unknown is if she suspected they might kill Darnley and, like Moray, turned a blind eye to the possibility. But if she did insist at Craigmillar on Parliamentary ratification and nothing that would offend her conscience she did, in effect, veto murder on at least one occasion. Her role was to bring Darnley to Edinburgh, which would prevent him from either plotting revolt or fleeing abroad, quite apart from making him available for murder; her supporters were able to argue that her intention was the former, not the latter. But quite apart from assessments of Mary's character and whether the devout queen would have risked committing a major 'sin' by taking no steps to make sure that her helpers would spare her unwanted husband's life, it made no sense to act physically against Darnley (murder or exile?) unless a divorce-plan had already been blocked by his family or the church.

In December 1566, Darnley was relatively safe in his family stronghold of Glasgow, near his father's earldom of Lennox, and surrounded by family retainers, and was plausibly rumoured to be – sporadically? – plotting against his wife again, presenting himself as a potential Catholic champion to the pope and Philip II. Around the new year De Silva in London was told that information had come from Paris to King Philip's aunt and regent in the Netherlands, Duchess Margaret of Parma, that Darnley was plotting to put his son James on the throne as his puppet. There is also the matter of a warning delivered to the queen by a man called Shaw shortly before the killing (according to Nau, who Mary presumably told this) that one of Ruthven's worst ruffians involved in the attack on Riccio, Kerr of Fawdonside who had waved a gun at her stomach, was back in Scotland boasting of an immanent change in affairs at court.[34] This may imply that Darnley was engaged in his own plot and had hopes of replacing his wife with his son as sovereign, with himself as regent backed by international Catholic troops – though his immaturity and lack of political skills make it implausible that he could ever have run a coup effectively. (Could his father have acted for him in staging a revolt?) He and Lennox had also been warned by an agent/retainer of his family who was used to collect intelligence, William Hiegait, that Mary had considered having him arrested and imprisoned and that her nobles had gone to her with a plan to have him arrested and if he resisted, killed, but she had stopped them (presumably a garbled account of the Craigmillar meeting). Hiegait was called before the council after his story about the 'Darnley plot' was betrayed to the queen by his friend William Walker, and denied it all – and this occurred before Darnley's return to Edinburgh so Mary had reason to fear him and take drastic action. Yet, he consented to come to Edinburgh to complete his convalescence after a bout of 'pox' that was probably measles or, as Nau and the English ambassador Bedford assumed, smallpox. His enemies, like Bothwell, said syphilis, and a 1928 examination of his remains by pathologist Sir Daniel Wilson confirmed odd pits in his skull that were consistent with the disease – in which case his deteriorating condition might have partly caused his erratic and paranoid behaviour. Ironically, if he did have syphilis he might have soon been too ill to pose a threat to his wife or his noble rivals and died within a few years, so saving his enemies from the risky plot to kill him.

Darnley returned to Edinburgh without armed protection which would imply that he trusted Mary with his security. He had complained of the ill-will shown to him by herself and assorted lords and made vague references to the 'Craigmillar Bond' plot in their tense interview in Glasgow on 23 January, before he agreed to return with them so he was clearly fearful – as was Mary who at the same interview asked about the Hiegait story of his plotting and the rumours that he planned to flee to England by ship. It appears, however, that both of them were satisfied with the other's explanations on that occasion, and had some sort of reconciliation which led Darnley to underestimate the threat that others still posed to him. (The 'reconciliation' theory is backed up by accounts of this agreement by an independent French agent, Seigneur de Clernault, as well as by the less trustable accounts of Lennox and of Darnley's servant Crawford who wanted to blacken Mary's name).[35] Not to accept her request or to travel with armed retainers would have been expected of someone less naïve however 'insulting' either measure would be to his wife. If either had happened, the chances of his enemies smuggling a large quantity of gunpowder into his residence and exploding it undetected would have been small.

The house at which he chose to stay on the outskirts of Edinburgh, the former provost's residence at the dissolved collegiate church of St Mary-In-The-Field, known as 'Kirk O'Field', was part of a quadrangle of buildings open to easy outside access and he did not take any armed guards there. This was a serious mistake on his part, but shows his trust in his wife who had been acting in an unusually friendly manner during her visit to Glasgow in order to make sure he came with her to Edinburgh. He had apparently heard a rumour of the events at Craigmillar, as seen above; his wife's refusal to agree to the suggestions of arresting or killing him duly reassured him that she did not have hostile intentions or intended violence (as testified to later by his servant Crawford). But rumours that a plot against him was underway, though Mary had refused to assist it, had reached the Spanish ambassador De Silva in London by his letter to Philip II of 18 January, and Darnley's lack of precautions against attack by one or more of his lordly rivals is surprising. Had he had bodyguards, even the boldest plotter might have hesitated about removing him by dumping a pile of gunpowder in a ground floor room under his bedchamber and blowing up the house. This is not to say that the Mary-Darnley marriage would have lasted beyond spring 1567 but for the murder, however, the chances are that Mary was determined on divorce if at all possible, which may explain apparent unspecified overtures to Archbishop Hamilton of Glasgow that midwinter. Another interesting and possibly significant detail of the rumours circulating in Europe just before the murder is that on 27 January, Archbishop Hamilton in Paris wrote to Mary to warn her that the Spanish ambassador Alava had told him that she was in danger from some unclear source – which may reflect the interpretation of the murder-plot as a plan to ruin her reputation by making it appear that she was involved in the assassination.

The murder

The events surrounding the choice of Darnley' s destination make it clear that she did not lure him to his death at Kirk O'Field, a small and isolated house on the outskirts of the capital suitable either for convalescence from an infectious disease or for murder. The house had been granted by Mary in December to Robert Balfour, brother of leading plotter and murder suspect Sir James Balfour, but as she did not choose it for her husband's residence this was clearly not part of a plot to isolate him ready for the assassins to act. Her choice for Darnley's residence was Craigmillar Castle, which he refused, and once he was at Edinburgh the choice of Kirk O Field was his. Bothwell's retainer, John Hepburn, significantly claimed later that Darnley's choice was guided by Sir James Balfour, which may suggest that the latter was the mastermind behind the choice of site for the killing as convenient for himself to smuggle in the gunpowder from his house next door. Paris, the page named the source of the idea as Maitland, also a lead contender for the organiser of the killing, and Nau later claimed that Darnley had warned Mary against Maitland's real intentions towards her and the necessity for the pair of them to beware the troublemakers who wishes to divide them on the evening of 7 February, shortly before he was killed.[36] If Nau is correct that he also promised to name the latter, this might have encouraged any plotter who was tipped off about the conversation to act quickly.

The mysterious events of the night of 8–9 February have been explored exhaustively ever since, but the basic details and 'timeline' of what happened as it involved Darnley and Mary are generally agreed; what is unclear is motives and the identities and movements of the killers. The subsequent official history of the incident, the 'Book of Articles'by George Buchanan, containing the results of the investigation of the crime carried out during the legal enquiry into it when Mary had fled to England in 1568 and been detained by Elizabeth – in effect Mary's 'trial' – cannot be trusted. Both the regency regime for James VI then in power in Edinburgh (led by Buchanan's employer Moray) and the investigating Elizabethan government had reasons to blacken Mary's name and keep her out of power in Scotland. If she was acquitted Elizabeth had no obvious reason to continue detaining her in England; if she was either found guilty or kept under a cloud of suspicion Elizabeth could claim that it was her duty to her own 'honour' not to allow or assist Mary to return to her throne. Blackening her name would excuse the action of the power-hungry junta led by Moray in deposing her – but this is not to say that all the 'evidence' was faked and a totally innocent. Bothwell was framed for a murder he had not committed. Modern rival theories about the responsibility for the explosion include one suggestion (by General R.H. Mahon in his *Indictment of Mary Queen of Scots*, 1923) that Darnley intended to murder one of his rivals by luring them into the house and blowing it up and/or (as suggested by R. Gore-Brown in *Lord Bothwell*, 1935) was detected and punished for his plot by Bothwell who set off the explosives early. Darnley had intended to flee the house with plenty of time and leave a rival to perish, but was caught in his own trap.

Mary's own knowledge of the plan, let alone her assistance in it, is unlikely given her actions at the time. Darnley moved in on Saturday 1 February, with furnishings supplied by Mary from Holyrood Palace, and she slept at the house on the night of the 5th-6th, in a room on the ground floor under his bedchamber. Otherwise she was as usual resident at Holyrood but she visited her husband regularly, and on the 7th, Darnley apparently confided in her that he had heard of plots against him which he begged her not to listen to and also said that he had himself been advised to have her killed. This may be correct, or reflect a literary attempt by the story's recorder (the pro-Moray and rabidly Protestant Buchanan) to present Darnley as a sympathetic figure, an unworldly and pacific victim of evil plotters led by his wife. Sir James Balfour later told the official enquiry (as recorded by the 'Book of Articles') that he only found out about the plot on the 7th. Morton admitted in his confession after his arrest in 1581 that he had been told of it shortly before the event by Archibald Douglas which may also point to this day, and John Hay of Tullo told the enquiry that Bothwell told him that Darnley was to be killed on the 7th and that Darnley's death was the only way to save himself.[37] (This might seem to hint at Bothwell fearing vengeance from the paranoid and unstable husband of the woman with whom he was having an affair and so acting first, meaning a personal not exclusively political motive, but the evidence is unreliable.) The murder was supposedly planned for the 7th but had to be postponed as preparations, presumably meaning installing the gunpowder, were not complete. There was also a suggestion that the original plan had been for the implicated nobles to send a posse of their chosen servants. selected to involve all of them via their employees so nobody could back out or claim ignorance. to murder Darnley in the nearby fields, presumably after kidnapping him.[38] The explosion may thus have served to enable more canny or nervous participants to hide their involvement – so did they suggest this form of murder to Bothwell? John Hepburn claimed to the enquiry that his employer Bothwell had chosen the means of murder so as to hide his own involvement – possibly in case Mary turned on him as she had turned on the men who murdered Riccio. Other evidence, by Mary's page Paris, may have been forced out of him by torture and so been 'planted' by the investigators to blacken Bothwell's name; this claimed that Bothwell (his own former and abusive employer) had lured Paris aside at Kirk O'Field while Mary was there a few days before the killing and bullied him into assisting as his duty to help his mistress rid herself of her unstable and dangerous husband.[39]

The day before the attack, Saturday 8 February, an English spy in Edinburgh wrote to Cecil in London that Mary's sojourn with Darnley the previous evening had involved him telling her that he had been warned by her half-brother Robert Stewart, illegitimate son of James V (and hence half-brother to Moray as well), that if he did not move from Kirk O'Field quickly he would be killed. Mary then apparently summoned Robert to question him on the Saturday, but he denied the story fiercely (or in a panic lest he be silenced by his conspirator friends for betraying them?). Darnley, Moray, and Bothwell were witnesses of this, and Buchanan also referred to this incident in his biased and lurid account, alleging that Darnley and Robert confronted each other and drew their swords but were restrained. Buchanan cannot be trusted, and neither can the account of the page Paris that Mary incited the confrontation in the hope that the skilled swordsman Robert would kill Darnley – who was probably too weak from his illness to fight in reality – in a duel. If the account preserves any truth (and Robert Stewart was quick to retreat to his new lands on Orkney after the 1567 crises as if fearing he was in danger), Darnley, and Mary, would now have been aware that there was something dangerous going on. Mary does not seem to have become worried, but the incident may explain why Darnley's servant was more alert than usual afterwards and so spotted the sinister figures out in the garden a few minutes before the explosion.

A few hours before the attack, on Sunday 9 February, Mary and her courtiers rode from Holyrood to the house so she could spend the evening with Darnley, who was due to leave for the palace next day. While they were with him the conspirators, possibly led by Bothwell, were piling up gunpowder in a room on the ground floor ready to blow up the house. Lennox later claimed that the house had been mined for days before Darnley moved in, but in fact this is impossible as the choice of residence was made by Darnley himself at short notice. Paris, the page, claimed that Mary ordered him to move out of the room where the gunpowder was to be piled up, i.e. that she knew what was to happen there, but his evidence to the anti-Marian regime after June 1567 was both 'forced' and contradictory. Paris also claimed that Mary had the keys to the rooms at Kirk O'Field so he was ordered by Bothwell to acquire those needed to carry out the explosion beforehand; in fact Darnley's surviving servant Thomas Nelson, who would have known the situation, said that Darnley's household had them. The 'official' story about a heap of loose gunpowder is dubious; this would not have caused such a large blast if it had ignited at all. The explosion in fact demolished the house, suggesting a concentrated charge placed in the centre of the ground floor ready to blow the walls down. Moray had left Edinburgh that day to allegedly visit his pregnant wife, which seemed sinister in retrospect as if he was keeping clear of the scene of the crime which he knew was about to occur. Bothwell, Argyll, Huntly, Maitland, and the thuggish young Catholic Lord Cassilis were all in Mary's party at Kirk O'Field. Mary had intended to stay the night, but was reminded that she had promised to return to Holyrood to attend the wedding-masque of her French valet Bastian and left some time between nine and eleven o'clock. Bothwell was among those who did the reminding; a Captain Cockburn wrote to Cecil later that Maitland and Bastian had been responsible. Buchanan typically assumed that the story of her intending to stay the night was an alibi to cover her 'coincidental not deliberate' departure and make it appear that she had nearly been killed too so she could not have been the perpetrator of the attack. As she left, she reproached her page Paris, one of Bothwell's helpers, for his dirty face and clothes – which were due to the gunpowder he had been handling so she evidently did not know what he was up to.[40] This confirms that Paris was definitely involved in the plot, though his later statement as to what occurred and who hired him (i.e. Bothwell alone) was 'forced' and so probably left out some facts embarrassing to senior regime figures in 1567–8.

In the early hours of the following morning, the house exploded. At least three of Darnley's servants, possibly more, had been killed though one (Thomas Nelson) was blown clear of the house by the explosion and survived to give an account of Darnley's last hours. Some local women later confirmed that they had seen at least eleven men running down the street a minute or two after the explosion, though it is unclear if these were the men who set the explosives or those who caught Darnley when he tried to escape. Darnley and his attendant Taylor were found dead a couple of hours later in their nightclothes in the orchard outside, apparently caught and strangled while trying to escape. They had a chair and a rope with them, as when they had run for their lives they had had to get out of the house through an upper window from the gallery adjacent to Darnley's bedroom onto the adjacent town wall and thence climb down into the orchard. The killers were identified as a party of Douglases from a nearby house, kinsmen of Morton who Darnley had betrayed over the Riccio murder (and who had not been invited to the party at Kirk O'Field the previous evening so he had an alibi). Darnley had presumably seen the murderers lurking outside the house and believed they had come to kill him more conventionally. According to later statements by local residents, he had been heard begging for mercy as they caught him.[41] The 'whitewash' of the resulting official enquiry, which cleared Bothwell to the murder-victim's father Lennox's fury, and the subsequent blackening of Bothwell's name once he was safely exiled, have muddied the waters concerning the facts.

It is far from clear that Bothwell was the only, or the principal, murderer and all his nine supposed accomplices were his own retainers so expendable as far as the other lords involved were concerned. The 'anti-Bothwell' evidence from one of them, William Powrie, his porter, that these lackeys brought the gunpowder publicly through the streets in barrels carried on horseback from Bothwell's apartments at Holyrood is unlikely, as for one thing the decision to blow up the house was not supposed to have been taken until the 7th and somehow Bothwell had had the gunpowder all brought from Dunbar in two days, had it carried into Holyrood Palace, and stored in his lodgings without any enquiries, and then had it carried openly to Kirk O'Field. Nor did Powrie stick to his story as to details, changing his initial account of one journey through the streets with the gunpowder all piled in one trunk or barrel on each of two horses to two journeys involving one horse. He and his crony Pat Wilson, a dubious merchant who helped Bothwell conduct illicit love-affairs, then took the empty trunk back to Holyrood on horseback along the same route, arriving as the queen's party was leaving the palace for Kirk O'Field at around eight or nine that evening. If Bothwell was supposed to be keeping his involvement secret, it was surely risky to use men known to be his retainers for any open transfer of goods on horseback through the streets – and one or two trunkloads of gunpowder were too little to blow up the entire house, as happened.[42] When the earl of Morton was arrested in 1581 he was accused of mining the cellars of the house at Kirk O'Field; by this time he was in disgrace so expendable and this cannot be trusted as in any case he was banished from Edinburgh as of early 1567, but he cannot be ruled out as a suspect if only acting by proxy. Also, the villains would have had to transport the gunpowder past the sentries at the Holyrood Palace gates and at the Netherbow Port (the gate out of the walled city to the suburb where Kirk O'Field was situated), plus assorted members of the 'Watch' on patrol in the streets, and somehow none of these men noticed or stopped them. How did they, or their supposedly efficient employer, know they would not be stopped, or that these witnesses would not report on their identity later and get them arrested? The Bothwell lackeys' story also has them meeting with Bothwell near the murder-site to confirm the procedure of the attack during the late afternoon or early evening when in fact other, and more reliable witnesses, have Bothwell at a banquet given by the Savoyard ambassador Count Moretta from around four that afternoon to seven in the evening – and nobody later came forward to confirm seeing Bothwell in the streets near Kirk O'Field around this time. The dodgy story of the gunpowder's removal indeed raises the possibility that the lackeys, though implicated in the killing, were also lying about Bothwell himself being there – though this is more uncertain. The Balfour brothers could more easily have moved a larger quantity of gunpowder from Sir James' house next-door, whether or not Bothwell's associates helped them. Indeed Sir James was pardoned by the 1567 regency regime so they had to avoid implicating him, and the English ambassador heard that he had in fact purchased a large quantity of gunpowder before the murder. The 'Holyrood gunpowder store ' claim was also alleged by the arrested page Paris, who no doubt was 'persuaded' by the regency to implicate their enemies Bothwell and Mary to the full. But it was unlikely that even a notorious risk-taking hothead like Bothwell either risked taking the gunpowder openly through the streets or, later as he allegedly headed from the palace after the queen's masque there to Kirk O'Field to set off the explosives, went openly along the main street between them (the Canongate) and identified himself to an enquiring watchman.[43] This detail was probably added by his enemies to definitively put him on the scene of the crime.

That Bothwell was involved seems probable, and those minor figures who were indicted for the explosion were his kinsmen and lackeys. The only detail of the lackeys' later account of the 'run-up' to the killing that was confirmed independently was that a party of around eleven of them walked up the Blackfriars Wynd towards the site of the murder before getting into the house to light the fuse. Several local residents (led by Mrs Merton) said that they had seen a party of this number at this time. If Bothwell's men were indeed there, then they were presumably acting on his orders and probably he was there too – though their 'confessions' may have left out the truth that they were there to help the Balfours move the gunpowder from the adjoining house or that someone else lit the fuse. Lennox's version of events has it that there were sixty men involved in the attack and Cecil heard that there had been thirty – though they were not named this number probably included the party of Douglases who ended up strangling Darnley and his servant after they escaped.

One version which reached the English had it that Bothwell and his men murdered Darnley and his servant in their beds and then took the bodies out of the house (why?). A more plausible version by his servant John Hepburn, apparently told to a fellow-prisoner who gave evidence at the annulment of the Mary/Bothwell marriage in France in 1576, had it that Bothwell lit the fuse from a distance and was about to investigate why the house had not blown up on time when the explosion occurred.[44] Ironically, as Sheriff of Edinburgh, he had the judicial duty of dealing with the bodies and instigating the first enquiry. This was suspiciously slow in coming to any conclusion or even questioning those who were rumoured to be involved, and angry members of the public put up placards naming suspects (a recently imported French custom), the first on 16 February naming Bothwell and Balfour plus David Chalmers (a friend of Bothwell's and witness at his wedding to Lady Jean Gordon, and accused by Buchanan of assisting Bothwell and Mary's adulterous meetings in autumn 1566), and 'Black John' Spens (Mary's lawyer), with Mary as an accomplice. Mary's foreign servants, including Riccio's brother, were later accused too. As reported by ambassador De Silva in London to Philip, the first reaction of the English regime and the Protestant elite around it was to assume that Mary was an accomplice and this was their broadcast conclusion, though Cecil would only say in public that there was some deeper collusion in it behind the scanty known facts. Shortly after this Moray, no doubt stressing his own innocence and Bothwell's and Mary's guilt, and Mary's envoy Melville, arrived in London to put their differing 'spin' on the rumours. But the absence of a vigorous and impartial enquiry in Edinburgh as urged by Elizabeth would have added to the latter's suspicions of Mary.[45] On 24 February she sent a famous and irritated letter to her cousin, warning her that 'I cannot but tell you what all the world is thinking' and 'Men say that, instead of seizing the murderers, you are looking through your fingers while they escape'. Elizabeth both urged Mary to act as her friend as well as her relation and warned that even Christ had had his Judas among his close followers, which presumably implied that Elizabeth regarded Bothwell in this light (and as acting without Mary's permission in killing Darnley). She did not appreciate, or chose not to accept, the reality of what little Mary (already depressed and confused) could do if Bothwell refused to co-operate with any enquiry that threatened his own men, the Balfours kept a low profile, and Lennox and the Moray/Morton ultra-Protestant faction started slandering her.[46]

The first official account of the murder by the Scots regime, sent in a letter to Mary's ex-mother-in-law Catherine de Medici by the Privy Council after a meeting at the Tolbooth the day after the murder (and in the absence of the queen who was confined to her rooms at Holyrood with shock), had it that it was merely chance that Mary and her entourage had not been blown up too, and that they had all been among the intended victims. This was therefore the conclusion reached by a wide variety of senior nobles and clerics within hours of the event, not a 'cover-up' ordered by Mary to protect Bothwell or anyone else, and it duly promised a serious investigation as to who had been responsible – tying in with the suggestions of how to proceed made independently in London by the realistic politician Elizabeth. The problem was that this was not followed through. Despite all the rumours and the angry demands of Darnley's father Lennox (safe in Glasgow surrounded by armed tenants) for a full judicial enquiry with all necessary powers to act, it was not until the 28 March that the Privy Council set a formal date for an enquiry to commence on 12 April. Mary had followed all the required rules of courtly etiquette, gone into deep mourning for her husband, and issued a promise of a reward of £2,000 (then a huge sum) for information as to the names of the perpetrators, but it was widely known that the culprits were great figures at court who were openly at large and in her favour. Indeed, Bothwell, the main focus of these stories though the first rumours had spoken of Moray's involvement, had been heard promising to murder anyone who accused him. Meanwhile Mary was being accused openly of being the assassin and Bothwell's mistress, and Moray was in London making his excuses to Elizabeth – and possibly manoeuvring to acquire English help for the next stage of a plan to remove Mary. That Mary was involved in the murder is very unlikely, though she may have suspected that something was being planned and was agitated at likely plotter Moray's leaving Edinburgh to visit his wife the day before (to give himself an alibi?). A 'cover-up' of the part played by figures prominent in the post-1567 regency (e.g. Morton) and their ally Sir James Balfour is very probable.

The aftermath: A royal 'cover-up' and colossal mistakes, or was Mary caught in a nearly hopeless situation?

Whatever the truth, the scandal was immense and Mary mishandled it; Elizabeth wisely advised her to take concern for her honour as well as for revenge in her first letter of condolence but this was ignored, as was Archbishop Hamilton's advice to take rigorous public revenge. Given that she now faced the inevitable enmity of, and probable revolt, from Lennox who would believe that she was behind the murder given her actions in early February, she needed a strong military protector and could not rely on Moray who might well be implicated in the murder. The Protestant 'Lords' were already anathema to her given the murder of Riccio, and even if she had Argyll and Huntly with their armed troops to aid her, they were not based close to Edinburgh. She had already decided to rely more on Bothwell, whether or not sex also played a part in this though it is unlikely that any 'affair' was going on, and given his violent and unstable reputation she could not 'throw him to the wolves' without fear of revolt. But her presumed decision to treat him as if he was innocent and let him go free in the hope that the scandal would 'blow over' – after all, Darnley had been widely loathed and a political liability was disastrous to her reputation for a start. It fuelled rumours of a 'cover-up' and popular anger in Edinburgh, and was to damage her reputation in London and overseas too. Bothwell was allowed to swagger around the streets of Edinburgh proclaiming his innocence with a large body of armed retainers and threatening violence on anyone who accused him, and no attempt was made to require him to disarm his men or to ask him to stay away from the city for a few months and call in a less contentious military ally like Argyll. (Huntly was too Catholic and the Hamilitons might try to depose her and take the throne or the regency for James.) Indeed, as the Earl of Mar, head of the Erskines, now took up his family's traditional role as guardian of the heir to the throne at Stirling Castle and duly became governor of that castle, the governorship of Edinburgh Castle was vacant so Mary gave it to Bothwell. He passed it on to his nominees, firstly Sir James Cockburn but soon to Sir James Balfour – who if he had not actually killed Darnley seems likely to have provided the gunpowder and who was shortly to betray both Bothwell and Mary. This was a fatal blunder given what was to happen in June, and Mary did not stop it – though possibly she did not know the details of who had done what in the murder so she did not realise how deeply Balfour was involved.

Nor was Lennox allowed to bring a large armed escourt to Edinburgh for the prosecution of Bothwell which he launched before Parliament on 12 April – he reasonably insisted this was needed for his safety, so when it was refused he did not turn up. The putting up of placards in Edinburgh denouncing Bothwell as the murderer showed stong public feeling – and one which appeared on 1 March, the famous ' The Mermaid and the Hare', showed the queen in company with the Hepburns' family symbol of a hare in the form of a mermaid which, in contemporary terminology, meant a prostitute. The implication was clear. Nevertheless the official 'trial' of Bothwell for murder quickly cleared him, and within a week (Saturday 19 April) a group of prominent noblemen and clerics, among them Morton, Argyll, and Huntly, were signing a 'bond' at a party at Ainslie's Tavern in Edinburgh (or possibly at Bothwell's apartments at Holyrood) with their host Bothwell, agreeing to his plan to promote his candidacy as Mary's next husband. Argyll, Huntly, Lords Cassilis and Rothes, Maitland, and the earl of Sutherland all signed, so this represented a (temporary) alignment by several factions and normally independent 'players'.[47] Whether they were threatened, blackmailed, or cajoled by strong drink and forceful logic into it is unclear. One visitor heard that Moray, who was still in London, and 'signer' Morton wanted Bothwell to marry Mary because it would incense the populace and they could then dispose of them both. Bothwell then proceeded to follow the queen to her country 'retreat' at Seton, accompanied by his new ally Maitland (who as a strong pro-English Protestant and a veteran wily politican may well have thought Bothwell the 'best of a bad bunch' as a new husband, being noble, Protestant, and militarily strong) and less tactfully Riccio's murderer Patrick Bellenden, a former 'sidekick' to the now deceased Ruthven. He then told Mary that the nobles had chosen him as the best candidate to be her next husband and pressed her to marry him, which Mary later claimed was the first she had heard of this idea. Maitland advised agreeing, on the logical grounds that the country was in chaos and needed a strong hand. Writing in the 1580s, her then adviser Claude Nau pointed out as an explanation for why she eventually went along with Bothwell's idea that she was in a state of confusion, did not know what to do or who could be trusted, and was presented with the idea as that of a united opinion by most of her noble elite, which rings true. But a wiser person would not have taken Bothwell's word for it and would have delayed a decision and consulted far more widely on her own initiative.[48] Bothwell was as capable of deceiving her as her late husband or Moray, but she does not appear to have considered the possibility that a trap was being laid for her despite the widespread hatred already shown to Bothwell in Edinburgh during the weeks after the murder.

Bothwell may well have felt aggrieved that he alone of the plotters was being blamed for the murder, and that as Mary's husband he would be safe from his treacherous ex-colleagues sacrificing him to save their own reputations. At the least it seems probable that the Balfour brothers were being protected, along with the Douglases who had done the actual killing in the orchard, and whose kinsman Morton may have arranged their presence to help in the assassination. Behind them lurked Moray, though his complicity may have been more as an 'enabler' who brought the murderers together and assured them that he would help protect them after the killing than as a participant. Bothwell could provide strong and Protestant leadership as Mary's husband, and was a capable soldier and a vigorous leader, so his and Maitland's reasoning was correct – but in terms of international politics it would be disastrous for Mary to be seen to marry her previous husband's reputed murderer. Moray was away in England at the time, assuring his patrons about his innocence of Darnley's murder.

Mary's principal non-noble adviser and confidante, Secretary Maitland, might have provided words of advice to Mary to be more cautious and seem rigorously even-handed after the murder, and unlike the equally wise Elizabeth he was 'on the scene' and trusted. But he had loathed Darnley and was involved in the murder-plot to some degree, so he was not willing to ask the queen to be more even-handed in the enquiry and allow Lennox to bring the armed men he wanted for his protection. But even if Mary was determined to support Bothwell, and could not 'target' anyone else (e.g. Sir James Balfour, who Elizabeth's chief minister Cecil was told had purchased a large amount of gunpowder in early 1567) without the fear that they would reveal embarrassing details, the failure to convict any 'scapegoat' (even a minor henchman) at the April 1567 enquiry added to international disquiet. The group of Bothwell retainers who were to be accused later, most notably John Hepburn, may have been 'scapegoats' and others may have taken part in laying and setting off the gunpowder. As supposedly related by Hepburn in prison months later to his cell-mate Cuthbert Ramsay who then told the story to the 'Mary/Bothwell' divorce tribunal in Rome in 1576, he and his colleagues had helped Bothwell to lay and set off the gunpowder train.[49] Assuming that they were involved, a proper legal investigation could have arrested and accused one or more of them without specifically naming their employer – this would have been obviously a 'cover-up' but at least it would have provided some degree of retribution. Bothwell's presumed refusal to sacrifice any of his men was to his personal credit as an 'honourable' lord who looked after his retainers. but the lack of any serious attempt to press charges against anyone at the enquiry was a farce. It was worse given Bothwell's provocative armed stance and bold threats at the time. His behaviour was outrageous, even for a notoriously arrogant hothead used to intimidation, and if Mary had had any sense of self-preservation she would have steered clear of him for a few months. The speed with which Bothwell and Mary acted was disastrous, though their collusion in it remains uncertain. Instead of keeping her distance from him for a few months, Mary chose to run off with him – officially 'abducted' against her will at the Bridge of Almond on 24 April as he and his armed retainers intercepted her and took her to the castle of Dunbar while she was returning from visiting her son, James, at Stirling. Possibly this was collusion arranged beforehand to exonerate her in the eyes of her supporters, or Bothwell's bold interpretation of her agreeing in principle to marry him earlier by forcibly speeding up the timetable.

Apparently Bothwell's retainer Ormiston had been secretly to visit her at Linlithgow Palace the evening before the abduction, or so the royal page Paris (one of the Darnley murderers) recalled later. Though Paris may have been 'lent on' to incriminate her and there is no proof that the visit was to arrange the interception rather than on some other matter.[50] Rumours of the attack reached both Maitland and Lennox beforehand, or so they recalled later. and the violently anti-Bothwell Kirkcaldy of Grange had warned English ambassador Bedford that Mary had said that she would follow Bothwell in her underwear to the end of the world if necessary.[51] She did not seem too outraged when Bothwell intercepted her entourage and demanded that he accompany her, though she may just have been shocked – and his then forcing her to have sex with him is highly probable and would amount to rape by modern standards.[52] Her hysteria and apparent threats of suicide followed her return to Edinburgh with Bothwell and her marriage (at Holyrood on 15 May) by some weeks, probably once she had realised the damage it had done to her reputation.[53] Typically, the marriage had been delayed while Bothwell rid himself of his current wife which Archbishop Hamilton obligingly arranged with a public annulment on 7 May on the grounds that they had been within the prohibited degree of cousinhood. By this point, an assembly of Bothwell's aristocratic enemies was already gathering at Stirling on 1 May, led by Morton, Argyll, and Mary's distant Stewart cousin the Earl of Atholl – all signatories of the 'Ainslie Tavern Bond'. So they had either changed their minds since that or had signed in order to lure Mary and Bothwell into a trap. This gathering and its personnel was adequate warning to Mary, had she cared to listen, of the danger she now faced. Also, when she had the banns read in Edinburgh for her forthcoming marriage the priest involved, John Craig, expressed his disgust to the Privy Council at the impropriety of the arrangement and his fear that it would confirm public suspicion of the queen's collusion in murdering her previous husband. Typically, Bothwell then threatened to hang him.

It is unclear whether or not the impatient Bothwell forced the issue to make Mary carry out an earlier agreement to marry him by raping her or making it look as if this had been why she had married him – i.e. she had had no choice but to marry him to save her honour. By Borders brigands' standards this was a logical solution to her hesitation, and it is possible that he quickly made her pregnant-though the timing suggests that she would not have known this by the time she married. Her decision to put herself totally in his hands cost her her political credibility and made it far more likely that her critics would be able to accuse her of murdering Darnley as Bothwell's ally – and to be believed. Her subsequent tearful depression and threats of suicide imply that she soon had second thoughts. Worse, some of her leading supporters fled from the newly-weds – Maitland claiming that Bothwell had tried to murder him, which, if true was a disastrous miscalculation by the hot-tempered thug about keeping a valuable and ruthless ally 'on message'.[54] Worse, Maitland then reported the alleged attack on him to Cecil so Elizabeth was left in no doubt of what sort of violent brigand Mary had married. A revolt by Bothwell's aristocratic enemies followed which had clear popular support within the capital. And thanks to their ally Mar being in charge of Stirling Castle, they had Prince James as their figurehead so they could depose Mary and acclaim a new sovereign. The future (and life) of the current Scots ruler was always in trouble if rebels had possession of their heir, as James III had found in 1488; the deposed sovereign was likely to meet with a violent end. Lennox ostentatiously used an emotive banner, portraying the infant prince praying by his murdered father's body under the words 'Judge and avenge my cause, O Lord', and now Mary had married the presumed murderer she could be placed with him in the popular mind and her deposition as a murderous whore seem a holy duty.

The rebels' party was based on the nucleus of the Moray faction from the 'Chaseabout Raid' revolt in 1565 which may suggest that the hidden hand of Moray lay behind it, now allied to the vengeance-seeking Lennox. Worse, the shameless and devious Sir James Balfour, now placed in charge of Edinburgh Castle, apparently secretly promised to desert to the rebels when needed but Mary and Bothwell continued to trust him. Mary's defeat was probably inevitable, but her capture, the decisive move in marginalising her from power, was her own fault and not inevitable. Firstly, she allowed herself to be caught unawares by the rebel advance in early June at isolated Borthwick Castle where Bothwell had taken her while he raised a Borders army (where were her husband's scouts?), and had to parley while Bothwell slipped away to raise more men. The rebels hesitated in attacking as they had not brought their full strength and Bothwell might counter-attack, and when they pulled back, Mary slipped out disguised as a man.[55] Mary and Bothwell then accepted an offer from the double-dealing Balfour (who had not officially defected yet) to advance from Bothwell's 'safe' Borders region towards Edinburgh to join him at the Castle – which was a trap to lure them within reach of the advancing rebels. They moved forward to Leith, and a confrontation with the larger rebel army followed on 15 June at Carberry Hill. Caught outnumbered by the rebels, Mary parleyed for hours with the superior rebel army but refused an offer to protect her crown if she abandoned Bothwell (which the French ambassador was willing to guarantee) while Bothwell swaggered around offering to have 'single combat' with any rebel lord. As her men started to desert, she accepted an invitation to surrender.[56] Her husband, who had more sense of reality, fled and failed to rally an army in the north-east to come and rescue her. He ended up fleeing to Denmark, where he was imprisoned for life by the embarrassed authorities. Rumour had it that this was the revenge of the relatives of Anna Throndsen, his Danish mistress who he had discarded in Scotland in 1563, and he ended up insane in a dungeon, chained to a pillar.

Possibly Mary's surrender was because she hoped to gain time for Bothwell to raise an army in Moray and rescue her. Instead, she was treated with ignominy by her ex-father-in-law and his allies and exposed to her subjects' anger. Having been greeted with public vilification and, on her arrival, been booed as a whore in the streets of Edinburgh, Mary was locked in the provost's house overnight within earshot of the baying crowd (presumably to unnerve her). Moved to Lochleven Castle in Fife, she was deposed by her council in favour of her infant son James VI under the legal fiction that she had willingly abdicated rather than been told (by one of the delegation sent to force her to abdicate on 24 July, Lord Lindsay) she would be killed if she did not. Her abdication was also forced on her while she was confined to bed ill and in a state of collapse, probably after she had miscarried of the baby or twin babies which Bothwell and English ambassador Bedford independently mentioned her carrying in mid-June. Her worst mistake had been her choice of protector after Darnley's murder, which in turn has influenced attitudes to the question of who was implicated in the killing and why ever since. She needed a capable and ruthless political 'operator' to rely on in spring 1567 and so chose Bothwell (who had a private army of tenants to hand), but Moray would have been a less controversial choice and also a potential threat as a man of semi-royal blood and so a possible regent if he decided to depose her later. In choosing Bothwell, she probably put sexual preference above politics unlike the wiser Elizabeth; but Bothwell may have forced her hand in the matter of a quick marriage.

Notably, as the new regime made their excuses for arresting and imprisoning Mary to the furious Elizabeth (but had not yet deposed Mary) the latter's ambassador Bedford write to Cecil on 23 June that they would act according to her wishes which, if true, may imply that Elizabeth approved the deposition in private whatever she said in public. Would the new regime have forced Mary's abdication and risked Elizabeth invading if they knew she was vehemently opposed to their deposing Mary? Had Elizabeth and Cecil also given the plotters the 'go-ahead' to overthrow Mary by force?

The enquiry, in England, and its context; the 'Casket Letters'. Blatant falsification of evidence plus a political 'show-trial' designed to incriminate Mary?

Mary would have been well advised to follow the precedent of evicted young King David II Bruce in 1334 and flee the country, sailing with Bothwell to the Continent if she could not trust Elizabeth. Instead, she was able to feature for the rest of her life as a romantic 'lady in distress' and persuade a succession of impressionable young men to attempt to restore her to the throne, starting with her captor's assistant George Douglas at Loch Leven Castle. The new, Protestant regency by a clique of pro-English nobles, led by Moray, was always going to be at risk from power-hungry rivals given the normal turbulent history of past Scot regencies, quite apart from the added 1560s elements of religion, foreign intervention, and the sort of romantic support that Mary was already attracting. Elizabeth was initially so angry at the idea of a crowned queen's deposition that she threatened invasion to restore Mary, which would have been likely to lead to the implacable Moray faction executing their captive to prevent her rescue. Elizabeth's suggestions of joint government by Mary and (nominally) her infant son James, with the new regent Moray guaranteed the continuation of his regime, was unlikely to have been acceptable to Moray's faction and would have had to be enforced by an English army allied to the pro-Marian faction, led by the Hamiltons. But the danger of either a Marian revolt by her remaining, mostly Catholic allies (possibly aided by an outraged foreign Catholic power like Spain), or the intervention of Elizabeth out of monarchic solidarity, now required the new regime to tackle the question of finding and punishing the 'guilty' for the Darnley murder as a matter of urgency – and also the political necessity of diverting attention away from Moray, Morton, the Balfours, and any other participants or encouragers who had joined the new government.

As Bothwell had been driven out of the country and vilified as the murderer, he and his lackeys could be safely indicted, and the more Mary was implicated the less likely it was that the politically fastidious Elizabeth or Philip II would intervene to restore her. Accordingly, the regime now went after the minor presumed participants in the murder, and rounded up as many accused who were connected to Bothwell (and Mary) as they could. Bothwell's henchman, Captain William Blackadder, who was apparently the first on the scene after Kirk O'Field exploded and who maintained that he had just been drinking in a nearby friend's house, was accused of being a participant, tried, and hanged. Also accused, convicted, and executed was Bothwell's retainer William Powrie, the man who had allegedly been seen transporting barrels or trunks (i.e. full of gunpowder) through the streets of Edinburgh a few hours before the explosion – though his two successive 'confessions' contradicted each other about how many horses he had used and how many journeys he had made. A copy of his first 'confession', made on 23 June 1567, was sent to Cecil four days later, showing the regime's need and desire to keep the latter and Elizabeth 'in the loop' about the current official explanation for the murder. The two retainers who had supposedly helped Bothwell to lay the train of explosives, John Hepburn and John Hay, were imprisoned and later executed, and other victims included Mary's (French) attendants Bastian and Busso. Busso was released after some weeks and not prosecuted, and 'Black John' Spens was released rather more quickly after handing over Bothwell's chest of treasure to the new government. Some or all of the convicted may have been guilty, or just scapegoats – the political need to establish a 'narrative' blaming Bothwell and Mary to the exclusion of everyone else makes the investigation suspect. The trials were notably carried out by a 'secret committee' of the regime's lords, not the full council – i.e. only those who could be relied upon to keep 'on message' and not quibble about inconvenient details and contradictions in the evidence?

It was also at this point that the mysterious 'casket' containing alleged letters implicating Mary and Bothwell in a toxic mixture of adultery and murder surfaced. They will be dealt with below, but it should be pointed out here that when the story first appeared it was seen as a minor detail and the contents of the casket were not specified; the casket was discovered in Edinburgh in the possession of Bothwell's just-captured tailor, George Dalgleish, on 17 June 1567 and opened by a committee of privy councillors on the 20th according to Morton's December 1568 declaration. But no mention of it or of its contents were made in Dalgleish's detailed statement about his part in and knowledge of the murder to the council on 26 June, suggesting that if the casket had genuinely been found and opened, its contents were in reality not that crucial. It might have been referred to obliquely in the Council proclamation of that day which announced that proof, written as well as verbal, had been collected of Bothwell's part in the murder. But it was not mentioned in a long list of Bothwell's alleged crimes read out by regime members to a crowd at the Tollbooth three weeks later (plenty of time to read and transcribe them) which suggests that there was no 'smoking gun' but at most, a number of suggestive details which the regime's adherants then 'improved upon' over the next year to blacken Mary's name. When Elizabeth referred to the casket's contents in an audience with De Silva in London on 22 July, she said that she was not convinced that Mary was guilty and that Maitland had acted badly – so did she suspect him of forging some or all of the letters? Significantly, although there has been speculation that the account of the current situation sent by Maitland to Cecil with ambassador Melville, which arrived in London on 26 June, may have included early details of the casket's contents (and Cecil apparently sent the data brought by Melville to Moray, who was now in France) Moray did not quote more than one of the 'Casket Letters' in his own letters in subsequent weeks.[57] If he had had such incriminating 'evidence' at his disposal in July and August, surely he would have used it? So was the majority of the 'sensational' written evidence only doctored or created after Dalgleish had handed the casket over?

Mary's subsequent unexpected escape from her captivity at Loch Leven to head a revolt did not attract major backing apart from the Hamiltons, and owed much to luck and the slackness of her captor, Moray's half-brother. A kinsman besotted with Mary managed to smuggle her out of the castle in a rowing-boat during May Day celebrations on 2 May 1568 and steal the bungs in the bottoms of all the other boats. His cousins had horses waiting on the shore, and Mary then rode to Hamilton to join a rally led by the eponymous family – who in return insisted that she name them as her heirs after her son. The rebels included an impressive nine earls and had a larger army (c. 6,000) than Moray, but were intercepted *en route* to Marian-held Dumbarton and defeated at Langside near Glasgow. The regent's army had a more coherent force with more modern weapons and was led by a better general (Kirkcaldy of Grange), but their victory was by no means assured and they might easily have failed to catch Mary's army on the march and had to blockade her in impregnable Dumbarton instead. One of the Marian commanders, Lord Herries, failed to rout the regent's disciplined pikemen with his Galloway cavalry, and the earl of Argyll put the matter beyond doubt by failing to act decisively on the battlefield and withdrawing from the fight (alleging that he had been taken ill). Coincidentally or not, he was Moray's brother-in-law and had been reported as hoping that once Mary was rid of Bothwell she would marry his own brother.

Riding south to the coast of the Solway Firth, Mary now made the decision to go to England and seek Elizabeth's aid – though at the time she could easily have decided to go to France instead with the proviso that she did not have a large ship to hand and it would have been risky to try to sail all the way in a fishing-boat.[58] She was assured of a comfortable material existence in France as a dowager queen, if not much military backing from the embattled Guises whose priorities were the continuing religious struggle (halted by a truce in 1568). Catherine de' Medici was unlikely to welcome her re-emergence in French public life as a Guise ally. Seeking an immediate divorce from Bothwell would have been politically necessary, and even as events turned out with her going to England, instead Mary made her position worse by not doing this or seeming at all repentant of her past mistakes. The embarrassment of giving her sanctuary and hopefully aid thus fell to Elizabeth; and the queen's fellow-feeling for another crowned monarch was unlikely to prevail over Mary's threat to the established orders of both England and Scotland. The Moray regime was Elizabeth's ally, and had no desire to risk Mary's return home given her recent revolt against it and her international Catholic backing.

When Mary arrived at Workington, Cumbria, by boat from Dundrennan Abbey in Galloway on 16 May asking for help, the English monarch showed her usual caution by putting the issue 'on hold' and refusing her an interview or immediate aid. She was lodged in Carlisle Castle rather than being invited to court.[59] The Scots regency was Protestant and well-disposed towards Elizabeth, its weakness implying that it was malleable,and Mary was a Catholic, the close relative of the anti-English 'ultra' Catholic leadership in France (the Guises), and accused by her supplanters of murdering her last-but-one husband. Mary was specifically told that Elizabeth would not allow her to bring in France to help her too, which would have saved the parsimonious Elizabeth from having to pay for a large-scale invasion and would have tied France into a policy of stabilising Scotland but would have brought the ultra-Catholic Guises back into Scots (and English?) politics.[60] Elizabeth seems to have preferred to send Mary home, hopefully as queen, rather than to keep her in England or let her go on to hostile France (which might revive her claim to the English throne), but that must be with her subjects' consent. So her representative, her staunchly Protestant cousin Sir Francis Knollys, reminded Mary at Carlisle Castle in a tense interview on 30 May 1568, that monarchs could be deposed for murder.[61] Elizabeth required that Mary be cleared of murder before she would let her into her presence or help her, as a matter of 'honour'. As Cecil saw matters in one of his famous and exhaustive lists of the reasons 'pro' and 'con' a major policy decision, the only legal and practical reason to keep Mary off her throne was moral depravity, as she had come to England of her own free will seeking aid from her cousin the queen, she had been deposed illegally by her subjects, the charges about her involvement in the Darnley murder had never been tested in court, she had been denied the right to defend herself, and she had offered to explain her conduct personally to Elizabeth who had expressed her support on numerous occasions. Law and honour both necessitated helping Mary, or at least investigating what her subjects alleged to her detriment, and she should have the right to conduct an untrammelled defence.[62]

This might seem to point to Elizabeth and Cecil conducting an 'honest' and open investigation into the Darnley murder and doing so free of Scots elite political machinations – but the latter could affect politics in England too. Mary had claimed Elizabeth's crown in November 1558 (though under orders from her father-in-law Henri II) and still claimed to be her heir, and as a Catholic she could be used by English Catholic plotters or by a hostile foreign power. Caution was needed, and Elizabeth's solution for a major problem was usually to impose a delay and see how events turned out. Accordingly the ex-queen was moved away from the frontier to Bolton Castle while an enquiry was set up at York to look into the question of Darnley's murder. Moray quickly started to 'smear' Mary to justify keeping her off her throne, and sent his secretary John Wood to London on 21 May 1568 (a mere five days after Mary had fled the country). He assured Elizabeth that he had the documentary proof that Mary was guilty,[63] and in a letter on 22 June even asked her to confirm that Mary would be found guilty and not allowed home if he could prove in the copies of her letters which he would be sending to London that she was involved in the murder – i.e. that the queen and her council, not the judges, were to make a decision on the sole basis of his own 'evidence' and the actual trial would be a 'fix'.[64] He duly secured her unofficial assurances via Cecil that if the case was proved, Mary would not be aided by England; though Elizabeth was theoretically opposed to the idea of anyone being able to judge a sovereign the enquiry could be used as an excuse for preventing Mary from returning to Scotland.[65] The depth of hostility to the ex-queen by her opponents should show if it was too risky to restore Mary in any case. This was confirmed by Elizabeth in a personal letter to Moray on 20 September after the vicious 'Book of Articles' by Buchanan had been sent to London and a new edition, mentioning the 'Casket Letters' in more detail than the mid-summer Scots edition, had been prepared there ahead of the trial.[66] Was Elizabeth persuaded to be harsher after reading the Buchanan 'data' and copies of the letter sent to her by Moray? Meanwhile, Moray also commissioned the dour and fanatically anti-Catholic scholar George Buchanan to write his vituperative 'Book of Articles' against Mary, which would seek to allege that she had not only been involved in the murder but had been Bothwell's lust-ridden and adulterous lover for months beforehand.

Accordingly there were 'sub-texts' to the commission's work as it met at York to examine the 'Casket Letters'. An English board, headed by Thomas Howard, duke of Norfolk (born 1536, a noble of royal blood, head of England's most notable Catholic dynasty though not himself one, and an eligible widower soon to be shown to be interested in marrying Mary, so not hostile), were to preside, and the letters' authenticity would be argued by the regency's representatives (including Moray and Maitland) and denied by Mary's (including Bishop Leslie of Ross and Lord Herries). Moray was determined to ruin his half-sister's reputation and keep her out of Scotland, but Maitland was open to a compromise that restored her in name but not complete power and offered to show her some of the 'evidence'. Some of Mary's commissioners who had disliked her falling for the unsuitable Bothwell were prepared to see her restored without real power. The possibility that some of the letters had been forged to incriminate Mary was recognised by the English commissioners, particularly the earl of Sussex who frankly admitted that their authenticity mattered less than the political usefulness of keeping Mary out of power.[67] What mattered was the 'political' imperatives rather than the facts, and Moray 'upped the ante' by showing copies of the 'Casket Letters' to the English commissioners on 11 October 1568 ahead of the trial. These seem to have taken the politically-naïve Norfolk in, and afterwards he expressed his horror at the contents and declared that such a large number of documents could hardly all have been forged' – if they were true Mary should be found guilty. But interestingly he abated his hostility to her after a private meeting with Maitland a few days later, and subsequently did not object when the possibility of his marrying this alleged adulterous murderess was raised.[68] Did Maitland assure him that most of the letters had been forged and Mary was in reality suitable to become his wife but had had to be 'smeared' for political reasons?

Elizabeth now transferred the initial October 1568 enquiry at York to London in November and added her most loyal councillors, led by Cecil and Leicester, to the commissioners. The 'originals' of the letters were apparently now shown by Moray to the English commissioners, but not to Mary's representatives – and Moray had earlier referred to only one letter of Mary's having been found in the casket so others may have been forged especially for the enquiry. Mary's representatives were quickly sidelined and ignored. Mary was refused permission to come to

London to speak (though the snow would have delayed her anyway) and was told to send written answers to a list of English queries from Bolton as her means of participating. Extra English judges were appointed after the initial proceedings had commenced, and her commissioners did not follow her instructions to walk out if she was not allowed to come and give evidence in person.

On 14–15 December, the enlarged group of English commissioners met at Hampton Court Palace and studied the evidence, including the 'Casket Letters', concluding (though it is not clear if this was unanimous) that the case was proven enough that Elizabeth could not, in honour, admit Mary, whose conduct was clearly reprehensible, to her presence. On the 16th, Elizabeth met the Scots commissioners and told them that she was still willing to listen to Mary's defence if she would either send this in writing to the full commission, to the Scots part of it for them to deliver to the others, or to a delegation of English nobles who would call on her at Bolton. Mary's representatives duly advised her to obey, but she refused on the 19th (saying that she would need to examine and reply to the evidence in person) and so excused the English commissioners not bothering to seek her reply to Moray's 'smears' any longer. Elizabeth, however, sent a letter back to Mary on the 21st inviting her to submit her written reply to the charges, and claiming she would be only too glad to acquit her – though the following day Cecil was writing a memorandum advising Mary's detention in England indefinitely as the best outcome for the crisis so he seems to have made his mind up. The question is whether Elizabeth had done so too – even before the enquiry – and Moray's 'evidence' in the form of the 'Casket Letters' were only pushing at an open door. Noticeably, there was a lack of any serious attempt to examine their contradictions with the actual course of events, e.g. 'Casket Letter III' which had 'Mary' writing to 'Bothwell' a few days before the assassination of Darnley about her regret at his long absence when they were in fact both at Holyrood in close proximity – as any of the Marian court or royal household could have told the enquiry. The English commissioners now acted as judge and jury, and made no effort to include the Marian delegates in their 'out of court' private deliberations. The final result was announced by Cecil on 10 January 1569. But even so it was not decided that the letters were definitely genuine, merely that nothing could be proved to the dishonour of either Mary or the nobles who had deposed her.[69]

The letters were returned to Moray's custody in Scotland, passed on to his successors as regent, and after the final regent, Morton was overthrown in 1581 were given by his bastard son to the Earl of Gowrie, heir of the Ruthven line. They mysteriously disappeared after Gowrie was arrested and executed in 1584 for kidnapping and ruling in the name of the teenage James VI, and may have passed to one of his relatives or been seized by King James and destroyed as embarrassing. The then head of the Hamiltons acquired and may have inherited the eponymous silver 'Casket' as he was later spoken of as its owner, but this is no proof that the letters were with this item. Historian Walter Goodall, who published the first major study of the letters in 1754, claimed to have discovered that at the time of the Restoration in 1660 an unnamed historian had declared that the Marquis of Douglas (a Hamilton relative) had possession of them. By the 1750s they were in the hands of the then head of the Hamiltons – whose ancestors were the marquis of Douglas' son William (third duke of Hamilton) and the first duke of Hamilton's daughter so either of these two could have passed them on in the family. He did not cite specific details and the original letters (which were in French) have since never reappeared; neither have the Scots copies made by the Scots privy council in 1567.

The copies which survive were those translations into English and French made for the York/London investigation in autumn 1568, and they cannot be a full 'set' as in 1571 Morton identified the letters to Darnley's father Lennox as twenty-one in number – letters, marriage-contracts, and love-letters. Eight letters plus two marriage-contracts and one love-letter survive, so what happened to the rest of the (copies of the) documents? An alleged letter from Mary referring to how she had caused the pre-murder row between Darnley and her half-brother Robert Stewart (in the alleged hope of Darnley getting challenged to a duel and killed) was quoted by Moray at the initial English enquiry at York but was not referred to in the meetings at Westminster. There is also the question of the inconsistencies in the longest and most damning of the letters, 'Letter II', seemingly written by Mary to Bothwell while she was in Glasgow with Darnley on the night of 23–24 January 1567. Much of it appears to be a genuine report by Mary of her meetings with her husband, but not as claimed a report to her 'lover', Bothwell, as he appears in the third person in the narrative; nor is the tone adopted by the writer consistent throughout though it could have been composed in two sessions hours apart. The 'report' part has been reckoned by modern commentators as probably taken from a report by her to one or more of her council about her meeting Darnley. The part where 'Mary' ceases reporting events clearly and appears to be obsessed with her lover and her rational approach in the script is suddenly much reduced would appear to be taken from a separate letter, of unknown date. So it may be a much later letter of hers written after Darnley's death or a complete forgery. The style of this section is similar to Mary's, but this may only mean that the forger copied out parts of genuine letters of hers which the regency regime had seized on her deposition. Other emotionally charged letters, particularly 'Letter V' which appears to refer to the dismissal of one of the queen's attendants a few days before the murder for becoming pregnant, were declared by the regency regime to be addressed by Mary to her lover but could just as easily have been really addressed to Darnley.[70] None of these possibilities were looked into in 1568 as they were too inopportune and the fact that her partisans Herries and Leslie were later unable to claim that the letters were definitely forgeries may just reflect the fact that they included (parts of?) genuine letters plus samples of her style mingled with outright inventions.

The 'status quo' was upheld in early 1569, with Moray returning home as regent (with a loan of £5,000 and the 'Casket Letters') and Mary being kept in England. Modern examination of the copies made at the time which still survive have suggested that genuine love-letters by Bothwell to another woman and extracts from letters by Mary on unrelated matters (quoted out of context) were 'tampered with' to make it appear that Mary and Bothwell were committing adultery and planning murder in Darnley's lifetime, and that her handwriting was forged in places by someone familiar with it. Maitland or another close adviser may have been the forger. But even if the English commissioners were suspicious of Moray's and Morton's accounts, politics required that Mary be kept out of Scotland under some excuse as the regent was adamant not to have her back. Maitland, who was more inclined to have Mary restored (as co-ruler with James?) under some form of compromise that kept her rights to the crown of England alive for the future, may already have 'floated' the idea of marrying her to a loyal Englishman to reassure Elizabeth – and Norfolk seen himself as that man. If so, Elizabeth and Cecil did not back them and on his return home Moray proceeded to arrest leading 'Marians' like Chatelherault (her nominee to be regent for James). Mary was moved to Tutbury Castle in the custody of the earl and countess of Shrewsbury, and the long saga of her confinement and apparent threat to Elizabeth as the hope of English Catholic rebels commenced. But the 'romantic novel' interpretation of this saga as a vindictive and unjust persecution of an honest and ill-used woman by her jealous cousin and the latter's obsessive or scheming ministers ignores the real threat that Mary posed to Elizabeth's regime – and thus the stability of England – if there was another Catholic rising and/or she was assassinated by anyone from a maverick 'home-grown terrorist' Catholic fanatic or an agent of the Catholic 'ultras' in France or Spain. If Mary was allowed to go home, even as co-sovereign to an under-age James and his 'hard-line' Protestant ministers, there was no guarantee that she would not get a priest to absolve her of any promises to co-operate with England and stage a Catholic coup, which from the later 1570s was likely to be backed by the increasingly antagonistic Spanish government.

It should, however, be remembered that there were to be several international diplomatic efforts to help Mary from the mid-1570s by insisting that her release and her return to Scotland be included in vital treaties with England, including moves by influential figures in the French government – which was strongly Catholic in tone and had been behind the St Barthrolomew's Day Massacre of Protestants in 1572, but was still needed as a potential ally by Elizabeth. Despite the anti-French and anti-Catholic vigilance of the Elizabethan spymaster and Secretary of State from 1572 Sir Francis Walsingham (a witness of the Massacre), who loathed and distrusted Mary, he was not the only political 'actor' to dominate foreign policy in London and Elizabeth herself was more interested in keeping up the ancestral rivalry of Valois (France) and Habsburg (Spain and the Empire) so that England could play one off against the other – her father's policy. She was not as ideologically minded as Walsingham (or Cecil), and in the search for a way to stoke the Dutch rebellion against Philip II and keep him preoccupied in the late 1570s and early 1580s it was easier – and cheaper – to get France to do the fighting for her, hence her interest (real or feigned?) in a marriage to the new French King Henri III's brother, Hercule Francis, duke of Alencon. The Queen's search for a French alliance duly gave France an important way of helping their king's ex-sister-in-law Mary – and the chances of this leading Elizabeth to have to release Mary in an Anglo-French treaty should not be regarded as minimal. There is more to the 'inevitable' road to the block for Mary than meets the eye, as the next chapter will show.

Chapter Five

Two Queens, One Crown. Was Mary Really Set on Murdering Elizabeth, or Was She 'Framed'?

Elizabeth vs Mary: Round One. The failed marriage plans of Mary and the Duke of Norfolk, 1569–72.

Was Norfolk unacceptable as a consort for the heir to the Queen's other advisers, or did they only back away and blame him once Elizabeth showed her opposition to it? And was he then 'framed' of treason to remove him from politics?

Contrary to the determinist narrative of popular romance, the cause of Mary Queen of Scots' death was not 'inevitably doomed' in England – or Scotland – after the 'Casket Letters' trial (see previous chapter) failed to exonerate her. Her cause retained widespread popular and elite support in Scotland together with the increased backing through the 1570s of Spain, and a coup, invasion or political agreement could still have restored her to power – if in name only in the latter case. Nor was Queen Elizabeth determined to keep her prisoner in England and out of Scots politics; there is plenty of evidence that by the early 1580s she was fed up with having to pay host to her and her meddling supporters and more than ready to send her home provided she would 'play ball' and not oppose Tudor/Protestant interests. After all, King James I of Scotland had been held as a political hostage in England for eighteen years (1406–24) then allowed to return home under an Anglo-Scots treaty, so such an agreement was not new – and executing a crowned sovereign, Mary's eventual fate in 1587, was unprecedented. The devious and ultra-cautious Elizabeth usually preferred the course of action of putting off a decision for as long as possible, 'sitting on the fence' on major issues and avoiding offending factions that were pressing their favoured solutions on her. This even extended to the vitally important issue of a military response to the rising ideological threat of Catholic Spain to her regime in the 1580s, with the meddling of hostile Spanish ambassadors in English Catholic plots by 'home-grown terrorists' to kill her (which would save their master Philip the cost of having to mount an invasion) and even preparations for the Armada in 1587 not causing her to break off relations. The queen was still negotiating with designated invasion-leader Duke Alexander of Parma as the Armada moved up the English Channel in 1588, and Elizabeth being prepared to abandon her Protestant Dutch allies to their detested ex-overlord Philip, despite her ministers' and admirals' frantic appeals to take invasion more seriously. She did not view international politics in the same mould of an existential 'Catholic vs Protestant' struggle for survival, as ministers such as William Cecil (Secretary of State 1558–72, and Lord Treasurer 1572–98) and Sir Francis Walsingham (Secretary of State 1572–90) did. Nor did she view the shocking co-ordinated mass-killings of French Protestants by Charles IX's regime in 1572 (the St Bartholomew's Day Massacre) as a 'game-changer' and break off relations with the regime; instead she was still negotiating with the French government into the early 1580s to get the new King Henri III, Charles' brother and successor, to help her prop up the rebel Dutch regime and keep Philip from reconquering the Netherlands. In that cause she was even prepared to seriously consider marrying his younger brother and heir Francois Hercule, Duke of Alencon/Anjou, who she received warmly in England as he came to woo her, and treated him as a favoured court 'pet' and her 'Frog'. She did actually agree to the marriage in principle at one point and asked her doctors if she could still have children, in her late forties.

The resulting possibility of the 'Virgin Queen', champion of Protestantism, marrying an under-sized and gauche Catholic prince young enough to be her son touched off frantic attempts to persuade her not to do it, and the zealous 'Puritan' polemicist John Stubbes wrote a vituperative pamphlet about the 'Gaping Gulf' in which England was about to be swallowed up – and had his hand chopped off for seditious libel on the queen's orders. In these circumstances, Elizabeth thought in terms of the old 'Habsburg vs Valois' international rivalry – Philip versus Charles and then Henri – rather than of religious 'solidarity' preventing any alliance with a Catholic regime. In similar vein, she was capable of sending the unwanted Mary Stuart back to Scotland as (titular) queen if this would shore up Scotland's shaky post-1568 stability and she could be sure that Mary would not ally to Spain and seek to overthrow her. In that vein, as of 1569–72 determined efforts were made to consider the viability of finding Mary a new and reliable husband who would govern Scotland with her and 'control' her in Elizabeth's interests. This would probably be an Englishman and not necessarily a Protestant, not least as Mary would still loath to marry a non-Catholic – but could Elizabeth trust any of her great men to become 'King Consort' of Scotland and stay loyal to her? Events were to show that the latter was a major problem, though the wary Elizabeth was likely to delay making a choice as long as possible so the opportune moment for acting might well pass. For that matter, was the failure of this plan at least partly due to English politics and the undermining of potential candidates to marry Mary by their local foes?

Mary's triumphant half-brother Moray had had Mary's legal case adjusted so that she had not been implicated in Darnley's murder, and 'rubbished' at the enquiry into the 'Casket Letters', and as she had not been cleared of suspicion she had to stay in England as Elizabeth's 'guest' while he returned to Scotland early in 1569 as regent. He was still determined to keep Mary off the Scottish throne although he made favourable noises about the idea of a marriage of Mary to the likeliest English candidate, the widowed duke of Norfolk who as seen in the previous chapter had been one of the nobles sitting on the enquiry into the 'Letters'. Presumably this was to avoid seeming obstructive in case Elizabeth backed the marriage. Until his murder (early 1570) Moray would have been blocking any attempt by Elizabeth to negotiate Mary's restoration, assuming that the tribunal had been more explicit in finding nothing to Mary's detriment. It is unlikely that Elizabeth would have pushed matters to the extent of sending troops to install a compliant Mary in Edinburgh if this would face strong resistance, and procrastination was always her favoured 'default' course of action. In addition, there was a rising problem of tension with Spain over its repression of autonomist struggles in the Netherlands (from Catholics in the south, now Belgium, as well as Protestants in the north) and a sporadic religious civil war in Catholic-led France. Wary and ideologically-minded 'internationalist' ministers in London, such as Cecil, regarded the existential religio-political struggles on the Continent as more of a priority for England than Scotland once the 'dangerous' Catholic Queen Mary had been deposed and her supporters' revolt in 1568 had been crushed. Sending an army to Scotland would thus be a dangerous distraction, and it appears that once Elizabeth had got over her initial indignation at Mary's deposition as an affront to all sovereigns, she accepted this. As seen above, the English government may even have 'spun' the narrative of the 'Casket Letters' trial to make sure Mary was not exonerated and restored to her throne. But the situation in Scotland was still fluid and armed Catholic magnates like Huntly were far from reconciled to the regency, which depended on an uneasy alliance of Protestant rivals such as Lennox (Darnley's father and so grandfather and nearest surviving male kin to the infant James VI), Moray, and Morton – not to mention the ultra-devious royal secretary, Maitland. These men were old rivals and their alliance could easily break up; once Moray and his successor as regent, Lennox, were dead in the complex coups of 1570–2 (see below) the Marian revival had an extra impetus in offering a greater chance of stability that would bring in more nobles than the narrowly-based regency. Could this affect Elizabeth enough to negotiate with Mary, given that if she did not help the exiled queen the latter and her allies could call in French or Spanish help instead and so threaten England?

The crucial question here is whether Mary would have been allowed to marry a 'safe' English peer who could be seen as 'controlling' her once she was restored to Scotland. Given her insistence on defending her queenly status by marrying someone of suitably elevated dynastic connections and preferably a royal, alongside her concern to marry a Catholic (though as we have seen Bothwell had been neither), the number of suitable candidates to marry Mary in England were limited. Until 1569, no Catholic peer had risen in rebellion against Elizabeth and until 1570 the pope had not declared Elizabeth definitively a usurper and it as the duty of all loyal Catholics to depose her – two actions which made the position of Catholics in England much more problematic. Since summer 1559, the official religion of England had been Protestant again and the remaining Catholic bishops had been deprived of their sees, but in effect Elizabeth – an 'inclusive' ruler in religious matters who ostentatiously declared that she 'did not want to create windows into men's souls' – had allowed private Catholic worship to continue. The majority of the population in northern England (which the Protestant Reformation in the late 1540s had barely touched), and in other remote areas such as Wales and

Cornwall remained Catholic in the 1560s, and as long as the local priests were loyal to their new queen and conformed to her political demands – and the local gentry did not start sacking those who owed their parish appointments to lay patronage – the situation only slowly altered. The mass seems to have been celebrated 'on the quiet' after 1559 by parish priests in some churches in these areas as well as by Catholic chaplains in private households, and illegal Catholic 'recusancy' was to remain a problem for decades to come. This was eventually tackled by intrusive government action and encouragement for defaulters to be reported and prosecuted was led in the north by the local ruling regional 'Council' of great nobles and state bureaucrats. Pro-Catholic JPs (who would let defaulters off or levy minimal fines) were duly replaced by zealous Protestant activists, local priests who refused to or avoided performing the Anglican Communion were replaced, and the Protestant local gentry and urban merchants known for religious zeal were called on to help establish new Protestant religious lecturerships (whose incumbents gave sermons to the public) and schools. The council itself had to be 'weaponised' under determined Protestant leadership to achieve this, and due to the risk of any harsh repression driving Catholics to rebellion, this was not a priority in Elizabeth's precarious early years.

At that time the sole duke in England, the queen's cousin Thomas Howard, Duke of Norfolk, born in 1536 (a descendant of Edward I in the female line) and usefully socially important and well-resourced, had regional connections as leader of the 1560 English expedition to Edinburgh to help the 'Lords of the Congregation' overthrow Francophile regent Marie de Guise. He was agreeable to becoming nominally Protestant when the 'Reformed Religion' was restored in 1559, and was trusted by the queen, showing his reliability in helping to overthrow the Scots regency. Furthermore in 1567, a complex marital legal arrangement with the north-eastern landed dynasty of Dacre (see below) brought him extensive local lands and thus clients. Though now technically a conformist Protestant, he had been brought up as a Catholic and favoured the Catholics, and most of his family remained Catholic led by his elder sister Jane (wife of the young earl of Westmoreland, principal magnate of north-west England). His grandfather the third duke, Henry VIII's powerful conservative minister and the uncle of his queens Anne Boleyn and Katherine Howard, had been a hard-line Catholic and had led the late Henrician repression of Protestants in 1540–6 with Bishop Gardiner, before being defeated in a faction-struggle with Edward VI's uncle Somerset. He was subsequently thrown in the Tower, had nearly been executed in January 1547, and had spent Edward's reign in the Tower before being rehabilitated under Mary Tudor. His father Henry Howard, the famous 'Poet Earl' of Surrey, had been executed at the end of 1546 in the purge of the Howard family as a result of Somerset's reformist faction working on the fevered suspicions of the paranoid Henry VIII – technically for having used the royal heraldic arms of Edward 'the Confessor' without royal permission, but in effect to stop him and his father attempting to secure the regency for the soon-to-succeed Edward VI. Surrey's combination of haughtiness, aristocratic disdain for lower-ranking courtiers, and occasional law-denying hooliganism, had helped to undermine his reputation with King Henry and his potential support at court, and though, his son the fourth and current duke was a less 'political' or violent character he was equally certain of his status. Living an ostentatious aristocratic existence at his Howard ancestors' grand Kenninghall Castle in Suffolk (where Mary Tudor had based herself in her successful rebellion in July 1553) or the converted ex-monastic 'Charterhouse' outside the northern walls of London, the fourth duke maintained a large household and had the confidence to 'speak truth to power' like a late medieval magnate. (This family tradition also seems to have affected the equally assertive earl of Essex, heir of the semi-royal Devereux and Bourchier lines, another executed victim of a clash with the queen in 1601.)

Norfolk presumed to defy the queen's known wishes to avoid marriage by openly supporting the agitation for her to find a husband in the 1566 Parliament. Complaining at the queen's taking no advice but her own and ignoring her subjects' wishes in that body's House of Lords debates, he had been threatened with arrest by his cousin, the infuriated queen – but luckily many other great nobles at court had shared his views. They had argued that he had only spoken out of his sense of duty and concern for the succession, and Elizabeth had let it pass. Giving him a leading role in the delicate business of handling her refugee fellow-queen and potential successor showed that she still trusted him.

Norfolk's late first wife Mary Fitzalan (died 1557) had been the Catholic daughter of Mary's conservative Catholic minister and Elizabeth's unsucessful suitor, Henry Fitzalan, earl of Arundel (d 1580); their son Philip was to be a devout and unflinching Catholic who refused to convert to reassure the queen of his loyalty and ended up in the Tower as a 'martyr' (and to be canonised). Norfolk had then married a second time, and after his new wife's death, had married in early 1567 Elizabeth Dacre nee Leyburn, offspring of one Catholic north-east England family and the widow of the head of a second, Lord Dacre of Gilsland. The Dacres were a major and titled regional dynasty, and the acquisitive Norfolk had become guardian to (and hence administrator of the family lands for, Elizabeth's under-age son, George, by Lord Dacre and had had his sisters married off to his own three sons – Philip (later Earl of Arundel and heir of the Fitzalans), Thomas (later Earl of Suffolk), and William (later Lord Howard of Naworth, one of the Dacre estates). The accidental death of George Dacre in a bizarre 'vaulting-horse' fall while exercising in 1567 left the two surviving Dacre girls, Philip and William Howard's wives, as the Dacre heiresses, and their estates were duly passed to Norfolk's family. His wife Elizabeth then died in childbirth in autumn 1567, which unlike her two predecessors' deaths seems to have been a major shock to him and made him something of a recluse. He subsequently re-emerged in 1568 to receive a ceremonial award of an MA by Oxford University and was then called on by the queen to go north and head the enquiry into the charges against Mary Stuart when she was forced to flee her homeland after the battle of Langside. He may have been chosen as his sister Lady Scrope was already helping her husband as Mary's 'host'/captor at Carlisle, so she had presumably been informing him of what was happening there.

By this point the queen was acting to assert her authority over the turbulent and pro-Catholic northern borders where once there had been 'no king but a Percy' and the local gentry were still used to their own way. The headship of the governing 'Council of the North' had been handed to the reliably Protestant and aggressively centralising earl of Sussex, a more capable general experienced in fighting guerrilla Catholic revolt in Ireland. Norfolk had probably been passed over for important roles such as this until 1568, as he too inexperienced and hot-headed and a known foe of Elizabeth's trusted confidante Robert Dudley. As seen, he had been one of the peers suspected of secretly paying Robert's brother-in-law John Appleyard to investigate the strange death of Amy Robsart in 1566–7, logically in the hope of 'digging up dirt' on Robert. He had been known for years for his antagonism to the latter, not least as an 'upstart' of lower social class origins who was presuming to throw his weight around at court as the queen's intimate adviser and potential husband, and had also been backing an English alliance with Spain (despite its aggressive Catholicizing policies) rather than France. By 1566–8, the supporters of the latter included Robert Dudley, now earl of Leicester as of 1564, a former Hispanophile, as well as William Cecil and his protégé Nicholas Throckmorton, and Norfolk's and Leicester's supporters had even taken to wearing rival colours of outfits at court and ostentatiously confronting each other. Norfolk's genetics and his religious pedigree made him seem a possibly acceptable husband for Mary, and his journey north to head the initial enquiry in to the 'Casket Letters' at York on Elizabeth's behalf in early autumn 1568 brought them into political contact, if not yet personal proximity. (Mary was currently being kept away from the enquiry at Bolton Castle.) This then led to the devious William Maitland, who had been one of the leaders of her overthrow in 1567 (and as we have seen had probably been deeply implicated in the Darnley murder) and was now one of his ally Moray's commissioners at the enquiry, getting involved. His past record would have suggested mutual enmity and complete mistrust by him and Mary, but instead he seems to have offered the latter's commissioners – including Lord Herries who Moray's troops had recently faced across a battlefield at Langside – his help. Possibly, he reckoned that the regency was dangerously unstable due to its leaders' mutual enmities and the number of pro-Marian lords still resisting it, and that a form of reconciliation was advisable if Mary could be induced (or blackmailed?) to co-operate – or that Elizabeth would support her fellow-queen if Moray was too obstinate.

Accordingly, Maitland appears to have kept the Marians informed about what Moray was up to, e.g. in showing the 'Casket Letters' to the English commissioners as proceedings opened on 11 October 1568, but not to them. They then hastened to Bolton and warned Mary about this. To add to complications, Moray also relied on Maitland to let him know how the English commissioners reacted to the apparent 'proof' in the Letters that Mary had been engaged in a steamy love-affair with Bothwell while Darnley was alive and plotting the latter's murder. Indeed, the 'Mary/Norfolk' marriage possibility nearly did not take off at all, as Norfolk professed himself, horrified at what the Letters seemingly revealed about

Mary's character. He further added that their sheer quantity meant that they could not have been faked and if they were accurate and in the ex-queen's own hand Mary should be convicted, and be shunned by all good and godly men, and could not be restored to her throne. He requested Moray to suppress the letters sooner than expose Mary and her son James VI to public dishonour, not least as the scandal would damage their claims to the English throne.[1] Clearly he was not opposed to the latter. But a few days after this, probably on 16 October on a private hunting-trip to Cawood near York, Maitland apparently took Norfolk aside and suggested to him that one solution for the dilemma of what to do with Mary might be for him to marry her.[2] Norfolk could then act as consort in Scotland, and keep it and Mary loyal to Elizabeth, and the latter would be agreeable to stabilising her neighbouring kingdom and Mary being controlled by a loyal Englishman. Norfolk was at least not inclined to dismiss it out of hand, and it is possible that as he had been so disgusted with Mary a few days before he was assured that the Letters were faked (or exaggerated) and that Mary was not as bad as they portrayed her. As suggested earlier, Maitland may have faked the Letters himself and if not had probably been involved with the 'smear' on her reputation planned by Moray, so he should have known the truth about Mary's alleged guilt.

The prospect of becoming a royal consort undoubtably appealed to the vain and status-conscious Norfolk, and there is no reason to think that at this point he was less than totally loyal to Elizabeth. When he arrived back in London to head the revised and extended enquiry into the 'Casket Letters', the queen questioned him semi-jocularly about the rumours that he wanted to marry Mary, and he assured hastily that it had not originated with or been encouraged by him. (The latter was not exactly true.) She asked if he would marry Mary if this was to the security of herself and the country, and he insisted that:

> 'no reason would move him to like of her that hath been a competitor to the Crown, and if Her Majesty would move him thereto he will rather be committed to the Tower for her never meant to marry with such a person, where he could not be sure of his pillow…'.[3]

The implication was that he still feared that Mary had murdered her husband Darnley and he could not be sure that he would not go the same way if he married her – or at least that he was too cautious and too loyal to risk the queen's anger by promoting the match. If he had kept to this position, the resultant estrangement between him and Elizabeth, and his arrest and execution would have been unlikely – though great nobles with their own priorities and an over-familiar attitude to their sovereigns could be brought down by jealous rivals on the minimum of flimsy evidence, as his father and grandfather had faced in 1546. Unfortunately he had enemies at home who already hated him and would look askance at any potential addition to his power, and as such were bound to oppose his marrying Mary even if the queen changed her mind and considered it – and Elizabeth was as suspicious once aroused as her father had been. Norfolk had proved his enmity towards the powerful and ruthless Robert Dudley, earl of Leicester, in and after the Amy Robsart mystery of 1560 (see Chapter Three), and at one point had come close to physical violence against Leicester during a tennis-match between them, which the queen was watching as his rival used the queen's proferred handkerchief in a gesture of over-familiarity. Elizabeth had then forced the two petulant courtiers into a public reconciliation. He does not appear to have ever met Mary although some have suggested that their paths had crossed briefly when she was being held at Carlisle soon after her flight to England in 1568, but this did not stop him entertaining hopes of her and he went as far as to send her a diamond which she subsequently wore. Their awkward 'wooing' extended to Mary sending Norfolk a pillow embroidered with a hopeful motto about her fortitude in the face of adversity, and she started to refer to him familiarly as 'my Norfolk', at the least grateful for his support at a largely hostile English court which she had clearly expected on her arrival to treat her with more chivalry and eagerness to help.

In more reflective moments, Mary led her trusted Scots ally Bishop Leslie to understand – as he told the Spanish ambassador in August 1570 – that she had not really wanted to remarry when she arrived in England but began to consider Norfolk seriously because Elizabeth clearly wanted her to marry an Englishman. This implied that the marriage was partly a bid to win over the hostile and suspicious queen who had shocked her by not helping to retrieve her throne in 1568, but instead held her captive and conducted a 'rigged' enquiry into the 'Casket Letters' that did not exonerate her. Mary could well have decided on this course of action in ignorance that her allying to a powerful – conservative and pro-Catholic

– courtier with important enemies would both upset the latter's rivals and make Elizabeth suspicious as to why she was seeking favour in the English elite. Was she after Elizabeth's throne? Thus Mary would have misread Elizabeth's mentality and English court politics for the second time – but it is equally important to note that if she did this, she did not back down when she found herself to be wrong about what would please Elizabeth. By this point, she may have been so dispirited about her continued incarceration that she assumed that she would now have to 'force' her restoration to a position of political and personal liberty on Elizabeth and so encouraged both Norfolk and her northern English Catholic backers. She certainly turned down the naïve but well-meant suggestion by her captor at Bolton in autumn 1568, the fervently Protestant Sir Francis Knollys (Elizabeth's cousin), that she should marry his young cousin Sir George Carey, who called in on her in October *en route* to join his father Lord Hunsdon, the new governor of Berwick-upon-Tweed. This would have tied her to Elizabeth's maternal family and to their Protestantism, but Carey (not of royal blood, unlike Norfolk) and his religion were not to her liking and she ignored him. However, choosing Norfolk had its problems; he was only nominally Protestant, rich enough to keep her in the style that she was accustomed to, and of royal blood. As we shall see, in 1569 Norfolk clashed politically with the even more influential and vehemently anti-Catholic, anti-Spanish Cecil. This clearly damaged his chances of the privy council, dominated by his personal foes, accepting him as a suitable husband for Mary – and it is possible that his opponents now actively undermined his chances. But what if another, 'tamer' great peer had been available as a loyal, Protestant widower of high rank to marry off to Mary? Would Elizabeth have shown more enthusiasm for this? It should be noted here that Elizabeth was as parsimonious about creating peers as her grandfather Henry VII had been – Norfolk was the only duke in England as of 1568.

Contrary to retrospective patriotic Protestant myth, the queen was far from an assured backer of the anti-Spanish and increasingly anti-Catholic faction in her council in the 1560s or 1570s, and so immune from the suggestions of more emollient men such as Norfolk. A split between the personally antagonistic anti-Spanish Cecil and Leicester led in 1569 to an unlikely temporary re-alignment of the latter, with Norfolk as the leading Council conservative. The seizure of the Genoese funds on Spanish ships which put into Plymouth late in 1568, *en route* for the Spanish army in the Netherlands, brought confrontation with King Philip and potentially between the rival groups of councillors. Elizabeth's dominant financial concerns (amounting to parsimony as with Henry VII) added to her irritation with Spain in this first major Anglo-Spanish crisis in November 1568. She agreed to order the confiscation of the contents of four Spanish treasure-ships driven into Plymouth by northern Netherlands (Dutch) rebel privateers, the 'Sea Beggars' – an £ 85,000 loan from Genoese bankers to the Spanish governor and army commander, the duke of Alva, to fund his armies in the Netherlands. Technically the money was Genoese, not Spanish, and the Genoese were at liberty to cancel their arrangement; they were induced to transfer the loan to the English government. But the politico-military intention was to hamper Alva's campaign, and presumably Leicester, Cecil, and the other anti-Spanish Councillors hoped to provoke a reply, ruin good Anglo-Spanish relations and Elizabeth's accompanying laxity on English Catholics, and force their queen into a more vigorous defence of the Protestant cause. At this point Cecil at least did not envisage open war with Spain but merely 'proxy' conflict in the Netherlands, as seen by his correspondence with the Dutch rebels and the French Huguenot leader Coligny; he accurately thought Philip was too preoccupied for open war.

The seizure was masterminded by Cecil, and was intended by him to damage Philip's ability to wage war on his restive Netherlands subjects. This was a struggle now becoming mainly religious as led by the Protestants in the northern (Dutch) region, but still encompassing those 'autonomist' Catholics in the southern Netherlands who were used to a more relaxed and 'hands-off' rule than that imposed by the centralising and religiously persecutory Philip. The region had long been a jumble of aristocratic duchies and autonomous mercantile towns ruled by their own sovereign, the duke of Burgundy, before it had been inherited by Philip's grandfather Philip (I) of Habsburg from his late mother Duchess Mary, and so passed via his son Emperor Charles V to Philip II. The 1560s rebellion had indeed originally been a 'devolutionist' one against oppressive Spanish governors led by nobles such as count Egmont, one of Philip's most famous executed victims, not a religious war, and Queen Elizabeth was uncomfortable at any such defiance of a legitimate sovereign by rebels, be it in the Netherlands or Scotland. Ministers like

Cecil, however, saw it as a chance to weaken Spain and tie down its large, competent and aggressive army of skilled military phalanxes (the famous '*tercios*'), who might turn on England next – hence seizing the Genoese money sent by Philip to pay his army under their fanatically Catholic and atrocity-committing commander, the duke of Alva. The current Spanish ambassador in London, Guzman de Spes, reckoned in spring 1568 that if Cecil had not been blocked by other councillors, he would by now have had declared open war on Spain. So did Cecil see the chance of acquiring a large sum of Spanish cash for England that November as a way of luring the fiscally cautious (if not stingy) Elizabeth into taking action over the Netherlands crisis at last, or even of hoping that Philip would declare war over it and so force her hand?

Philip, like Elizabeth, was too cautious to rush into war with his rival, however damaging and insulting the seizure of the Genoese ships was – and he may also have reckoned that declaring war would only strengthen the hands of anti-Spanish councillors in London. It could also drive England into alliance with France (always a major fear for a strategy-conscious Habsburg ruler), as despite being a hard-line Catholic and the main influence on the weak-willed teenage king Charles IX, his mother Catherine de Medici, was an Italian heiress who distrusted Spanish domination of her homeland. The commercially crippling Spanish Netherlands embargo on English trade which followed the seizure – eased once alternative buyers could be found for their goods – avoided declaring open war, and brought embarrassment to and pressure on the chief mover in the seizure, Cecil, in spring 1569. Cecil was also unpopular with great nobles fond of allowing the regional magnates traditional semi-autonomy for his centralising aims, especially in the north – where Norfolk now had a major stake as controller of the Dacre of Gilsland lands. A Council plot followed to have him arrested, in which Norfolk was a prime mover. Like Thomas Cromwell in 1540, he was condemned by nobles like Norfolk (grandson of Cromwell's arch-enemy, the third duke) as a low-born 'usurper' of the nobility's rightful role in council and a religious fanatic. Norfolk was the queen's closest male relative and was generally trusted at this point, though his occasional physical clashes with his rival Leicester – son of a major foe of the Howards from the 1540s – were politically dangerous. Leicester, a dangerous foe to Cecil as the queen's favourite, joined in Norfolk's campaign and even now suggested to the queen, in a stormy meeting of senior courtiers in her chambers, that the realm was not safe until Cecil was beheaded. The queen threatened to send him to the Tower for his impertinence, and Norfolk – who would normally have been only too glad to see Leicester in trouble – grumbled to some other listeners that clearly even Leicester only kept the queen's favour as long as he agreed with Cecil, and the latter's power over her was too much to be tolerated. One of them agreed with Norfolk that they had to seek some remedy for this, and the duke then went over to the queen and told her that he hoped that she would realise when she calmed down that Cecil's power was causing disunity and she needed to seek another way to preserve her and her subjects' safety. He and his friends on the council would be willing to help her do this when she asked them.[4] She did not reply directly and left the room in some distress – but clearly Norfolk was hinting at helping in a 'coup' to have Cecil arrested and sacked if not executed. Was Leicester partly motivated in his evidently increasing antagonism towards Cecil by knowledge that Cecil had ruined his chances of marrying the queen in 1560 by interfering in the Amy Robsart scandal?

Had Elizabeth given the 'go-ahead' as her father had done in 1540, council foes were evidently more than ready to have Cecil kidnapped or arrested at the council and dragged off to the Tower – and once an enquiry into a fallen minister was underway they had their own momentum. But Elizabeth was not her father, and she trusted more of her closest advisers than he did; she continued to give Cecil her unswerving backing,[5] and he survived the crisis. If he had been arrested in spring 1569, the uneasy alliance of Leicester (normally a militant Protestant by now) and Norfolk would have been likely to see a more pro-Spanish policy in the 1570s, with the replacement of the determined, methodical, well-organised, and ruthless Cecil's unwavering pro-Protestant 'line' in foreign policy by a more uncertain one. That could in turn have led to a move to get Mary released and sent home, albeit as a 'puppet' of pro-English lords, to reassure France (or even Spain); Mary's continued detention was not just due to Scots and French politics sidelining rather than helping her. Cecil, a superb administrator and effective chief minister to Elizabeth for forty years (as Secretary of State to 1572 and Lord Treasurer 1572–98), was a force for stability and consistency; either the hot-tempered, extravagant, 'showy' Leicester nor the arrogant and politically naïve Norfolk were likely to prove as consistent in determining international policies had they had Cecil's influence removed. Nor was there any guarantee that their alliance would continue for long, as quite apart from their sporadic personal tensions, their religious interests were at odds (Leicester was a patron of 'reformist' Protestants and Norfolk was not).

The unexpected political ruin which befell Norfolk in 1570–2, in the aftermath of the reign's first Catholic revolt, the rising of the 'Northern Earls' (to which his attitude was alleged by his enemies to be equivocal) has a new explanation if the events of 1569 are considered. Did the cunning and ruthless Cecil now turn his attention to undermining Norfolk, as successfully as he had once undermined Leicester's chances of marrying the queen? As of late 1568, into early 1569, Norfolk was showing his conspicuous loyalty and the queen was showing her trust in him in his leadership of the 'Casket Letters' enquiry, which as seen in the previous chapter, the queen moved from York to London and ensured that the letters did not clear Mary Stuart enough to allow her return to her throne. But now Norfolk was talked of as a potential husband for Mary, and was backed by his ex-foe Leicester. The latter encouraged the queen to allow Norfolk to marry Mary Stuart, apparently to the queen's anger.[6] The Spanish ambassador De Spes offered Norfolk his and Philip's support provided that the duke promised to work for the welfare of the northern English Catholics, who were being legally harassed and heavily fined for attending illegal masses instead of going to weekly Protestant services as required by law. Norfolk agreed and dared to put his offer to marry Mary to a privy council meeting called in the queen's absence. Evidently, the councillors had decided *en masse* that it was safer not to broach such a touchy subject in front of Elizabeth and to put up a 'united front' to her so she could not single out one or more of them as pressurising her and make them scapegoats for her wrath. With Leicester backing the proposal, even Norfolk's current '*bete noire*' Cecil carefully avoided antagonising him with an open refusal to consider it, and he promised to do what he could to help provided that the queen approved.

But now the question arose of who would speak to the queen, and as Leicester suggested a committee – again, to minimise the risk of Elizabeth blaming and victimising the 'spokesman' for their decision – this was agreed, but then nobody would agree to serve on it. Clearly nobody wanted to be put in the 'firing line' with the hot-tempered queen if they could find someone else to serve in their place, and Leicester accepted that perhaps Her Majesty would react badly to a group of them as a supposed plot to force her hand. It would be better for one or two to approach her, and he would be prepared to do so if Cecil went with him. But Cecil had already discreetly left the room, and was not seen at court for some days. Leicester promised to raise the subject on his own when the opportunity arose, but days passed without him doing so and eventually an irritated Norfolk, prodding him in vain to act and being told that the queen had not been in a good mood for days, agreed to his suggestion to talk to the queen himself. But when he did go to the queen's rooms, he lost his nerve and did not say why he had come, and he ignored opportunities presented to him by Elizabeth to speak of what was on his mind. Instead he became too afraid and went home without staying for dinner, and she left for her favourite residence up the Thames at Richmond next day. Norfolk made up his mind to go there and tell her and boldly set out, but *en route* he met Leicester out fishing in the river near Kew and the favourite told him that some gossiping court ladies had alerted the queen to what he had intended to say. Elizabeth was not too pleased and so Leicester declined to accompany Norfolk to Richmond and be blamed too and advised him not to mention it, and at the palace Cecil gave him similar advice. He still braved the queen's presence, but when asked by her what news he had brought from London he said 'none'. She retorted tartly that she had expected to hear news of a planned marriage which was being talked about in London, and at that his nerve failed and he made a hasty withdrawal. A similar failure of nerve occurred next time he encountered the queen, at Farnham.[7]

Norfolk's failure to tell the queen what he was planning seems to have aroused her suspicion that his silence must mean something underhand, which was to her detriment rather than her writing it off as awkwardness and nerves, and from then on the situation deteriorated. But the ambitious duke was too committed to his idea of marrying Mary to abandon it, and he was egged on by assorted friends and clients – including northern Catholics, nobles and gentry alike, who looked on it as a way to improve their religious situation by acquiring Mary, a committed Catholic (though she had been seen attending Anglican services when she first arrived in England, to please her Protestant captor Sir Francis Knollys) as their patron at court. Indeed, they – especially the leading anti-centralising Catholic nobles who most disliked Sussex's policies and resisted Protestantisation, the earls of Northumberland (Thomas Percy, born 1528) and Westmoreland (Charles Neville, born 1542) – saw Mary, once Norfolk's wife and so linked closely to court, as likelier to be named as Elizabeth's successor. They were backed up by their wives, both strong Catholics too – Anne Percy, nee Somerset, from the leading south-east Wales Catholic dynasty of Somerset of Raglan Castle and descended via the Beauforts from Edward III, and Jane Neville, Norfolk's sister and probably the main 'contact' between her husband and brother in championing the northern Catholics. In the fifteenth century the dynasties of Percy of Alnwick (Northumberland) and Neville of Raby (Co. Durham) had squabbled and fought over local and national office, but now they were allies in the causes of Catholicism, and were fighting for local autonomy from centralising and religiously alien government bureaucrats at the Council of the north in York. Also, in families proud of their history it would not be forgotten that both had once been involved in defying monarchs in London who had tried to rein them in – the Percies had helped Henry IV to depose Richard II in 1399 then turned on him in 1403, and the Westmoreland Nevilles' cousin had been Warwick 'the Kingmaker' who helped to depose Henry VI in 1460–1 then overthrew his replacement Edward IV in 1470. Treason – or patriotic resistance – was in their blood, and the present earl of Northumberland's family had lost most of their lands and power in disgrace after their involvement in anti-Henry VIII and pro-Marian plots in 1536–7.

Installing a new Catholic queen, or at least forcing Mary Stuart on Elizabeth as her heir, was in the local family traditions. Once she was queen, she and Norfolk would act decisively in favour of Catholicism and restore the 'True Faith' to which Elizabeth herself had once belonged under Mary Tudor. Some of the Catholic peers were now so annoyed at Elizabeth and her ministers for standing in the way of the marriage that they began to plan to rescue Mary by force so that she and Norfolk could marry without royal permission. The leading light in, or brains behind this daring plan, was probably the person who offered to carry out the original scheme, Northumberland's wife Anne, who it seems was intended to use her physical similarity to Mary to change clothes with her on a visit to her 'court' – now usually at Tutbury Castle in Staffordshire from February 1569 but at easier-of-access Wingfield Manor when the castle had to be shut up for cleaning. The excuse for the visit was to be Anne's friend with one of Mary's ladies-in-waiting, now married to Mary's French page Bastian and pregnant; once the women had changed clothes Mary would slip out of the castle disguised as Anne and be escourted to safety at the Northumberlands' home. That was only one step from a treasonous plan to put Mary on Elizabeth's throne, and it amounted at the least to coercing the sovereign to change their ways by an armed demonstration of power. Such a showdown (again by conservative Catholics in the north against the London government) in the 'Pilgrimage of Grace' in 1536 had been interpreted by Henry VIII as treason – once his local commander, Norfolk's grandfather, had had the time and troops to reverse his initially conciliatory offers to the rebels – so it was logical to expect Elizabeth to react the same way. It is not clear how many of them were now aiming at removing Elizabeth in favour of Mary, rather than just forcing Mary's marriage and restoration to favour on the English queen, but this would be the way the Tudor regime interpreted it. Given his priorities, it is clear that Norfolk was not aware of this yet – so was he dangerously naïve?

Elizabeth's fear of Mary ran too deep to allow the aggrandisement of her potential successor in any circumstances. This made any attempt to coax, let alone force, her to accept the marriage to Norfolk political dynamite, even if the council had unanimously and genuinely backed it as a way to 'control' Mary. A figure who was now seen as a 'loose cannon', attracting ambitious and dubiously loyal local northern Catholic gentry visitors to her exiled and supervised 'court'. This was now at Wingfield Manor in Derbyshire, one of the many manor-houses of her current captor Gilbert Talbot, earl of Shrewsbury and husband of the famous 'Bess of Hardwick'. (Mary was normally kept, as of February 1569, at the more secure Tutbury Castle, isolated and strongly fortified in rural Staffordshire, but this was being cleaned up as was regularly necessary during a long residence by a large household there.) As shown above, the queen's temper, paranoia and habit of blaming others as scapegoats induced caution in them and none of them wanted to seem to be the plan's fervent backer and so risk her wrath. This even applied to Leicester, hence his refusal to accompany the nervous Norfolk to Richmond and speak to the queen with him – and as Norfolk's encounter on the Thames riverbank with Leicester *en route* to Richmond was coincidental this failure to act was not a 'careful plan' to let Norfolk risk disgrace and ruin, but spontaneous. In the event, a dangerous stalemate saw the northern Catholics continue their plans to rescue Mary, some sort of contacts between them and Norfolk (probably on his part rashly seeking their support to put pressure on the queen and show her how granting his wish would bring them peacefully into line), and the queen aware that Norfolk favoured the match but for some reason was not telling her about it.

Given the duke's apparent enthusiasm for the match ahead of the next council meeting (he was said to have claimed he would rather lose his life than this match), he clearly failed to read the 'danger signs' that the northern Catholic support he had been canvassing could be interpreted as treasonous plotting. He still had the backing of Mary herself, who as late as January 1570 – with the 'Northern Rebellion' in full swing and widespread suspicion of their involvement or encouragement for it – was declaring in a letter that she was sure that most of England would approve of their marriage. But the tide now began to turn against Norfolk's always slender hope of success, commencing with Leicester falling ill (or so he alleged) at Titchfield, the home of the earl of Southampton, during the royal summer 'Progress' round southern England in late summer 1569. He asked the queen to come and see him privately, stressing the seriousness of his condition and that he had things to confess in case he died. Given the speed of his recovery when she arrived, he may well have been pretending to be more ill than he actually was, to cause her panic and to ensure that she treated him sympathetically rather than having one of her rages when she discovered what he was about to say. She arrived to see him in an anxious mood and was relieved to see him improved and out of bed, probably as he had intended, and he used their private meeting to tell her all that had been going on between him and Norfolk and the latter's firm intention to seek Mary's hand but failure to confide in her. He theatrically claimed that he had been anxious not to die without confessing to and being pardoned by the queen, and she duly forgave him.

As Leicester had no doubt hoped, she transferred her wrath at the defiance of her wishes to Norfolk. Encountering him later that day, she ordered him sharply to leave off his plans for Mary, and he hastily assured her that he would do so and claimed that in any case the impoverished nation of Scotland was worth less than his current estates, so he would have had no material gain from the marriage. When he was on his tennis-court in Norwich (where he had a grandiose town house) he already felt like a king, so he had no need of marrying a queen.[8] Having dealt with Norfolk, the next day the queen made her opposition to the match clear at the planned council meeting and told her councillors that if she agreed to it she would be in the Tower in four months, i.e. as a result of a Catholic plot to put Mary on her throne. One councillor dared to present a petition from Spanish ambassador De Spes for Mary's liberation, at which Elizabeth said angrily that she would advise Mary to have more patience or some of those on whom she was relying would lose their heads.[9] This effectively presented the supporters of the plan with a major blockage in the form of a royal veto; even though the queen might change her mind later, discretion and postponement for the moment would be politically advisable. But instead the obstinate Catholic plotters continued their plans to liberate Mary by force, and Cecil and his spies had good enough intelligence on what was intended to forestall this. Crucially, the now shunned Norfolk left the unwelcoming royal court for his house in London, the Charterhouse – without royal permission, which for an arrogant noble of semi-royal blood used to doing what he liked was a minor matter, but which in the circumstances of immanent rebellion assumed an ominous explanation. The queen feared the worst, and sent her ultra-Protestant and totally loyal cousin Huntingdon to Wingfield with soldiers to take charge of Mary and remove her back to the safer Tutbury Castle, behind strong walls that could keep 'rescuers' out and in a more isolated hilly district so that arriving intruders could be spotted easier. Mary was furious at being transferred from the relative comforts of Wingfield back to a cold and draughty medieval castle, and to have the rough and distrustful Protestant Huntingdon rather than the more courteous Shrewsbury in charge of her, apparently fearing that as another royal cousin Huntingdon had claims on the throne and might seek to do away with her as a rival. She complained that his men had searched her rooms and questioned her servants at gunpoint, but was ignored. The search was apparently aimed at finding incriminating correspondence between her and Norfolk, but if there was any she was already adept at hiding such evidence. Whether the story about Anne Percy planning to swap clothes with Mary and have the latter spirited away to Northumberland had 'leaked out' is unknown, but the Countess' visit to Mary's cancellation in September appears to have been due to mischance, not the danger – the friend she was due to visit in Mary's household had her baby early so she was unable to receive visitors.

With rebellion rumoured to be immanent and Norfolk under suspicion the latter was summoned back to court, but in a probably fatal miscalculation and/or panic he refused to come. Instead, on 18 September 1569 he bolted from London to his main East Anglian residence at Kenninghall in Suffolk – the seat of Mary Tudor's mainly Catholic rebellion against the Protestant regime of Jane Grey in July 1553.[10] This was a public relations disaster for his already tarnished reputation and for the queen's ability to trust him, not least as failure to come to the embattled sovereign when summoned at the start of a rebellion, which had been Elizabeth's own reaction to her half-sister's command to attend her at the opening of the Wyatt Rebellion in 1554. She had ended up in the Tower under suspicion of treason with councillors urging Mary to execute her, and although she had eventually been cleared, as no evidence could be found of her plotting, she had remained in exile and disgrace for over a year and only she knew what exactly her attitude to the rebels had been. The same fear of treason, arrest, and vigorous interrogation could be expected to be Norfolk's fate, so logically he was at least gambling that the rebels would rescue Mary and/or hold out against the government and, as with the 'Pilgrimage of Grace' in 1536, negotiations would have to follow. The latter could lead to his being called in to help the government and being able to insist that he was allowed to marry Mary; if he was under arrest already he might be 'framed' and executed by his enemies. Whether he had any serious hopes of Mary gaining the throne, perhaps with Spanish military help given the latter's interest in her role as a Catholic champion and Philip's anger at the 1568 treasure-seizure, is dubious. But he had now put his neck on the line – literally – and rumour assumed that he would flee to the north and aid the rebels. The queen moved to well-guarded Windsor Castle and sent an army north to tackle the rebels. Rather than joining the plotters, Norfolk wrote anxiously to the queen on 24 September that he had 'never entertained a thought against her Highness, her Crown or her dynasty' and was grieved that she was angry with him. He had 'preferred to withdraw' from court only because he had found that he was receiving cold looks from everyone and he had feared that he could not get a chance to show his innocence to the queen.[11] If so, he had gone the wrong way about it – but if he had temporarily reckoned on bold defiance serving him best, he had clearly lost his nerve (again). His letter crossed with one from the queen summoning him to court in firm but not hostile terms, and with Leicester writing to assure him that he had 'nothing to fear in submission, but would be proclaimed a traitor by disobeying' he agreed to come to court. He wrote to the leading plotters, the earls of Northumberland (head of the long-dominant but now somewhat eclipsed local north-east English dynasty of Percy, lords of Alnwick Castle) and his own brother-in-law the earl of Westmoreland (head of the senior branch of their main rivals the Nevilles) on 30 September asking them to cancel their planned rising, and a day or so later rode to court as the queen had demanded.[12] He arrived at Windsor on 8 October, but now he was safe in government hands, the queen refused to see him. She summoned her council and ordered him to be taken to the Tower, and his conservative allies, the earls of Arundel and Pembroke and Lord Lumley, were placed under house–arrest. A mixture of the evidence amassed by Cecil's spies, the extent of danger from the rebels, and high politics would now determine if Mary Stuart's planned fourth husband would now go the same way as her first three.

The 'Northern Earls' now rose at the head of their armed tenants and other allies in November 1569, with a pre-arranged overnight peal of bells at Topcliffe in Yorkshire on the night of 8–9 November announcing the rising and and the rebellion breaking out the next day with assorted local assemblies. The rebels' imagery was the same as that of the 'Pilgrimage of Grace' and explicitly catholic with them wearing the crosses of Crusaders and marching under banners of the 'Five Wounds of Christ', a subject of popular rural devotion, and their manifestoes similarly declared that the sovereign was being deceived by evil advisers into attacking the 'True Faith' and dishonouring the realm and the ancient nobility. Cecil and Leicester now assumed the 'bogeyman' role of jumped-up and greedy 'arrivistes' previously awarded by Northern conservative rebels to Thomas Cromwell in 1536 (and by Warwick 'the Kingmaker's followers in 1469 and 1470 to the Woodvilles), and the faithful were summoned to defend their religion and force the queen to rid herself of her crooked councillors and rely on the old nobility instead. On 14 November the rebels ceremonially entered Durham Cathedral, an ancient symbol of the faith in the region and headquarters of its medieval palatinate – bishopric, to burn the current ruling religion's official service-books and celebrate an illegal Mass. One body of rebels then headed south for York and another for Tutbury to free Mary Stuart, but her captors had been forewarned and had time – just – to move her hastily out of harm's way south to Coventry (where there was clearly no 'pre-planning' for her evacuation as the disused castle was still uninhabitable and she had to be put up at an inn). In fact, her follower Bishop Leslie later testified that Mary had disapproved of the rising as untimely, unlikely to succeed, and probable to end in bloodshed and damage to her reputation and she had asked him to write to the earl of Northumberland to have it postponed – showing that neither she nor Norfolk were the masterminds behind it, whatever their foes might hope to prove.

The rebels reached Tutbury to find Mary gone and rumours that the earl of Warwick (i.e. Leicester's brother Ambrose Dudley, commander in the French expedition to aid the Huguenots in 1563) and Hereford (i.e. Walter Devereux, a veteran and brutal commander in Ireland), plus Lord Clinton (the Lord Admiral of the fleet) were *en route* with a large army. They gave up and headed back north to the port of Hartlepool where hopefully Alva might send Spanish ships to help them, but in fact the cool-headed and realistic Spanish commander had refused to have anything to do with the rebellion as hopeless and had turned down De Spes' suggestions. Instead, the only ships in Hartlepool were government ones which fired on the rebels on shore; they had to retreat north, and as the regime's army approached, Northumberland lost his nerve and fled to Scotland. (He was later extradited to England by the regency and executed in 1572.) Westmoreland fled to Flanders and was to spend the next thirty years there as a Spanish pensioner, and the rebellion collapsed though the experienced and well-supported Lord Dacre, Norfolk's father-in-law, held out into January 1570 at isolated Naworth Castle on the Borders with bitter snowy weather aiding him. The rebellion also had the unexpected advantage that in Scotland Elizabeth's ally, Moray, was assassinated by one of his Hamilton enemies, being fatally shot while riding through Linlithgow on 23 January, and the lack of certainty about who would take over the regency enabled assorted Marians to make for the Border and help the rebels in Northumberland hold out for a few more weeks. But as soon as the queen's cousin Lord Hunsdon arrived at Naworth with his army in February the assembled rebels there were defeated in a pitched battle, 300 or so being killed, and Dacre fled into

Scotland. The usual round of executions (over 750) and heavy fines – and an even harsher imposition of Protestantism on the region – followed, with many Northern landed families, with any possible connection to the rebellion, stripped of their lands and replaced by loyalists; the old 'feudal' world of loyalty to the ancestral lord and the ancestral religion was to be destroyed. At the Percies' castle, the exiled earl's nephew, Sir Henry Percy, arrived to check on the rebel leader's abandoned daughters to find the girls shivering in the half-empty, robbed building with no money for food or fuel, while the bodies of their executed servants swung from the trees outside. In Durham Cathedral the priest who had celebrated the illegal mass at the start of the rebellion was hanged at the site. The purge left any ambitious English Catholic peers who aimed at reversing the Reformation by force with no physical basis of armed support to do so.[13] In effect, any restoration of Catholicism would now have to be by outright invasion – and in retrospect, the defeat of the rebellion and deliberate wrecking of the local old social/religious order deprived the Spanish Armada of crucial potential support in 1588.

Elizabeth could not be certain until the rebels were finally defeated that the revolt was containable, or that Spain or Marians in Scotland would not aid it, and her weeks of anxiety increased her vindictiveness – and her 'focus' on Norfolk for encouraging the rebels. Before Moray was murdered she wrote to him offering her increased goodwill if he could prove that Norfolk was behind the rebellion,[14] but no such proof was forthcoming. Norfolk had been naïve and rash rather than a competent or committed plotter and had at the most hoped to coerce the queen into letting him marry Mary Stuart, but he had corresponded with and initially encouraged the Northern rebels, which amounted to treason. The question now arose of whether he would escape execution on account of a lack of 'hard evidence', despite some ill-will from both his sovereign and assorted ruthless councillors, as Elizabeth had done in 1554. And would any reprieve only prove temporary, given that his reputation and standing at court were now ruined and he was under permanent suspicion? This is where the central part of the mystery surrounding Norfolk's execution arises – the question of whether he was really stupid or desperate enough to dabble in further plotting, as was alleged at his later trial. Any serious hope of political support in the north had vanished, his sister and brother-in-law were exiles in the control of Spain, and his fellow-councillors were too keen to save their own skins from the wrathful queen to dare to admit that they had tentatively accepted the idea of him marrying Mary in 1569 when Elizabeth seemed not too hostile to this. Dangerously for him, the plot earlier in 1569 to unseat Cecil had the crucial result that the latter now took the offensive against his council foes – and he was the person who controlled the nascent Elizabethan intelligence service. This was small and inexperienced in the 1560s and nothing as wide-ranging as it was to become as Spain. The threat of a catholic invasion became serious and papal-sponsored Jesuit missionaries started to come into England to win back converts to the faith – and in some cases to persuade them that it was their religious duty to help remove the 'heretic' queen as the Holy Father Pius V had ordered in 1570 in the Bull '*Regnans In Excelsis*'. The Papal Bull presented devout Catholics with a dilemma, and anti-Catholic English ministers and writers with an opportunity to argue that in theory all Catholics were now traitors who regarded the queen as a usurper. (In fact, the vast majority of English Catholics were unswervingly loyal and regarded the Bull with embarrassment, as did most of Europe's Catholic sovereigns – even Philip of Spain did not act on it for years.) Now a Catholic rebellion had actually occurred and had been linked to the cause of Mary Stuart the threat could recur and have overseas support next time – and Norfolk was 'on the radar' for his involvement with the 'Northern Earls', even if in the event he had asked them to call off their rising.

The Ridolfi Plot: an unrealistic scheme, but who was conning who?

In August 1570 Norfolk was released from the Tower of London, this was probably sped up due to the presence of the plague in London and his poor health. He was remanded under house-arrest to Howard House in the suburbs under the guardianship of Sir Henry Neville, who no doubt passed on details of his correspondence and visitors to Cecil (who urged Norfolk to prove his loyalty by marrying his own widowed sister-in-law Lady Hoby), but his problems were not over. He had not learnt from his arrest, and seems to have continued to maintain secret correspondence with his allies and clients – and with Mary – during his imprisonment, smuggling out coded messages hidden in leather bottles.[15] The letters to and from Mary seem to have been innocuous enough to suggest mutual encouragement so they could keep their spirits up, but any contact was grist to the mill of those seeking to ruin him as an unrepentant plotter who was only awaiting the opportunity to commit more treason and needed to be executed. The chief of these enemies was clearly his 1569 foe Cecil, who seems to have been the prime mover behind Norfolk's disgrace and execution over the forthcoming 'Ridolfi Plot'. Norfolk was clearly naïve if not worse, and wrote enthusiastically of his continuing hopes to marry Mary at a time when it was anathema to the suspicious Elizabeth. Indeed, he had had to promise in a written 'submission' not to continue that plan before she would release him; he broke this pledge and even sent Mary a copy of the document so she could see what he was being ordered to do but was nobly resisting. But it is important to remember that, as with other memorable Elizabethan plots, the account which we have of what transpired next comes from state documents, all of them based on the alleged discoveries of the secret intelligencers employed by his foe Cecil. Early students of these papers in less troubled and intrigue-riven times than our own tended to take them at face value, as the honest recordings of upright and patriotic intelligencers seeking to defeat sinister Catholic plots against queen Elizabeth. But this is much less certain in an era of 'fake news' and double or triple-agents, and it is not clear if any of the details were embellished or even invented to 'prove' the guilt of the accused beyond all reasonable doubt and show them up as unrepentant villains. Was Norfolk lured into a 'honey trap' by Cecil and his allies in order to ruin him, and did they genuinely believe that he was a public danger who had to be removed for the safety of the nation – as arguably happened to Mary herself later. Was the evidence exaggerated, or was he as duplicitous, treacherous, arrogant, and foolish as the 'official line' put out?

The plot centred on the activities of an Italian Catholic banker, the Florentine Roberto Ridolfi, a theatrical character and master of exaggeration who seems to have been as over-ambitious and confident that a precariously planned 'master-plan' to aid Mary would work as much as Norfolk or the 'Northern Earls' had been in 1569. Having come to London to secretly distribute copies of the Papal Bull deposing Elizabeth to the Catholic community and so incite rebellion, he extended this to dabbling in a plan to free Mary in association with an invasion by the Duke of Alva with his Spanish army in the Netherlands – forgetting that Alva had turned down the chance to assist a rebellion which was already underway in late 1569 as too risky. Supposedly, both the pope and the fanatically Catholic king Philip would assist the plot and fund the plotters and the invasion, and now that Elizabeth had been declared deposed by the pope, assorted councillors were bound to have second thoughts about defending her from a Catholic attack and would join it instead. Mary would be rescued and married to Norfolk, and the Catholic cause would triumph. Mary's restoration to the throne of Scotland was the aim, and what exactly was to happen to the queen of England seems to have been more ambiguous beyond coercing Elizabeth to help Mary and make her her heir.

Ridolfi had himself smuggled into Howard House for secret talks with the probably very bored and worried Norfolk, who Elizabeth was refusing to receive at court again. It was a major act of folly for the duke to receive him or not to throw him out in ostentatious horror when he heard of Ridolfi's plans, and apparently the plotter had to ask his patron Bishop Leslie (the man whose literary defence of Mary he had been printing abroad) to intercede for him and had no success for some time. Possibly Leslie – who Norfolk later blamed for his ruin – 'had his own fish to fry' and was using Ridolfi to press a version of his own plans to restore Mary to power (in Scotland and probably in England too) on the duke as his best hope of armed assistance from a leading magnate. If the duke was with him, the plan would sound more impressive to the Pope and King Philip. This also arouses the possibility that Mary – on her own volition or as prompted by Leslie – was actively encouraging the duke to listen to Ridolfi, and so to convert his interest in marrying her into armed political help. (The contemporary plans of romantic young northern English Catholics to rescue her from custody, e.g. a vague plan to 'snatch' her while out hunting with her guardians near Chatsworth, may have improved her confidence of success.) At the eventual meeting with Ridolfi, the duke apparently approved a plan to release Mary by force, arrange his marriage to her, and then force her restoration to Scotland and to the heirdom of England. But he would not countenance Elizabeth's deposition or murder, and had the sense to refuse to sign any incriminating documents.

Norfolk's position does not seem to have gone beyond the basics of what he had approved of in the late 1569 'Northern Rebellion', i.e. rescuing and marrying Mary in defiance of Elizabeth and having her chosen as the heir to England, and logically his isolation from court and continued disgrace had been preying on his mind. As with other marginalised and disgraced, but not yet legally charged ex-ministers at the febrile Tudor court (e.g. Wolsey in 1529–30 and Somerset in 1549–50), the natures, of competitive politics and of the 'suggestible', paranoid sovereign were such in 1570–1 that Norfolk could easily imagine that his enemies were building up a 'dossier' of his alleged crimes (probably mostly invented) to have him charged so he ought to take measures to save himself. Such fallen ministers often ended up charged with treason some time after their removal from court, probably due to a mixture of their enemies methodically compiling 'evidence', them indulging in indiscreet 'soundings' to see what was really going on or to regain influence, and the monarch suspecting what they might be up to. The accuracy of the charges that were eventually laid for 'treason' is also often suspect. Wolsey does not seem to have been engaged in any serious activity against Henry VIII's ministers while exiled to his see of York in 1529–30, but in 1551 Somerset he was allowed back onto the privy council by his foe Northumberland but kept 'out of the loop' for major decisions, may have been planning to remove the latter. The question of what Norfolk was up to is also unclear, but his removal from court and the queen's favour, alongside placement under 'house-arrest', was not unusual for a senior figure under royal disfavour – Elizabeth had suffered this under Mary Tudor, firstly at isolated Woodstock in 1554–5 and then unofficially at Hatfield in 1555–8. Some strong or wily characters like Elizabeth could keep their nerve and give no evidence to their enemies of further plotting, but Norfolk seems to have been more inclined to panic or affronted at the disgrace, and as the leading magnate of a major region (East Anglia) and a rich noble of semi-royal blood, he had a host of tenants and other clients to impress and 'lead'. If he could not gain access to the queen and have favours to distribute, he was politically and socially useless in the competitive world of Tudor patronage – so did he resort to a gamble to force himself back into the limelight with the help of Ridolfi and hopefully De Spes? Was he genuinely angry at the purge and mass-executions of Catholics in the north in winter 1569–70 and so found that his ancestral faith meant more to him than it had when he had 'conformed' in 1559–69, so he now set himself up as a Catholic champion?

Norfolk may have exaggerated his Catholicity to win the favour of the pope and the anti-heretic champion King Philip, or decided that it would win him the backing of the surviving, and now presumably even more fearful Catholics across England, who presumably would be the alleged army of 20,000, who his 'letters' (if they were genuine) said he believed would rally to him. But there remains the possibility that the letters were not actually written by him but by the over-enthusiastic and poorly-informed Ridolfi, who was less likely than Norfolk to realise that the suppression of the Northern Rebellion meant that raising an army of 20,000 rebels was extremely implausible. Ridolfi had every reason to exaggerate the number of potential rebels to reassure King Philip and the cautious Alva to back the rebellion this time, unlike in late 1569. Plus, Norfolk had refused to sign any incriminating documents when he first met Ridolfi why should he suddenly change his mind and put his life at risk? The duke's caution at the start of the conspiracy is much more in keeping with his awkward and hesitant character – he was a man who had been too nervous to tell his hot-tempered and unpredictable cousin the queen about his plan to marry Mary, even when she was giving him several opportunities to do so in private in 1569. Did his isolation and/or coaxing by Ridolfi lead him to take a gamble if it was insisted that the king of Spain would need his personal written commitment to the plot (and to his Catholic beliefs) before he sent in troops – or is this just too implausible?

It is apparent if the 'official' papers from and account of the conspiracy are accurate that Ridolfi and at least some of his backers intended to overthrow the 'illegal' queen and probably to murder her too (at least if she resisted arrest).[16] The version of the plan supported by Norfolk, i.e. with no regicide, was presumably agreed with him in order to keep him 'on board' with the plot as he would not countenance the capital crime of killing his sovereign, and possibly this version was also 'dangled in front of' others with qualms too. Included in the overall plan for a combined revolt and invasion were both Spanish ambassador De Spes, who was to get the King of Spain and Alva to support the plan with troops, and Mary's Scots ally Bishop Leslie; they duly wrote letters to overseas heads of state and government including Philip, Alva, and the Pope confirming that the plan was genuine and supported by them and asking for help in carrying it out. Ridolfi would then act as their 'postman' and argue their case with the potentates in question – and Norfolk was supposed to be ready to lead an army of 20,000 men and supply 3,000 horses to help the rebels take over England. He allegedly wrote his own letters to the potentates for Ridolfi to take, assuring them that he was ready to venture his life in this cause of the true religion and could hold out with his 'army' for forty days to give Spain time to land 6,000 men to aid him. Subsequently, he was accused of selling some of his more valuable possessions (including family plate and jewellery) to raise cash for the military supplies they would need. Mary also wrote letters approving of Ridolfi's plans and asking for Catholic potentates abroad to help him, and her train of admiring (often young) Catholic gentry in the north and midlands, who regularly called on her 'court', were large enough for De Spes (prone to over-optimism about the strength and will of the English Catholic community) to write admiringly that with a little help she and her friends could easily take over the kingdom. One question is to what extent the apparent violent and regicidal plans of Ridolfi himself were genuine (if naïve), as opposed to the invention of the English intelligence service aimed at blackening his and his allies' names and ensuring a maximum public reaction of horror and fury at the plotters – and a watertight reason to execute Norfolk. He may have exaggerated numbers and the ease of success to lure Philip and the pope into aiding him, and seems to have played up the Spanish fear of Elizabeth turning to an alliance with France instead and marrying Charles IX's brother and heir Henri, duke of Anjou, if she was not stopped. (This was the period of tentative Catholic/Huguenot reconciliation but also mistrust before the August 1572 'St Bartholomew's Day Massacre' plunged France back into civil war.) The other main question is whether all or some of the letters were compiled by Ridolfi, who seems to have been a vain, erratic and wayward character who believed his own 'hype' and played up the ease of success to impress Spain into aiding him. The question of the documents' authenticity has been examined in Francis Edwards, *Dangerous Queen* (London, 1964).

Norfolk's alleged treasonable conversation with the plot's 'leader' Ridolfi before the latter left England to seek foreign aid rests on the circumstantial evidence of later second-hand summaries, filtered through the prism of Cecil's agents. Notably, when Ridolfi, apparently already under suspicion, applied to the government for a passport to go back to his native country Italy, this was speedily granted – in a personal interview with the queen at Greenwich. There was no concern over hauling him in for questioning despite his association with both De Spes, a man known to be a fervent Catholic and antagonistic to England's current Protesantism and anti-Spanish diplomatic alignment, and Mary's meddling representative Bishop Leslie who was currently publishing a book defending his ex-sovereign's conduct in the 1560s and implying that the 'Casket Letters' enquiry had been rigged. Logically, Cecil and his allies wanted Ridolfi to take the treasonous correspondence which he was suspected of having solicited to its targets, so that the suspects – led by Mary and Norfolk – could be caught red-handed and charged with inciting a foreign invasion. But in fact, Ridolfi had a poor reception when he did call on his targets to seek aid for an invasion – Alva regarded him as an impractical and hopeless 'babbler' who had little precise and proveable evidence of English rebelliousness to offer and advised Philip to wait for a rebellion to start before intervening, and warned that if the scheme went wrong Mary, Norfolk, or both could be executed. Furthermore, in Alva's opinion, if the first blow, i.e. the combined revolt and Spanish landing in eastern England, failed to destroy Elizabeth, she would throw herself into the hands of France – it was safer to wait until someone had assassinated her and then intervene in the inevitable civil war in what would now be called a 'peacekeeping mission', i.e. to back up Mary and Norfolk. Only the poorly-informed pope seems to have believed Ridolfi's bold claims. King Philip offered him £50,000 to assist his schemes, but practically preferred to launch chaos in England before sending in 10,000 troops – which should cut his risk and costs – and arranged for a violently Catholic Italian intriguer in his service, the Marchese of Cetona, to plan an assassination-bid against Elizabeth. Cetona believed the queen was so lax with her security that attacking her would be easy, possibly at the next Parliament; Philip was more cautious and was still uneasy about having his wife's half-sister, a reigning sovereign and former ally, murdered.[17]

According to the official English account, however, Ridolfi himself had already endangered his cause by talking too freely about the plot and who was involved in it *en route* to Spain at the Grand Duke Cosimo de Medici's court in Florence, and that ruthless and security-conscious Spanish client had not been impressed with its plausibility. A trading-partner of England, he had sent a warning to Elizabeth about what was going on, and Cecil's spies in Rome, Brussels and Madrid supplied other details of the talks held there with the pope, Alva and King Philip. Letters sent from the Continent by the exiled earl of Westmoreland, the countess of Northumberland, and others were conveyed by a young Scots-Flemish 'Marian' enthusiast, Charles Baillie, to England along with Ridolfi's letters about how the plans were going to Norfolk, Mary, and Bishop Leslie, and the copies of the latter's book defending Mary which Leslie had been having printed in Flanders.

But Cecil's spies were keeping an eye on Westmoreland and other exiles in Flanders and warned him that a packet of treasonous letters were *en route* to England. Baillie was intercepted at Dover, probably around 10–12 April 1571, and taken to the Marshalsea Prison, across London Bridge from the capital in Southwark, to be questioned. He was threatened, probably with torture on the rack, but managed to smuggle a packet of letters out via Lord Cobham to Bishop Leslie – who apparently feared what the other documents might say if they were deciphered, and so approached Cecil for help pretending that some letters sent to him had been stolen and might be tampered with to his detriment. Leslie might have got away with his ingenious plan to discredit the missing letters, but the watchful Cecil had apparently 'planted' a fake prisoner who was really a government agent, a cousin of Lady Northumberland's called Thomas Herle, in the Marshalsea to gain Baillie's (and others') confidence. Called in for interrogation by the council and threatened with a racking by a 'furious' Cecil for obduracy, Herle seemed to be a genuine 'Marian' political prisoner; but in fact he was a double agent and when the agitated Baillie confessed to this new 'friend' about his other documents and the cipher he possessed, Herle duly told Cecil. Baillie ended up in the Tower of London on the rack being persuaded to reveal all, with his scribblings on the wall of the Beauchamp Tower (where eighteen years earlier Robert Dudley and his brothers had been imprisoned by Mary Tudor) surviving to testify to his ordeal. Baillie's letters were duly deciphered and read.

In late August, another alleged 'lucky coincidence' saw a Shrewsbury draper (Thomas Browne) employed by Norfolk's household 'trusties' William Barker and Robert Higford become worried at the large amount of silver in a supposedly 'routine' bag-load of material being sent north to the duke's agent in northern England. He opened it to find £600 in silver from the French embassy and a cipher which were being sent to the Marian rebels still at large in Scotland – a powerful contingent of disgruntled (mostly Catholic) foes of the regency who had now been joined by Moray's ex-henchman, the general Kirkcaldy of Grange who commanded at Edinburgh Castle. The latter now used the castle cannons to fire on a regency Parliament held in Edinburgh in May 1571 and called in his allies to hold a rival one, so the shaky regime led by Darnley's father Lennox could still fall to the Marians, and in September a rebel attack on the pro-regency lords as they met at Glasgow was to leave Lennox shot dead. This material was then passed on to London, and the cipher was used to decode various relevant and incriminating letters showing that Norfolk was busy assisting the Marians and dealing with the Spanish concerning an invasion.

While the plot was being unravelled in London, Norfolk was permitted to leave Howard House for a change of air, and while he was away the residence was searched by Cecil's agents and his servants were interrogated to find out where he hid incriminating documents and the crucial cipher for decoding them. The latter was apparently found hidden between two tiles in the roof. Ironically, while this was going on the queen was visiting Norfolk's younger son Thomas Howard, later Earl of Suffolk, at his heiress wife Margaret Audley's home of Audley End in western Suffolk, and being lobbied by her hosts to free and pardon Norfolk, who would allegedly steer clear of Mary Stuart in future. Bishop Leslie was arrested and interrogated by Cecil's aide Thomas Wilson, who, terrified and keen to clear himself at all costs, or 'repentant', babbled about what a wicked woman his employer Mary Stuart was. Allegedly, she had poisoned her first husband Francis II of France, hired Bothwell to murder Darnley and watched the murder, married Bothwell only to abandon him to his enemies at Carberry hill, and was now intending to marry Norfolk but could be expected to turn on him too. Leslie's testimony was clearly worthless – but on 7 September Norfolk was arrested and sent back to the Tower.[18]

Ridolfi never testified, and remained safe in Italy. The government's case against Norfolk relied mainly on the documents allegedly discovered at Howard House along with the material disclosed by Charles Baillie and Thomas Browne, and such evidence can easily be manufactured – or, more charitably, 'improved' to fill in gaps in the narrative which the intelligencers investigating it suspected but could not yet prove. Any reasonable view of the situation that Norfolk was in during his 'house-arrest' would ask why such as notoriously nervous and wary person, who had long been careful to avoid antagonising the queen or seeming to aim at her throne, would throw in his lot with the ill-informed and wildly optimistic Ridolfi? Why would he do this at a time when the main hopes of a successful Catholic revolt had been brutally crushed or – even if he was desperate enough to do so as a gamble – why would he break the habit of a lifetime and write incriminating letters to foreign sovereigns? Why was he doing this, implying that he had given up hope of winning Elizabeth round to his marriage or even allowing him back at court, at the same time as his son Thomas Howard was entertaining the queen and interceding for him? Should he not have waited for Thomas' report on Elizabeth's reaction to the request before pledging to aid an invasion – or was he so worried and insecure that he was running two contradictory lines of action at once? What exactly his 'plot' consisted of, and if it was at odds with Ridolfi's (and De Spes') intentions, remains unclear; he does not seem to have been 'in the loop' regarding the Spanish plan to hire a professional assassin to murder the queen though he was to be charged with plotting her assassination. He was a magnet for current dissidents and foreign meddlers given his prominence and his devotion to Mary Stuart, and as such he was politically doomed whether or not the danger he posed (latent or real) drove the Tudor regime to destroy him with exaggerated evidence.

There is also a question about Mary's allegedly incriminating letters to Philip and the pope, not only saying wildly that English Catholics were suffering unprecedented persecution and needed rescuing (which she may have been told by her alarmed Catholic visitors in the aftermath of the suppression of the Northern Rebellion) but that Norfolk was the chief organiser of the plot and would lead the rebel army so he knew much more about the plans than her. At the same time, in more obviously genuine letters, she was asking the French government, Philip's foes, for help instead via their ambassador in London, La Mothe Fenelon – and this approach involved the latter winning Elizabeth's goodwill for her release, which was incompatible with Mary simultaneously planning (as her zealous but politically naïve representative Bishop Leslie alleged) to overthrow her.[19] Possibly, Mary exaggerated her hoped-for ally France's involvement or committedness to armed insurrection in order to impress Philip, so that they had so much English support that not many troops would be needed to help – but did she genuinely believe from Norfolk's chivalrous letters and gifts that this was true, or was it 'spin' by Ridolfi and/or Leslie to enrol her for their plans? Norfolk's crucial retirement to his Norfolk home at Kenninghall and failure to turn up quickly at court when summoned as the northern revolt broke out in 1569, had politically ruined him with his royal cousin, who from then on was ready to believe the worst of him. Now the machinery of a state trial for treason and execution were set in motion, as inevitably biased as a Stalinist 'show trial', although notably almost all the English peers were summoned to act as the jury – in order to show outsiders that the entire landed elite denounced the plotters and would never aid Spain?

An 'official' explanation of the plot's discovery and Norfolk's wickedness was read out to a public assembly in the Guildhall during the trial, apparently due to popular interest (Norfolk being a well-known figure in London and a major and generous employer) and to bring the public 'on message'. The prosecutor, Sergeant-at-Law Nicholas Barham, alleged that the charges of treason (which extended to plotting against the Scots as well as the English regimes) encompassed Norfolk's plan to marry Mary as he who tried to marry a lady claiming a crown made himself complicit in her endeavours to gain it. After a unanimous verdict of 'guilty' from his peers at Westminster Hall, a death-sentence, and a long delay that shows that Elizabeth had qualms about implementing it, on 16 January 1572 Norfolk was finally executed. He chose to die as a Protestant, which may have been politic caution to avoid the queen and Cecil writing him off as a 'Papist' and confiscating all his estates from his children, but implies that any assertions he made of being a committed Catholic in 'his' letters were fake. So had he even made them, or had Ridolfi, Leslie or Cecil invented them? The trial was a 'showpiece' of justice on a proven traitor rather than a serious attempt to investigate the evidence – though normal for the era. His planned marriage to Mary, overthrow of Elizabeth, and regicide had been lumped together in the charges as if all were inevitably linked – which they may well not have been in his own planning. Notably, in his final letters to his children he forgave most of his accusers but not Bishop Leslie, the most vehement, who he charged with falsely blaming him for Leslie's own treasons.[20] Possibly Leslie only said what the English government required, in a failed attempt by Cecil to have Mary as well as Norfolk arraigned for treason, or else he went beyond what Mary wished in his enthusiastic plans to attract foreign help. But he was certainly incorrect in alleging that Mary and Norfolk had been behind the Northern Rebellion, and this and his other exaggerations point the finger at him for being a suspect if Norfolk was 'framed' – though if he did forge evidence this may have been to reassure King Philip about the wisdom of becoming involved in a risky plot, not to ruin Norfolk. It is far from certain in this murky episode that the 'evidence' of Norfolk's involvement with the Ridolfi conspirators, especially incriminating documents conveniently found at his London residence, were not 'planted' by Cecil's agents to incriminate him, or that the promises he allegedly made to Ridolfi were not invented by that ill-informed enthusiast or by Bishop Leslie.

The Road to Fotheringay, 1572–87. Was Mary really guilty of treason and intended regicide or just a political scapegoat?

In the aftermath of the Ridolfi Plot, Anglo-Spanish tension seemed to ease temporarily, but the potential for overseas Catholic aid to Mary's supporters – and thus her destruction by the Elizabethan regime in 'self-defence' – continued. Elizabeth now responded to Philip's seeming goodwill in avoiding war over the 1568 treasure-seizure, and in spring 1572 she finally expelled the Dutch Protestant 'Sea Beggars' privateers as a goodwill gesture to Philip. They proceeded to take over the Dutch ports of Flushing and Brill in open revolt against Spain, and in the coming years several thousand English volunteers, including Drake's half-brother Sir Humphrey Gilbert, joined their struggle for independence. Gilbert had his own reasons for hating Spain, as much to do with money as Protestant idealism; he had been conducting a technically illegal but usually tolerated private mercantile trip to the Spanish imperial viceroyalty of Mexico (and selling slaves there) in 1568 when the local authorities had attacked his ships without warning at San Juan de Ulloa. He had escaped, but ships and men had been lost, and after that he was out for revenge, in alliance with Drake and others (mostly expert west country gentry or merchant captains with local crews) who ravaged the coasts of the 'Spanish Main', now the Caribbean coasts of Venezuela and Colombia. Both at sea and on land in Holland, the English volunteers fighting Spain acquired crucial military experience that would prove invaluable in the Armada invasion crisis of 1588 – as England was not engaged in 'up to date' European wars with modern armies (or in a major naval Mediterranean war with the Ottoman Turks) unlike Spain, its fledgling army and navy lacked the Spaniards' large-scale and prolonged military experience. Most of the English volunteers in the Netherlands were recalled by the queen in 1573–4 as the immediate crisis with Spain eased. In association with this policy of weakening Spain by proxy, a naval campaign began to stop the flow of South American silver to Spain to fund their warfare and Drake was despatched to raid shipping and ports on the 'Spanish Main', without any official backing.

The concomitant English effort to patch up relations with France and use the latter against Spain seemed viable as the 1560s religious conflicts there were temporarily in abeyance and Catherine de' Medici's government had patched up an uneasy truce, and in spring 1572 an alliance was agreed at Blois. This assured the support of either signatory to the other if the latter was attacked by a third party (i.e. Spain).[20] This seemed to give hopes for English Catholics of England having to ease off repression – and even release Mary Stuart? – if Catherine de' Medici demanded this. In the period after this treaty the conditions that Mary was kept in eased as the threat of revolt lapsed for a few years.

Mary was usually kept at the isolated but well-furnished original Tudor mansion of the Cavendishes (her hostess the Countess of Shrewsbury's previous husband's family) at Chatsworth House. She was allowed a suite of thirty and from 1573 was able to make visits to the newly-popular medicinal springs and hot baths of Buxton. She also received visitors including both potentially supportive Catholic gentry and what would nowadays be thought of as celebrity-hunting sightseers, and was able to go hunting with the local gentry and take up archery – but was watched closely by the earl of Shrewsbury and his servants for any potential conspiracy, with regular reports being made to the Privy Council. Her health was uncertain and she suffered from a mixture of aliments which were not all traceable to her sporadic lack of exercise, boredom, and the anxieties of constant confinement under watch by government agents. A mixture of arthritis and stomach problems plus pains in her legs and apparent over-eating can be detected, but the severity of some of her collapses and her extreme mood-swings and manic behaviour at times have been suggested as indicating signs of the porphyria that was presumably in the medically-afflicted Stuart family before descending eventually to George III.[21] Her father died surprisingly young at thirty with apparent depression but no obvious underlying medical condition, and her son James VI and I suffered from arthritis and assorted other ailments; and she had already had earlier bouts before she was afflicted by internment, as at Jedburgh in 1566. Whether or not she had porphyria and this worsened during her captivity, in political terms her problems may have made her less cautious and more susceptible to taking unwise risks in communicating with potentially 'double agent' supporters.

The danger of Philip backing the Catholic 'ultras' in France, led by the Guises, against the French government as too tolerant of the Huguenots seemed to impel the queen-mother Catherine's faction into alliance with the latter in 1572. Hence the projected marriage of Catherine's daughter Margaret to the Huguenot leader Henri of Navarre and the despatch of the English Protestant zealot councillor, future spymaster Sir Francis Walsingham, to Paris as ambassador to organise pan-European Protestant alliances between England, the French regime, the Huguenots, and the Dutch. The 'Massacre of St Bartholomew' in and around Paris in August 1572 ended that prospect in a spectacular manner as the most violent and confrontational Catholics were given their head to slaughter the Huguenots.[22] As far as the French regime was concerned, it literally decapitated a 'treacherous' as well as heretical faction who could ally with England again and overthrow the faith, and military commanders such as Admiral Coligny (nearly killed already in a failed assassination-bid and feared to be out for revenge) were hunted down and killed as a priority. The notion that the French government would put religious fanaticism above the usual imperative of the traditional Valois/Habsburg antagonism was unsuspected by and unwelcome to Elizabeth. Had Catherine de' Medici and her weak-willed, impulsive son Charles IX not listened to their more fanatical advisors and decided to destroy the Huguenot 'threat', by eliminating their leadership when the latter were in Paris for the Henri /Margaret wedding, a return to the Anglo-French alliance of the early 1550s would have been expected. The fervent Protestant Walsingham clearly favoured a new-style, ideological rather than a traditional dynastic alliance, which would have been profoundly uncomfortable to the devout Catholic Catherine. In the event, the massacre wrecked the alliance plans – but only for the moment as unlike the religiously-minded Walsingham his queen still favoured a French alliance to constrain Philip. Hopefully, the weak and fanatically Catholic Charles IX died young in his early twenties in 1574 and was succeeded as king of France by his more pragmatic and open-minded brother Duke Henri of Anjou (as King Henri III), though he had recently been elected king of Poland so he had to sneak away from Cracow and get home before his subjects found out.

The traditional 'narrative' of Mary's role in Anglo-Scottish affairs after 1568 has her totally marginalised as a result of the 'Casket Letters' trial and reduced to being a powerless pawn of events, held captive in England at Elizabeth's mercy and abandoned by her people. The latter was not actually true as a substantial amount of Marian resistance by friendly nobles continued into the early 1570s and came near success in ousting the regency at times, and also in the early 1580s there was the possibility of Mary being restored to nominal power as co-ruler with her son James – despite the blackening of her character in the 'Casket Letters' trial. Her role in the 1570s-80s is often treated as if it was all part of the long road to the execution-block at Fotheringay Castle in February 1587, and the planned 'Association' of herself on the throne with James is either forgotten or treated as a fantasy scheme that stood no chance against the odds. In fact, the actual chain of events in Scotland between the 'Casket Letters' trial verdict and the execution of Mary was less clear-cut and 'inevitable' than it seems, and the hostility of Elizabeth to releasing her was not steady. The Marian plans did go wrong, but Mary was more than a passive 'victim' if not the scheming Catholic murderess lusting after Elizabeth's throne that many Protestant MPs in England believed. Her failure was due to a mixture of bad luck, misjudgement, and betrayal – and not only in the British Isles. The regency for James VI in Scotland was in a precarious position in the early 1570s, its original leader Moray having been fatally shot by one of the Hamiltons in an ambush in the street in Linlithgow in January 10 1570. This deprived the mistrustful coalition of Mary's foes of its lynchpin, and king James' guardian at Stirling, the earl of Mar, hastily asked Elizabeth for help.[23] Its leadership changed several times thereafter, with Darnley's father the Earl of Lennox (as implacable towards Mary as Moray had been) being appointed the new regent – as was his right as the king's nearest male kin – after the divided Scots Protestant nobles had been lobbied strongly for this solution by Elizabeth. Her success in this blow to Mary's fortunes owed much to the nobles' need of her military help against the 'Marians', including the earl of Huntly and

Lord Herries, who despite the disaster at Langside still held Dumbarton and were to add Edinburgh Castle. Lennox was still disliked by some major political 'players' from his activities against Mary's regency in the 1540s, principally his then foes the Hamiltons, but he managed to take Dumbarton Castle from the latter and executed archbishop Hamilton; the earls of Argyll, Eglinton and Cassilis now defected from Mary's cause to him. Unfortunately, Lennox was then murdered too, in August 1571 in a botched 'Marian' attempt to kidnap him and other council members during a meeting of the regency leaderhip at Stirling. The ambushers had the element of surprise as they rode into the town and seized Lennox and other councillors at gunpoint, but their targets were rescued by loyal troops and Lennox was shot in the melee.[24] The attackers had nearly made a 'clean sweep' and killed or captured the regency leadership, and control of King James' person and his residence at Stirling Castle would probably have been in their grasp – enabling negotiations to restore Mary from a strong position. Or would the surviving anti-Marian lords (e.g. the Earls of Mar and Morton) have summoned English help first? Mar then died suddenly in October 1572 soon after dining with Morton, leaving the latter with allegations of poisoning him but now in power as the fourth head of the regency council in four years. Another crisis erupted when the shaky regency held a Parliament in Edinburgh city centre; their Marian foes were now holding the castle above the streets (Kirkcaldy of Grange having defected to them) and were able to fire their cannons down at the meeting, disrupting proceedings. The Marian lords then marched into Edinburgh and held a rival Parliament of their own under the protection of the Castle guns, before being driven out later.[25] The two sides were militarily evenly matched so the regency had to call on Elizabeth to send in troops with long-range artillery, which duly battered the Castle into submission in May 1573. Kirkcaldy was forced to surrender and executed, and Mary's ex-secretary Maitland killed himself before the castle fell to avoid execution.[26] If anyone knew the secrets of who exactly killed Darnley and who had forged the incriminating portions of the 'Casket Letters' it was him, and he was never a reliable ally for Mary. This was a final blow to the armed Marian cause in Scotland as events turned out, putting Mary's cause into the hands of her potential allies in England (a medley of ill-equipped and over-optimistic Catholic gentry and individualist enthusiasts) and her more powerful overseas fellow-sovereigns. But at this time Philip was not ready to intervene openly in British affairs, while Mary herself refused an offer of help to escape in 1570 because she was still hoping that either Charles IX or Philip would put diplomatic pressure on Elizabeth to release her.[27]

The nucleus of the 'Association' plan for Mary and her son – Protestant and hopefully more reliable – to reign jointly, the ex-queen probably just nominally at the head of a Protestant council, came from a surprising source – the English government. The crucial English 'hard-line' Protestant minister Cecil took part in a formal mission from his queen to visit Mary at Sheffield Castle and discuss a treaty with her in October 1570, despite the effective blackening of her reputation by the rigged 'Casket Letters' investigation. He was assisted by chancellor of the exchequer (i.e. deputy treasurer) Sir Walter Mildmay, another determined evangelical Protestant who loathed international Catholic revanchism. The proposed terms would have involved Mary's restoration to Scotland in return for her formally renouncing her claim to England and allowing Elizabeth to choose any future husband of hers, plus James VI taking her place as a hostage in England.[28] These three concessions would place Scots policy as affecting England under Elizabeth's veto, and counter the papal declaration that the queen was a bastard who should be removed in Mary's favour. James would be available to be placed on the Scots throne as an English puppet if Mary reneged on the deal (or had a priest absolve her from any promises). In effect, Mary would be a puppet of her council – all or mostly strong Protestants, allied to England. There was little fear that James would grow up to support and restore power to his mother, as his fiercely Protestant tutor George Buchanan, the historian and author of an rabidly anti-Marian book on her 'misrule' and deposition, was one of the hard-liners who believed she was a 'Papist whore' who had murdered her husband in league with her lover Bothwell, and he had been indoctrinating James in this vein. At this point James was only four, the regency was distinctly shaky, and Marian loyalists still held Dumbarton where French or Spanish troops could land to aid Mary. In retrospect, this was probably Mary's best chance of returning to rule Scotland, albeit as a puppet of Elizabeth who would have to come to terms with Mar and Morton and keep Spanish or French offers of help at bay. It would have prevented the fiasco of the Ridolfi plot if not the ban on Norfolk marrying Elizabeth, but although Cecil seems to have been won over to some degree by Mary's charm and may have offered to arrange for her to see Elizabeth, the Council could not agree on proceeding. The plan was shelved for the moment and the Ridolfi plot revived fears of Mary's alleged plotting and untrustworthiness.

The alternate possibilities of Mary either being restored to (nominal) power by the grace of Queen Elizabeth or implicated in a worse scandal than the Ridolfi plot and executed, continued through the 1570s into the early 1580s, and were both subject to the ebb and flow of international politics. Elizabeth was not seeking a confrontation with Spain despite the later myths of her as the dauntless Protestant warrior-queen who stood up to the might of Spanish Catholic imperialism (which owes much to hindsight and how events turned out in 1588). Saving money and avoiding provocation came first to this scrupulous and parsimonious granddaughter of the equally cautious Henry VII, and aggressive Protestant ideology was absent from her motives; such swashbuckling but expensive attitudes to foreign policy were left to Leicester and his nephew Sir Philip Sidney. She was quite prepared to marry a Catholic French Valois prince, Henri III's younger brother and heir the much younger Francois Hercule, Duc d'Alencon, in 1579 – only seven years after his mother and brother had been involved in the St Bartholemew's Day Massacre. Cementing an Anglo-French alliance came first, to the despair of anti-Catholics such as the pamphleteer John Stubbes. His indignant literary reply, the *'Gaping Gulf'*, implied that she was willing to risk abandoning the national interest for her would-be suitor's – and he was promptly mutilated with the full rigours of the law for libel. Unlike her spymaster Sir Francis Walsingham (Secretary of State in succession to Cecil in 1572–90), she did not let the events of 1572 in Paris turn her into a foe of the Catholic government of France; *'realpolitik'* and cost trumped ideology. Even when her potential French husband, for whom she felt a degree of affection, Alencon/Anjou, died (1584) she was prepared to assist his his more explicitly Catholic brother Henri III to rule of most of the Netherlands to avoid a costly English war to defend them from Spain.

In a similar vein, Elizabeth's attitude towards war at sea was no more belligerent than that concerning war on land, although 'long-distance' colonial attacks far from England might usefully employ hotheads, undermine Spain's financial sinews so its army was unable to put down the Dutch rebels, earn treasure so taxes did not have to be raised by

Parliament, and avoid open conflict closer at hand in Europe. Naval encounters could be excused as accidents or replies to provocation if both parties to an incident were so minded; and even Drake's famous privateering expedition to the Spanish colonies in 1577–80 (which turned into a round-the-world voyage) was marked by a desire to avoid open confrontation with Philip. Her role in financing Drake was kept secret and she was clearly ready to deny any involvement with him were he captured or killed. It was not clear on Drake's return whether he would be rewarded, ignored, or arrested. However, in the event, Elizabeth graciously went on board his flagship to greet him and knighted him in a public seal of approval.

Throughout the early-mid 1580s Elizabeth avoided retaliating for Spanish armed interference in Ireland, where Philip landed troops to aid Catholic Gaelic rebels against her colonial authorities with the technical excuse that these men were private citizens who had volunteered to fight for an expedition paid for and authorised by the pope.[29] This was a shrewd 'tit for tat' to Elizabeth for allowing thousands of English volunteers to fight for the Dutch rebels, and was replied to by an aggressive English 'plantation' of Protestant settlers in affected areas such as Munster – and was later to be extended to Ulster once the O'Neills there revolted. Philip was at this point wary of open embroilment with the private initiatives of enthusiastic English Catholic militants to overthrow Elizabeth in Mary Stuart's name, counselling caution on his ambassador Mendoza in London;[30] if the queen were deposed or killed Spain could then take advantage of the chaos and install Mary as its candidate for the throne without the expense (or embarrassment if things went wrong) of initiating the revolt with its troops. The Spanish embassy might unofficially encourage such plots, but only in a climate of 'plausible denial' – and the enthusiasm of exiled English Catholics (and more recent converts) to return England to the faith in an era of rising missionary activity could be used to send Catholic priests to England to assist local plots as part of their 'holy' duty. As a result, in England it was assumed that all incoming Catholic priests were not just ministering to their 'underground' flock and holding illegal masses, but sponsoring and inspiring rebellion and probably regicide too, and a major 'cat and mouse game' to find them commenced for Walsingham's intelligence service. Parliament, the forum of public opinion among the landed classes, made it a capital offence to convert to Catholicism in 1581 and now linked the religion explicitly with treason. The fines for not attending weekly Anglican services were dramatically increased from one shilling to twenty pounds per offence (a ruinous amount for anyone who was not rich), and dedicated regional 'pursuivants' were employed as informers to hunt down and round up Catholic priests for trial and execution. This equated peaceful and loyal Catholics of ancient hereditary allegiance to both crown and Catholic church, people who would not dream of rebelling and who were embarrassed by the papal declaration deposing Elizabeth, with fanatical young converted zealots. These had been reclaimed for Catholicism in the 1570s-80s by a new Jesuit missionary campaign masterminded from Rome, and the college was set up for educating Catholic exiles and training future priests at the university of Douai in the Netherlands in 1568 by a self-exiled English Catholic scholar from Oxford, Dr William Allen.

Ministering to a mixture of English exiles from Mary Tudor's 1550s Catholic church (illegal since Protestantism was restored in 1559) and the sons of English Catholic gentry who were sent abroad to get a Catholic education, the college was regarded as a nest of 'Papist' traitors even though Dr Allen initially banned any discussion of politics, Elizabeth's legitimacy as queen, or the alleged duty of Catholics to obey the Pope (and later to depose her), and once its graduates started becoming priests and returning to England to convert others, the authorities' hostility worsened even more. The college was later moved to Reims in France after the suspicious local authorities shut it down, and another college was later opened in Rome. Its most famous member was the former Oxford scholar Edmund Campion (later executed and canonised) who had given an official welcome address to the queen when she visited the university with its Chancellor, Leicester, in 1565. This campaign of Catholic conversion was in Philip's strategic interests (as was Elizabeth's murder), and as he saw it the campaign was carrying out a sacred duty in returning England to the faith – his late wife Mary Tudor's aborted mission which he had aided as her consort – even before the 1568 'treasure ship seizure' crisis and the English meddling in the Netherlands turned him to thoughts of removing Elizabeth. Once Mary Stuart was available as an alternative and Catholic monarch for England and Pope Pius V had declared Eliabeth's regime illegal in 1570, that added a 'political' role for Catholic converts and priests as potential agents to overthrow her, and from the mid-1570s Allen's zealous new priests were backed up by a missionary role in England for the militant 'Society of Jesus' (ie the Jesuits) based in Rome. Their efforts had the potential to save Philip from a costly frontal attack on a united England by creating 'terrorists' who would obligingly murder Elizabeth and thus cause chaos in England, hopefully rescuing Mary Stuart too. Catholic priests were now banned from England and were to be executed when caught as of 1581, and although many were not involved at all or interested in the cause of Mary Stuart, the temptation to see her being put on the throne of England was viewed as a great advance for the persecuted faith. At a time when the frequently ill and depressed Mary was becoming more openly religious herself and steeling herself as suffering for her religion, she became an icon for admiring, and not very practical young Catholic enthusiasts and the danger of them becoming what would now be called 'home-grown terrorists' multiplied. It gave the cause of the imprisoned 'Catholic martyr' glamour and potential recruits, but it could be fatal if she was proved to be embroiled in such a plan.

The destruction of Mary in 1586–7 could have been avoided if her own plan for her titular restoration as co-ruler of Scotland, the 'Association', had been acted upon in the early 1580s – the failure of which was beyond her control, and partly due to French inaction. Once her son James VI was a teenager and was able to act politically without his anti-Marian regents (and once Mary's arch-foe Morton, regent until 1579, was sidelined and then executed in 1581) Mary conceived the hope that James would help her return home as his co-ruler but without impinging on his authority. For one thing, as she had renounced her abdication in 1567 as forced and illegal during her Langside campaign in 1568, she could claim to be still legally queen and so offer her son the bonus of an end to the uncertainty over his reign's legality in international Catholic eyes. This plan was to be promoted by her representatives in Paris, using her family link to the Guises so the latter could insist on her freedom as part of any of the current Anglo-French negotiations (which centred on England and France working together to keep Philip from conquering the rebel Netherlands). France would then stand as guarantor that Mary would not become involved in politics again. The French had been supporting her claim that her detention was illegal and pressing for her release since 1568, but their government never made it a '*sine qua non*' of a treaty with

England. Arguably this was a serious if not fatal blow to her chances of release, given Elizabeth's need of French help in 1579–84.

Nor did her son James take up her cause eagerly; he had been educated by his ferociously anti-Catholic tutor Buchanan to hate his mother and Catholics, although this was eased and his attitude appears to have changed after his entourage was freed from Morton's and Buchanan's influence. He became an eager friend and patron of his pro-French cousin and adviser from 1580/1, Esme Stuart, a dashing, handsome, courtly and charismatic French-educated nobleman with a broad international education and sympathies, who he soon looked up to as a model to follow and who he made Duke of Lennox to the horror of ultra-Protestants. Esme Stuart was looked on as the same sort of 'Papist subversive' who was too close to his suspiciously fond sovereign as Riccio had been to Mary, and some zealots wanted to deal with him the same way. He was then, and later, suspected of a homosexual liasion with James, whose interests ran to handsome young men throughout his life. However, hero-worship for the first sophisticated and sympathetic older man the awkward young king had encountered is more likely. Stuart and the other rising figure at court, the swashbuckling young guards-officer and Gentleman of the Bedchamber' Captain James Stewart of Bothwellhaugh (son of Lord Ochiltree and a former soldier against Spain in the Netherlands), encouraged James to reject the narrow thinking and political alignment that Morton's regency had thrust on him, and Morton himself ended up in prison and beheaded with accusations from Captain Stewart that he had murdered Darnley. The most that he would admit was that he had known about the plot beforehand.

This reassessment of the kingdom's international stance could benefit Mary and lead to her recall, but despite now having second thoughts about the tone of his education, James appears to have preferred to leave her in captivity rather than risk alienating Elizabeth and jeopardising his chances of the English succession. Also, Elizabeth and her ministers turned against Lennox as a potential channel for international Catholic conspirators (or a renewal of the 1550s French domination) in Edinburgh and her ambassador Randolph demanded his exile, working with the new duke's Protestant noble foes. The exile of Lennox, after a coup by jealous Scots Protestant nobles led by the Ruthven family (under the earl of Gowrie) in August 1582 weakened Mary's chances. Their leader, the ultra-Protestant Gowrie, led a posse to intercept James while out hunting and 'invited' him to his castle (the 'Ruthven Raid'), not taking 'no' for an answer and then forbidding him to leave; the king was in effect held hostage and the Gowrie-led junta, backed by the Presbyterian church who hated Lennox as a Catholic, demanded that James exile him. After a 'stand-off' in which Lennox, holding out in Edinburgh but with the Kirk whipping up anti-Catholic paranoia against him, was deserted by most of the nobles, James had to give way and the Gowrie group ruled Scotland in his name until he was 'rescued' at his own wishes from their guards by the earl of March and others on a journey in Fife in June 1583, and escourted to safety. The junta were banned from his vicinity and a shaky mixture of Protestant and moderate Catholics now assisted the understandably wary and devious young king in ruling. Adding Mary to the mixture would be a risk given the fears of any Catholic or pro-Catholic figure among both ultra-Protestant nobles and Kirk. Elizabeth and her ministers were probably involved in the fall of Lennox and in backing Gowrie, as the queen had been denouncing Lennox as a French agent and demanding that James remove him from power to no avail.[30] Had he stayed in power, this French-educated Guise confidante might have talked James round to supporting the 'Association'. Instead, he died in France in 1583 while expecting his recall – as a Protestant.

Crucially, Mary's choice of envoy to James to persuade him to press Elizabeth for her restoration was of uncertain reliability. Like others of her showy but blundering partisans in the 1570s and 1580s, the French-educated and ultra-devious young 'Master of Gray', Patrick the eldest son of minor peer Lord Gray, had his own agenda and was so complex a character that his true allegiances are still a matter of debate. The subject of a trilogy of novels by the late twentieth-century author Nigel Tranter, he was capable and highly intelligent but unprincipled and capable of deceit and manipulation to benefit his own career, though he probably 'drifted with the tide' and took up the most profitable cause at any one time rather than having a 'master-plan'. Having worked for Mary's agent the archbishop of Glasgow in France and been connected to the ultra-Catholic Guise dynasty there, he returned to Scotland in 1583 and started to pass on intelligence about what was going on in Mary's entourage and among her overseas backers to James. Elizabeth had now abandoned her initial hostility to the post-Gowrie regime and reopened negotiations with James' envoy Captain Stewart (now made earl of Arran though the title's insane previous holder was still alive) via her cousin and veteran diplomat Lord Hunsdon, probably spurred on by having had to expel Philip's ambassador, Mendoza, in London for plotting her overthrow. With Spain now proveably hostile, England might shift to an alignment with France and Scotland, and in this 'opening' James used Gray (or Gray used him?) to press the English to release Mary and take up the offer of 'Association'. But it seems that the data that Gray (a Protestant by religion) was giving James about the 'ultra' Catholic aims of many of Mary's closest supporters and the regicidal hostility of their zealot members to Elizabeth, plus possibly Mary's own incautious words and letters, alarmed James. Motives on all sides are unclear in this murky world of intelligence, 'spin', and rumour and double-crossing, but logically James feared that the recent Marian plots in England (e.g. the Throckmorton conspiracy) would put Elizabeth off backing him if he took up her cause and that his mother was a 'loose cannon' and a political embarrassment.

James chose Gray (presumably thinking him reliable in resisting temptation to link up with the 'ultra' Catholic Marians in England or the Spanish) as his ambassador to London to propose the 'Association' plan to Elizabeth in summer 1584. This was a time when Mary's French representative Fontenay, Henri III's ambassador in London, believed that the situation had never been so favourable for her restoration.[31] At this point Elizabeth was reliably said to be so fed up with Mary's presence in England that she would release her if France and James would agree to guarantee her goodwill and political marginalisation.[32] But the plan did not win favour in London, and Gray failed to back it with any enthusiasm – though it is unclear if this was on James' wishes or his own initiative. This has been seen by subsequent pro-Marian authors as a Machiavellian betrayal of Mary by Patrick Gray, and the lack of simultaneous insistence on her release by the Guises finally ended the plan's chances of winning Elizabeth's consent. Gray went home empty-handed, and in November Mary's secretary Nau drew up a list of her proposals for the 'Association', which would entail her agreeing to renounce both her claims to the English throne (which would reassure English Protestants by transferring these to James) and the Papal Bull of 1570 deposing Elizabeth. She might be prepared to stay in England, and would even sign up to an alliance with

England against France if it refused to back the 'Association' – provided that England then reimbursed her for her income from France as Francis II's widow which would be confiscated – although there was an element of arrogance in her agreement to avoid claiming compensation for her 'illegal' detention in England and to make James' current 'illegal' regime fully legal by not pursuing her 1568 cancellation of her abdication.

Mary's offer would have amounted to her abandoning the disastrous schemes of her current admirers, but in fact the ground was being cut from under her by her son – possibly due to his fears of the ruinous links of these same people. James now broke off correspondence with his mother, and so ended her hopes of his support.[33] This in turn made her restoration seem less worth pursuing. In spring 1585 Elizabeth sent a new ambassador to Edinburgh, Sir Edward Wotton, with an offer of a pension of £4,000 per annum – effectively bribing the impecunious king to abandon his mother's cause. James took the bait, though in terms of hard politics his decision was logical, as the impractical plans of Mary's wilder supporters for regicide and revolution plus Spanish invasion in England were unlikely to succeed, and if they did, would thrust it into a fixed Catholic alignment hostile to James' own religious leanings. Had James and the Guises both insisted on Mary's release, could she have been returned to Scotland as nominal co-ruler in an Anglo-French treaty in 1584 or 1585 and so been safe from implication in any more English Catholic plots? Would Philip have persuaded Mary, back in Scotland, to offer herself as his puppet-queen in 1588?

Mary's route out of a probably doomed link to her more impractical English followers and their dreams of a coup was now blocked, but it is unclear whether her fatal approval of the Babington Plot scheme for killing Elizabeth was a rational choice, a 'honey-trap' by Walsingham, or (less likely) a case of forgery of her writing. The setting for such a scheme was set by greater Spanish engagement with such plots. In 1583 Philip's attitude towards Elizabeth's regime and the chances of overthrowing it seems to have hardened, and Spanish involvement in usually vague and impractical plots went beyond cheering them on in private but not providing much help. His embassy was embroiled in a complex Marian/Guise/Spanish/Papal project for both Spain and the Guises' French faction to land troops in England to liberate Mary. This is generally known as the 'Throckmorton Plot' from the identity of the main English Catholic 'go-between' and eventual victim, Francis Throckmorton.[34] Ambassador Mendoza ended up expelled and the role of the Spanish embassy as a honeypot for disaffected English Catholics (and 'double agents' sent by Walsingham) came to an end. But Elizabeth's reaction to all this was more limited than that of her xenophobically Protestant Parliament, who demanded the execution of the plotters' wicked 'mastermind' Mary Stuart. The rising English Protestant paranoia about Catholicism '*per se*' and alarm at the treasonable potential of all its adherants resembles the manner of post-'9/11' Westerners equating all Muslims with 'Al Qaeda', and as with modern Britain there was always a danger that a plot by men not on the English secret service's 'radar' would escape detection and carry out an atrocity. If Elizabeth had been murdered as William of Orange had been in Holland, from 1584 a formal plan existed in legislation (the 'Association') for the assumption of full power over the leaderless country by her privy council.

Walsingham had to push Elizabeth into trying and then executing Mary Stuart, the act which at least provided an excuse for, if not directly causing, Philip's decision to invade in 1587. Walsingham's agents in Mary's increasingly circumscribed and infiltrated household provided the incontrovertible 'proof' that Mary had actively encouraged her hot-headed ultra-Catholic admirers to murder Elizabeth in the Babington plot, so she could take her throne; she had apparently been aware of the Throckmorton plot plans and written letters of approval but was not definitively involved in planning. The viability of the scheme of the naïve and fanatical young Warwickshire Catholic convert Francis Throckmorton, if not its malign intent, was, however, dubious. One of the chief 'plotters' involved, Charles Paget, was a double agent working for Walsingham and he first used a trip to Paris to ask the duke of Guise to bring in Spanish military help to try to talk him out of it and then used his mission to the supposedly pro-plot Earl of Northumberland (the nephew of the 1569–70 rebel) to talk him out of joining it too. The allegiance of 'Marian' chief cipher organiser Thomas Morgan, a former employee of her captor the earl of Shrewsbury and now of her ambassador in France, James Beaton, was also dubious – his Catholicism was suspect, he was the man who signed up the later arch-betrayer George Gifford for her cause, and he and Paget were said in France to have been left out of the most secret part of the Throckmorton Plot deliberations as suspect.[35] There is also the problem in interpreting who amongst the plethora of alleged Marian agents was loyal to her, due to the mutual suspicions and slanders of rival Catholic groups. The Jesuits were regarded as being 'unpatriotic' agents of the papacy and Spain by some of the trainees of the Douai/Rheims and Rome priestly seminaries/colleges set up by Dr/Cardinal Allen who had a more independent mindset. By the latter's reckoning, the allegiance of the pro-Spanish groups to current Spanish policies towards England made them 'sitting ducks' for the Elizabethan regime's accusations of treason, and so undermined their religion's success at conversion among the politically non-committed. These disputes and mutual slanders were stirred up enthusiastically by Walsingham as a means of undermining the Catholic mission and 'smearing' its membership, (though his main agent was only at work in the college in Rome from 1586), and it spilled over into the 'internment camps' in England where the regime dumped arrested priests, converts, and attendees of illegal masses (e.g. Wisbech Castle in the Fens). As a result, we cannot be sure if one of the 'Marian agents' alleged to be a secret agent working for Walsingham by fellow-Catholics was just being slandered by someone in a rival group. Once the Throckmorton group had been exposed and liquidated amidst the usual uproar in England, Mary would have been well-advised to distance herself from all treasonous talk and dubious young admirers, particularly given their division into rival groups. Even if she did not realise how many of her servants and visitors were working for Walsingham this was an obvious precaution. However, she seems to have been trapped in her own little world and increasingly oblivious to the threat that the English regime posed to her and the unliklihood of her allies' schemes succeeding.

As the post-Throckmorton furore fed into Parliamentary fears of a coup, and the murder of the Dutch leader William of Orange inflamed opinions further, it was even legislated that if another regicidal plan was launched she would be assumed to be guilty of it even if there was no direct evidence. By implication, the beneficiary was as guilty as the actual plotters and if Elizabeth was to be killed she would then be executed in reprisal. To add to the severity of the threat, she was then moved to stricter incarceration with a reduced, heavily supervised household at isolated Tutbury Castle in the care of the rigorously Protestant officer Sir Amyas Paulet, who unlike the genteel and kindly aristocrat Shrewsbury, loathed her and was determined to treat her as a felon. She then (presumably) fell into the same trap as with Throckmorton when the next plot was hatched by another impractical young Catholic squire, the Derbyshire landowner Anthony Babington, in 1586. The romantic and wildly optimistic Babington, a well-connected and naive young man who had been a page of Mary's some years before and had been devoted to her ever since (and who she trusted), was not a natural 'terrorist' let alone a competent planner and indeed appears to have had qualms about the moral rectitude of starting a civil war and causing mass bloodshed. He was worked on and manipulated by a far more hardened and ruthless character, who deserves the role of the plot's mastermind more than Babington does – the fanatical priest John Ballard, a troublemaker of long standing who had been plotting a coup for years. So much so that in 1584 had visited Rome with his protégé Anthony Tyrrell (another well-connected young landowner, from the Essex gentry family of Richard III's henchman Sir James Tyrrell) to call on the pope and swear an oath to him to overthrow the 'heretic' Elizabeth. Tyrrell, a detained Catholic 'recusant', had escaped from custody in the Gatehouse prison in Westminster and gone into hiding in 1582, probably helped by his 'contact' and adviser Ballard, and the latter also had access to a fanatical ex-soldier in the Spanish army, John Savage, who had sworn to assassinate Elizabeth.

Ballard thus brought his own network of fanatics, arguably more deadly than Babington's own small group of naïve young Catholic gentry (including one of the north-east Wales Salusburys and one of the Hampshire Tichbornes),who so far had not planned anything serious, into alliance with the latter in 1586. The 'six gentlemen' who Babington assured Mary were dedicated to putting her on the throne, i.e. his own small group of Catholic friends, were joined by more serious and ruthless 'terrorists', and the plot took shape, and as Mary's ex-page, Babington could persuade her to rely on and communicate with him. But his activities do not suggest a 'hard man' doggedly planning regicide and rebellion, as with the plot already underway he applied to Walsingham for a passport to leave the country and go abroad to Catholic France – leading to an odd personal interview between him and the secretary, who was probably already aware of his intentions and refused him permission to leave the country. Was Babington losing his nerve and ready to 'bolt', and did Walsingham want him to stay around, under surveillance and available to be arrested and 'persuaded' to name his comrades? There was clearly some 'double agent' in the group, and it is unlikely to have been Ballard who at this stage was abroad collecting more letters to be delivered to Mary, and on his return in late summer 1586 was arrested and tortured into confessing. He was then put on trial and executed, and Walsingham retorted to alleged rumours that Ballard had been one of his agents by pointing out that in that case he would have been reprieved. Meanwhile, Walsingham sent a forged request at the end of a genuine (intercepted) letter from one of the conspirators to Babington to write out a list of the band of plotters apparently ready to assassinate Elizabeth, but he had enough sense not to do so. This suggests that the secretary's 'informer' was not so senior a plotter that he was in Babington's confidence, or the list would have been known to him.

The vital written evidence of Mary's approval for the murder-plan by this group of hot-headed and impractical English conspirators was apparently now acquired by Walsingham's secret agents, who controlled and read all letters passing to and from Mary in custody. They deliberately let a letter containing an adherant's provocative request for this approval get through to her (in a beer-cask). The 'middle-man' in the transmission of the message, Mary's supposed loyalist Gilbert Gifford who had trained as a Catholic priest at the college for English exiles in Rome, was actually an agent of Walsingham's, at least from the time that he was 'arrested' and brought to see the spymaster when he arrived in England in December 1585 and possibly earlier (even in Rome?).[36] Gifford, from an old Staffordshire Catholic family, was a dubious but talented character who had already been expelled from the Catholic college in Rome, roamed Europe with uncertain adventures and paymasters, and then was apparently coaxed back to the 'fold' in Rome by the college's head Cardinal Allen and sent to England to help Mary. Instead he ended up working for Walsingham as well and now offered the new French ambassador, the Marquis de Chateauneuf, to use his knowledge of the Tutbury/Chartley area from his upbringing in the district to smuggle letters from France to Mary. Supposedly, he had been away so long that his family would not recognise him and report his presence, though he had also (contradictorily) claimed that his father had invited him home so he could have a legitimate reason for being there. The French embassy later claimed that Gifford had never been fully trusted and the fact that he was lodging in London with Walsingham's master decipherer Thomas

Phelippes did not help, but he was entrusted with taking letters that had been piling up waiting for a chance to be delivered to Mary, succeeded in this, and was duly hired to take more on a regular basis.

Gifford was chosen to take the partially forged message in the beer-cask asking for Mary to approve the latest regicide plan, the 'smoking gun' which would condemn her – which raises the possibility that he or Phelippes may have forged her secretaries' handwriting to incriminate her. (Mary could only write French, so her English letters to the conspirators and others were physically written by her secretaries Nau and Curle.) Walsingham admitted his plan to trick her into incriminating herself into committing a capital offence, some days ahead of this in a missive to Leicester in the Netherlands, but this of course was never revealed at the time. After the arrests Nau and Curle were questioned and intimidated by the government's representatives – Nau apparently had Walsingham shaking his fist in his face and threatening execution – into 'confirming' that the writing in the inflammatory letter was genuine, and Nau was reported to have claimed that Mary had written out what he was to say in a memorandum but destroyed it. The 'proof' that if Nau or Curle had written the incriminating document, it was as good as a written statement of guilt by Mary in condemning her for intended regicide and was accepted by the court – though in any case the 'Association' legally made it possible to execute her for any plot to kill Elizabeth whatever her guilt. The question of the forged addition to the letter to Babington requesting the name of the would-be assassins was never raised or admitted. Mary may have been so desperate to be out of custody that she jumped at the chance and excused her willingness to accept murder as being necessary in the overall 'good cause' of the triumph of the Faith – an argument for justifying extreme violence that was currently promoted by some of the Jesuits.

Mary (probably) fell into the trap of putting her willingness to have Elizabeth killed in writing, despite knowing that Phelippes had been to see her gaoler Paulet so some plot to entrap her was possible. The plot already being hatched by Gifford's dubious cousin George Gifford, Tyrrell, Savage, and other associates of Ballard to murder the queen – under Gifford's watchful eye and with him reporting on it to Walsingham so containable – had now become entangled with the initially separate and vague schemes of the impractical dreamer Babington, and the latter's enthusiastic letters to Mary offering to help her were read by Walsingham *en route* to her. Mary's apparent permission for Elizabeth's murder, in her (or more accurately Nau and Curle's) letter to Babington drawn up on 17 July, could be used as proof that she was planning regicide and was thus guilty of treason. Walsingham's agent Phelippes,superintending the transit of the vital letter in the beer-cask, notoriously did a 'doodle' of a gallows on the incriminating document before he sent it on to Walsingham.[37] This left him for London on 26 July, and as soon as it had been confirmed, Walsingham had the plotters rounded up – though in the event Babington and some others eluded his agents for a few days after bolting so they had not been closely enough watched. Given Mary's isolation and lack of clear news on what was happening in England and how strong her supporters were in reality, which was in itself a deliberate ploy by Walsingham to trap her into being less cautious, her approval for the regicide plot was certainly plausible, and she was 'set up' for execution as a political act to rid the realm of the intended beneficiary of regicide, and so put off further plots. But it cannot be taken for certain that the letter was not at least partly a forgery, and (as usual for 'terrorist' trials in this and other eras) the public hysteria at the plot and demands for exemplary punishment helped to prevent the trial examining the holes in the prosecution's evidence .

Mary was supposed to have given written approval for the Ridolfi plot to murder her cousin in 1571, but the document (forged or not) has not survived; this one was more damning as the political situation was more dangerous. A pre-prepared plan to remove Mary could go according to the script, with lurid details of her wickedness released to inflame Parliament and put pressure on Elizabeth to act. Mary was put on trial, with conviction a certainty in the inflamed atmosphere of rising inter-religious and international confrontation. But Elizabeth had been reluctant to put a queen on trial due to the precedent, and notably did not sign the death-warrant until repeatedly reminded to do so – and then she claimed that she had not meant it to be sent out and acted upon and 'scapegoated' the unfortunate official (William Davison) who had done so.[38] Philip's fury at the execution then probably pushed him into the final decision to invade England himself, at a time when Elizabeth was endeavouring to wind down her involvement in the Netherlands, negotiate a truce with Spain keeping English troops in vital ports, and withdraw her troops after Leicester's failure to make any impact on the war there. Her decision to put naval preparations for a war with Spain underway and allow Drake to make a pre-emptive raid on the Spanish naval headquarters at Cadiz in 1587, only followed incontrovertible evidence that Philip had played her false and was preparing an invasion. But the way that events developed after February 1587, not least in the Low Countries where the coast of Flanders was now partly under Spanish military occupation so that two ports (Dunkirk and Ostend) were available for the Armada to use, was arguably more crucial to Philip's decision to – finally – turn a 'Cold War' of espionage and propaganda into a 'Hot War' of invasion than was the execution of Mary. Had the Spanish not had any ports ready to embark their Continental forces in 1588, the chances would have been against Philip taking the gamble as he would have had to use exclusively troops sent directly from Spain and so not call upon his best commander, Alexander Farnese (Duke of Parma), and his far more 'war-ready army in the Netherlands. He might still have taken this risk, though, given his intense and stubborn religious belief that God was on his side, so that he would be guaranteed good luck, good weather, and an easy landing in England; he was physically as well as mentally isolated in his forbidding, fortress-like palace of El Escorial outside Madrid and for all his obsessive reading and stockpiling of documents sent from across his Empire his knowledge was not matched by his willingness to draw the correct interpretations. Elizabeth and Philip were both seriously over-confident about the military abilities and logistic capabilities of their forces and the flexibility and genius of their chosen commanders – but we can see this far better from the distance of centuries, with the evidence in front of us, than contemporaries could do. The failings and blunders of state military machines were as many and varied in 1588 as in more modern times – and though the miscalculations of the men (and women) in power then is not exactly a 'mystery', it is something that is not generally realised. Elizabeth I was not quite the 'Winston Churchill' figure in 1587–8 that is often assumed, given her willingness to compromise to avoid war with Spain – and her public fury at the actual execution of Mary (as opposed to the legally and politically necessary death-sentence) may well be partly due to her having been forced to take irrevocable action at last. The characters and motivations – and mistakes – of both Elizabeth and Mary seem to have been more complex than they are usually portrayed in modern media, and in many history books too.

Notes

Chapter One

1. Desmond Seward, *The Last White Rose* (Constable 2010) pp. 15–16.
2. S.R. Chrimes, *Henry VII*, pp. 73, 75–6.
3. Polydore Vergil, *Anglica Historia*, ed Hay, pp. 12–26.
4. See John Ashdown-Hill, *The Dublin King* (History Press 2015).
5. Chrimes, p. 76.
6. Vergil, op. cit.
7. First stated in Gordon Smith, 'Lambert Simnel and the King from Dublin' in *The Ricardian*, vol x, no. 135 (December 1996) pp. 498–506.
8. As n. 4.
9. Analysed in Fields, Royal Blood, pp. 203–4, and David Baldwin, *Elizabeth Woodville: Mother of the Princes in the Tower*, pp. 211–17.
10. *Rotuli Scotiae*, ed D. Macpherson et al, (2 vols, Edinburgh 1814–19) vol ii pp. 475–7. The marriage had however been suggested in 1486, before Elizabeth's alleged disgrace.
11. John Leland, *Collectanea*, ed T Hearne (6 vols, London 1770) vol iv p. 249.
12. Fields, pp. 203–5.
13. Anne Wroe, *Perkin: A Story of Deception*, pp. 525–8 for a transcript of the 1496 'Setubal Testimonies'. For the 1497 'confessions by 'Warbeck' see *Great Chronicle*, pp. 284–6 and Hall, *Chronicle*, pp. 488–9, with analysis in Wroe, pp. 48–53.
14. Wroe, pp. 77–8.
15. Ibid, p. 77.
16. *Rotuli Parliamentorum* vol 6, p. 194.
17. B.L. Additional Mss. 46435, f. 1371.
18. Polydore Vergil, p. 89; Bernard Andre, Historia Regum Henrici Septimi, ed J. Gairdner (Rolls Series, vol 10, 1858) pp. 65–6.
19. C S L Davies and Mark Ballard, 'Etienne Frion: Burgundian Agent, English Royal Secretary and "Principal Counsellor to Perkin Warbeck" ' in *B I H R*, vol 1989)
20. Christine Weightman, *Margaret of York, Duchess of Burgundy* (Leicester UP 1989) p. 158.
21. *Accounts of the Lord Treasurer of Scotland*, ed Thomas Dickson et al (Scottish Record Series, 1877 ff) vol 1. Wroe, pp. 89–90.
22. John Ashdown-Hill, op. cit.
23. A.F. Pollard, *The Reign of Henry VIII from Contemporary Sources, Vol 1: Narrative Extracts* (1913) pp. 82–3; Rotuli Parliamentorum vol 6 pp. 454–5.
24. BL Additional Mss. 46454, f.61.
25. Campbell, *Materials*, p. 328.
26. Wroe, pp. 94–5.
27. Ibid, pp. 114–17.

28. A Morel-Faro, 'Marguerite d'Yorke et Perkin Warbeck' in *Melanges d'histoire offerts a Charles Bemat* (Paris 1993) p. 414.
29. BL Egerton Mss. 616/3; Frederick Madden, 'Documents relating to Perkin Warbeck, with Remarks on his History' in *Archaeologia*, vol 27 *1838) app. 2, pp. 198–200.
30. Bertram Fields, *Royal Blood*, p. 220.
31. Livia Visset-Fuchs, 'The Divisie Chronicle' in *The Ricardian*, vol 9 no. 118 (September 1992) pp. 119–22; also P.W. Hammond and Maaike Lulofs, 'Richard III: Dutch Sources' in *The Ricardian*, vol 3 no. 46 (1974) pp. 11–13.
32. Molinet, *Chroniques*, vol 2 p. 402–3.
33. Ibid vol 5 pp.46–7.
34. Wroe, pp. 201–2.
35. Molinet, vol 5 pp. 49–50.
36. Wroe, pp. 165–6.
37. Wroe pp. 222–5.
38. Wroe, pp. 180–92; Seward, p. 166.
39. Molinet, *Chroniques*, vol 5, pp. 47–8; Polydore Vergil, pp. 71–3; N A : DL: 28/2/2, letter of 22 October 1494 to Henry VII.
40. Wroe, pp. 182–4; W.A.J. Archbold, 'Sir William Stanley and Perkin Warbeck' in *E H R* vol 19 (1899) pp. 530–3; *Rotuli Parliamentorum*, vol 6 p. 504 .
41. Wroe, p. 198.
42. Ibid, pp. 219–21.
43. *Calendar of Patent Rolls Henry VII*, vol 2, p. 13.
44. *Polydore Vergil* pp. 73–4.
45. *Excerpta Historia*, ed S Bentley (London 1831) pp. 100 and 101.
46. Molinet, p. 48; *Chronicles of London*, ed H. Kingsford (1905) pp. 203–4.
47. Molinet, pp. 50–1; Andre, pp. 67–9.
48. Archbold 'Sir William Stanley and Perkin Warbeck', as n. 40, p. 531.
49. Molinet, vol 5 p. 48; *Chronicle of London*, ed C.L. Kingsford (London 1905) pp. 203–4.
50. Polydore Vergil, pp. 83–4.
51. Molinet, vol 4, pp. 339–40; J. Gairdner, *Richard III and Perkin Warbeck*, pp. 320–3; Carew Mss: *Book of Howth*, p. 472; R.H. Ryland, *The History Typography and Antiquities of the County and City of Waterford* (1824) pp. 30–3; Calendar of Patent Rolls Henry VII, vol 2 p. 42.
52. *Accounts of the High Treasurer of Scotland*, pp. 296–300; Polydore Vergil, pp. 85–9, 105.
53. Polydore Vergil, pp. 85–7; Wroe, pp. 258, 262–71; Norman Macdougall, *James IV* (Edinburgh 1989) p. 121; David Dunlop, 'The masked comedian: Perkin Warbeck's adventures in Scotland and England from 1495 to 1497' in *Scottish Historical Review*, vol 70 no. 190 (October 1991) pp. 100–01; Wendy Moorhen, 'Four Weddings and a Conspiracy: the Life, Times and Loves of Lady Katherine Gordon, part 1 ' in *The Ricardian*, vol 12, no. 156 (March 2002) pp. 202–3.
54. Wroe, pp. 308–10; *Calendar of State Papers Spanish*, pp. 73n, 81 and n, 91–2,, 98, 103, 141; Garret Mattingley, 'The reputation of Dr de Puebla' in *E H R* (1940) pp. 30–4.
55. See G.R. Elton in *Annali della Fondazione Italiane della Historia Administrativa*, vol 1 (Milan 1964) pp. 116–19. *The Letters and Papers of Henry VII*, vol I p. 231–40.

56. Polydore Vergil, pp. 104 and n, 105–6, 109; Davies Gilbert, *The Parochial History of Cornwall* (4 vols, 1858) vol 2 pp. 187–9; Andre, p. 71.
57. Polydore Vergil, pp. 105–7; *Great Chronicle*, p. 282; *Calendar of State Papers and Manuscripts in the Archives of Milan*, ed Allen B. Hinds (1912) vol I, pp. 327–8, 331; A.F. Pollard, Henry VII, vol I pp. 167–8; Alexander Jenkins, *Civil and Ecclesiastical History of the City of Exeter* (1841) pp. 91–2.
58. CSPM pp. 326–8, 331; Pollard, vol I pp. 174–5; *Calendar of State Papers Venetian* p. 265.
59. CSPM p. 329; *Great Chronicle* p. 282; Andre, p. 71.
60. BL additional Mss. 46454, f. 61; Wroe, pp. 195–7.
61. Pollard, pp. 173–6.
62. The 'confession' in English: *London Chronicle*, pp. 219–22; Hall, *Chronicle*, pp. 488–9; *Great Chronicle*, pp. 284–6. The 'confession' in French: *Courtria Codex*, vol 111, f. 1881v.
63. Wroe, pp. 404–5.
64. Wroe, pp. 383–4, 394–5.
65. Molinet, vol 5, p. 80; Bacon, *Henry VII*, pp. 195–6.
66. Wroe, pp. 525–7.
67. Wroe, pp. 208–9; CSPV vol 4, pp. 482–3.
68. *Courtrai Codex*, 8840, f. 581; 8841, f. 50v; 8842, f. 53v; 8843, ff. 62v – 63r; 8844, ff. 54v – 55r; 8845, f. 59v; 8846, f. 53v.
69. Wroe, pp. 422–32.
70. *Courtrai Codex*: 111, ff. 188v – 189r; Wroe, pp. 412013 and 415–17; Gairdner, pp. 329–30.
71. Polydore Vergil, pp. 114n, 115; Wroe, pp. 448–50, 452, 456–8; CSPV p. 269; N A: E101/414/16, f. 30 r and v.
72. Molinet, vol 5, p. 120; CSPM p. 329; *Calendar of State Papers Spanish* pp. 185–6.
73. *London Chronicle* p. 225; *Great Chronicle*, p. 289; polydore Vergil, p. 117; PRO Fifty-Third Report, app. 2, pp. 30–6; PRO Third Report of the Deputy Keeper of Public Records (1942), app. 2, pp. 216–18.
74. BL Additional Mss. 46455, ff. 136r – 137v.
75. Molinet, vol 5 p. 121; *London Chronicle*, pp. 226, 227–8; *Great Chronicle* p. 291; N A: KB 8/2, mem. 3v.

Chapter Two

1. Eric Ives, *Anne Boleyn*, p. 230
2. Ives pp. 210–12; Nicholas Harpsfield, *A Treatise on the Pretended Divorce Between Henry VIII and Catherine of Aragon*, ed N. Pocock (Camden Society, second series, vol 21, London 1878) pp. 234–5 for a Catholic view. On Warham, see Scarisbrick p. 429, Ives p. 191.
3. *CSP Spanish* 1531–3, p. 699.
4. Ives, p. 207.
5. *Letters and Papers of Henry VIII* vol v, no. 216; also Ives, pp. 172 and 175–6 on instances of Anne's arrogance and bad temper after 1533 which may have seemed more significant in retrospect than at the time. Some accounts are from her enemy Chapuys, hopeful of the king tiring of her .
6. Ives pp. 199–201; *CSP Spanish* 1531–3 pp. 609, 625.

7. Nicholas Sander, *The Rise and Growth of the Anglican Schism*, ed. D Lewis (1877) pp. 93–4 for a later Catholic view.
8. Ives p. 230; Scarisbrick pp. 421–2.
9. See *CSP Spanish* 1531–3 p. 788 for Chapuys' reaction.
10. *CSP Spanish* 1534–5, pp. 67 and 234; *Letters and Papers of Henry VIII* vol vii, nos. 556, 958, 1193.
11. *CSP Spanish* 1531–3, p. 760; and for the story of Henry fancying another woman at court in 1534, see *Letters and Papers of Henry VIII*, vol vi no. 1534. Analysis in Ives, pp. 240–3.
12. *CSP Spanish* 1531–3, p. 788 for a September 1534 report by Chapuys which he admitted was over-hopeful (p. 788). Chapuys' first mention of Jane Seymour, *CSP Spanish* 1536–8, pp. 39–40; see ibid pp. 81, 84–5, 106–7 on her and the King in spring 1536. For 'back-dating' the king's disillusionment once Anne had been executed, ibid p. 127.
13. *CSP Spanish* 1536–8, p. 54, 89, 91, 93; *Letters and Papers of Henry VIII*, vol x pp. 351 and 699.
14. *CSP Spanish* 1536–8, p. 98; *Letters and Papers*, vol x p. 699.
15. *CSP Spanish* 1536–8, p. 106; *Letters and Papers* vol x p. 752.
16. *CSP Spanish* 1536–8, p. 98; *Letters and Papers* p. 699.
17. *Letters and Papers* p. 720.
18. Ibid, pp. 688, 748, 752; *Lisle Letters* vol iii p. 748; *CSP Spanish* 1536–8 pp. 99–102, 105.
19. *Letters and Papers* vol x, p. 700.
20. Ibid p. 601; *CSP Spanish* 1536–8, pp. 81–2.
21. *Letters and Papers* vol x p. 908.
22. Ibid pp. 141, 351, 494, 601, 699, 782.
23. Lehmberg, *Later Parliaments of Henry VIII*, pp. 15–16.
24. *State Papers of Henry VIII*, vol vii, pp. 683–8; *Letters and Papers of Henry VIII*, vol x p. 726.
25. Constatine article, *Archaeologia* vol 23, p. 64; Ives, Anne Boleyn, pp. 366–8.
26. *The Life of Cardinal Wolsey* by George Cavendish, ed S.W. Singer (1827 edition), p. 452; Ives, pp. 365–6.
27. NA SP 70/7, ff. 1–11; *CSP Foreign*, 1558–9, no. 1303; Ives p. 364.
28. Bodleian Library: Ashmole Mss. 861, f. 332.
29. *CSP Spanish* 1536–8, p. 359; *Life of Cardinal Wolsey*, ed Singer, p. 451. The story of the May Day 1536 tournament appears in the later sixteenth-century N. Sander, *The Rise and Growth of the Anglican Schism*, ed D Lewis (1877) p. 33.
30. BL Cotton Mss. Cleopatra: E IV ff. 109v-110; *Letters and Papers of Henry VIII*, vol xiii, pt 1, pp. 362–3; also Retha Warnicke, 'The fall of Anne Boleyn: a reassessment' in *History*, vol 70 (1985) pp. 4–6.
31. Ives, pp. 366, 364.
32. Alexander Ales' letter to Queen Elizabeth, 1559: National Archives S.P. 70/7, ff.1–11. For Anne's exchange with Norris, see The *Life of Cardinal Wolsey* by George Cavendish, ed G.W. Singer (London 1827) p. 452. See Ives pp. 370–4 on how the coup unfolded and how Cromwell barred access to the king. Also see Julia Fox, *Jane Boleyn: the True Story of the Infamous Lady Rochford*. Also Ives, pp. 376–7 and Herbert, *The Life of Henry the Eighth* (Bodleian Library Mss. Folio 624) p. 384.
33. G. Ascoli, *La Grande Bretagne devant L'Opinion Francaise* (Paris 1927) pp. 339–458.

34. N. Pocock, *Records of the Reformation*, vol 2 (Oxford 1870) pp. 574–5.
35. *CSP Spanish* 1536–8, p. 126; *Letters and Papers of Henry VIII*, vol x, p. 908.
36. *Gilbert Burnet, History*, ed Nicholas Pocock (Oxford 1865) vol I p. 316.
37. Ives, p. 377; Betha Warwicke, 'The Fall of Anne Boleyn: a reassessment', in *History* magazine, vol 70 (1985), pp. 607.
38. J.E. Paul, *Catherine of Aragon and her friends* (1966) pp. 34–47, 126–8, 131–2: *Letters of Royal and Illustrious Ladies*, ed M A Ellwood (1846) pp. 377–9; Ives, pp. 377–9.
39. *Lisle Letters*, vol iii p. 703a; vol iv, p. 847.
40. John Strype, *Ecclesiastical Memorials* (London, John Wyat, 1721), appendix, pp. 315–16.
41. State Papers 1/167, f. 148.
42. As n. 32; Ives, pp. 306–7.
43. Foxe, *Acts and Monuments*, vol v, p. 605.
44. William Latimer, 'Treatise', Bodleian Library Ms. Don C. 42, ff. 28v – 30.

Chapter Three

1. Victor Klarwill, *Queen Elizabeth and Some Foreigners* (London 1928) p. 93.
2. Ibid.
3. For the Thomas Seymour incident, see Frank Maumby, *The Girlhood of Queen Elizabeth* (London 1909) pp. 40–57. For Elizabeth's imprisonment in 1554, see Mary M. Luke, *A Crown For Elizabeth* (Michael Joseph 1971) pp. 386–99. For the 'De Vere was Elizabeth and Seymour's son' theory, see Paul Seitz, *Oxford: Son of Queen Elizabeth I* (2001).
4. Jasper Ridley, *Bloody Mary's Martyrs: the Story of England's Terror* (Constable 2001) pp. 215–17.
5. Ibid p. 212.
6. Alison Weir, *Elizabeth the Queen* (Vintage 2003) p. 120.
7. Porter, pp.271–2.
8. *CSP Spanish* vol I pp. 27 and 57.
9. *CSP Spanish: the Reign of Elizabeth*, vol I pp. 174–5.
10. Mary M. Luke, *Gloriana: the Years of Elizabeth I* (Gollancz 1974) p. 87.
11. Christopher Skidmore, *Death and the Virgin* pp. 137–8.
12. Wilson, p. 259.
13. As n. 6.
14. *CSP Spanish: Elizabeth*, vol 1 p. 27.
15. BL: Harleian Mss. 48023, f. 455r; Skidmore, pp. 255 ff. For the arguments of the first major supporter of the 'Bacon was Elizabeth's secret son' theory, see Orville Ward Own, *Sir Francis Bacon's Cipher Story*, vols 1–5 (Howard Press, 1893–5). Also see C.Y.C. Dawbarn, *Uncrowned* (Longmans, 1913). For the refutation of this, see William and Elizabeth Friedman, *The Shakespearean Ciphers Examined* (Oxford UP, 1913).
16. *CSP Spanish: Elizabeth*, vol I p. 57.
17. As n. 15.
18. Skidmore, pp. 255–60.
19. *CSP Spanish: Elizabeth*, vol I pp. 182, 197.
20. National Archives: SP 70/21, f. 177v.
21. BL Stowe Mss. f. 180v; *Conyers Read, Mr Secretary Cecil and Queen Elizabeth*, p. 199.

22. Skidmore, pp. 266–7.
23. *CSP Spanish: Elizabeth*, vol 1 pp. 174–5; D. Wilson, *Sweet Robin: A Biography of Robert Dudley, Earl of Leicester* 1532–1588 (Hamish Hamilton 1981) pp. 251–3.
24. Ibid.
25. G. Adlard, *Amy Robsart and the Earl of Leicester* (1870) p. 32.
26. *CSP Spanish: Elizabeth*, vol 1, p. 175.
27. Ibid, pp. 36–7.
28. *Hardwicke Papers*, vol 1 (1775) p. 123.
29. P. Yorke, ed, *Miscellaneous State Papers* (1778) vol I p. 167.
30. Skidmore, pp. 338–9.
31. Derek Wilson, *The Uncrowned Kings of England: The Black Legend of the Dudleys* (Robinson 2005) pp. 273–5.
32. Spain: Simancas Archives, AGS, E 815 ff. 76–7
33. BL Additional Mss. 35841, ff. 121–3. See also F. Chamberlayn, *Elizabeth and Leycester* (Dodd Mead and Co., London 1939), and Skidmore, pp. 45–6, 245, 303–4, 386–7.
34. Hatfield House: *Cecil Papers*, Ms. 153, d. 168v; HMC Pepys Mss. vol 1 pp. 111–12 (Blount's report to Leicester on Appleyard meeting the 'boatman').

Chapter Four

1. *Calendar of Scottish State Papers Relating to Mary Queen of Scots* 1547–1603, 12 vols, ed J. Bain (Edinburgh 1898–1969).
2. *CSP Scottish*, ibid.
3. *Calendar of State Papers Spanish, Simancas*, vol 1 p. 173.
4. *Calendar of State Papers, Foreign: Elizabeth I*, ed Joseph Stevenson and A.J. Crosby (London 1863 ff) vol 4 p. 102.
5. *CSP Simancas* vol I p. 144.
6. Antonia Fraser, *Mary Queen of Scots*, pp. 258–9, 263–4.
7. Conyers Read, *Mr Secretary Cecil and Queen Elizabeth*, p. 229.
8. Robert Keith, ed, *History of the Affairs of Church and State in Scotland from the Reformation to 1585* (3 vols, Edinburgh 1844–6) .
9. *CSP Scottish* vol ii p. 210.
10. *CSP Simancas* vol I p. 295.
11. *CSP Scotland* vol ii p. 170.
12. *CSP Simancas* vol I pp. 196 and 304; William Fraser, *The Lennox* (Edinburgh 1874, 2 vols) vol I p. 445.
13. *CSP Simancas* vol I p. 196.
14. Ibid pp. 305–8.
15. Keith, vol 2 p. 347.
16. *CSP Scotland* vol 2 p. 230.
17. Ibid p. 201; J. Knox, *History of the Reformation in Scotland*, tr and ed W Croft Dickinson (1949).
18. *CSP Elizabeth: Foreign*, vol 8 p. 885.
19. *SCP Scotland* vol 2 p. 213.
20. Herries, *Memoirs* p. 73.
21. *CSP Elizabeth: Foreign*, vol 8 p. 13.
22. P.F. Tyler, *History of Scotland (1841)* vol 5 p. 334.

23. A.I. Labanoff-Rostovsky, *Lettres et Memoires de Marie, Reine d'Ecosse* vol 1 p. 342; Robert Birrell, *Diary* 1532–1605, in *Fragments of Scottish History*, ed J.G. Dalrymple (1798), p. 5 footnote.
24. Fraser, *Mary Queen of Scots*, pp. 307–11.
25. *CSP Scotland* vol 2 p. 289.
26. J. Stevenson, *Selection of Unpublished Manuscripts*, p. 65; R. Mahon, *Mary Queen of Scots: A Study of the Lennox Narrative* (Cambridge UP 1924) pp. 122–3.
27. P Tyler, *History of Scotland.*
28. Keith, vol 1 pp. xcvii – xcviii.
29. *CSP Spanish*: *Simancas*, letter by De Silva to Philip II of 13 November 1566.
30. Keith, vol 3 p. 290.
31. Alison Weir, *Mary Queen of Scots and the Murder of Lord Darnley*, p. 165.
32. Herries, *Memoirs*, pp. 82–3.
33. As n. 30.
34. Claude Nau, *Memorials*, p. 31.
35. T.F. Henderson, *Mary Queen of Scots* (2 vols 1905) vol 2, app. C, p. 664.
36. Fraser, pp. 351–2.
37. Nau, p. 37.
38. Labanoff-Rostovsky, vol 2 p. 20.
39. Fraser, pp. 354–5.
40. Nau, p. 34.
41. Fraser, pp. 357–60.
42. R. Pitcairn, *Ancient Criminal Trials in Scotland* (Bannatyne Club, Edinburgh 1833) vol 1, part 1, p. 493.
43. Ibid, p. 495.
44. Fraser, pp. 362–3 and note.
45. Ibid, pp. 366–8.
46. Neville Williams, *Elizabeth I: queen of England*, pp. 146–7.
47. Fraser, pp. 375–6.
48. Nau, p. 37.
49. *Calendar of State Papers: Rome*, vol 2 p. 223.
50. Pitcairn, vol 1 part 1, p. 502.
51. *CSP Scotland* vol 2 p. 322.
52. Fraser, pp. 377–8.
53. Teulet, *Papiers d'Etat*, vol 2, p. 170.
54. *CSP Scotland* vol 2, p. 336.
55. Teulet, vol 2 p. 711; Keith, vol 2 p. 628; Herries, p.93.
56. Nau, pp. 47–8.
57. Pitcairn, vol 1, part 1, p. 495.
58. Labanoff-Rostovsky, vol 2 p. 76; Fraser pp. 431–4; Henderson, vol 2 p. 494.
59. Nau, p. 95; Labanoff-Rostovsky, vol 2, p. 117.
60. *CSP Scotland* vol 2 p. 409.
61. Ibid, p. 420.
62. Conyers Read, op.cit. p. 401.
63. R.H. Mahon, *The Indictment of Mary Queen of Scots* (1923) p. 3.
64. *CSP Scotland* vol 2 p. 442.
65. Conyers Read, p. 401.
66. *CSP Scotland* vol 2 pp. 509, 510.

67. *Calendar of Hatfield House Papers*, vol 1 p. 369.
68. Fraser, pp. 457–8.
69. Ibid, pp. 458–63.
70. Ibid, pp. 463–79.

Chapter Five

1. Neville Williams, *Thomas Howard, Fourth Duke of Norfolk* p. 137.
2. A. Fraser, *Mary Queen of Scots* pp. 457–8; *Calendar of State Papers Scotland* vol 2 p. 526.
3. Froude, *History of England*, vol 9 p. 427.
4. Derek Wilson, *The Black Legend of the Dudleys* pp. 303–4.
5. Mary M. Luke, *Gloriana*, pp. 343–7.
6. J. Martin Robinson, *The Dukes of Norfolk: A Quincentennial History* (Oxford UP 1982) pp. 160–1. See also article on the 4th Duke in *New DNB*, vol 28, pp. 429–36 by Michael Graves.
7. Luke, pp. 347–9.
8. Agnes Strickland, *Lives of the Queens of England*, vol 7 p. 301; Luke, op. cit., pp. 349–51.
9. Strickland, p. 302.
10. Luke, pp. 351–2.
11. Froude, vol 9, p. 488.
12. Ibid, pp. 489–90.
13. Luke, pp. 354–6.
14. Williams, op. cit., p. 166.
15. Luke, pp. 363–4.
16. Ibid, pp. 364–5.
17. Ibid p. 366; Fraser, pp. 502–3.
18. Wright, *Queen Elizabeth I And Her Times*, vol I p. 399; Williams, p. 213.
19. Labanoff-Rostovsky, vol 3 p. 115; D.M. Lockie, 'The Political Career of the Bishop of Ross, 1568–1590' in *University of Birmingham Historical Journal*, 1953.
20. L. Frieda, *Catherine de' Medici*, pp. 276–7.
21. Fraser, pp. 524–5; Sir Arthur Salusbury Martin, *Mary Queen of Scots* (London 1960) app. 1.
22. Freida, pp. 288–321; Wallace MacCaffrey, *Queen Elizabeth and the Making of Policy 1572–1588* (Princeton UP 1981) pp. 249–66.
23. HMC Manuscripts: Mar and Kellie, p. 28.
24. Bannatyne, *Journal of Transactions*, pp. 256–7; *Calendar of State Papers Scotland* vol 3 pp. 677–9.
25. Graham Donaldson, *Scotland: James V to James VII*, pp. 165–6.
26. Fraser, pp. 499–501.
27. Ibid, p. 511.
28. Ibid, pp. 502–3.
29. MacCaffrey, op. cit., pp. 293–4 and 318.
30. Alan Stewart, *The Cradle King: A Life of James VI and I* (Chatto and Windus 2003) pp. 64–8.
31. *Calendar of Hatfield House Papers*, pp. 46–7.
32. Fraser, pp. 541–5.

33. Labanoff-Rostovsky, vol 6 p. 58; Robert Rait and Annie Cameron, *King James' Secret: Negotiations Between King James VI and Queen Elizabeth relating to the Execution of Mary Queen of Scots* (Nisbet and Co., London 1927) pp. 10 and 101–2.
34. MacCaffrey, pp. 326–8.
35. Le Hicks, *An Elizabethan Problem* (1964) p. 7; Fraser, pp. 555–7.
36. J.H. Pollen, Mary Queen of Scots and the Babington Plot (*Scottish History Society* 1922) p. 1; Conyers Read, *Mr Secretary Walsingham and the Policy of Queen Elizabeth*, vol 3 p. 9.
37. J. Morris, *The Letter-Books of Sir Amias Paulet* (1874) p. 267; Fraser, pp. 555–6 and 567–78.
38. Luke, pp. 533–41 and 551–3.

Bibliography

Primary Sources

Bernard Andre, *Annales Henrici: in Memorials of King Henry the Seventh*, ed, J. Gairdner, Rolls Series (London 1858).

James Aske, *Elizabetha Triumphans* (London 1588).

British Library: Additional Mss. 35841, 48023 .

Cotton Mss. Julius, F X.

Harleian Mss. 787, 48023.

Stowe Mss.

Calendar of State Papers Domestic: *Edward VI, Mary, Elizabeth*, ed R. Lemon and R. Green (HMSO 1856–72).

Calendar of State Papers Foreign: *Elizabeth I*, ed J Stevenson and A. Crosby (HMSO 1863).

Calendar of State Papers relating to Scotland 1509–89, ed M. Thorpe (HMSO 1858–)

Calendar of State Papers Scottish Relating to Mary Queen of Scots, 1547–1603, ed J. Bairn (12 vols, HMSO 1898–1965).

Calendar of State Papers Spanish, ed. G. Bergenroth (HMSO 1862–6): especially *CSP Spanish* 1536–8 and *CSP Spanish: Elizabeth*, vol 1.

Calendar of State Papers Spanish: Supplement, ed. G Mattingley (HMSO 1868).

Calendar of State Papers: Venetian, ed. Rawdon Smith (HMSO 1864–98).

William Camden, *Annals of Queen Elizabeth* (London 1675).

Chroniques de Jean Molinet, ed G Dutrepont and O Jourdogne (3 vols, Brussels 1934–7).

Robert Fabyan, *The New Chronicles of England and France*, ed H. Ellis (London 1811).

Correspondencia de Gutierre Gomez de Fuensalida, ambassador en Alemania, Flandes e Ingleterra (1496–1509) (Madrid 1907).

The Great Chronicle of London, ed A.H. Thomas and I.D. Thorne (London 1938).

Edward Hall, *Chronicle* (London, 1806 edition).

Nicholas Harpsfield, *A Treatise on the Pretended Divorce Between Henry VIII and Catherine of Aragon*, ed. N Pocock, Camden Society, second series, vol 21 (London 1878).

Hatfield House: *Cecil Papers*.

HMC Manuscripts: *Mar and Kellie Papers*; *Pepys Papers*.

Edward, Lord Herbert of Cherbury, *The Life and Raigne of King Henry the Eighth*: Oxford, Bodleian Library Mss. 624).

John Herries, *Historical Memoirs of the Reign of Mary Queen of Scots* (Edinburgh 1836).

Historical Manuscript Commission Reports: Hatfield House; *Pepys Papers*, Magdalene College Cambridge.

Raphael Holinshed, *Chronicles*, 6 vols (1807–8 edition).

R. Keith, *History of the Affairs of Church and State in Scotland*, ed. J P Lawson, Spottiswoode Society (Edinburgh 1844).

John Knox, *History of the Reformation in Scotland*, trans and ed. W Croft Dickinson (Edinburgh 1949).
John Leland, *De Rebus Britannica Collectanea*, ed. Thomas Hearne (London 1774).
——, *Antiquarian Repertory*, ed F Grose and Thomas Astle, 4 vols (London 1807–9).
Letters and Papers Illustrative of the Reigns of Richard III and Henry VII, ed. J. Gairdner, 2 vols, Rolls Series (London 1862–4).
Letters and Papers of Henry VIII, eds. J.S. Brewer, J. Gairdner and R.H. Brodie, 21 vols (London 1861–1932).
Letters of Royal and Illustrious Ladies, ed M.A. Elwood (1846).
The Life of Cardinal Wolsey by George Cavendish, ed G.W. Singer (London 1827).
J. Lilly, ed, *Black-Letter Ballads and Broadsides Printed in the Reign of Queen Elizabeth Between the Years 1558 and 1597* (London 1870)
A Lobanov-Rostovsky, *Lettres et Memoires de Marie, Reine d'Ecosse*, 7 vols (Paris 1844).
Dominic Mancini, *History of the Usurpation of Richard the Third*, ed and trans C A J Armstrong (Oxford UP, 1969).
Sir James Melville, *Memoirs*, ed. Francis Stewart and T. Thomson, Bannatyne Club (Edinburgh 1827).
Sir Thomas More, *The History of King Richard III*, in *The Complete Works*, ed J.S. Sylvester, vol 2 (Yale UP 1963).
J. Morris, *Letter-Books of Sir Amias Paulet* (London 1874).
National Archive: State Papers CCXII, CCXIII, CCXIV, CCXV, CCXVIII (1588).
Claude Nau, *Memorials of Mary Stewart*, ed. J Stevenson (Edinburgh 1883).
R. Pitcairn, *Ancient Criminal Trials in Scotland* (Edinburgh 1933), vol 1.
Nicholas Pocock, *Records of the Reformation: the Divorce*, 1527–32, 2 vols (Oxford 1870).
A.F. Pollard, *The Reign of Henry VII From Contemporary Sources: Vol 1: Narrative Extracts* (1913).
Thomas Rymer, *Foedera, Conventiones, Litterae* etc, 20 vols (London 1704–35).
Nicholas Sander, *The Rise and Growth of the Anglican Schism*, ed. D. Lewis (Oxford 1877).
The State Papers of Henry VIII, 11 vols (HMSO 1830–52).
John Strype, *Ecclesiastical Memorials*, 3 vols (Oxford 1820–30).
Three Books of Polydore Vergil's English History, ed H. Ellis (Camden Society 1844).
Charles Wriothesley, *A Chronicle of England under the Tudors From AD 1485 to 1559*, ed. W. Hamilton, Camden Society (London 1877).

Secondary Sources

G. Adlard, *Elizabeth and Leycester* (Dodd Mead and Co, London 1939).
S. Alford, *The Early Elizabethan Polity: William Cecil and the British Succession Crisis, 1558–69* (Cambridge UP 1998).
Francis Bacon, *The History of King Henry the Seventh*, in *Works*, ed J Spedding (10 vols 1858), vol 6.
G.W. Bernard, *The Tudor Nobility* (1992).
L. Boynton, *The Elizabethan Militia* 1558–1638 (1967).
Gilbert Burnet, *History of the Reformation of the Church of England*, ed N Pocock, 7 vols (Oxford 1865).
Jessie Childs, *Henry VIII's Last Victim: the Life and Times of Henry Howards, Earl of Surrey* (Vintage 2008).

C. Coleman and D. Starkey, *Revolution Reassessed: Revision in the History of Tudor Government and Administration* (Oxford 1986).
Claire Cross, *The Puritan Earl: Henry Hastings, third Earl of Huntingdon 1536–1595* (Macmillan, 1966).
A.G. Dickens, *Later Monasticism and the Reformation* (Hambledon Press 1994).
Gordon Donaldson, *The Scottish Reformation* (Cambridge UP, 1962).
Scotland James V to James VII: the Making of the Kingdom (Mercat Press, Edinburgh, 1965).
G. Elton, *Reform and Renewal: Thomas Cromwell and the Common Weal* (Cambridge UP 1973).
——, *The Parliament of England 1559 to 1581* (Cambridge UP 1986).
Anthony Fletcher, *Tudor Rebellions* (1983).
Julia Fox, *Jane Boleyn: the True Story of the Infamous Lady Rochford* (2007).
Lady Antonia Fraser, *Mary Queen of Scots* (Granada 1970).
Leonie Frieda, *Catherine de Medici* (Phoenix 2003).
J.A. Froude, *The History of England* (London 1870).
Thomas Gainsford, *The True and Wonderful History of Perkin Warbeck, Calling Himself Richard IV* (London 1618).
Peter Gwyn, *The King's Cardinal: the Rise and Fall of Thomas Wolsey* (1990).
Christopher Haigh, ed, *The Reign of Elizabeth I* (Athens, Georgia 1987).
Alice Hogge, *God's Secret Agents: Queen Elizabeth's Forbidden Priests and the Hatching of the Gunpowder Plot* (Harper Perennial 2005).
The Horizon Book of the Elizabethan World (Paul Hamlyn 1967).
R.W. Hoyle, *The Pilgrimage of Grace and the Politics of the 1530s* (Oxford UP 2001).
Eric Ives, *Anne Boleyn* (Blackwell 1986).
Paul Johnson, *Elizabeth I: A Study in Power and Intellect* (1974).
Michael Jones and Malcolm Underwood, *The King's Mother: Lady Margaret Beaufort, Countess of Richmond and Derby* (Cambridge UP 1992).
Robert Keith, *History of the Affairs of Church and State in Scotland from the Reformation to 1585* (3 vols, Edinburgh 1844–6).
Victor Klarwill, *Queen Elizabeth and Some Foreigners* (London 1928).
R.J. Knecht, *Francis I* (1983).
Mortimer Levive, *The Early Elizabethan Succession Question 1558–1568* (Stanford UP 1966).
Jennifer Loach and T.R. Tittler, eds, *The Mid-Tudor Polity* (London 1980).
D.M. Loades, *Two Tudor Conspiracies* (Cambridge UP 1965).
Mary M. Luke, *A Crown For Elizabeth* (Michael Joseph, 1971).
——, *Gloriana: the Years of Elizabeth I* (Gollancz 1974).
Wallace MacCaffrey, *The Shaping of the Elizabethan Regime* (Princeton UP, 1968).
—— *Queen Elizabeth and the Making of Policy 1572–88* (Princeton UP, 1981).
Diarmaid MacCulloch, *Thomas Cranmer* (Yale UP 1995).
——, *The Reign of Henry VIII: Politics and Piety* (Macmillan 1995).
P. McCullough, *Sermons ar Court: Politics and Religion in Elizabethan and Jacobean Preaching* (Cambridge UP 1998).
R.H. Mahon, *The Indictment of Mary Queen of Scots* (1923).
A. Martienssen, *Queen Katherine Parr* (1973).
Sir Arthur Salusbury Martin, *Mary Queen of Scots* (1960).
Garrett Mattingley, *Catherine of Aragon* (London 1942).

J. Maumby, *The Girlhood of Queen Elizabeth* (London 1909).
Geoffrey Moorhouse, *The Pilgrimage of Grace* (Phoenix 2003).
Adrian Morey, *The Catholic Subjects of Elizabeth I* (Allen and Unwin 1978).
F.A. Mumby, *The Fall of Mary Stuart* (Constable 1921).
Beverley Murphy, *Bastard Prince: Henry VIII's Lost Son* (Sutton 2001).
J.E. Neale, *Queen Elizabeth* (Harcourt, New York/London 1934).
N. Orme, *From Childhood to Chivalry: The Education of the English Kings and Aristocracy 1066–1530* (London and New York 1984).
Geoffrey Parker, *The Dutch Revolt* (Penguin 1977).
Geoffrey de C. Parmiter, *The King's Great Matter: a Study of Anglo-Papal Relations 1527–34* (Longmans 1959).
J.E. Paul, *Catherine of Aragon and Her Friends* (1966).
Thomas Penn, *Winter King: the Dawn of Tudor England* (Penguin 2012).
Alison Plowden, *Lady Jane Grey and the House of Suffolk* (Sidgwick and Jackson 1985).
J.H. Pollen, *Mary Queen of Scots and the Babington Plot* (Scottish History Society, 1922).
Robert Rait and Annie Cameron, *King James' Secret: Negotiations Between King James VI and Queen Elizabeth Relating To The Execution of Mary Queen of Scots* (J. Nisbet, London 1927).
Conyers Read, Mr. Secretary Cecil and Queen Elizabeth (London 1955).
——, *Mr Secretary Walsingham and the Policy of Queen Elizabeth.*
Jasper Ridley, *Bloody Mary's Martyrs: The Story of England's Terror* (Constable 2001).
D.E. Roberts, *The Battle of Stoke Field* (Newark 1987).
J. Scarisbrick, *Henry VIII* (Methuen 1968).
Desmond Seward, *The Last White Rose* (Constable 2010).
Christopher Skidmore, *Death and the Virgin: the Mysterious Fate of Amy Robsart.*
L.B. Smith, *A Tudor Tragedy: the Life and Times of Catherine Howard* (1961).
Anne Somerset, *Elizabeth I* (Doubleday 1991).
David Starkey, ed, *The English court from the Wars of the Roses to the Civil War* (Longman 1987).
Alan Stewart, *The Cradle King: A Life of King James VI and I* (Chatto and Windus, 2003).
Agnes Strickland, *Lives of the Queens of England.*
J. Martin Robinson, *The Dukes of Norfolk: a Quincentennial History* (Oxford UP 1982).
Alison Weir, *Henry VIII: King and Court* (Jonathan Cape 2001).
——, *Elizabeth the Queen* (Vintage 2003).
Neville Williams, *Thomas Howard, Fourth Duke of Norfolk.*
Derek Wilson *The Uncrowned Kings of England: the Black Legend of the Dudleys* (Robinson 2005) .
Anne Wroe, *Perkin: A Story of Deception* (Vintage 2003).

Articles

S.L. Adams, 'The Accession of Queen Elizabeth' in *History Today* (May 1953).
I. Aird, 'The death of Amy Robsart' in *English Historical Review*, vol lxxi.
W.A. Archbold, 'Sir William Stanley and Perkin Warbeck' in *E H R* vol xiv (1899).
J.Arthurson, 'The Rising of 1497' in J. Rosenthal and C. Richmond, eds., *People, Politics and Community in the Later Middle Ages* (Sutton 1987
David Baldwin, 'What Happened to Lord Lovell?' in *The Ricardian*, no. 89 (June 1985).
G.W. Bernard, 'The fall of Anne Boleyn' in *English Historical Review*, vol cvi (1990).

——, 'Anne Boleyn's religion' in *Historical Journal*, vol xxxvi (1993)

E. Cavell, 'Henry VII, the North of England and the First Provincial Progress of 1486' in *Northern History*, vol xxxix (Sept 2002).

Patrick Collinson, 'The Politics of Relgion and the Religion of Politics' in *BIHR* vol 82 (2009).

C.S.L. Davies and M. Ballard, 'Etienne Frion: Burgundian Agent, English Royal Secretary and "Principal Counsellor to Perkin Warbeck" ' in *Bulletin of the Institute of Historical Research*, vol 62 (1989).

Jane Dawson, 'Sir William Cecil and the British Dimensions of Elizabethan Foreign Policy' in *History* vol lxxiv (1989).

M. Dowling, 'Anne Boleyn and reform' in Jounral of *Ecclesiastical History* vol xxv, part 1 (1984) pp. 30–46.

G. Elton, 'Thomas Cromwell's decline and fall', *Cambridge History Journal* vol x (1951).

——, 'The political creed of Thomas Cromwell' in *Transactions of the Royal Historical Society*, fifth series vol vi (1956).

J. Gairdner, 'Mary and Anne Boleyn' in *E H R* vol viii (1893) pp. 53–60.

P.W. Hammond and M Lulofs, 'Richard III: Dutch Sources' in *The Ricardian*, vol 3, no 46 (1974) pp. 11–13.

P.W. Hammond and W.J. White, 'The Sons of Edward IV: a Re-examination of the Evidence on their Deaths and the Bones in Westminster Abbey' in C.Ross (ed), *Loyalty, Lordship and Law* (1979).

W.J. Haugaard, 'Katherine Parr: the religious convictions of a Renaissance queen' in *Renaissance Quarterly*, vol xxii (1969) pp. 346–59.

R. Koerner, 'The imperial crown of this realm: Henry VIII, Constantine and Polydore Vergil' in *BIHR* vol xxvi (1953).

J. Leslau, 'Did the Sons of Edward IV Outlive Henry VII?' in *The Ricardian* vol iv (1978): the theory of 'hidden meaning' regarding the Princes living under assumed names seen in Holbein's portrait of the More family.

A.J. Loomie, 'The Armadas and the Catholics of England' in *Catholic Historical Review*, vol Lxix (1973) pp. 385–463.

D. Luckett, 'The Thames Valley Conspiracies Against Henry VII' in *BIHR* vol lxviii (1995) pp. 164–92.

Frederick Madden, 'Documents relating to Perkin Warbeck, with Remarks on his History' in *Archaeologia*, vol xxvii (1838), appendix 2.

W.E. Morehen, 'The Career of John de la Pole, Earl of Lincoln' in *The Ricardian* vol xiii (2003).

A. Morel-Faro, 'Margeurite d'Yorke et Perkin Warbeck' in Melanges d'Histoire Offerts a Charles Bernat (Paris 1992).

R.B. Reid, 'The Rebellion of the Earls, 1569' in *TRHS*, second series, vol xx (1906) pp. 171–203.

C. Roth, 'Perkin Warbeck and his Jewish Master' (i.e. Sir Edward Brampton), in *Transactions of the Jewish Historical Society of England*, vol ix (1922) pp. 143–62.

A.L. Rowse, 'The Turbulent Career of Sir Henry de Bodrugan' in *History*, vol xxix (1944).

S.J. Smart, 'John Foxe and the Story of Richard Hun, martyr' in *Journal of Ecclesiastical History* vol 37 (1982) pp. 205–34.

G. Smith, 'Lambert Simnel and the King from Dublin' in *The Ricardian*, vol x (1994–6) pp. 498–536.

L. Baldwin Smith, 'The Last Will and Testament of Henry VIII: a question of perspective' in *Journal of British Studies* vol ii (1962).

Livia Visset-Fuchs, 'The Divisie Chronicle' in *The Ricardian*, vol 9 no 118 (September 1992) pp. 119–22.

Retha Warnicke, 'The fall of Anne Boleyn: a Reassessement' in *History*, vol lxx (1985) pp. 1–15.

B. Williams, 'Lambert Simnel's rebellion: How Reliable is Polydore Vergil?' in *The Ricardian*, no. 6 (1982).

C.H. Williams, 'The Rebellion of Sir Humphrey Stafford in 1486' in *E H R* vol xliii (1928).

Index